Praise for Clifford Beal

Also by Clifford Beal

Quelch's Gold
Gideon's Angel
The Raven's Banquet
The Witch of Torinia (forthcoming)

Tales of Valdur:
Book One

The Guns of Ivrea

Clifford Beal

SOLARIS

First published 2016 by Solaris
an imprint of Rebellion Publishing Ltd,
Riverside House, Osney Mead,
Oxford, OX2 0ES, UK

www.solarisbooks.com

US ISBN: 978 1 78108 347 5
UK ISBN: 978 1 78108 348 2

10 9 8 7 6 5 4 3 2 1

A CIP catalogue record for this book is available from the
British Library.

Designed & typeset by Rebellion Publishing

Printed in Denmark
by Nørhaven

To the good gentlefolk of
the Barony of the Bridge,
Anno Societatis IX–XXI,
for recreating the Middle Ages
not as they were
but as they ought have been.

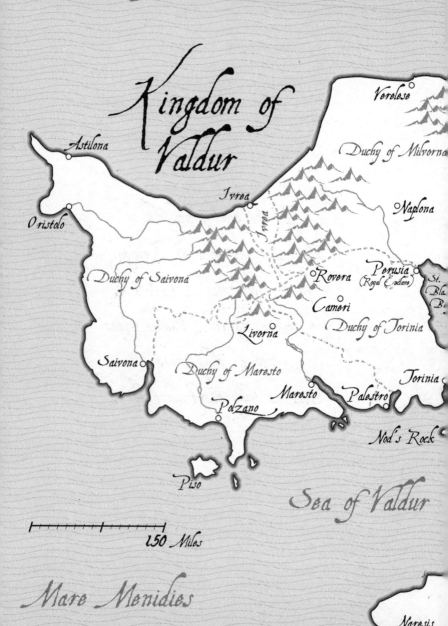

Imperium Serica
(the Sinae)
and lands East

N
W
E
S

Gorviatas

Duchy of Colonna

Miluorna

Colonna

Telas

Tetrarchy of Keres

Kerespura

Darfan

Azilas

Naaman

Kingdoms of the Southlands

One

THE SECOND TIME he entered the tomb, the air was just as musty, leaden and sweetly cloying as it had been the first time. Even so, this was not why his stomach roiled and tugged, a sick taste rising in his mouth, dry as dust. His sandals scuffing the rough-hewn stone steps, he descended again into the crypt; descending for the second time ever, and in the very same day. He was one of the first living souls to take those steps into the pitch blackness in four hundred years, his ears ringing in the muffled silence. When first he had stepped down into the darkness it had been shortly after dawn. Brother Kell, an old blackrobe and a tutor of catechism to the novices, had put an arm around his shoulder as the two led the way with tallow rag torches.

"Acquel," he had said, a ghost of a smile on his lips, "it is an honour we've been given—a sacred honour. Something that you will forever remember. A memory that will strengthen your faith in the Lord." That promise had turned out to be half true. He now fervently wished he had never been chosen, never to have had the ill luck to be where he was. Never to see beyond the oak and iron door that led to the tomb of Elded the Lawgiver.

His legs were trembling even as he gripped the sputtering torch. Ten steps, then a gentle cobbled slope, then ten more steps. He remembered this from earlier in the day. Hard sharp edges rasped under his feet, for these steps had never been given the chance to soften, to round down and hollow out like those leading to the Temple Majoris far above them on the plateau of Ara.

There had been six of the brethren chosen to go down into the tomb that morning—two blackrobes and four greyrobes, including Acquel. No whiterobes were to join them. The Magister had forbidden it. It was far too holy a place to allow novices, requiring the reflection and maturity of more senior brethren. Acquel shot a glance over to Kell who was carefully shuffling down the steps, one foot at a time, his left hand gathering up the skirt of his woollen robes. Acquel could see his face in the orange glow of the torch. There wasn't the trace of a smile on his lips now, and whatever thoughts ran through his mind were his own, in no way betrayed by outward expression. Two days before, when the tremors began deep in the bowels of the earth below Livorna, pediments and walls had come crashing down and clay tiles had showered the streets, striking man and beast alike. The great east tower of the city gates had cracked like an old walnut, leaving a gap wide enough to walk through. Mercifully, very few in the city had died and the merchants, eager to stop looters, had begun clearing the debris within the hour. The High Priest, Brachus, grew fearful that the crypt itself had been shattered by the force of the tremor. He had ordered Magister Kodoris to send some brethren down into the tomb. And that is how Acquel, a greyrobe of no particular skill, an indifferent scribe and even worse chorister, found himself chosen this morning to explore the tomb of the great Lawgiver, Saint Elded, dead for seven centuries. What they had discovered necessitated a second trip into the caves and this time accompanied by no less than the Magister himself.

Acquel looked to the faces of the other greyrobes. Worry on all of them and a mask of outright fear on one. No one spoke. It was a far cry from earlier that day when they had joked and laughed, Brother Kell even suppressing a chuckle as he scolded them into a more pious demeanour. Brother Silvio, a wise-cracking greyrobe who Acquel knew well, kept talking of ghosts that were watching them and waiting for their moment to pounce; creatures that would wrap their long bony hands about you as they sucked out your lifeblood. Anything left would be a meal for the fat-bodied cave spiders as big as your fist. Acquel had grinned in the torchlight, exchanging a wink with gap-toothed Silvio. Now their voices were silent. The echo of their footfalls seemed deafening and the only other sound was the snapping and hissing of the torches as they made their way further into the cavern.

A strong scent of mould filled his nostrils and, unbidden, a memory came to him.

He was in the market in the low town, stalking carefully among the stalls and tables. He was eleven. Crouched down, his eyes peered over a table edge as townspeople bustled around him. The skinny baker in a silly slashed cap was fumbling for coins in his pouch while he laughed with a customer. The boy's gaze settled upon warm steaming loaves of rye bread an arm's reach away. He had gathered two up to his face, inhaling deeply, before laughing and tearing down the alley with his prizes. Even now, in the darkness, he felt a thin smile part his lips. A hacking cough echoed on the stairs and the reality of the present pressed down upon him.

Four paces behind them was Magister Kodoris himself in his robes of burgundy, and arrayed on either side a contingent of the Temple guard. As they made their way down, the roof of the cavern changed to stone of reddish hue. They were deep underneath the Ara monastery but just how far down Acquel could not even imagine. It was a miracle that the way in front of them was not blocked by fallen stone. Somehow the passage had stayed intact. As if, thought Acquel, they were meant to find what they had found.

The air was colder and more damp. Above their heads a strange-greenish, white glow clung to the rock. Brother Kell had calmed them earlier, explaining it was only some mushroom that produced this effect, offering them a natural light along the way, a gift of God.

Acquel remembered the awe he felt that morning when they reached the burial chamber and lifted their torches, the ceiling of the cavern suddenly soaring upwards, high over their heads, its true height lost in shadows. A flat-topped pyramid of carefully laid white limestone rose up some twenty feet high, topped by a large rectangular sarcophagus of beautiful marble, swirled black and cream white. Ceaseless dripping from the cavern ceiling had created rust red rivulets of slime down the sides of the marble, making it look as if blood had been spilt.

Even from where they stood at the base of the pyramid, they could see the great crack that had sundered the tomb of Elded. The lid was broken too, casually ajar and precariously balanced. They had all ascended the limestone stairs, the blackrobes first. The stones were slick with ooze. At the top Brother Kell went to his knees in prayer, as did the other blackrobe. Acquel, slack-jawed in wonder, was too carried by the moment to even think of prayer. He held out his torch to view the fine carvings in the marble, sinuous designs of ancient foliage, delicately worked into the stone by the master masons of antiquity. His feet carried him around the side, and here the quake had dislodged the entire end stone. A large slab lay broken, halfway down the pyramid dais.

He had knelt down, holding out his torch in front of him, moving closer to the aperture, almost forgetting to breathe. His eyes took in the sight before him, dimly illuminated. But he saw. The skeleton of the saint was laid out, feet foremost to him, wrapped haphazardly in faded cloth now tissue thin with the passage of time. Perhaps his heart should have been filled with piety then, but he had taken to monkhood in the same way as many men had to their professions whether tiler, baker, or blacksmith. He had just fallen into it. Or rather, to be more exact, his mother, a washerwoman for the Count's household, had forced the issue a few years previously, demanding he offer himself as a novice to the church. His casual thieving in the streets of Livorna had grown less casual and more accomplished. She had told him she'd be damned if she was going to be thrown out of the palace for his sake. It was join the Church or she would call the watch to haul him off to the magistrate and from there to a hole of a gaol in low town.

The habits of the street die hard, even in an indifferent greyrobe like Acquel. And before he had even really thought about it, his hand had reached into the sarcophagus and grasped the thing that had truly caught his eye. It was a gold amulet, its chain sparkling through the dust. He thrust it into the pocket of his robe in an instant, the automatic reflex of long practice. He threw a rapid glance over his shoulder. The brethren had not come around to the foot of the tomb. The price on the market for a saint's knucklebone was a small fortune but to have a relic from the Lawgiver himself was too tempting an opportunity to be denied. On both knees, he leaned further into the tomb, the torch nearly burning his face. The flickering light shone harshly on the mortal remains of Elded and Acquel saw how very tall he had been. He tried not to look at the skull which was turned towards him, jaw dangling in a silent cry.

"Brother Acquel! Have you found something?" It was Silvio's hand on his back. "Can you see the Lawgiver? Let me have a look."

And that was when Acquel saw what he had first overlooked. It struck him like a hammer blow, but only after a few moments had passed, as if his brain would not allow him to recognise what his eyes had seen. He fell backwards and into Silvio's arms, stuttering. Brother Kell was suddenly there, shoving them both out of the way, frothing with anger over their sacrilegious foolery. Kell's tongue-lashing died away when he saw Acquel's frozen face. Acquel's voice was a strangled whisper. "The Lawgiver... His *body.*"

Brother Kell thrust his torch into the tomb. There was cry of anguish and confusion as the blackrobe sank to his knees.

That had been some four hours ago. Brother Kell had duly made report to the Magister who had demanded to be brought to the place to see for himself. And now the whole numbed party, joined by the Magister and his guards, were standing once again at the foot of the pyramid.

This time, Acquel had no desire to ascend. Brother Kell whispered something to the Magister and the two slowly climbed the steps. Kodoris paused halfway up, knelt, and began to pray aloud. Brother Kell followed his example. The greyrobes exchanged nervous looks.

Acquel felt a tinge of sadness for Magister Kodoris. For what he was about to see. He liked the old man, and although he had never exchanged a word with the priest who ruled them all, he thought of Kodoris as though he was some aloof grandfather. He would always be given a kindly nod when he passed by and a twinkle of acknowledgement from large brown eyes and bushy brows. Kodoris rose and continued up, while Brother Kell, somewhat stooped, followed, holding aloft the torch to guide the way. Acquel lost sight of them as they reached the foot of the sarcophagus, and he looked around in the nervous silence. The five guardsmen stood in their crimson waist sashes, hands resting on the hilts of their short double-edged swords. Had *they* been told, wondered Acquel? Not if their bored expressions were anything to go by. One of the guards wiped his mouth and cheek with a gloved hand and pulled his cloak closer about his studded red leather jerkin to stave off the damp.

Silvio glided to Acquel's side and leaned in to whisper, "Maybe the saint's body was stolen years ago and they left *this* in its place. That must be what happened, right?"

Acquel shook his head. "Either way this will not end well. I wouldn't want be the one to tell the High Priest."

The blackrobe standing behind Acquel had overheard their exchange. "I saw the unbroken seals at the entrance above this very morning," he said, his voice drained of emotion. "We are the first—and only ones—to come into the crypt. God save us all."

Silvio started slightly, taking a half step closer to Acquel. The magister and Brother Kell had re-emerged from the sarcophagus and begun to descend the pyramid. Kell was ashen, as before, but Magister Kodoris was an absolute blank. Not just expressionless as if pole-axed, thought Acquel, but blank as if he was thinking about what to do next. Thinking like mad.

When they reached the uneven earth of the cavern floor, Kodoris, a head taller than Brother Kell, turned to him and tenderly cupped his hands about the monk's face. He leaned in and whispered earnestly, He then stood back and looked at the others. Acquel watched as Brother Kell's eyes welled with tears.

Magister Kodoris's voice was strong but calm; soothing and reassuring. The grandfather Acquel had never known. "Brethren, this revelation has set us a terrible challenge, it would make you lose heart. But do not let your faith fail you. Our faith must be sustained and we must all do what must be done to preserve that faith." Kodoris nodded, as if to affirm the correctness of what he was saying. Acquel thought that *what must be done* was just a polite way of saying that they would have to lie about what they had seen. But what else could the Magister say at such a moment of shocking revelation?

"Now, my brothers," continued Kodoris, "were any others amongst you this morning when you entered the tomb?"

"No, Magister. We are all," replied the blackrobe behind Acquel. Brother Kell's chin had dropped to his chest. He was silent, not confirming the monk's words. Kodoris nodded gravely and walked to the guards who stood off to one side, all attentive now that they could tell something had gone darkly wrong. Kodoris put a hand to the shoulder of one, leaning in to speak rapidly and quietly.

Brother Kell spoke up then, his voice quavering. "Brethren, to me!" He lifted both arms wide as if to gather the greyrobes to him; an act of fatherly consolation. But a street thief has a sense for the unspoken, the tell-tale movement of hand and foot as if joined by an invisible silken strand. And Acquel had not forgotten these things. The greyrobes shuffled towards Brother Kell but Acquel moved more slowly, letting the other monks move past him.

At the same time, Acquel saw the Magister step to one side, joining with the guardsmen. Without even thinking, Acquel stopped and took small steps backwards.

Silvio turned his head. "Acquel?"

That was when the cloak of the first guardsman was swept aside, revealing the silver flash of naked steel. His left arm pulled in Brother Kell while his right rammed the short stabbing sword upwards into Kell's belly, the force pushing the monk backwards. Brother Kell did not cry out, it was more of a loud exhalation, as if willing his soul to take flight. He collapsed silently, sinking to his knees and falling forward. He had let himself be the first sacrifice.

The guardsmen were on the others without hesitation. The greyrobes were frozen into terror, easy marks for wide blades that plunged past collarbones and into their hearts. Only the other blackrobe fought, pushing away the soldier that moved upon him. It mattered for nothing. He was quickly overwhelmed and dispatched. All this happened in an instant. And for an instant, Acquel locked eyes with a guard who was also caught in the terrible moment's strange dreamlike quality. The young guardsman's eyes were huge in the torchlight and the look he wore was one of almost nervous frenzy, poised as he was to leap forward. Acquel whirled, his long legs propelling him towards the steps leading out of the chamber. The cries of the dying greyrobes sounded like foxes screeching in the night.

A monk's robes are not made for climbing, let alone running in, and even as Acquel made it to the second tier of steps, he could hear the footfalls and jangling harness of his pursuer closing on him. He'd never outrun him, he knew that. Halfway up the third tier of steps he turned and flung his torch at the guardsman. More by luck than design, the flaming head struck the man in the face, splashing him with burning tallow. The soldier's hands flew to his head as his shin struck stone, and he was down. Acquel gathered up the skirts of his robe and bounded up the steps.

Half a moment later, the toe of his sandal caught an edge and he too was down, briefly, before leaping up and moving forward out of sheer terror. Cries below told him that the others were now joining the chase. The darkness of the passage gave way to faint light. They had shoved torches into the iron wall sconces as they had descended and these lit his way to the top. After a hundred stone steps he burst into the antechamber, gasping for breath, his mind racing: hide or run? Hide where? Run where? He clutched at his sides, eyes searching the room. *Run.*

He reached the large black oaken door that led to the vaulted passage back to the monastery. His left hand was covered in blood, palm stripped of skin from when he had tripped below. Breaths came in great heaves as he opened the door and went into the passageway. There were two doors here. One led back to the centre of the monastery and the dormitories, the other out to the physik gardens. He darted to the door that led to the dormitories. Smearing his shaking, bloodied hand on the door frame, he left that door ajar and ran not through it but instead back into the passage and to the door that led to the gardens. Using his unbloodied right hand, he pulled the door open. As soon as he had passed through the threshold he slammed the door shut with his back.

The warm rays of the summer sun struck him full on the face even as his nostrils filled with the scent of rosemary. But the horrors below still filled his mind's eye.

I have seen Saint Elded, the Lawgiver and prophet of the Lord. And I am a dead man for doing so.

And he ran again.

Two

To be sure, Valdur was not a happy kingdom. Five fractious duchies, three free cities, and a royal enclave not much bigger than a market town made the prospects for prosperity and *concordia* rather slim. Nor did it help that the king of Valdur was a distracted, vain, and rather stupid man, content to let the dukes and high stewards of the land conspire and scheme.

But at least he has me, thought Captain Danamis as he stood at the taffrail of his vessel looking out onto the rocky headland just over a league and a half away to the north. Nicolo Danamis, more than a pirate and less than a prince, commanded a sizeable fleet which had come into his hands as a result of inheritance, brashness bordering on insolence, and a smidgen of blind luck. And this fleet, a collection of great carracks, caravels, and cogs, was now the largest in Valdur. His flagship, *Royal Grace*, a heavy three-masted carrack built before he was born, was the mightiest of the fleet. Her stout oaken hull, broad and apple-cheeked at the bow, carried sixty sailors and over two-hundred soldiers. This vessel, and her sisters, gave some semblance of spine to a weak king. The royal bargain struck with the Palestrian pirates had survived more than twenty years. Signed between

Danamis's father Valerian and Sempronius II in the royal city of Perusia when the king was new to the throne, the deal had made the pirates wealthy, the king secure, and raiders from the Southlands wary to linger in Valdurian waters.

It would be unseemly for the king of Valdur to depend solely upon a mercenary fleet, and for that reason the king maintained a modest fleet of his own—twenty narrow-hulled and centipede-like galleys propelled by oars nearly as long as the ship itself. Not the idea of Captain Danamis, but a good one nonetheless as those ships required no wind to move and only the sinews of a few hundred miserable rowers, most harvested from the prisons of the land. No good in rough open sea but useful in coastal waters where a dash of speed and a good ram from a beaked prow could hole a sailing vessel with terrifying ease.

As the mild west wind blew across the sterncastle, riffling the full sleeves of his white cambric shirt, Danamis felt rather pleased even if the rest of the kingdom was miserable. He had the royal warrant giving him stewardship of the port of Palestro, he held a commission as king's admiral, and he had no shortage of comely women or coin of the realm. This day, he had even more reason to be in good spirits. Today was the appointed day to meet with his most lucrative trading partners. A transaction that would take place in open sea.

He turned his head at the sound of the ship's master, who stood centre on the main deck, barking orders to seamen who were scrambling in the rigging to stow canvas fore and aft. Sweating soldiers in their studded and quilted jerkins, steel sallet helms upon their heads, scuttled across the deck bearing breech pieces charged with black powder for the swivel guns perched on the gunwales. Higher up, in the towering fo'c'sle, painted in garish red and green, crossbowmen readied their weapons, arms straining as they hauled on the drawstrings. All as it should be, he thought.

The trade always went smoothly but better to be sure with a readied volley of arrows or good-sized stone shot.

Nico Danamis was dark. Dark because his mother was swarthy and because he had been tanned since a boy, it was undoubtedly a combination of the two. Long black ringlets surrounded his olive face, a face surmounted by a strong nose and outlined by a jaw that lightly carried a thin chinstrap of a beard. His blue-grey eyes, the colour of a winter sea, were arresting in a face so brown and so hawk-like. He had been born to the sea, and to command. Some said this he wore too proudly. It was a quality Danamis himself was sometimes aware of, when in quieter moments a mocking inner voice would chip away at him. But battle had never even once unmanned him. He'd taken more than a few punches, an arrow in the hip and a sword cut to his arm that now was marked by a seared gulley of a scar. Yet in his heart, he knew he had two things counting against him. First, he was too young, and though he did not know exactly when he was born, he was the youngest commander the fleet had ever seen. Second, he knew that his father's legacy to him—ships, command, money, and even the rule of Palestro itself—was not the result of his arduous labours, but rather, the outcome of tragic happenstance. One day his father had sailed off to explore the south seas and had never come back. And for six years Danamis had held the fleet together and upheld the rule in his father's name. But there were those who never agreed with that arrangement and dark rumour was never far from his ear. But today, the sun bathing all in warm rays, the winds light and favourable, and his precious cargo waiting to be offloaded, today was a day to revel in.

Danamis turned back to the railing and watched as a small boat pulled away from the nearby carrack *Firedrake*, oars rapidly rising and dipping, making its way towards his ship. Even at this distance he could see the gleaming bald pate of the passenger shining like a beacon. He smiled to himself. *Suppose I'd better steel myself for an endless night of hard drinking and twice-told tales.*

"Captain, we're on the banks now and ready to drop anchor." It was Gregorvero, the ship's master and his second-in-command, standing at his shoulder. "Nico? This *is* the place, is it not?"

Danamis turned, almost absently, and gave his friend a weak smile. He looked out to starboard to check their distance from Nods Rock, an uninhabited island and its smaller siblings which themselves lay some seven leagues from the shores of Valdur. They were just level with the largest of the islets, a roiling cloud of seabirds swirling around its white cliffs. "Aye, this is the spot. Drop anchor when you're ready." Gregorvero nodded and turned for the stairs down to the main deck. Danamis called after him. "And Gregor, summon me the captains of the castles when you get below."

Already descending, Gregorvero managed to whirl around smartly to face his captain, no small feat given his ample bulk. "I'll toss them up over the rail to you if I have to!" He grinned broadly at Danamis but still he felt the tickle of a small but persistent niggle at the back of his head. A captain distracted was a captain not in command.

"THERE'S THE BOY! There's my bonny buccaneer!" Danamis found himself briefly in the grip of a bear then found himself grasped on both sides of his face while his head was rattled like a dicing cup. Giacomo Tetch released Danamis then tenderly placed both his hands on the younger man's shoulders while he spoke.

"It will be a good haul today, my boy! I feel it in my bones. My very bones, sir." The commander of *Firedrake* smiled broadly. "Any sign of them yet? Half my crew jabbering away like children. All eager for a look-see." He leaned back and beheld Danamis. "By God you look well, sir!"

Danamis clapped a hand on Tetch's shoulder in return, his face breaking into a grin. "Well met, uncle! We are waiting on *Salamander*. She fell behind but is catching us up fast."

Captain Tetch shook his head. "Bassinio ought to throw his ship's master over the side. He's never been a judge of windage. Too damned lenient with his crew. Be the death of him it will." Tetch wiped the sweat from his tanned scalp and smoothed his pointed chin beard, bright ginger red. This day his right eye socket held his alabaster eye, milky white and cold, staring. Before battle was joined, he would swap it out for one of red marble, something that usually gave a charging enemy pause. Just long enough for Tetch to run a sword through him.

Tetch was not his uncle. But Danamis had called him that since he was a boy. Captain Giacomo Tetch had been his father's lieutenant and only by getting himself a broken leg had he avoided the ill-fated expedition that had claimed the life of Danamis's father. He was now vice-admiral of the flotilla, sworn to uphold the law laid down by House Danamis, father and son.

"What news in Palestro? And has our friend the Duke of Torinia and his overfed knights been busy along the border?"

Tetch snorted. "Bah! They're still making noise but haven't tried having much of a go in the past month. The Duke knows better than to pick a fight now. And what of you in the past three weeks? How have you fared?"

"Chased two Southland raiders out of our waters and well down their own coast. Took one and burned it but they had bugger-all in their hold for all our trouble."

Tetch grinned. "Aye, well, will give the one that got away something to think about will it not?"

"Sail Ho!" Both men followed the gesturing arm of the

lookout to see a ship well-up on the horizon to their stern.

"Well, shit, we know who *that* is. They should rename her *Snail*, eh?" Tetch shook his head in disgust.

Danamis smiled and tutted. "Easy, uncle, give a sea brother some grace. The winds may have shifted on them."

"Maybe you're too lenient," said Tetch, wagging a finger. His blackened pegs of teeth looked so rotten that Danamis wondered how he managed to eat his meat.

"Not lenient, uncle. Only reasoned. And prudent."

Tetch nodded, his one good eye meeting Danamis's regard; a look of mild, grudging apology. A gust picked up and inflated the red and white striped canvas tilt that shielded the stern deck from the sun. It rippled and flapped, lines creaking. Two soldiers came up the ladder and approached, swords and harness jangling. One tipped his helm up and gave a curt bow of his head.

"Captain, the fo'c'sle gang is at the ready. Guns charged and bows cranked as ordered." His companion raised a gloved hand to the peak of his iron barbute. "Same below us, Captain. All at the ready."

Danamis nodded. "Good. And remind your men that we are trading with *friends*. No taking aim at them. No shouting or cursing. Silence. Do you understand?"

Both captains-at-arms nodded earnestly. Danamis shifted the belt that held his single-edged falchion. "Very well, then. Break out the cargo on the main deck. I expect our guests to be arriving soon." The two bowed in unison and withdrew below.

Tetch moved to the ornately carved blackwood rail that overlooked the deck and placed both hands upon it as he watched the sailors and soldiers begin to raise the hatch grating. Soon, large bundles of tarred canvas, tied stoutly with hempen rope, came up from below, passed hand to hand.

"You truly speak their tongue?" remarked Tetch. "I always

marvelled at how your father could manage that. Reckon he learned you, eh?"

Danamis joined him at the railing. "He did."

Tetch's gaze remained focussed on the men below as they laboured to shift the cargo. The last of the five bundles was brought up and laid out below the fo'c'sle. "Many of the men still don't like this trade. Grumbling below decks on *Firedrake*. Your vessel too, from what I hear."

Danamis felt himself begin to bristle. "They like the gold well enough."

"Oh, aye, that be true. But it's trade with *heathen*, my boy. And we've all been to temple, haven't we? Damned priests hectoring us about the wicked spawn of the sea..." He shook his head slowly. A loud splash sounded on their larboard quarter as the *Firedrake* dropped anchor a cable length away.

"And I hope your lads know *their* orders. And their place," said Danamis.

"I'd trust my lieutenant to escort my own wife," said Tetch, turning to him. "He knows how to run a ship with or without me."

"You don't have a wife," replied Danamis, his voice flat. Tetch swallowed a chuckle.

"Captain Danamis!" The captain of the fo'c'sle yelled up to them. "Broad on the starboard bow!"

It could have been taken for a broaching whale but Danamis and half of his current crew had seen this before. The sea bubbled and foamed about a hundred yards away, a circle as big as their ship was wide. And then another, this time on their stern quarter. Men went rushing across the deck to catch sight of the arrivals. Danamis felt his heart quicken. As always, this would be delicate business. A third area of the sea boiled, this time dead ahead of the *Royal Grace*. For a moment, his eyes met those of Gregorvero down on the main deck. Gregorvero gave him a wink and a nod of encouragement.

Danamis moved to the starboard side of the ship and watched as four dolphins broke the surface. And behind them (for they were each in harness of woven sea grass) rose a chariot, fashioned of whalebone jaws and the shell of some vast mollusc, all bone white. It seemed to float just at the surface, though how it managed this Danamis did not know. But it was the chariot's riders that drew the attention and marvel of all aboard. Two more shell and bone chariots broke the surface, each bearing three or four occupants. A conch horn sounded and was met by another and then a third. The middle chariot slowly turned as its dolphins were given rein, and it made way to the side of *Royal Grace*, bobbing abeam of the carrack.

Clever, thought Danamis as he slowly made his way down the ladder to the main deck. *They are shielded from* Firedrake *if it all goes tits up*. He reached amidships and then turned to face the new arrivals. He raised his arm, palm extended, in greeting. Below him, the tallest of the mer raised a hand in reply, webbed fingers spread wide. Without waiting for leave, the creature leapt from the chariot and seized a thick rope that dangled over the side of the ship. Danamis took a few measured steps backwards as the mer warrior pulled himself up over the gunwale and stepped onto the deck of the *Royal Grace*.

He was blue-grey, the colour of death itself, and he towered over Danamis, nearly seven feet if not an inch. He was naked except for a loincloth made from some strange brown fabric that looked like fine glove leather. His skin was smooth and shiny like the dolphins that bore them, and not scaled like that of a fish; it fair bulged with sinews and muscle, for these creatures were unnaturally strong and powerful. Behind him, four more long-fingered and webbed hands reached up over the railing. His companions clambered aboard, lithely and with no visible effort. Both bore thin black blades that were fashioned from the bills of swordfish. They were hideous to behold. Eyes that were somewhat larger than a man's, almost like a sheep's, a flattened nose and a mouth that was wide and nearly lipless, they resembled some monstrous frog. They had small rounded ears and even something upon their heads resembling hair but which was not as men had. Yet they were manlike just the same: they stood upon two legs and bore no tails as in the legends of old. Even so, more than one sailor aboard could tell a story of a fisherman tipped out of his dory and dragged down to the depths for no more cause than the sheer fun of watching a man drown, the merman no doubt smiling as the last bubbles of spent air exploded from the fisherman's lungs. God had created mankind; Belial and Beleth had chuckled and created the mer. Or so said the priests. A low murmur rippled through those men who had never before seen the mer and they who had been so eager to gawp from the starboard rail now found themselves backtracking to the other side.

"Stand fast!" said Danamis, without turning to his crew. "They are here to trade. I'll kill the first man who gives them cause to panic." The crew instantly became quiet, some faces turning up to their captain for reassurance, others wide-eyed and staring at the new arrivals who dripped seawater onto the decks.

Danamis took a step forward and his lips struggled to form the words his father had taught him. He barely knew more than a few phrases of their tongue; just enough to conduct the trade and very little else.

The words left his mouth sounding like a baby's babble and God knew if they could even understand him. But the lead warrior nodded and replied with something similar though more musical and accompanied by clicks of its tongue.

Danamis recognised very well one of the mermen who

stood before him, the tallest of all of them. He spoke the creature's name: Atalapah. He followed this with the word for 'trade' and gestured to the sacks upon the deck. Atalapah gestured to one of his men-at-arms who moved forward, his long feet slapping the deck planks. With one thrust and twist, he ripped a hole in one of the canvas sacks, knelt, and removed a large leaf the size of a man's hand, waxy and bright green. This he handed to the chieftain. Atalapah took it, held it out briefly towards Danamis. The pirate smiled his reassurance. The merman slowly folded the leaf upon itself, opened his mouth, revealing a row of short pointed teeth, and thrust the packet into his cheek. He inclined his head as if tasting—or thinking—and then withdrew the leaf which he dropped onto the deck.

Atalapah spoke. "It is good." A spontaneous sputter of surprise spilled out among the crew for the words were in the high tongue of Valdur. Danamis realised he was gaping like a landed mackerel. He stuttered a reply.

"Then... we may trade?"

Atalapah nodded. "Yes, Danamis, son of Danamis." He turned and spoke to one of his men, who in turn moved to the side of the ship and signalled his comrades. Tetch moved alongside Danamis to whisper, "Just as well I didn't call him ugly. Tell me you knew they could speak as men."

"I did not. They did not do so last time."

"I wonder what else they know."

A few moments later two more mer came up over the side, bearing a new arrival. This time a gasp exploded from the crew and the mer men-at-arms stepped forward, swords in front to protect their charge. Boldly, she pushed her protectors aside and stepped forward next to Atalapah. A mermaid. Danamis had not even imagined he would ever see one. He awkwardly bowed in acknowledgement. She was nearly naked, only her loins covered in the same fashion as the others. Her breasts, pointed and firm, were bared to the world and the hundred men who watched, unsure whether to be repulsed or aroused. Mermaids were certainly the comelier of their kind. Blue-grey as the menfolk but not as tall, her features were far gentler, eyes more human—almost violet; a nose and dark lips where the men had almost none, and long tresses of white-blonde hair. *Just* as the old legends told.

"By all the saints," muttered Tetch.

Her voice was like liquid silver. "I am the daughter of Atalapah. I am named Citala. I speak your tongue better than he." She paused and moved to behold the sacks upon the deck. "Five bundles of myrra leaf? No more than that?"

Danamis stuttered again. "It... it was difficult enough to get even this, my... lady."

Her eyes narrowed, purplish lips pursing in frustration. "Then the trade will be... amended. Three chests only." She raised an arm and, at this command, the mer behind her pulled on sea grass ropes that had been flung up over the rail. Danamis could see the soldiers in the fo'c'sle tensing, crossbows shifting as they sensed the trade might be about to go awry. He turned and thrust out his arm. "Damn you, dogs! Hold fast there!"

Tetch followed his lead. He rounded on those behind him, pushing men backwards and bellowing. "You heard your captain! We are here to trade in peace so stand down or I'll have your heads!"

The mermaid showed no fear or apprehension despite the tension on deck. She stood tall, emotionless, and almost regal, and she signalled the mer men-at-arms to continue their labours. Soon they bore up three blackened and splintered wood caskets, two feet wide and one deep, lashed with sea grass to stop them from spilling. These were placed on the deck at Danamis's feet. The mermaid gestured to him to open one. Two dozen helmeted heads in the fo'c'sle craned to get a look as Danamis drew his dagger and knelt to cut the lashings. The lid disintegrated as he lifted it, for in truth it had lain waterlogged for years at the bottom of the sea. Even after all that time in the bowels of a shipwreck, lying in the deepest fathoms, as he pulled away the lid the gold coin within sparkled and blazed in the burning rays of the sun. It was brimming. As were the other two caskets. Coin and gemstones both.

Atalapah stepped forward and placed his arm about his daughter. "Good enough, Danamis?"

Danamis looked down upon the treasure—more than sufficient to buy three new ships and the crews to sail them—and then over to the Mer chieftain.

"Indeed. Good enough. The bargain is struck."

The mer chieftain waved his arm and the sacks of myrra leaf were effortlessly hefted by the others.

"They actually *like* chewing that leaf?" muttered Tetch. "Tried it once in the hills. Nearly split my skull in two from the inside."

"They like the leaf the way you like your wine, uncle" said Danamis. "Too much."

They watched as the sacks were thrown over the side and into the sea for the other Mer to drag down to the depths. Tetch put his hands on his hips. "I cannot even figure out how they can breathe air never mind chew myrra."

Atalapah turned to face Danamis again. "More trade in two moons. In this place."

Danamis nodded. "I will be here." But he was looking at the mermaid. She was smiling at him, eyes and cheeks creasing in good humour; a spontaneous reaction and with an almost strange affection. How could they look so different from their menfolk?

When the crossbow bolt struck the deck at her feet,

Danamis felt the world hang for a moment, suspended like the time between a lit taper and the explosion of the gun. But he was already moving forward as the second bolt struck. It hit the thigh of a mer man-at-arms and his cry was a high-pitched strangled croak. Danamis threw himself in front of Atalapah who had already folded himself over his daughter, to shield them both. He caught a glimpse of the maid—eyes wide in surprise and then narrowed in rage. He wheeled and spread his arms wide, crying "Hold!" at the top of his lungs. The archers in the fo'c'sle were pointing up and away to the larboard side of the ship as cries echoed across the deck of *Royal Grace*. And Danamis found himself looking across to the crow's nest on the mainmast of *Firedrake*. For that was from where the shots had come. All was a swirl of madness and shouting men. Tetch's face was purple, his bellowing curses booming across the vessel.

Danamis turned again to see the mer plunging over the side, father and daughter first and then the others supporting their wounded comrade. It had all lasted but seconds. Now there was silence as he surveyed the faces of his sailors and soldiers. Fear, confusion, disbelief. Danamis's arm shot out towards *Firedrake*, his hand reaching as if to pluck the crow's nest from off the mast and crush it in his grasp. "Bring me those men!"

Royal Grace bobbed and rolled in the gentle swell, the afternoon sun beating down upon the deck. All the ship's company was arrayed on deck from stem to stern. *Firedrake* was tied fast abeam, all her complement lining the railings of main deck and fo'c'sle. Even poor *Salamander*, which had missed it all, was only half a cable length away, her deck enveloped in silence except for the creaking of stays and lines. Two crossbowmen were side by side upon their knees on the deck, faces bloodied. Captain Tetch jerked one's head up by a handful of lank and sweaty hair. Tetch hefted his blade in the other and looked over to Danamis. He then tossed the sword upwards lightly and reversed it. He extended it to Danamis.

"Your law and your right, Admiral," he said quietly.

Danamis looked down at the pair, disgusted and still oblivious as to why they had done what they had. These two simpletons had ruined it all. Tetch gave the man's head a vigorous shake. "Who's running this venture, you little piece of dung!" The man was drooling, eyes tightly shut. But the other next to him spoke up, a broken voice stuffed full with rage.

"Blasphemy!" he spat out. "Blasphemy! And dead men's gold! Taken from their graves by heathen *fishmen*!"

Danamis moved a step closer to the bowman, slowly drawing out his own falchion from its scabbard. He handed Tetch's sword back to him. A low burble moved among the crew. And then someone cried out, whether on *Grace* or *Firedrake* Danamis knew not. "Dead men's gold!"

"Belay that!" bellowed Tetch. "Goddamn you, I'll rip you if I hear another word!"

The crossbowman looked up at Danamis with one remaining good eye, the other swollen shut. "Goddamn blasphemy it is." His voice was quiet and unafraid. "Your soul is damned and I curse you and your house."

Danamis's jaw clenched. His sword arm flew back and then delivered the blow with all the force his anger could impart. The man's arms shot out in a spasm, his head flopping to the side and rolling onto his shoulder, the cut nearly severing it completely. A great gout of blood fountained upward, pulsing, covering Danamis and the other shivering would-be assassin. A few nervous coughs echoed from castle to castle.

Danamis's sword clattered to the deck as he moved to reach

for a discarded helm that lay on the planks. Tetch stood back as Danamis rammed it down upon the head of the remaining crossbowman then lifted the whimpering wretch by the back of his gorget and coat of plates and marched him to the side. With a grunt of rage he upended him and tossed him into the sea where he sank so fast not even a single bubble rose up.

Danamis turned to face his crew, wiping his bloodied sleeve across his mouth. "Get this deck cleared and prepare to make sail!"

Gregorvero stood expressionless, his normally scarlet face near ashen. Tetch looked at Danamis, the slightest hint of a grin on his lips. "Palestro?"

"Aye, Palestro." And he scooped up his dripping falchion before moving to the stern, the crew receding before him. As he pushed his way back to his cabin, his mind raced to think of a way he could salvage the trade that had made him rich. And he cursed himself for thinking he could have gotten away with it for so long by merely paying off those around him. For some men, gold was not enough.

Three

Captain Julianus Strykar yanked hard on his reins, pulling his mount up so sharp that those following behind nearly careened into one another since they were, for the most part, all dozing in the saddle.

"Goddamn you!" he said to his lieutenant. "How many times do I have to say no? I swear you're worse than children, you lot!"

Lieutenant Poule was instantly apologetic. "No disrespect, Captain. It's just that we're close to the city. Some of the men want to make... pilgrimage."

Strykar let out a such a roar of laughter it belied his outrage. "Pilgrimage? This lot?" He jerked his thumb back towards the three hundred and ninety soldiers that trailed behind. "Do you really think I just stopped sucking at my mother's tit? Count Malvolio graciously keeps us on a very long leash as it is. If this company stops in Livorna we might not see half of them back on the road again the next day."

"Well..." said Poule, "and by your leave, sir, I reckon if we were to make camp in the valley below the town walls, have the field sergeants set up pickets and let only a few out at a time—"

Strykar's scraggly-bearded face leaned in towards Poule, whose mouth slammed shut with a clack. "You really do want me to knock your head in, don't you?"

The lieutenant's chin drooped as he cinched up his reins.

Captain Strykar resumed his pace and the others in the column followed suit. "We'll find a good place to make camp off the road ahead when the time is right," he said. "It'll be a place where the only unhealthy diversion on offer will be you lot buggering each other. No wine and no whores... At least no *new* ones." One could never forget the gaggle of hangers-on that piggy-backed in the baggage carts.

He chuckled to himself. "As a matter of fact, we'll send the quartermaster up ahead now to find a suitable campsite." And he turned in the saddle and despatched a rider who was sweating heavily in the midday heat in his padded doublet, breastplate, and sallet helm. Strykar grunted as he swung his steel round shield further over on his back. He shook his head. "Pilgrimage!"

The company rode on. They were a day out of the mountain passes to the north where the Duchy of Maresto bordered the territory of the Free City of Ivrea. Patrolling the hinterlands showed the Count and *his* employer, the Duke, that he had initiative (unlike the heavy cavalry of their company who squatted in Maresto city, polishing their armour and waiting for the next war). It was also the perfect pretext for him to carry on his personal commerce. A trade that made him a valuable middleman indeed.

Strykar caught wind of a few grumbled curses as they reached the crossroads where a left fork and a rising road led to the ancient holy city of Livorna. But the column carried on, following the wide road as it dipped down, the forest giving way ahead to rolling hills and a gentle golden plain that led eventually to the sea. As he was about to chastise Poule for no particular reason other than for his own diversion, he saw a large bundle of grey rags roll out of the bramble and bracken to his left, thirty feet ahead. He raised an arm to halt the column, even as the bundle came to life: a man, a *holy* man, staggered to his feet, arms stretching out to steady himself. Poule shot a look of pure confusion over to his captain but before either could say a word or give a command, at least a dozen riders appeared ahead, riding full tilt. From where the monk had tumbled out into the road, four crimson-sashed men-at-arms, swords drawn, extricated themselves from the clinging undergrowth and poured into the open. The lead soldier had already grabbed the monk by the back of his cowl before he noticed he had an audience of a considerable number of mounted *rondelieri*—sword and buckler men—standing still in their saddles mouths gaping. He froze in his place, sword arm extended.

Strykar recognised the men and the riders that had now reined-in up ahead. Temple guard. In an instant he turned and gestured to his flanking crossbowman. The crossbowman deftly swung up the already spanned weapon as he reached to his saddlebow and drew out a bolt from his pouch. In but a moment it was laid in the dark ash stock which he then tucked in tightly to his shoulder. The hapless monk was pushed to his knees and the cloaked guardsman cranked his sword for a full arcing blow. But his eyes swiftly took in that he was in the sights of the crossbowman and he hesitated. Strykar gently kicked his horse and moved forward, closing the distance.

"Since when are monks open sport?" His voice carried beyond the now worried guardsman and over to the man's mounted comrades.

An officer in blackened plate and chainmail answered Strykar calmly. "When they are defilers of the Holy Temple—and murderers."

Strykar laughed and leaned forward in his saddle. "Surely you can find some other young monk to fondle. What's he done?"

The front line of the guardsmen edged forward, cursing loudly, until their captain held up his hand. "This is no business of an *aventura*. The man is a murderer who has had sentence of death passed upon him. So stand aside."

Strykar could hear his men in the front files drawing steel. "I think you got it backwards. Livorna is *that* way. The Temple guard has no authority here on the Duke's road." Strykar could see the captain's eyes looking past him, counting the numbers and probably also noticing other crossbowmen raising their weapons. "Whereas we *aventuri*—or to be more exact, we of Count Malvolio's free company—have *every* authority to do as we please outside Livorna."

The guardsman had already calculated his odds but tried again anyway. There was a lot riding on this one. "The High Priest knows the Duke Alonso very well. And if you make incident here I reckon your next pillow will be on the scaffold in the square at Maresto. End this and give us the monk."

Strykar smiled as he slowly drew his blade from its scabbard. "But *we* need a monk. Ours died a few months ago." A rumble of laughter broke out among the men of the Black Rose who were close enough to hear the exchange.

The captain of the Temple guard again looked beyond Strykar and took in the levelled crossbows and hefted swords. More than that, he could see the looks of absolute calm—almost insouciance—on the faces of the mercenaries. There was a pause and then the mount at his left farted loudly, a rather drawn out affair. Again a ripple of laughter spilled from the men of the Black Rose. The captain of the guard cursed under his breath and called over to his man, still gripping the ripped and mud-stained cassock and the shivering youth inside it. "Release him!" The order was barked with an exasperated fury.

"Sir?"

"Release him, goddamn you!" The soldier lowered his sword, pushed the monk over into a heap, and backed away towards his compatriots, all the while staring down Strykar. The four soldiers faded into the mass of horsemen, pulled up onto the cruppers of their comrades. The captain of the guard gave Strykar one last look of contempt and then jerked his reins, nearly snapping his horse's neck and scattering the men around him. They pounded up the road from where they had come.

Strykar leaned over his saddle and peered into the grey pile of rags below him. And Acquel, his face covered in scratches, welts, black mud and dried blood, looked up into the relatively clean but mildly astonished face of his saviour.

REFRESHED BY A mug of water but still looking like a beggar (despite his tonsure, which had yet to grow out), Acquel stood in front of Captain Strykar who was seated on a three-legged camp stool as tents were noisily hoisted around them. The company had found a large field by very late that summer's afternoon, far enough away from Livorna to make a Temple guard assault less likely. Strykar leaned back and stretched his legs out in front of him. He had not yet taken off his steel breastplate and cuisses but gauntlets and helm lay tossed at his feet.

"Now, monk, remind me why I prevented your head being lopped and kicked into the road. I *think* it was because I was intrigued to know what a monk could possibly do to so piss off the Temple priests." Strykar waved to a boy to bring him over a large silver basin and then proceeded to splash his face and his lank greasy hair. He yanked the boy's tunic and dried his face with a quick swipe. "I mean, thieving from the Holy Temple I might understand but *murder*. That's a bit dramatic for a greyrobe."

Acquel had by this time stopped shaking, allowing only an occasional weak shudder of his shoulders. He had run and hid for hours only to find the Guard still pursuing him and gaining. Now, as he stood before Strykar, his wits regained, he realised he must have been easy prey to track with his bumbling branch-breaking tear through the forest. He was now in an altogether different but equally dangerous situation than his flight from the guardsmen. His eyes darted nervously around him, taking in the laughing and cursing soldiers as they made camp. These kinds of men he had never known, never spoken with or even robbed from. He had to be careful and measure each word. He clasped his hands contritely in front of him, his chin practically touching his chest. "I am no murderer, sir. I've not harmed a soul."

"So the guard are liars?"

Acquel knew that he had to be guilty of something. Why else would a squadron be sent in pursuit of him? Admit to thievery he could, but that would lead to even more explanation. He could almost feel the amulet and its golden chain weighing heavy in the deep pocket of his cassock. That it was still there was amazing in its own right, given his scrambles over tiled roofs, a drop of some twenty feet over the city wall and a tumble into the stinking ditch on the other side. The headlong rush down the sloping forest floor had nearly killed him and he had spent more time crawling than running. He looked at his feet as his mind raced to come up with an answer. One of his sandals was missing. Magister Kodoris could never have known that he had taken the amulet. The Magister, who he had placed blind trust in, had probably just heaped on as many plausible outrages as possible to justify his summary execution. But that didn't matter now. He could never tell them what he had seen in the saint's tomb but he could admit his mercenary actions there.

Acquel looked up again. "I robbed a tomb in the Ara. Saint Elded's tomb."

Strykar whistled. "A very *ambitious* greyrobe." Lieutenant Poule had wandered over in his short padded arming doublet, his hole-shot hose, one leg white and the other red, dangling loosely over one thigh. His cod-piece was half-untrussed and urine had splashed his leg.

"So what have we caught here, Captain? Is the bird singing his song?"

Strykar laughed, his deep crow's feet creasing as he did so. For his thirty-six years, he looked older than he was, black hair streaked lightly with grey and already receding. "He's been grave robbing from some very important dead. The Lawgiver himself, he says."

Poule snatched an apple from a wicker basket on the back of a camp cook who was hurrying past. "So... where's the swag? Up his arse?"

Acquel reached into the pocket of his cassock. It was no use now, he thought. He could not conceal it if they searched him and, he reasoned, it might just buy him an ounce of gratitude from the *rondelieri*. He held out the golden amulet, set with ten tiny stones of lapis, and let it dangle from its chain as he extended his hand towards the captain.

Strykar raised an eyebrow as he extended his palm and Acquel dropped the shining treasure gently into it and let the chain follow, coiling into the mercenary's large hand. He picked up the amulet and examined it. It was round and no more than a thumb length in diameter, intricately and delicately etched with what looked like a sunburst. The round shape was complemented by the tiny cut lapis stone, deep ultramarine blue. The reverse was also etched along the border, in fine black enamel, and it held some writing on it—ten small lines of text. Although Strykar held it up and squinted, he could not recognise the tongue. Old

Valdurian perhaps. But he knew gold when he saw it and this was pure.

Styrkar looked at Poule and then back to Acquel. "You lifted this from the Saint's tomb? From his bones?"

Acquel quickly realised he had to weave a story that was believable if not completely true. "Well, it was in the cavern below the Ara... near the tomb. I stumbled on it and... lapsed into sin."

Poule was soon ogling the amulet over Strykar's shoulder. "And what the hell was a greyrobe like you doing skulking down in the tombs?" he asked. Strykar nodded in agreement.

There was a sudden crash and clanking of poles as a large round tent of green canvas collapsed behind them, followed by much cursing and swearing by the men underneath. Acquel prayed his story would not end up the same. He spread his hands, almost in supplication, and spoke firmly, his voice as assured as he could make it sound. "There was an earth tremor a few days ago in the city. Bad enough to topple some buildings and crack the town walls. The High Priest sent the Magister to arrange a party to delve into the caverns to see if the tomb of the Lawgiver had been sundered. I was chosen to go down there and that is how I found the amulet. I was wrong to have taken this thing."

Strykar swung the amulet gently at Acquel. "You are a *very* bad monk, my friend. But I can relieve you of this burden, have no fear."

Acquel's heart sank a little—not too much—but enough, as he knew he was penniless with no chance of a return to his previous life. A golden amulet could have helped him along. "You have saved my life, sir. I have nothing else to offer you in return than this." And he tipped his head downwards.

Strykar smiled. "Poule... get one of the sergeants to take our monk here—" And he turned his head back to Acquel. "What is your name, brother monk?"

"Acquel."

"Tell him to take Brother Acquel over to see the Widow. Put it on my account."

Poule nodded quickly enough, but his eyes had narrowed slightly. "Aye, sir."

A minute later Acquel was led off, bowing profusely, and not really knowing where he was going, who the Widow was, or what would befall him by sundown.

Strykar turned the amulet over, studying it. It smelled old and acrid... of the tomb. Poule had finished lacing up his hose and codpiece and was now hollering for his doublet. He looked back at his captain.

"Do you believe him?"

Strykar shrugged and placed the amulet into his pocket.

Poule turned to face him squarely. "I think it stinks of deceit. And I'm not sure keeping him is worth having Temple soldiers barging into the camp around cock crow."

Strykar looked up, expressionless, his deep-set eyes boring into those of his lieutenant. "It's a puzzle, Lieutenant Poule. A puzzle. Don't you like puzzles?"

Poule inclined his head slightly and grinned a little. He knew when to leave well enough alone. "Aye. I suppose so."

Strykar nodded slowly. "We'll just have to see what happens next. I don't think our Brother Acquel will be going very far without us. But for now—for now at least—the company has a holy man again. And we have a delivery to make in Palestro, don't we?"

"That we do, sir."

Strykar waved him off, but then called after him. "And lieutenant... double the guard tonight." He then threw up his arms expansively over his head, twirling his hands in mock submission. "See, I *do* listen to my officers' counsel!"

*   *   *

ACQUEL'S HEAD SWAM with dozens of images of the last day—all nightmarish. He was led through the still-rising maze of tents accompanied by a cacophony of shouts, laughter, hammerings and clangings. Just what had happened to him, and was still happening, he had barely begun to digest. Only the rank fear of the chase, his near execution, and his timely rescue kept filling his mind's eye, fogging his capacity to think his way out of the situation in which he now found himself.

Where could he run to now? Not having yet taken his final vows to become a blackrobe, was he even still a monk? His guide turned left behind a cook wagon and Acquel followed. The soldier stopped and turned back to him, roughly pulling him by the shoulder with one hand and pointing to a large painted wagon.

The Widow was not what he expected. As Acquel drew near to the red and yellow wagon, a woman emerged from the rear and stood, hands on hips. She took off her wide-brimmed straw hat and watched as the newcomers approached. She could not have been long a widow. She was young and slim, her smallish bosom cinched into her bodice, hips round but not matronly. The faded skirt of the ankle-length kirtle she wore, once russet red and now a pale brown, swished through the trampled dry grass as she moved to meet them.

"Who have we got here then, young Ricardo?" she asked, a sly grin forming on her browned face.

The sergeant threw a comradely arm around Acquel's neck. "We've got ourselves a holy man for the road. The captain wants him…" Ricardo trailed off, slightly unsure of his orders. "Hell, he's a right mess and at the very least he needs some shoes."

The Widow looked Acquel up and down, shaking her head. Whether in disgust or wonderment Acquel was not quite sure. Looking at her he reckoned she was young—probably no more than a few years older than he. She was also comely, he thought, staring at her perfectly formed nose and full lips. She wore her dark red hair coiled up tight in a whirl of a plait, revealing a long neck. Still, a few ringlets had escaped to dangle about her cheeks. He had not been a monk for all *that* long. Her green eyes widened slightly as she spoke.

"Money?"

"Captain's account, my lovely. Just get him road ready."

A not so gentle shove from behind propelled Acquel even closer to the Widow, and Ricardo was gone to find supper and beer.

"A greyrobe? Our last monk died on the march six months ago."

Acquel nodded, not really knowing what to say. "Yes, I was told that," he ventured, voice croaking.

"Keeled over on the march. But... mind you, he was a fair bit older than you. How did you end up here, Brother..."

"Acquel."

The girl nodded. "Acquel. Looks like you've had some rough treatment of late."

"Truth is, I'm not quite sure what's happened to me. I only know I can't go back to the Temple Majoris in Livorna."

She raised her chin, contemplating his mystery. "I'm the Widow Pandarus. My shit of a husband got himself killed in a knife fight with a customer in Maresto. But, at least I got the business out of it. Let's see if we can find you some shoes."

The sutler's widow turned and made her way to the rear of the long wagon. It was tall, its peeling painted wooden panels topped with a grey canvas cover over stays to form a tilt to keep out the weather but still let in light. She motioned for Acquel to wait while she nimbly pulled herself up the steep stairs and into the dim, musty treasure trove of stores. She kept talking all the while she rummaged about and Acquel moved closer to the opening, the floor of which was level with his chest. He could see her clogs and ankles as she moved about the tightly packed wagon.

"If you stay, it will be a good thing. More of these soldiers have a religious itch that needs scratching than you'd guess." The widow thrust her head out and looked down at Acquel. "Show us your feet, Brother Acquel!"

Acquel awkwardly raised up his tattered robes and extended his bare foot. She gave a quick nod and disappeared into the gloom again. "My old father took me to temple every new moon for high prayers. We had a good priest there in my village when I was little. Aha!" She stood again at the opening and leaned down towards him. "Try these," she said, tossing down a pair of green leather flats. Acquel fumbled the catch and bent to retrieve the shoes. "Don't know whose they were but they likely don't need them now."

Acquel sat in the grass and slipped on the well-worn shoes, fastening their single straps with horn buttons that thankfully still clung on to their sides. They actually fit him. He looked up at the woman and smiled. "My thanks." He was now starting to realise just how hungry he was, not having eaten since early that morning. That meal, eaten in the early dawn light of the refectory, seemed like a week ago not a day.

The Widow leapt down in a single bound to land next to him, her purse and belt knife jangling. "So, what was it you *did* do to find yourself on the run? Surely that pair of shoes is worth the tale."

Acquel stared down at his new shoes. God, how he ached to tell her—to tell anyone—the things he had witnessed that day. But who could he trust to tell the entire truth of what he had seen? For all he knew, this Captain Strykar might just as soon turn him over to the Temple guard in the morning. The widow was standing over him, a smile still on her lips, and waiting for his story. A loud grumble from his stomach made her laugh. "Come on, then! The sooner you confess the sooner I can get you fed."

"You would not believe it all. But I can tell you I am a thief. I took something this morning from a great tomb in Livorna, something very old... a golden amulet of sorts. That is why I was pursued out here. If I hadn't blundered into your company I'd probably be dead by now."

"A thieving monk? Not especially rare I would think."

"I was a thief before I was a monk. Come to think of it, I was probably a better thief."

"Not that good if you got caught."

Acquel chuckled, more at himself than at her remark. He rubbed the stubble of the hair on the back of his head. "Are you still as devout as you were when you were a little girl, mistress?"

The Widow Pandarus snorted. "Mistress? Just call me Timandra. And I do still wear my faith openly. I follow the seven holy laws. Or at least I keep trying to follow them. When we're in billet I go to temple. Why? Do you want to pay for those shoes with some absolution?"

Acquel picked himself up and straightened his mud-stained robe. "No. It's just that I would not want to rob you of your faith as I robbed myself today."

Timandra Pandarus shook her head as she looked into Acquel's face. "You are a curious man, whether thief or monk. Tell me your story later if you like. I'm not going anywhere and I doubt you'll be straying far if Livorna and the guard are still looking for you. I'll take you up to the cook wagon so you can fill that empty stomach." She pulled up the little hinged gate at the back of her wagon and latched it. She turned back to Acquel with a grin. "So... you don't have a coin to your name then? No other golden trinkets to pay your way?"

Acquel tilted his head and reached into his pocket in order to pull it inside out to show her the depth of his poverty. But his hand touched metal and a fine chain instead. His mouth fell open as he pulled forth Elded's amulet from his robes. Timandra's eyes suddenly grew large but as for Acquel, he felt his balls shrink into his belly as naked fear gripped his heart.

Four

Magister Lucius Kodoris placed both hands on the stone window ledge and looked out over the courtyard and beyond to the red terracotta roofs of the palace. Below him the open space blazed with colour in the heat of the summer day: the bold lush green of the palms, orange and yellow flowers bursting proud on the spreading branches of the *nutaris* trees brought from lands to the east. From a perch tucked up in the highest palm, he could hear the voice of a jubal bird, harsh and insistent. It left its place and flew to one of the roofs, settling upon the pediment of a milky marble column. Kodoris eyed it absently as its long iridescent purple-blue tail twitched in agitation.

He drank in the scent of the garden but his thoughts were far away and deeper than the High Priest's palace where he now stood, high upon the Ara. He had relived the moments of yesterday once again: the discovery in the tomb of the prophet, his shock, and then the overwhelming fear. Fear for the Faith, the faithful, and everything he had ever believed in. Once again, the screams of the brethren filled his head and he turned to face the interior of the high-ceilinged room, brushing away the sweat on his upper lip. Two attendants, no more than boys, watched him, expressionless, from near the double doors. Dressed in black pinch-waist doublets and red hose they, like him, awaited the arrival of the High Priest, Brachus. Their pudding-bowl haircuts reminded him of his youth—and lost innocence. Without those double doors stood four soldiers of the Temple guard, *his* guard. Kodoris walked to where two chairs and a table were placed, his steps echoing across the high-ceilinged reception chamber. Despite the heat of the day, it was cold in the room, the red marble walls and floor practically oozing a chill one could see.

On the far wall, over the hulking yet delicately carved blackwood fireplace, hung a tapestry depicting a scene from the life of the great prophet—Elded giving a sermon to the children of Livorna, one arm raised to heaven, the other resting paternally upon the shoulder of a boy. He had to avert his gaze. It would be hard to look upon any image of the prophet from now on.

At the opposite end of the chamber an even larger tapestry hung, and this one—another devotional scene depicted many times by countless Valdurian artists—elicited particular heartache in the Magister in light of what he had discovered. It was old and dark with caked dust. Where bright reds and blues had once stood proud, it was all browns and greys. Yet still, the depiction was clear. Again, Saint Elded was the focal point. He stood near the centre, surrounded by his disciples, their voluminous robes sweeping to the ground. Next to Elded was a man attired in beautiful garb, the real gold thread worked into the weave brighter than the rest of the tapestry. His tunic was more ornate than Elded's or any of the others and his pose, hand on hip, marked him as well-born and proud. But the drama of the story was something more. Elded held in his hand the mask of a beautiful young man, fair and graceful; the mask he had just torn from the face of his elegant companion. And what he had exposed was the face of a beast: darkly jagged with wild eyes, goat ears, and small horns protruding from the forehead. Saint Elded had revealed the Great Deceiver. The Trickster. Berithas. But who was the deceiver now?

The loud clank of a door handle brought him back to attention. To the left of the hearth, the wall swung inwards as the concealed door opened. The High Priest of Valdur shuffled into the receiving room, his bright purple robes trailing behind him. Upon his chest he wore a great gold medallion, a sun in splendour with seven long rays emanating; a symbol of the seven commandments of the Lawgiver Elded. Before Kodoris could move, the attendants were with Brachus, each taking an arm and gently, wordlessly, guiding him into the chamber. Kodoris approached, knelt on one knee and reached to kiss the right hand of the old man.

"Ah, Magister Kodoris!" Brachus's reedy voice trembled slightly. "It gives me pleasure to see you again." As he bent forward to offer his hand, his flat-topped gold and satin embroidered mitre toppled to the side, saved only by the quick reflex of one of the boys.

Kodoris stood and bowed his head. "Your Holiness, I am grateful for the granting of this audience."

Brachus nodded, his mitre wobbling precariously. "Yes, yes, Kodoris. It is the report of the quarterly tithes, no doubt. I knew it must be about time."

Kodoris looked into the watery eyes of the old man and winced internally. "No... Your Holiness. It is the matter of the tomb... The prophet's tomb." Kodoris could almost see the ancient clockwork struggling to turn inside the High Priest's head.

"Yes, I knew that, Magister. Don't confuse me with talk of the tithe collections!" The little party continued to shuffle to the chairs and table.

Kodoris gathered up the skirt of his burgundy robe as he walked at the side of Brachus. "With respect, Holiness, would it not be better if we continued our discussion *in camera*—in your private chamber?"

The High Priest stopped and looked to his attendants before turning his attention back to Kodoris. Only now did it seem that the old man was beginning to understand, or remember, the nature of the audience. "Very well, Magister," he replied, giving Kodoris a look that suggested he did indeed remember and that he was loathe to have to discuss it at all. "Boys, get me turned around!"

Once Brachus was seated on a cushioned chair near the foot of his heavy four-poster bed, he motioned for Kodoris to sit in another. Without waiting, the youths manhandled the gilded oak monstrosity into position next to the High Priest.

"That will do now. Go and fetch the wine and the goblets." The boys bowed, their grease-slicked hair unmoving, and hurried from the bedchamber. They came back bearing a finely engraved silver ewer and two large goblets which they set to filling.

"I need to confide the further details of the matter to you, Holiness." Brachus took a proffered goblet in both hands, the better to keep it steady. Kodoris looked to the attendants before continuing.

Brachus glanced up. "Eh? Ah, yes, I see." He waved one hand to the boys who bowed and left, shutting the door behind them. Kodoris set his goblet down upon the table. He leaned in towards Brachus and spoke, his voice firm but quiet. "I have made a discovery in the tomb. Something that could bring ruin on the Temple Majoris. It is something that requires your... guidance."

Brachus raised the goblet to his lips with both hands and took a long drink.

"You sent me down into the tomb of the prophet because you feared there may have been ruin after the earth shook. You were correct in your assumption and the tomb has been broken. Broken such, Your Holiness, that the remains of the prophet could be easily seen." Kodoris swallowed hard before continuing. "I do not know how to relate this to you but the prophet was... not wholly a man. I don't know what kind of deformity afflicted him but, his bones... his bones appeared to be like those of a fish-man. A *mer* creature." Even the act of giving voice to these words brought him nausea and he shifted his weight and took in a deep breath.

"At first, my thought was that it was a cruel blasphemous jest, carried out many years ago but undiscovered until now. But I came to see that it is truly the prophet's remains. Everything else in the sarcophagus pointed to it being he. But you... you must tell me otherwise."

Brachus looked down into his goblet which was moving almost rhythmically in his palsied hands. Kodoris leaned forward again, looking into the face of the High Priest. He found little reaction.

"Your Holiness, did you understand what I have told you?"

"Mer," Brachus mumbled thoughtfully, as if to say, *That makes sense.*

Kodoris gripped the fabric of his robe in his right hand and squeezed tight. "My god. You *knew*. You knew all along and yet you sent me down there without a word of warning?"

Brachus had turned slightly flush now. He did not look at Kodoris but instead worried his wine goblet. "I did not actually know. But I am not surprised by what you have found."

Kodoris could feel the anger welling up inside him. "You sent me down there without telling me you had suspicions?" He had always had contempt for Brachus; far too old to be running the Faith anymore yet yielding to no one or no counsel. And now, in this moment, any vestige of respect he had harboured for the High Priest was scattered like dust blown in the wind.

Brachus took a long sip of his wine and set his goblet on the table. "The rumours of Elded's lineage had all but died out two centuries ago. I myself had almost forgotten."

"But *you* knew of the rumours?"

"Take some wine with me, Magister. It is very sweet. The best of Milvorna." Brachus strained to prop himself up again to reach for the table.

Bumbling old fool. Has he half-forgotten or is he lying?

"Your Holiness. How do you know of such rumours? I have lived for sixty winters in Valdur and have never once heard the like." Kodoris lowered his voice to a whisper. "Was the prophet a mer? Half-mer?"

Brachus rubbed at the centre of his forehead with the back of his hand. A weak rumbling in his throat meant he was trying to come up with something to say. "There are some things, Magister, that only the Nine are allowed to know."

"The Nine Principals? They are privy to this revelation?"

Kodoris was not among them. It was rumoured he was to be elected to the Grand Curia of the Holy Temple within a few months as at least two of the principals were not likely to survive the summer and most definitely would not see the coming winter out. But he was still waiting.

"The Nine decide the governance of the Faith and they hold its secrets. You know this, Kodoris. And you also know that you yourself are near to joining our table." Brachus shook his head. "Would that your discovery had not come now."

Kodoris stood up. Slowly, he moved to the blackwood table, so close to Brachus that his robes nearly touched the garments of the High Priest. He grasped the silver ewer and refilled the goblet as Brachus shifted his small frame and lowered his gaze. Kodoris leaned over and gently pushed the brimming cup to Brachus.

"It is too late for regrets, Holiness." He set the ewer down and then leaned closer in, his meaty hands flat upon the inlaid table. "There is a dagger poised over the Faith and I must be told the truth if I am to defend it. You must confide to me what is known."

Brachus looked up into Kodoris's face, his mitre slipping backwards slightly. "You are the Magister of the Temple Majoris... but I would need to consult with the others."

"You are the supreme head of the Temple Majoris, Holiness. And as commander of the Temple guard, I must know what is known. And I must know now."

Should I kill him now? I've already killed innocents for what has been exposed. He could have a fall—here in this chamber. Break his neck.

The High Priest leaned back, cradling the wine. Kodoris could see the signs of growing alarm on the old man's face but he was past caring about protocol. "What you say you have seen in the tomb," the High Priest said, "it is borne out by the Black Texts."

Kodoris straightened up. "The Black Texts?"

Brachus nodded. "Those certain books of Elded that have been suppressed for centuries." His voice was practically a whisper. "His early gospels, the annals of his pilgrimages, and the seven laws he revealed are all sacrosanct. But these others were dictated by the prophet in his last years. After the Temple had been built but before it was finished. After Elded died, they were deemed heresy and the scrolls were taken away."

"You mean locked away," said Kodoris, his voice quiet, urging more revelation.

Brachus nodded again. "Yes. Locked in a secret vault in the undercroft with all other suppressed texts. These scrolls are all that remain of the later words of the prophet. Words that proved he had fallen under the sway of the evil Trinity or that his mind had fled the paths of reason."

Kodoris's head swam. "I have served the Temple my whole life not knowing any of this. The faith of my father is..."

"Is kept safe by our actions," finished Brachus.

And kept from ruination by a gaggle of senile old men, he thought. *God help us.* He was feeling sick again. He reached for the wine goblet he had thus far spurned and brought it to his lips. New terrors seized his mind. *Was the prophet cursed—bewitched—at the end of his life? Was he enchanted into a fish-man and not born one?* He shuffled to the window. He needed to see light and trees and birds once again.

"Magister, were there others who beheld the saint's bones?"

Kodoris turned, wine spilling down his robes. "Others? *Others* you ask, your Holiness. There were others. But I have defended the Faith."

Brachus frowned. "Kodoris, this truth cannot be entrusted to the brethren. It is how we have guarded the Faith all these centuries. You do understand that?"

A fall upon the marble floor, making sure his head strikes first. It happens to the old all the time.

"Yes, your Holiness. I have taken measures." The weedy rumbling began again in Brachus's throat. "*Definitive measures,* your Holiness."

The High Priest blinked, gave a small nod, and sipped his wine. Kodoris placed his goblet on the table and loomed over him again. "And you will convince the eldest of the Nine to step down tomorrow due to infirmity. I will be elected in his place."

The eyes of the High Priest glistened and Brachus gave an even smaller nod than before.

And Kodoris felt suddenly lifted. As dark as the revelations he had just heard were, they confirmed the correctness of the actions he had taken. He had not overreacted. Kodoris retreated and gave a court bow. "I am the Magister of the Temple and I will defend the One Faith with all in my power."

He had reluctantly dispatched the four guardsmen who had done the first deed at his secret behest. A generous measure of foxbane in half a rundlet of wine, offered in a private chamber as reward for service, had seen to that. One at a time, dragged in a blanket, he had taken them down into the tomb in the night. Their absence was put down to desertion.

Brother Kell, good brother Kell, served a second purpose. His heart had nearly burst as he laboured to bring Kell's body up the stone steps, depositing it at the door to the physik garden. So too the body of the other blackrobe. And young Acquel was playing his part too in saving the Faith. Kodoris had made it plain to all that Brother Acquel Galenus must have led the other three greyrobes into murder and flight. A necessary lie. But their bodies, still deep in the crypt, would not be found in his lifetime. Blackrobe and greyrobe alike agreed it had been the mad desperate crime of young men who wanted escape from the drudgery of a monk's life. The tomb of Elded was now sealed up tight once again and with it the dark secret. He had seen to that.

But Acquel had to be found, and soon. He needed a Seeker.

Five

"HE WILL KILL me." Acquel stared at the amulet that lay heavy in his palm. The Widow Pandarus stared too, then looked up at the monk.

"What have you done?"

Acquel shook his head. "He took this from me! How did it end up with me again? By God, he had it in *his* hand when I left him."

Timandra stepped forward and grasped his wrist. "This is the amulet you stole this morning? And you say you gave this to Strykar?"

"He took it from me, I tell you. I've got to give it back. He knows I'm a thief—he'll think I stole it back off him!"

Timandra looked him in the eye. "Did you?"

"By all the saints, no! Why would I do that? He'd run me through or else drag me back to the Ara!"

She took the amulet from his hand and studied it. "It's very old workmanship. I've never seen the likes."

Acquel's reply was barely above a whisper. "I took it from Saint Elded. I took it from his bones."

Timandra's free hand flew to her mouth and then, quickly, she blessed herself, touching forefinger and middle finger to forehead and right breast. She thrust the amulet back into Acquel's palm and stepped back. "You're a monk! You *stole* it from the fucking tomb of the Lawgiver?"

Acquel collapsed onto his backside and buried his head in his hands, the golden chain of the amulet dangling down. "The captain took it from me. How did it get into my pocket?"

Timandra squatted down next to him. "Listen, I'll take you back up to Strykar. You can explain."

Acquel raised his head and looked at her like she was a simpleton. "Explain? How do I explain? I was standing six feet away from him when he held the amulet. I didn't take it back. I swear to you!"

"And this is why you were chased out of Livorna by the Temple guard?"

Acquel's shoulders shook and his head flew back as he laughed. "They don't even know it's missing. They don't even know it was there." Tears filled his eyes.

Timandra placed a hand on his arm. "Tell me the truth. What happened to you?"

Acquel rubbed a sleeve across his face and cleared his throat. He turned and looked at Timandra. "I saw the Lawgiver's body. And everyone else who saw the Lawgiver's body is dead now. They murdered them all. Except for me."

"What are you saying? Who was murdered?"

"My brothers. The greyrobes and blackrobes. We saw something in the tomb that we should not have. And they killed us."

"Who killed who?"

"The Temple Magister gave the order. He told the guardsmen to slay the greyrobes and Brother Kell. But I ran."

"Acquel, why did the Magister do that? What did you all see?"

Acquel's voice lowered and his words came out calmly. "I saw the saint. I saw his bones. And he wasn't a man. I mean, he wasn't completely a man. He... was a fish-man. A merman."

Timandra's right hand shot out and grabbed Acquel's face, pinching his cheeks. "You listen to me, man! Start making sense or I will drag you feet first to Strykar and watch while he guts you."

Acquel batted her hand away. "He was a mer! He was a goddamned fish-man."

Timandra sank back and leaned against the wagon. "It must be a mistake. His body must have been stolen and replaced with another."

Acquel shook his head. He'd already thought of that. "No. It was he. Still in his burial robes, thin as gauze and practically dust. I swear to you."

Timandra looked straight ahead, silent for a moment. If she was to believe the tale then her entire upbringing was now exposed as a lie. Her faith was built upon a dreadful secret that somehow had never been revealed. If it was true.

She stood up and brushed off her skirts. "Very well. I believe what you say you saw. But I'll need more proof than your word for what it means."

Acquel looked up at her. "You think the Magister would order the deaths of six innocent men for no good reason?"

She had no quick answer to that. "Come on, get up. I'll take you back to Strykar. We'll figure something out."

HE HAD MADE the mistake of holding out the amulet before making an explanation. Strykar's eyes flashed anger and as he snatched the chain with his left hand, his right gave a cuff to Acquel that sent him sprawling.

"So much for gratitude!" Strykar seized him and hauled him upright to land another blow.

"Jules!" cried Timandra, as the burly soldier shook Acquel like a rabbit in a hound's jaws. She grasped the back of the captain's doublet. "Cousin! Stop!"

Strykar half-turned towards her and then released the monk with a disdainful push.

"Let him explain what happened," she said.

Lieutenant Poule stood near the back of the large field, tent near the table, leather jack in hand and a barely suppressed smile on his face. Acquel stood up, rubbing his cheek and thanking his stars that Captain Strykar had some respect for blood ties. And *this* tie he had not expected.

"How did you manage that, monk?" Strykar jerked his doublet back down over his exposed linen and hose. "I put that thing in my belt pouch after you left here. How in hell's name did you learn that little trick?"

"I swear to you, in the Lord's name, I did not steal that from you. I don't know how it found its way back to me."

Strykar moved to retrieve his wine cup. "So I suppose you will tell me that Poule here lifted it from me when I took my belt off earlier and slipped it into your arse crack when you weren't looking?" Poule grinned and held up both hands in surrender.

Acquel felt a flush of anger in spite of his fear. "I did not steal it from you. If I had why would I have come back to hand it to you?"

Strykar nodded. "Very well then. Start explaining." The golden amulet clattered to the table.

Acquel looked over to Timandra, not knowing how much to reveal to the captain and fearing that his precarious situation might be made even worse by what he had to say.

"Tell him," she said softly. "Tell him everything you told me."

Acquel stood straight as he could, arms at his side. "You know what I have stolen. But I didn't tell you everything about how it happened. I didn't break into Saint Elded's tomb. I was *chosen* to go down there by the blackrobes."

Strykar nestled his brass goblet in the crook of his folded arms. "Keep going."

"I was one of a party of greyrobes and blackrobes sent below to see if the recent earth tremor had collapsed the tomb of the saint. It had, at least partially. The tomb was smashed and that is how I saw—and took—the amulet."

"And who else saw you do this?" asked Strykar. "Why did the Temple guard say you had killed someone?"

Acquel bristled. "I've killed no one. And no one saw me lift the amulet either. They still don't know."

Strykar gestured with the goblet. "So now we get to the heart of the matter. What exactly did you do down there?"

Acquel again looked to Timandra. She was tense, he could tell, even in the poor half-light of the tent. But she nodded at him, urging him to continue.

"I saw something—we all did—something that we should not have. The Lawgiver's bones were exposed where the sarcophagus was broken. I saw him. He... was not like you or me. I mean, not like *us*."

Poule chuckled. "Of course not, you fool. He was a fucking saint, wasn't he?"

Acquel shook his head. "You don't understand. He was a merman. Or half a merman... I don't know."

Strykar laughed and Poule echoed him. "Good one!" the lieutenant chuckled.

"I saw him with my own eyes. We all did. More too, so did the Magister Kodoris after we fetched him down. As soon as he saw the truth of the Saint's bones he ordered all of the monks slain at the foot of the sarcophagus. His guardsmen saw to that."

Strykar wasn't laughing now. "But you got away. How did you manage that?"

"I was standing furthest away and as soon as I saw Brother Kell get run through, I ran for it. Got out before they could catch me and ran for hours. Until you found me."

Poule sidled up to Strykar. "See! I told you this one was going to be trouble, Captain. We should have turned him over to the Temple."

Strykar took two steps closer to Acquel. "You swear the Magister ordered everyone killed? You saw this?"

"I swear it. On everything that is holy."

Poule pointed at Acquel, his jack sloshing drink on the ground. "No wonder they wanted his skin so badly."

Strykar squinted. "The Lawgiver was *mer*? There was no mistake?"

Acquel nodded.

Strykar looked down. "Well, that is enough to blow the roof off the Temple or it's a full wagonload of horseshit." He looked to Timandra. "And I don't have a lick of proof to say either way."

"You can see what he's been through," she replied.

"Aye. And that could have a hundred explanations."

"And it doesn't explain our holy man's sleight of hand trick," added Poule.

Strykar nodded. "He's right, brother monk. You haven't given answer to that yet. Pretty trinket, worth keeping isn't it…." He turned to the table, only to find the amulet gone. Strykar looked down to see if it had fallen onto the floor and then over to Poule. "Did you pick that thing up?"

Poule shook his head.

Acquel knew even before he felt for it in his robes. "Captain Strykar, it is in my pocket." His voice was calm as he looked straight into the soldier's eyes. "May I?"

No one said a word as Acquel reached in and withdrew it, dangling from its golden chain. He held it out for Strykar. "I swear to you, sir. I am not doing this."

Strykar said nothing but reached out and took the amulet. He held it away from him as if it would bite. "Timandra, close the flap."

The Widow hesitated, still frozen by the surprise of what she had seen—or not seen, to be exact.

"Timandra, we don't want any unwanted eyes on this, so close the bloody tent."

With the flap closed, the light diminished. The sole lantern now illuminated the field tent. Timandra Pandarus was now staring not at the amulet but at Acquel, staring as if she had perhaps misjudged or misunderstood the monk.

Strykar rubbed at his beard a second and then let the amulet and chain coil itself in his outstretched palm. "Brother monk, I want you to place your hands on top your mangy scalp until I say so." Acquel did as he was bade. "Poule, I want you to watch this trinket like a hawk. Don't even blink. Do you understand? You too, cousin."

Strykar moved so that he was between the table and Acquel. He cautiously reached out and placed the amulet on the wooden plank, full in the glow of the lantern, and then withdrew his hand. There were no words exchanged. Acquel became aware of the noises of the camp around them: the cries, the laughter, the sounds of crockery clattering as the men gathered around the cook wagons. Strykar stared until his eyes began to narrow with the effort. Poule looked like a cat staring down a rat, rigid and intent. And when it finally happened, not a single one of them saw it. Strykar hadn't even blinked, but the amulet was gone.

"Aloysius and all the Saints!" Strykar took a step back. Poule muttered an oath, his jaw dropping, and Timandra could not move her eyes from the table.

Acquel swallowed hard as Strykar walked in front of him, his face hard as stone. Without asking, he reached into Acquel's pocket and Acquel watched as the captain's eyes widened. He pulled out the amulet and held it out towards Timandra. "Tell me you know how this is happening, cousin."

Timandra blessed herself, forehead and breast. "It's a miracle from God," she said softly.

Strykar pushed Acquel's arms down. "I've not seen any miracles in my time," he growled. "So is it the Lord's will or is it something else?"

"Sorcery," said Poule, the word almost catching in his throat.

Acquel looked straight at Strykar. "I have been a greyrobe these past two years and have devoted my life to the Faith. I did not ask for this to happen to me."

Strykar nodded thoughtfully and pursed his lips. "Or... is it the ghost of the saint himself?"

Timandra swore and stepped between monk and soldier. "It is a sign and you will give it back to him now!"

Strykar said nothing but slowly stretched out his hand to Acquel. "Looks like it might be best if you hold onto the Saint's trinket." As Acquel reluctantly took it, it felt as if it were a lump of lead in his hand.

Strykar turned to the Widow and to the lieutenant. "Not a word," he said. "Not a word to a soul or they'll burn the monk—and us too, more than likely."

Poule nodded. "But we still have to deal with him. If what he says is true... I mean, what we've just *seen*. The Temple guard will hunt him down and they know we have him. We should hand him over in the morning."

"Then they will kill him," hissed Timandra. "Another innocent slain for the High Priest."

Strykar put his hands on Acquel's shoulders. "Boy, look at me. Did you will this in any way?"

Acquel raised his chin slightly. "I did not, sir."

Strykar turned to Poule. "I believe him. I don't know why but I believe him."

Poule shook his head. "Captain..."

Strykar glanced down at the amulet grasped in Acquel's

hand. "This is beyond my cunning but I know it is grave. And it will not go away of its own accord. The Count will know what to do and if he doesn't the Duke of Maresto will."

"So what do we do with him?" replied Poule.

"Brother Acquel comes with us to Palestro first. Then we return to Maresto by the south road to give Livorna a wide berth. Timandra, put him into a proper shirt and hose and burn these rags he's in. And he's in your charge so put him to work."

Timandra nodded, fearful of what the young monk's presence meant for the company of the Black Rose. And fearful of the true nature of the force that had chosen him.

THE SUN WAS blood red and shimmering upon the horizon as it burned its last rays of the day. Acquel sat cross-legged on the grass near Timandra's wagon, distinctly uncomfortable to be wearing woollen hose again for the first time in three years. And his green shoes looked, well, just plain odd after years of being sandal-shod. Around them, the occasional guffaw or burst of laughter sounded, but for the most part, the company was settling down for the night, ragged after a day's march. He shovelled his evening meal of thick grey stew into his mouth and followed this with a hunk of black bread. After the ordeal he had been through, and what seemed the longest day of his life, it was a banquet.

Timandra sat nearby, watching. The warm evening breeze blew a few loose strands of her hair across her face which she absently brushed away. He was not a handsome man, she thought, but neither was he ill-favoured. Scruffy to be sure, and no doubt because of what had happened to him, but he would undoubtedly look better with more hair on his head. And he was young. She had not really thought about monks being young. Yet, why *this* monk? Why had he been singled out for the touch of the divine spirit?

"Is Acquel your true name or is that a monk-given name?" she asked.

Acquel took the spoon from his mouth and swallowed. "It's mine. The Temple let me keep it. They said it was probably short for Acquelonius, some great cleric who lived a few hundred years ago. It didn't much matter to me at the time. My family name is Galenus."

She smiled. "You don't sound all that dedicated to your calling. After today, I suppose I can't blame you for that."

Acquel set his empty bowl into his lap. "I told you I was a thief before I became a monk. And I only became a monk because I had to. I was older, the gangs were getting rougher. I knew I would end up caught and hanged or else knifed in an alley."

She reached for his bowl. "You needed that, I think."

Acquel nodded. "At least in the dormitory you get regular meals just for singing and praying, tending the gardens and binding books. Don't have to worry about a knife in..." He suddenly trailed off, his head falling as he looked away from her.

"You're with the Black Rose now," she said, trying half-heartedly to reassure him.

"Captain Strykar doesn't like me or believe me. Doesn't seem to like anybody as far as I can see. Has he always been so... grim?"

"There's more to it—more to *him*—than you know. Give it time."

"Is your cousin going to hand me back or is he going to give me over to his masters in Maresto as some pawn to be traded?"

"I won't let him do that."

"You shouldn't make promises you can't keep, Mistress Pandarus."

She knew that too. But she could not resist asking the one question that burned in her mind.

"Acquel, why you?"

He knew exactly what she meant. "It shouldn't be me. I don't even want the thing... anymore."

"But, it... it is like a miracle of old."

"I'm not a good monk. Haven't even taken my final vows as a blackrobe. So why has this happened to me? To teach me a lesson about stealing?"

"Maybe because the Lord sees something in you that you do not."

He smiled—but it was a smile borne of scorn. "It isn't from God, Timandra. It's from *Elded*. His ghost is following me. And I can't outrun it."

And he believed it.

Timandra didn't reply. She arose, brushed her kirtle and gathered up the bowls. She was growing fearful again of the amulet—and of Acquel. And she realized that he was no longer the frightened barefoot monk she had first met and shod like some deserving beggar. He was angry.

Six

DANAMIS STOOD FOURSQUARE on the sterncastle deck, hands on the railing as he watched the two great stone towers loom on either side of the harbour entrance. *Royal Grace* was easing forward under a light breeze, her lateen mizzen sheet unfurled and a small square sheet rigged up on her bowsprit. On the deck below where Danamis stood, he could hear Gregorvero barking commands to the helmsman as he gripped the long whipstaff pole. The mouth of the harbour was two hundred feet wide, not the smallest that he had ever sailed into but not especially large either. Not a worry on an incoming tide like now; most of the manoeuvring was done by some short sail with the helmsman correcting with a bit of heave on the whipstaff when needed. A well-judged heading to begin with, a good eye, and the tide flow did the rest.

She glided past the squat two-storey rectangular tower that lay off to starboard with twenty feet to spare. The giant links of a great cast iron chain, the thickness of a sailor's forearm, spilled down from the second level straight into the water. Like a monstrous black serpent, it wound its way upon the floor of the harbour mouth until it rose up at the opposite tower, disappearing into the capstan room there.

It was Palestro's great defence. Twenty men in each tower, straining on those capstans and bars, could raise the chain in a few minutes. And then, no ship was coming in or out.

Horseshoe-shaped Palestro rose up in front of him: the city of his birth and where he had spent most of his life. Bounded at the sea's mouth by the two towers, the twenty-five foot tall city walls extended from there, encompassing the town completely. On the north side of the city one massive gate stood, to the east and west two others, the only ways in or out other than by sea. The city itself was built upon a hill that rose steeply and suddenly from the quays of the harbourside. Narrow streets wound their way up, up to the summit where the great white stone merchant villas sat, nestled closely next to one another. The far side sloped down more gradually to the city walls and the plain beyond. Here lay another warren of alleyways and streets, the home of Palestro's, tanners, bakers, butchers, and other tradesmen. In all, some 40,000 souls laboured, loved, feasted, played, and died in the place. Danamis's heart lifted as he drank in the view from such a splendid vantage on his ship's highest deck, the sun beating down strongly against a sky lapis blue, the gulls dipping, diving and screeching overhead.

Already people were running along the quay: fisherfolk, lightermen, sailors, children too, yelling and screaming at the arrival. His personal standard waved gracefully from the top of the mainmast but most Palestrians knew the lines of the *Royal Grace* from a distance. They knew their High Steward had returned, the sole heir of Lord Valerian. Danamis turned to look behind them. *Firedrake* was just now entering between the towers of the chain. Beyond her, *Salamander* bobbed under full sail as she made a turn north to prepare for the run into the harbour mouth.

"Douse sail!" bellowed Gregorvero as the ship cleared the mouth and entered the harbour. The mizzen and foresheets fell and crew on the fo'c'sle and bowsprit readied the cables as the *Royal Grace* rapidly slowed to a drift. Gregorvero had piloted the ship to within a throw of its berth, and those on the dock stood ready to receive the line as it was heaved. On the main deck, a second cable was readied while a grapnel anchor at the bow was unchained. The ship's soldiers, shouldering their crossbows and clutching sword and axe, jostling each other as they crammed together on the main deck, eager to disembark.

"Cast your lines!"

The ropes were thrown and caught by the lightermen on the quay, and slowly the bulk of the vessel was hauled in, hand over hand. From his station high up in the sterncastle, Danamis reached into a canvas sack and palmed a handful of gold coins. As the assembled crowd cheered, he tossed the coins high, raining down treasure upon them and causing a mad scramble. He laughed and scooped another handful, flinging these after the first. It was what they were used to—and what they expected. It had been nearly three days since the disatrous trade with the mer. Three days of furtive glances from his soldiers and an unusual silence below decks.

But look at the lads now, he thought. Pushing and shoving to get off first, laughing and roughhousing; the events at sea were passing into hazy memory. And for Danamis, somehow just entering Palestro again cleared his head like a cold blast of winter air.

I've got time to make things right. Perhaps spread a little more of the treasure this time around. Smooth the feathers. Time to think of a way to regain the trust of the mer.

In the centre of the harbour, the remainder of the fleet lay at moorings. The great carracks *Fortuna*, *Hammerblow*, *Drum*, and *Bonadventura* clustered one to another. A short distance away the lighter and faster caravels rode low and sleek: *Swiftsure*, *Seafox*, *Seahawk* and *Unicorn*. On the opposite side of the harbour half a dozen tubby single-masted cogs lay tied up to the docks. These were the Palestrian trade ships (more were out at sea) but these too could be armed and fought when times required.

Danamis watched as *Firedrake* made stately passage into the harbour, dropping anchor somewhere between the other carracks and *Royal Grace*. Tetch must have arranged a tender before he had even left Palestro because the longboat was out from the quayside, sweeps pulling hard, even before the anchor hit the water. Poor old *Salamander* too had now entered the safety of Palestro and its master worked to guide the ship forward of *Royal Grace* to attempt a quayside dock.

Danamis leaned over the rail and surveyed his men.

"Well done, my lads! Well done for a hard run of it! Ship's master will give out your shares from the quayside so give him way. You there—let him through! There's a good fellow. Your woman will wait!"

Danamis searched out Ramus, the captain of the sterncastle, and gave him a sign. He then picked up the sack of coins, dropped down the ladder and made for his cabin. Inside the cramped and musty space, lit only by two small leaded windows, there were two small chests of stout seasoned oak and a much larger iron strongbox. He lifted the lids of the oak chests to count the canvas sacks tied up with twine: the remainder of the treasure haul. The bulk of it now lay in the strongbox, reinforced and riveted and with a rare and complex mechanism forged with Ivrean skill for which he and Escalus, his castellan, alone held keys. And the reality came back to bite him again. This could be the last of it. The very last. When Ramus knocked, his escort in tow, he was still staring at the chests. The party of soldiers had been hand-picked. Danamis indicated the oak chests for Gregorvero and the castle captains to distribute to the crew, archers, and swordsmen. His eyes fell again to the great black strongbox, its iron bars locked firmly by the clever puzzle of ratchets and pawls inside. He then motioned for the soldiers to pick it up and carry it away.

They manhandled the strongbox out of the narrow hatch of the stern cabin and out onto the main deck. Danamis put a hand on Ramus's shoulder and leaned in to speak into his ear. "Keep to the main streets and don't get distracted. If you beat me to the palazzo, Ramus, I'll double the coin for you and the men."

Ramus nodded and smiled, his leathery face creasing. "Very good, my lord. We shall be up the hill in a trice. Never you worry."

Danamis followed behind them and as he emerged into the sunlight he saw Escalus leading his retainers down the quay, the stable boys guiding his grey palfrey past the multi-coloured awnings of the chandlers' shops. It was time to go home and to his own bed. He drank in a chestful of sea air, tinged with fish, and let it out. The voyage had been intolerably long and fractious. And despite that he had brought treasure home, it had also been a failure, one that he had yet to fully come to grips with.

GREGORVERO WAS BREATHING hard as he reached the walls and the outer gate of the Danamis palazzo, the sun low in the sky as evening approached. He swept off his red felt hat and wiped his brow with the sleeve of his doublet. Despite the meagre ship's fare he never seemed to see his belly shrink out at sea, and if anything, he was larger than he had been before the voyage. If he hadn't been so winded he would have sighed. He was about to pull the cord on the bell but two guards had seen him and came to swing open the huge oak and serpentine wrought iron gate. Inside the courtyard, he again drank in the sight of the manse. It wasn't overly large as palazzos went: just two storeys high and made of rough-hewn yellow sandstone below and more elaborate brickwork above.

Situated in a large courtyard, it sat long and rectangular, more than a dozen large mullioned windows arrayed along its upper storey. There were fewer windows on the ground floor, ornate ones of lozenge-shaped leaded-glass, but these were faced with black iron grates cast to resemble a climbing rose. A large studded oaken door sat framed in an arch, the decorative brickwork in alternating colours of red and yellow. The low and lean terracotta roof was failing in a few places, but the octagonal brick tower that rose up at the south end of the palazzo still looked sound. Gregorvero knew from past visits how good the view was from its vantage. And above the orange terracotta roof of the tower flew Nico's personal standard: a dolphin and falchion, dark red upon white.

His boots crushed the pea shingle as he approached; already the great door was swinging inwards to receive him. All the way up to the palazzo, his mind had gone in circles about just how to say what he knew in his heart needed to be said. Trouble had come and could no longer be ignored or wished away.

Inside, the ground floor hall looked straight into a lush courtyard, surrounded by the beautiful stone arches of an arcade. A fountain whispered. Silks and cushions covered three large wood couches and there, reclining in the midst, was Captain Nicolo Danamis, a woman on either side.

"Master Gregorvero! You are most welcome." Danamis shifted himself and gestured with an arm towards a couch. A retainer stepped forward to pour a goblet of wine for the ship's master. Gregor couldn't suppress a smile as his eyes settled upon the two courtesans in their flowing gossamer gowns, breasts peeping out of the folds. Nico never wasted any time once back from a voyage, and he had only been back for a few hours.

Gregorvero grasped his goblet and sat uneasily in the centre of the couch facing Danamis. The young admiral of Valdur raised his cup while the jet-haired girl on his right stroked his thigh.

"Here's to another voyage ended! The coffers refilled!" He swigged back his cup. "It might just be our last for a while..."

Gregorvero could see his commander had been at it for some time already. He wasn't obviously drunk, just mildly cupshot—and loquacious. The ship's master nodded and raised his own cup to the toast. The wine felt good going down and, the saints knew, he needed it.

He leaned forward, trying to keep his eyes off the breasts of Nico's companions. "Ship is secure, everything stowed. I've paid off the men and left twenty aboard to keep watch."

Danamis nodded and extended his goblet to be refilled by the young man liveried in red and white. "You did well on this one, Gregor. Especially when all hell broke loose like it did."

Gregorvero acknowledged the praise with a modest nod, took a long drink and gripped the silver goblet with both hands, arms resting on his thighs. "We have to talk, Nico. About the trade. About... well, a lot of things."

Danamis frowned and pushed himself upright on the sofa. He lifted the arm of one lady and pushed the other's backside away from him. They took the hint and stood, giving a little curtsey and exiting the inner courtyard, bare feet slapping on the paving slabs.

Gregorvero managed to drag his couch a little closer to Danamis. Off on the far side of the loggia, he could see the castellan, Escalus, watching and fingering his gold collar of office. Gregorvero paused, made eye contact, and the castellan gave a brief nod and left them, understanding the need for privacy. As castellan of House Danamis, Escalus was a crusty and formal coxcomb of few words but Gregorvero had always known him to be honourable. He had remained with Nico long after it became clear that his master, Valerian Danamis, would never return from the sea. Gregorvero turned back to Danamis and leaned in, his voice quiet.

"Nico, I must speak my mind to you. I wanted to last night but, well, I thought it better to wait until we were at home. There is something not right. Now wait... I've sailed with you for many years. And I'm telling you the mood is as bad as I've seen in all that time. Belly-aching below decks. Grumbling. I'm used to that. But what I'm not used to is silence. And that's what I heard on the voyage home. Nothing."

Danamis took another drink and did not reply.

"Nico, I'm telling you this does not bode well. Something is simmering, I can feel it. And the cock-up with the merfolk is just the start."

"Go on," growled Danamis.

"You know most of the men have never liked the trade with the fishmen. And now, what with the priests at the Temple openly calling the seamen sinners for taking part in your little business, that's wound them up all the tighter."

"They looked happy enough on the quayside today."

Gregorvero shook his head slowly. "Don't be deceived by that. That was relief they were home, nothing more. And it doesn't signify that they're any happier."

Danamis raised his chin. "You think I should not have killed those two fools as I did?"

"I am not saying that. I probably would have done the same thing. There was no other punishment. What I'm saying is what happened that day has changed things... for the long term. It's been building for the last year or more. And the dam is ready to burst."

"So what is your counsel, good Gregor? Go ahead, tell me." Danamis drank again, his lips stained red.

"I'm saying that perhaps, just perhaps, what happened with the merfolk is no bad thing. It was a good run while it lasted but it's come to an end. It's time we went back to what we used to do."

Danamis laughed and leaned back into his cushions. "Yes! Go back to hunting dirt-poor Southlander merchants for a few more bolts of silk and a few jars of spice. How much cloth and spice do you think we'll need to steal to make as much as just one myrra trade? It would take fucking years!"

Gregorvero swallowed. He knew he was pushing his friendship probably more than he should. "You may not have a choice."

Danamis's annoyance flared and he flung his now empty goblet into the fountain. "We're hemmed in tighter than a nun's twat and it was the myrra trade alone that has kept us from going under. I get nothing from the king and only a pittance from Maresto. With no war in years we can't even pinch the damnable Torinians!"

"It was your father who accepted the title of admiral and the gift of this city from the king. It was a good decision then and a good one now."

Danamis looked upwards to the darkening sky, aggravated. "Well, he's not here anymore to sort things out, is he?"

"Nico, make an effort with the town. Announce the trade is done with and that we're going back to pirating the foreigners and defending the coast. In the meantime I will make sure my men and the dock scroungers keep their ears open for trouble."

"Boy! Fetch me my goblet back and fill it. Fill his as well!" Danamis smoothed back his hair and swore under his breath. "I'll think about it, Gregor. I'll think about it." He stood up and tugged at his short-sleeved brocade coat, now adorned with wine. The youth, ever patient, placed a full goblet in Danamis's hand. "Oh, and get those women back in here." The youth bowed and scuttled off.

Gregorvero opened his mouth, about to say more, but a commotion in the hall told them both that there were new arrivals to the palazzo. A stuttering armed retainer hurried into the loggia to announce the guests but it proved too late.

"By Elded's bollocks! Just the two of you! Where are all the women?"

Giacomo Tetch strode in, three whores in tow, the latter all giggles and smiles. Danamis shook his head in quiet surprise.

"A good evening to you, uncle."

Gregorvero was on his feet as soon as he had heard the ruckus and now he took half a step back and gave a curt nod. "Captain Tetch."

Tetch grabbed one of the girls around the waist and pulled her in. "Just as well I brought enough for everyone!" he roared. "The *Grace* has been at anchor for hours and you haven't dipped your wicks yet?"

Gregorvero's mouth twitched into a half smile. He didn't like Tetch's bravura—or him. He may have been a good captain, and he was most assuredly a good pirate, but Gregorvero always thought him as slippery as a hagfish and just as ugly. He found it difficult to stop from staring at that white glass orb in his head: the closed eyelid of a sleeping snake. He was dying to ask him more about the two bowmen who had shot at the merfolk and precipitated chaos. They had, after all, come from his crew. But that was a demand for Danamis to make and not him.

Tetch fell onto one of the couches, pulling a whore down onto his lap. "Where is the wine, then? I've brought the dessert."

Danamis motioned the servers and more drink was duly brought in. Gregorvero took his seat again and reached for his wine. *Might be better if I stay awhile,* he thought, as he watched the sweating pirate guffawing and pawing at the prostitute. But to his eyes, Tetch did not seem like he had been pouring it down his throat overly, at least not as much as Danamis.

Tetch snatched a goblet and took a long drink before wiping his doublet sleeve across his mouth. "Now, I don't believe in mixing business with pleasure but... it does fall on me to pass you a message. I came across a member of the Council of Decurions on the way up here. They are hoping for an audience with you on the morrow. I told them I was confident you could oblige."

Danamis's eyes narrowed. "The Decurions? And what do they wish to hear?"

Tetch shrugged. "It seemed an ordinary request. I think they wanted to hear how the voyage went. And... well, Elonis—you remember him I think—Elonis had heard that the trade did not go quite as planned this time. He said they just wanted to hear from you and not the rumours of sailors."

Danamis wasn't overly concerned. The Decurions of Palestro generally did what he asked of them to keep the city administered. And he compensated them handsomely for their allegiance. But giving the request via Tetch annoyed him.

"I'll speak with them, uncle. As soon as I get a proper request for an audience. Do they think me some town watchman they can call in for reports? No, I'll wait for a proper delegation to come up the hill."

Tetch nodded gravely. "Too right, too right, Nico. They must see who rules Palestro. Say, what's this then?"

Danamis's courtesans had reappeared and were now giving a curtsey. One of Tetch's whores made a sour face.

"Make yourself at home, uncle," said Danamis sounding bored but not a little irritated. "I'm for my own chamber.

Gregor, stay as you please. Escalus will look after you." He gestured to Tetch's ladies. "Or you can assist Captain Tetch here who clearly has far too much to handle."

Tetch laughed and nodded vigorously. "Aye! Share and share alike. That's the way of sailors, is it not?"

Gregorvero smiled and made a graceful bow from the hips, his belly spilling from underneath his belted doublet. "You are most generous, my lord. But I must get down to the harbour again or there will be hell to pay with my own woman."

As he walked from the palace, the sounds of high-pitched squeals followed him, Tetch and the women both. He pulled his cloak about him, glad he was out of there and glad that he was walking *down* the hill this time. He knew how to pilot ship, bark, or caravel in calm water and in the roughest sea. And his old father had always told him he had a nose for what was coming over the horizon. Now, his nose was itching again.

Seven

Lucius Kodoris pulled his cloak away from his arm and raised it across his nose and mouth, his left hand holding onto the reins of his mount. A swirling cloud of hot yellow dust flew into his face from the brick-hard road. Next to him his riding companion, Captain Flauros of the Temple guard, merely wiped a gloved hand across his narrowed eyes. He was sitting a head higher than Kodoris himself since the charger he rode was some three hands taller than the Magister's palfrey. Kodoris didn't like that much in a world where presence and perception were everything.

They were only five miles outside the walls of Livorna, heading east past the outlying farms and orchards of the city. And not far ahead, as the dust cloud whipped past them, he could just spy the large walled estate that was their destination.

Flauros cleared his throat and spat. "I've not heard of this priory before—Saint Dionei's. Not even heard of the saint. You have had dealings here before, Magister?"

Kodoris let his cloak fall back to his shoulder and turned to his companion. "I would have thought that knowing one's catechism was a prerequisite for becoming an officer in the Temple guard."

"That was a long time ago in my case, Magister."

Kodoris looked back to the road and the great house ahead. "Saint Dionei was a companion of Elded the Lawgiver. Surely you remember *that* saint."

Flauros bore the barb, his expression stoic.

"Dionei," continued Kodoris, "was the one who was instrumental in revealing the existence of the Great Deceiver who was amongst the followers like a wolf amidst the flock. She paid for that with her life. And yes, I have been a visitor here once before… when I needed the services of a Seeker."

"God willing they will do you good service again then, Magister."

It was Flauros who reached out to ring the priory bell at the gates. "These Seekers are canonesses you say? They take no vows?"

"They come and go as is their will. But their piety is not to be questioned. Nor their ability. They are high born—their father was the Lord of Rovera."

A servant girl came to greet them at the gate, dressed in grey and with a face as blank as an unwritten page. She led them inside to the courtyard where their horses were taken. They were ushered into the cool of the stone priory and into the main hall where a great oak table stood at its centre. Two dozen small windows, set high up the walls, illuminated the drab chamber. In a few moments the girl returned bearing an earthen wine jug and cups. She had no sooner left when an older woman, a cleric, and nearly as wide as the doorway, waddled in to greet them. Her round face looked like a full moon against the blackness of the wimple that surrounded her head and shoulders.

Kodoris bowed deeply, followed immediately by Captain Flauros, who had hastily removed his polished sallet helm. "Prioress, we are honoured that you receive us," said the monk.

She curtsied. "We are glad to offer the Temple Majoris any assistance when called upon. Our two ladies have been told of your letter and are eager to meet with you. In the meantime, please take refreshment. They shan't be long."

Flauros looked hopefully at the Magister.

"We thank you for your hospitality," the monk intoned before giving the nod to his eager captain. With barely contained restraint, Flauros poured out two cups and passed one to the Magister before raising his own to his lips without even a pause.

When two identical women entered the room a moment later, Flauros paused with his vessel halfway to his mouth. The Magister had not bothered to tell him that the Seekers were twins nor that they were young (no more than five and twenty summers, he reckoned). Dressed separately to be sure, but so strikingly similar in aspect that had they been attired the same he would have been unable to tell them apart. And they were beautiful. Hair golden, the colour of sun-bleached straw, eyes of blue, pretty noses, and perfectly formed thin lips framed by a strong feminine chin. They dwarfed the prioress as they stood next to her. Flauros set his cup upon the table without taking his eyes off the pair and gave a deep court bow.

They were dressed in satin, one blue, the other amber, the delicate cambric of their chemises showing at the slashed sleeves and the high, square-cut neckline, and enough golden lace to shame a prince. Their long hair was tied back and a transparent veil of tissue-like silk gauze covered the tops of their heads, ending in a peak and dangling pearl at the forehead. They belonged at a duke's court and not a priory.

Kodoris gave a deep bow. "My good sisters, it fills my heart with gladness to see you both again and in the bloom of good health." He half-turned and waved his hand. "And this is Captain Flauros of the Temple Guard. My escort."

The sisters smiled and gave a simultaneous, if shallow, curtsey and Flauros inclined his head in return. The one on the left spoke. "I am Lucinda. My sister is called Lavinia."

"Well then," puffed the prioress, clapping her hands together. "I have duties to attend to so I will leave you here to discuss your business. Please be seated." Flauros thought it strange she would not stay but she was gone in seconds, toddling out through the ornately carved archway.

The sisters walked across to the far side of the table and Flauros was about to seat himself on the bench at his side when Kodoris put a hand on his arm. "Captain, I would ask you to place yourself outside the door that no others may enter. I will call you in after I speak with the sisters." His look was steel; a look that Flauros had learned not to question. He gave a smart bow to Kodoris and the ladies and exited the chamber, now more eager than even before to uncover the purpose of this secretive enterprise.

Kodoris pulled in the skirt of his robes and sat facing the sisters. He laced his hands together and placed them on the table. "My letter to you was necessarily vague. That I am in need of a skilful Seeker you both already know. It remains for me to tell you the why." He reached into a deep pocket of his garment and withdrew a grey cloth—a monk's hood. "This belongs to a greyrobe who has fled the Ara. Someone who must be found and returned. For the good of the Faith."

Lucinda's eyes bored into him. "And what did this greyrobe do that he had to flee, Magister?"

"He killed a brother monk in his bid to escape the monastery. He was pursued by Captain Flauros and his men but he cleverly fell in with a band of mercenaries who have apparently given him shelter. He is probably on the road south as we speak."

Lucinda nodded, expressionless. "May I hold the garment?"

Kodoris pushed it across the scored planks of the old refectory table and Lucinda leaned forward to retrieve it. She shared it with Lavinia, the two of them kneading it gently in their long-fingered hands. They exchanged a knowing look and Lucinda's eyebrows arched briefly. She turned back to face Kodoris.

"He saw something. Something that frightened him. That is why he fled."

Kodoris sat back.

"And there is no blood on his hands," said Lavinia quietly. She turned to her sister. "The Magister is frugal with the truth."

Kodoris had always been unsure that he could conceal anything from the sisters for very long. But that they had seen through his lie instantly unnerved him to the point of panic. "There are some truths that can never be told—or shared," he said, thinking fast.

Lucinda shook her head slowly and gave him the look of an indulgent mother. "Magister, I can see into your soul from where I sit. We *know* what this man has seen. We know what you have seen too. And you want the greyrobe found before he can share this terrible secret with others."

Kodoris clenched his jaw and nodded.

Lucinda's eyes moved to the door. "*He* does not know the real reason why you seek this monk?"

"Neither Captain Flauros nor any of his men. It is a secret shared only by the High Priest and the Nine," replied Kodoris, seeing no further point in deceit.

"The Nine Principals... of which you are now a part," said Lucinda. "And of course, the greyrobe... Tarquel."

"No," interjected Lavinia, placing her hand over her sister's. "He is... Acquel."

Lucinda nodded. "Quite right, sister. *Acquel*." She crossed her arms and leaned forward, her face that of a perfect maiden of Valdur. "Do you wish the greyrobe purged? To defend the One Faith we all serve."

Kodoris felt a chill to hear such brutal frankness from so

beautiful a woman. "I want... I need to know who he has shared this secret with. For that reason he should be recovered to Livorna. With all due haste."

Lucinda nodded. "The righteous have the right, Magister. And it is we who must do the Lord's work on this plane of existence. Let not your heart be heavy with the decision. We will help you."

Kodoris felt a weight lift from him. "I knew you would. You have a gift given of the Lord." His mouth had gone completely dry. He reached for his wine. "Captain Flauros and a party of his men will accompany you both south."

Lucinda and Lavinia both broke into gentle smiles. "I will accompany the good captain. Lavinia will go with you to Livorna to keep you abreast on our progress."

Kodoris smiled awkwardly. He did not even wish to know how they would accomplish such a communication across the distances but he knew well enough it would not be by courier. He looked at them both, their composure, their *knowing*. And if they now knew the secret of Elded it appeared to move them not at all.

"Are you not distressed by the nature of the secret we now share?" he asked. "Is your faith not shaken?"

Lucinda and her sister exchanged a quizzical look. "Why should we be distressed?" said Lucinda. Her sister nodded sagely in agreement. "It is the Lord's will that we discover such things and the Faith can survive these revelations. The lies of a saint do not change the laws of God or the Faith. The heresy will be contained."

Kodoris had used the sisters two years before. And then, as now, it had been to find someone. Neither the guard nor the town militia had found a trace of the thief who had stolen the golden incense burners and the great staff of the High Priest. Yet these canonesses had done it in a day, and recovered them from where they had been buried. The man had never even opened his mouth to reveal the truth. He went to the hangman with the vacant look of an imbecile.

"Sisters, we should bring in Captain Flauros again to tell him of our plans."

Lucinda nodded. "Yes, I would gauge the measure of this soldier, Magister. We will be spending a great deal of time together."

Lavinia was running the grey hood through her hands again, staring off into the middle distance of the chamber. Lucinda touched her shoulder.

Lavinia returned to them. "Your greyrobe found something in the tomb. Something small. Something old." She looked directly at Kodoris. "Something rather important."

Kodoris froze. "Tell me. What did he find?"

The canoness's brow furrowed as her art endeavoured to pierce the veil of time and distance. "I think, Magister, that your young monk has found the conscience of Elded."

Eight

"Fifty soldi!" Lieutenant Poule took a step back from the wagon of the Widow Pandarus and held out the leather riding gloves he had just been given to try. "That's practically half a gold ducat you cheating harlot!"

Timandra shrugged. "You won't find another pair this side of Palestro and even then not of this quality. Soft as a baby's backside. You don't want them then give them here."

Poule swore softly. "For that money they ought to be *from* a baby's backside." He dug into his belt pouch and produced a handful of silver. "Here, take it." He thrust the coins into her hand and pushed back the large floppy brown beret that had fallen over his right ear, pheasant feathers all askew.

Timandra laughed. "Don't complain, Poule. It's a fair deal and they match your hat, you peacock."

Poule grumbled an obscenity and then looked to either side of the wagon. "Hey now, how is our monk getting on? Any more tricks? Must be a bit unnerving for you what with that—"

"Don't say it. Strykar doesn't want a word of that mentioned and you damn well know it." She scowled at him and climbed down from her wagon.

Poule lowered his voice. "I know, I know. It's just so... unnatural and all."

"He hasn't spoken of it and nor have I. But he's settling in. Not half as skittish as he was two days ago."

Poule grinned. "And he's up in there... with you, is he? At night and all?"

Timandra flicked Poule's long nose. "He stands a better chance of getting into my rack than you!"

Poule ducked and chuckled. "Have a care, Widow! No offense meant."

"If truth be told, he beds down under the wagon at night. I've got him doing chores during the day and he seems happy enough—if a little lost in his thoughts."

Poule nodded. "I'm still explaining why we have a monk who doesn't wear monk's clothes."

"Just tell them I'm out of monk's robes at the moment, and then change the subject. He's asking me if he thinks Strykar will let him train with sword and buckler."

Poule roared with laughter. "You're having me on, sister! Swordplay?"

"You would want to learn how to swing a sword if you had the Temple guard trying to kill you. Do you think Strykar will let him have a go?"

Poule pushed his oversized beret further back on his greasy head. "Well, it couldn't hurt to ask. One of the sergeants could run him through some drills with the lads." He chuckled to himself, imagining the scene. "Might even be good fun."

THAT AFTERNOON, TIMANDRA'S arm entwined with Acquel's, the two wended their way through the forest of tent pegs and guy ropes, making their way to the clearing used for mustering. Pennants snapped and flapped around them as the breeze picked up. This was the last halt before Palestro and already a salt tinge lay on the muggy air.

"Now, the captain *may* let you try your hand but I know him well and you'll not be coddled, whether you're a monk or no." Timandra's left hand reached over to pinch Acquel's bicep. "And I just hope you can heft a sword and a shield."

"I've had my share of brawls. Some of them even after I became a novice."

She looked up at him and smiled. He was certainly still a mystery—and a disturbing one at that—but she was developing a strange admiration for this man who was willing to stand up for himself. But his request had worried her. A worry that he was intent on leaving behind his vows to the church forever. She herself felt an ache for the comfort of the Faith, something she feared she would never be able to experience again, and often did she push back one dark memory that denied her peace. It had seemed almost divine providence for Acquel to fall into their laps when he did. But if he lapsed in his own faith, what then?

"Brawls?" she replied. "That may be true, but not with a sword I would venture. Nor a round shield."

Acquel looked at her and gave her a twisted smile. "True enough, mistress. True enough. But I'll not go like a sheep to the slaughter when the red capes next show up."

They reached the clearing to find a large group of soldiers gathered there. Two were squaring off against each other, armed with double-edged swords about a yard long and steel round shields that were two feet wide. A grey-bearded sergeant, in a multitude of colours and slashed velvets, swung his quarterstaff in an upward arc and struck the bottom rim of one of the soldier's shields.

"Get that fucking rim up to your eyes and keep it there!"

The soldier struck the rim on the cheek of his barbute in

his haste to comply. His sparring partner let out a laugh like a sneeze.

"And why are you fucking grinning like an ape?" snarled the sergeant. "Keep that hanging guard in place or I'll use your head as a temple bell! Now... lay on!"

And quick as you like the opponents were trading blows, sword hilts high, snapping their wrists in an overhand motion that brought their blunted practice blades crashing down on the top rims of the other's shield. Lieutenant Poule and Captain Strykar stood off to the side, silently watching. Poule, as per usual it seemed to Acquel, was hefting a leather jack, filled no doubt with ale.

Timandra guided him over to the captain and Acquel gave a curt bow with his head. Strykar folded his arms over his polished breastplate and smiled.

"So, the widow tells me you want to learn swordplay. My first question, brother monk, is why?"

"You saw how I fared a few days ago. Next time—if there is a next time—I want to at least give myself a chance."

"One does not learn this craft in a day. Or even a month. And a sword and shield only do you any good when you're actually carrying them." Strykar leaned forward and peered around Acquel's side. "And you don't appear to have either."

Acquel drew himself up, nearly eye-to-eye with the mercenary. "I am prepared to learn and carry them like a *rondelieri*."

Strykar smiled. "But you're not a *rondelieri*, Brother Acquel, nor likely to be one."

Acquel felt his face flush. Timandra had already receded from him, standing alone by the armourer's wagon, leaving him to plead his case.

"So, you're expecting me to be your meek and mild captive holy man. At least until you're ready to let me go."

Poule snickered into his jack.

Strykar gave Acquel a look of stone. "I'm not in the business of training holy men who want to change their profession," he replied, disdainfully. "You're here to serve the needs of the men in their Faith, at least until I decide what to do with you. Stay with the Black Rose and you'll be safe. There's no need to waste my officers' time with teaching you how to swing a sword." He then turned to face Poule, who rapidly lowered his ale. "Finish up here with the exercises for the new men and see that the camp is readied for the night."

"Wait!" Acquel took a step forward. "Surely you know of the fighting monks of Lessia, in Saivona. They still sing songs about their battles in the last war. So what is the difference now?"

Strykar turned back to Acquel. "I would say the difference is about forty years. And those left alive are now old men. You'll have to do better than that."

Acquel flashed Timandra a helpless look but she could only shake her head in reply as if to say, *I've got you this far.* Acquel held out a hand. "Very well, then. If you won't give me a sword and shield let me show you what I can do with a knife. I've fought with those before."

"You are a persistent one, I give you that," said Strykar.

"I'll give him a lesson." It was Poule. "By your leave, captain, of course."

Strykar shook his head and threw his hands up. "Well, you're itching for it, aren't you. The both of you." He turned to the old sergeant who had just knocked one of his slower charges on their helm, bringing forth a delightful ring. "Gillani! Fetch a pair of those wooden daggers. We have a knife fight to run over here."

Poule was smiling broadly now as he began to unbutton his doublet. "Come now brother monk, let's get ready to play."

Acquel nodded to the lieutenant and began undoing the small round wooden buttons on his own doublet. He walked over to Timandra, undoing the belt and pouch that she had lent him along with his clothes.

"Is this really what you want?" Timandra asked. "A knife fight like a couple of alley brawlers?"

Acquel held out the belt and pouch. "Three years ago I *was* an alley brawler."

Timandra eyed the worn brown leather pouch as if it were a poisonous toad. She knew what lay inside. She reached out and then hesitated to take it.

"Don't worry," Acquel said. "I don't have any pockets for it to appear in—unless you count my codpiece."

She nodded, and gingerly took the pouch in hand, still not entirely certain. Acquel then peeled off his hole-shot doublet. When he pulled his linen shirt over his head, she saw the marks of his escape from Livorna: yellowish bruises on his ribcage, welts and scratches across his arms and chest from grasping trees and thorn hedges. But she also spied two livid scars: one across Acquel's right breast, the other at his right collarbone. The marks of blade wounds.

"Have a care," she said as she folded his clothes over her arm. "You might have had some experience but he's had far more practice of late."

"Come, brother monk!" Poule was windmilling his arms in preparation for the fight.

The sergeant handed two rude wooden daggers with simple cross hilts to Strykar. The captain stepped forward and handed one to each of them. "Remember, no blows to the face or neck. Anything else is fair game. First who strikes thrice is the winner. Poule, you keep your head. Understood?"

Poule tapped the ash blade to his temple. "Understood, my captain!"

Acquel took a few paces back and hefted his practice dagger. It was a foot long and though of wood, had a diamond cross section like a real dagger. But the point was rounded and thick. Still, enough to break a rib and most certainly hard enough to bruise. Poule was smiling broadly as he cinched up the points of his hose and tied them to the points of his codpiece so as not to have them slip during the fight. Acquel tucked the dagger under his armpit and did the same.

He became aware that an audience of soldiers and camp followers had begun to gather. A small rivulet of sweat trickled down his side.

The sergeant stepped forward as Strykar receded. He raised his quarterstaff and signalled for Poule to move forward. He then did the same for Acquel. Poule took his station and immediately went into a crouch, holding his dagger point down in his fist. A good defensive guard and one natural for a soldier who knew how to fistfight.

But Acquel's craft was far different. Fighting in the narrow streets and alleys of Livorna had taught him the thieves' way of bladework. He gripped the dagger, point up. His stance was high and straight, his right arm along his thigh, the dagger just pointing down and touching near his knee. His left arm he held loosely at belly level. And when Poule came at him, wading in with both arms raised to chest height, he was loose, balanced, and ready to receive him.

Acquel held his ground. Poule lashed out with a cross swipe aimed at his shoulder or left breast and Acquel lifted his left foot and pivoted back and away, Poule's blade sailing past. As he did so, he thrust outwards and upwards with his dagger at Poule's ribs. The lieutenant batted his wrist down before he could land the blow. They had both now turned a quarter circle, eyes locked one upon the other. Acquel moved again, right foot circling so as to strike at Poule's back. But his shoe slid on the grass, and he lost a second. It was enough for Poule to strike. He drove his dagger down horizontally, skimming the cup of Acquel's left shoulder and juddering off a rib above his breast. Acquel exhaled loudly with the dull pain of it and drew back to recover.

Around him he could hear catcalls and encouragements, some for him and some for the lieutenant. Poule licked his lips and gestured with his free hand for Acquel to come on. In a slight crouch the monk moved forward, both hands low and his torso moving side to side. Poule's fists were up in a fighter's stance, his dagger hand poised to lash out. Acquel stepped forward on his right, dropping his right shoulder in a feint as he switched his dagger to his left hand. As Poule moved to block Acquel's right arm, Acquel shot out his left into Poule's belly. Poule cried out in surprise and pain and fell back. The soldiers roared their approval. Like a wounded bear, Poule growled and ran straight at Acquel, intent on bowling him over and stabbing him as he fell on top. Acquel dropped low, both hands in front of his stomach. Poule leapt forward, off balance, dagger poised to strike as he tackled the monk. As he piled into Acquel, Acquel seized the waist of Poule's hose and braes with his left hand, bent his knees, and rolled backwards. Poule continued overhead, tumbling, and Acquel's dagger raked him down his chest as he did so. Both men rolled to the side and were up without pause, Poule spitting and swearing and Acquel breathing heavily.

As laughter filled the air, Poule turned red. "Very well, brother monk! Let's stop being gentlemen." And he was quickly on the balls of his feet, closing the distance again. He took a swipe with the dagger—slower than normal thought Acquel—and the monk threw a block with his left wrist. But Poule had already stepped in with his left foot and sent an arcing left fist into Acquel's stomach that left him heaving for air. As he doubled, he felt the dull pain of the dagger point in his right bicep.

"That's two apiece, brother monk!"

Acquel fell back, trying hard not to be sick. He sucked in a deep breath and managed a broad smile to hide his pain. The soldiers were worked up now, crowding in and yelling for a good finish. Acquel again took his stance—not too low, torso working side to side, his dagger moving fast between hands to keep Poule guessing. Poule came on, lips drawn and teeth gritted. Acquel realised in that moment that a win for him in this circumstance might be no victory at all. Poule was bright red and glistening as he crouched. An instant later there was a flurry of blows and blocks from both men. As the lieutenant took a half step back to poise for a new attack, Acquel pivoted again off his left foot and followed up with a leap with his right. He found himself now with his belly pressing into Poule's left side, right leg stuck between both of Poule's and his own left arm wrapped around Poule's dagger arm as he prepared to drive in his right into the small of Poule's back.

What then happened was so quick that it was more reflex than studied attack. But it was by design. As Acquel struck his dagger at Poule's hip he also let his grip on Poule's right arm slip. Poule's hand shot down and drove his dagger into Acquel's left thigh even as Acquel's own blow struck home. The sergeant broke them apart with a push and the combatants threw down their wooden blades.

"Double kill!" he cried.

Acquel didn't take his eyes from Poule as the sound of whoops and clapping erupted. Suddenly Poule gave a roar and charged at Acquel, just a few paces between them. Acquel froze in place and raised up his arms but Poule pulled up sharp in front of his face and broke into a huge laugh before seizing the monk in a hug.

"Not bad for a little priest! Not bad at all!" He gave Acquel's hedgehog prickles a rub.

Acquel grinned with relief and looked over to Timandra. As their eyes met across the open space, she nodded and smiled.

Strykar gave a nod of respect and walked away. A few soldiers came up and clapped Acquel about the shoulders in comradely support. He thanked them and walked to Timandra to retrieve his clothes.

"Well done," she said, handing him back his linen. "I did not think it would end thus."

Acquel pulled on his shirt, wincing now as the pain began to flare with the heat of the combat passing. "Neither did I. Maybe now they will at least let me bear some steel to defend myself, even if it's just a knife."

Timandra handed him his belt and pouch. He shook it and heard the chain jangle inside. "See, nothing to fear," he said.

She offered him his doublet back. "*This* time."

A loud whistle came from across the field. Acquel turned to see Poule shaking himself like a dog, a bucket of water having been poured over him.

"Brother monk! Next time, perhaps, we will have a go with a proper sword!" He laughed and strode off, a camp boy in his wake bearing shirt, doublet, sword and harness.

"You may have found an ally," said Timandra, a note of disappointment in her voice. Disappointment that Acquel seemed to be straying further from the path of a man in holy orders.

"It was a bit of a gamble, I know. But maybe now I've earned the beginnings of some respect, no?"

THAT EVENING, TUCKED comfortably under the widow's wagon, Acquel sat and watched as Timandra, perched on a camp stool, mended a sword belt with stout thread, a thick needle, and a sailmaker's glove. The sun, gloriously huge and orange, hung low in the sky and as he rubbed onto his bruises some pleasant smelling ointment she had given him, he reflected on what lay ahead. He had never been to Palestro nor had he heard of this Captain Danamis, former pirate and the king's admiral. Timandra had been of few words when he had asked about the nature of the business that brought the company there. All he knew was that there were some valuable goods that Strykar carried, something that the pirates paid good coin for, and that it was a trade that had gone on for some time now. He still didn't trust Strykar. He knew full well that any mercenary worth his salt would opt for profit given the opportunity. What price had the Magister put on his head already?

Timandra caught him watching her. She set down her work in her lap and rolled her aching shoulders.

"So, brother Acquel, have you decided to throw away the greyrobe for good and take up the sword instead?"

Acquel shrugged. "You know what happened. I don't think there's much chance of a return to the Temple Majoris now."

"There are other monasteries in Valdur. You could go elsewhere."

"The Magister and the High Priest have a long reach. And there is only the One Faith."

"Well, you could stay here and administer to the company. You would do good work, I know it."

"You want me to stay?"

"I do. I've missed hearing the Word. Missed telling a holy man what troubles me. I've felt I have nowhere to turn for comfort. For… forgiveness."

He grinned. "And what would you need forgiveness for, mistress?

She suddenly looked down again at her work. "Damned stiff leather! I'm running out of needles."

"And you didn't tell me what exactly happened to your last holy man."

Timandra smiled, still avoiding his gaze, a slight look of embarrassment crossing her face. "I know. I did mean to tell you. He fell into strong drink and it killed him after a year."

"And you're recommending me as his replacement? Sounds like the office is too demanding for any cleric."

She laughed softly. "He was weak of will. You would do better from what I have seen of you."

"Somehow I don't think my wishes enter into any of this."

And she knew he was not just speaking of Strykar's intentions. He was frightened of what he carried, something he could not be rid of.

They spoke little after that as an awkward silence fell between them, born of uncertainty and worry for the future. As darkness descended, Timandra bid him a good night and returned to her wagon. Acquel listened to her feet scuffing the floorboards above as he lay in his woollen blankets, his head resting on a feather bolster (no doubt thieved from a Maresto nobleman's litter). He toyed with the idea of leaving, taking his chances on the road. But he would first have to steal money and a sword from the very people who had given him refuge. For the moment, far better to stay put and keep a watchful eye. And there was Timandra. He found himself thinking of her and of her long brown neck, her shapely body. Ever since he had flung away his greyrobe and donned the dress of real men, old feelings had returned. But fatigue quickly crept up on him and he was asleep before Timandra had ceased her rummaging inside the wagon. He dreamt long and deeply.

HE FOUND HIMSELF standing on the ocean shore on a stretch of grey sand under a clear azure sky. He had never seen the sea in his life but here it was in front of him in vivid detail, roiling whitecaps dancing far off and more gentle tumbling green waves breaking on the sand of the beach. And most strange of all, he was aware that he was dreaming as he marvelled at the scene before him. There were figures a short way off, further up the beach as it met the treeline of twisted windblown pine and cypress. He walked towards them. As he drew nearer, he saw that they were mainly children, perhaps twenty or more, most running and playing, but a smaller group gathered around a man in a long coarse linen robe.

The scene gained clarity and he saw that not all were the children of men. There were merfolk; young, laughing and playing with their human companions. They were grey of colour, some having no hair upon their heads and others having long, thick whitish-blonde strands like the strands of rope on a mop head. All were immensely ugly to his eyes, with bulging faces and near lipless mouths. A group of adults came through the trees, dressed in the tunics of antiquity he had seen in countless paintings in the great Temple. Some of the children recognised them and ran to them, reunited. And then *through* him passed another figure to join the group, a towering merman who stood nearly two heads taller than the rest, dressed only in a shaggy brown loincloth. His lanky, well-muscled arms held out a gift of a string of silver fish and he was, in return, clapped about his shoulders in a gesture of goodwill.

Acquel found himself standing over the robed figure who some of the children had gathered round. He looked into the face, dark and long. The man was old, wrinkles having creased his brow and cheeks but his eyes still shone with vitality. He was somehow—subtly—formed in a way that was not quite right. The eyes were too far apart, the mouth thin and wide. And his hands were long with fingers like birch twigs. Acquel knew he was staring at the Lawgiver, Saint Elded, as he had appeared in life. Elded looked up from the children and into Acquel's eyes. He smiled as if they were sharing the same thought. The thought that this was how the world lay seven hundred years ago when the Word was delivered to Valdur. A world very different from the one he lived in. A world where merfolk and humankind appeared to exist side by side.

A little mer boy approached him and took his hand. Acquel felt the cool dampness of the grasp and drew back, frightened that he was losing himself in the dream that he knew was no dream. He squeezed his eyes shut and opened them again to find himself on his back, the mudstained planks of Timandra's wagon a few feet over his head. He shivered. Never in his life had he had such a dream nor seen such things.

Breathing heavily, he rolled over and pulled himself out of the tangle of blankets. The dew-soaked grass drenched him as he crawled out from under the wagon into the faint beginnings of the dawn. He knelt, left hand resting upwards, flat in the open palm of his right. He began mumbling the morning prayer, line upon line as he had been taught, willing himself back to the certainties of the old way of life now taken from him.

Nine

NICOLO DANAMIS WAS also dreaming of the sea. He was drowning, tumbling end over end in a monstrous surf, unable to rise to the surface to draw breath. Someone or something was holding his ankles, pulling him down deeper. The grey-green waters churned and bubbled in front of his bulging eyes as panic overwhelmed him. He rose up out of the nightmare, surfacing briefly into wakefulness, before almost as quickly sinking back into slumber.

He was on the *Royal Grace*, but it was a ship empty of men. He alone stood on the main deck and around him lay a dozen sundered wooden chests, spilling gold coins across the planks. He called for Gregorvero, for the helmsman, for the captains of the castles. But he was alone on board the vast creaking vessel; dead in the water, its sheets furled tight to the spars.

A squadron of ships was bearing down on him under full sail, their bows dipping and rising as they neared. The mainsail of the lead ship bore the sign of the ram's head—it was a Southlands pirate ship out of Naresis. Danamis knew he was alone against them all, with no means of flying or fighting. He turned to look for his missing sword, only for his eyes to open in the waking world.

Through the long rectangular window the first delicate light of the day shone, illuminating his bedchamber in a faint purple hue. He rolled over on to his side, the silken sheets halfway down his body. His bedmate lay with her back to him and he reached to caress her bare buttocks, the sheets wrapped around her calves. His hand moved gently up her spine and he caressed the thick dark locks of her long hair that splayed wildly across her back. She stirred. His hand moved to her shoulder and he pulled her over towards him. Yet, as she faced him, he recoiled onto his back, crying out. For she was mer, her huge eyes white and staring, bulging out of the wet grey head, and the wide slit mouth gasping. Two small nostril holes flared open and shut as the creature moved to embrace him. The mouth opened fully to reveal needle-like teeth. Danamis screamed.

And awoke. He was alone in his bed, the rays of the morning sun spilling into the high-ceilinged bedchamber. He groaned and rubbed his face. He shuddered and threw off the sheets, rising naked from the bed. Kassia's gown and slippers were gone. She must have tired of his snoring. He had done nothing for two days except eat a little, drink a lot, and ride his courtesans until he was sore. He shuffled out into the adjoining antechamber, his head lightly throbbing from the Milvornan wine. The servants had left him a basin and water jug and he washed himself and pulled on a red silken gown, the tiles of the floor cold under his feet. As he opened the door to the hall, he saw Kassia standing against the wall near her chamber, her arms wrapped tightly about herself.

"Kassia, what are you doing over there? Come here."

The girl hesitated then slowly walked to him. Danamis reached out to stroke her long black hair but she pushed his hand away. Gently enough, but her anger was clear.

"What ails you, woman? What have I said now?"

Kassia's eyes filled with tears. "You have said nothing.

That is what is wrong. Since you've returned you've not been as you were when you left. You mount me like an animal and then leave me. You don't talk with me; I am as a side of meat to you. Talia is crying in her chamber because you can't even look her in the eye."

Danamis swore under his breath. "You want a fight this early of a morning? When my head is pounding away?" He reached out to take her arm and Kassia batted him away again.

"Now, you'd better settle down, my girl. I can damn well do as I please with the both of you. I may not own you but by God I can have you when I will it."

Her reply was soft spoken. "Nico, you could have had so much more. You could have had my heart."

And the look on her beautiful olive face was of such perfect sadness that Danamis was stopped short, lost for words. "Kassia..."

She backed away and walked down the wide empty hall, towards her own rooms.

"Kassia!"

Danamis stood, unmoving, as he watched the train of her robe disappear through the doorway. A loud clearing of a throat snapped him back to attention. Halfway up the broad marble staircase leading from the central courtyard came the castellan, his keys jangling at his waist.

Danamis folded his arms as Escalus drifted towards him, already immaculately dressed in a long russet velvet gown, his trim black beard glistening with oil. His father had brought him back from a trip to Perusia, the royal enclave, where he had been at the court. How he had ever become accustomed to a pirate's den like Palestro was something that Danamis had never understood.

"A good morning, my lord." Escalus gave a small bow of his head and then his eyes moved towards where Kassia had stood. "Problems?"

Danamis waved his hand. "Not of your concern. What is it you want—at *this* hour of the day?"

"A messenger has just arrived from the city gate. The company of the Black Rose is making camp on the plain just beyond the wall. We can expect Captain Strykar to arrive sometime later this morning."

Danamis's shoulders sank a little. "Hell and blast. I had clear forgotten about the new delivery. I don't know how I'm going to explain what the hell happened this time. And worse than that I'm sworn to buy the damned leaf from him with little fucking chance of selling it again."

"He's more than your partner in the trade, my lord. He is your friend, is he not? You should tell him everything that happened out at sea."

"And tell him I can't pay for the shipment? He won't be my friend long after that."

"You can pay him for the last shipment now at least. He'll have to be patient for the rest."

Danamis looked at Escalus. He was beginning to sound like his father had a few years before. "I'll have to come up with something. Maybe he'll take a ship instead… as collateral."

Escalus smiled. "See, many alternatives if you put your mind to it. Finish dressing and I will get the cook to prepare you smoked herring and some sops in wine."

"I was joking."

"You might not be later," replied Escalus. "Come, my lord, get yourself dressed."

Danamis mumbled a curse and returned to his bedchamber. Headache or not, and with his women in sullen rebellion, he was going to have to steel himself for what would be a very long day with the mercenaries of the Black Rose.

* * *

CAPTAIN STRYKAR WATCHED as the rope-bound oilcloth sacks were thrown onto the two mules and strapped down. He still found it near inconceivable that a mere leaf could be worth so much gold coin, and that he had managed to keep the knowledge of how to obtain it to himself. Around him, the sounds of a camp newly pitched rang out. There was more than the usual joking and camaraderie this morning: the men knew they would get to visit Palestro, in turns, and eat, drink and whore until their money ran out. He had chosen the first to go into the city along with the myrra shipment; forty strong and in full shining harness to impress the pirates if needs must, and he had decided that the greyrobe would come too. Besides, Timandra was coming along to buy her own supplies and the monk could not stay on his own, even with Poule to keep an eye on him. No, this Acquel was too much of a mystery to risk losing and his conjuring trick was still causing Strykar to lose sleep. The Duke would have to see the monk for himself and decide what to do. A few days in Palestro—no more—and they would take the coast road back to Maresto. A three day journey if the weather held.

He turned as he heard Poule's braying laugh.

"Don't go sticking that into just anyone, holy man!" said the lieutenant as he wrapped an arm around a beaming Acquel. Acquel was still dressed like a ragamuffin, but he held a shining dagger with a fine wooden and brass wire grip, balanced with a pretty silver pommel. Acquel slid it back into its leather scabbard and unfastened his belt in order to loop it through.

"The captain gave his permission," warned Poule, "but don't you fuck about and make me look a fool. No picking fights."

"I'll mind my business, lieutenant. And I thank you."

Poule shoved him away. "Go help the widow with her pack mule. And bring me back a woman if you find a good-looking one. No fishwives!"

When Timandra saw him and the blade at Acquel's hip, her face darkened; he seemed to be moving further away from his vows as a cleric. She cursed herself for having burned his robes, leaving him no alternative but to don some dead soldier's grubby doublet and hose. Perhaps, if there was time in Palestro, she could convince him otherwise. For now though, he was like a child proud of his new toy. She managed to brighten as he approached her.

"See what the lieutenant has given me!"

She pushed her straw hat back high on her forehead. "Yes, I can see that. Just don't go waving it about."

They finished loading Timandra's wares as the soldiers formed up for the march down to the city gate, the gently sloping plain a broad meadow shining with thousands of buttercups. Timandra passed Acquel the reins to one of the mules. "Here, you can lead him into town. I'll ride the other."

Acquel nodded. He was tense with excitement to see a city other than Livorna and to lay eyes upon the great sea for the first time. He remembered his dream again, becoming so lost in his reverie that he didn't hear Stryker coming up behind him.

"Are you well, Brother Acquel?" the captain said, sat astride a gleaming dark brown courser.

Acquel turned and looked up, shading his eyes against the glare of the sun. "I am, sir."

"I want you to stay close to the Widow Pandarus today—and me. Understood?"

Acquel nodded. Not much chance of anything else he reckoned, for he didn't know a soul where they were going.

Strykar tugged his reins and moved down the assembling column to seek out Poule. The chosen were now moving into columns of two, the old sergeant bellowing at the stragglers. Poule stood watching as Strykar approached, admiring his captain's embossed breastplate and jet black cloak that trailed over the horse's cruppers, fastened by a great silver chain and escutcheons to the leather breastplate straps. His round shield, embossed with some scene of great slaughter, hung at the high rear of the saddle. *Comes of having the right friends*, he mused, even as he broke into a broad smile.

"You look an imposing sight, my captain! I suggest you leave the harness on if you do business with Palestrian ladies. They're a rum lot and partial to sliding a knife into a ribcage." He took hold of the bridle and patted the neck of the fine mount.

Strykar surveyed the camp from the vantage of the saddle. "I'll send word back for you to send another party into the town. Once I see what Danamis has planned."

Poule nodded. "We'll await your orders. Expecting anything different from last time?"

Strykar leaned back, his saddle creaking. "No. But I haven't forgotten about the Temple guard in Livorna. I wouldn't put it past them to be trailing us. Don't let the watch sleep."

Poule moved a half step closer and lowered his voice. "I don't think the monk will run. He's a good enough sort. It's just I don't trust what he carries with him."

Strykar bent over, his steel vambrace clacking as it rested on his thigh armour. "You're the one who armed him," he said.

"I wasn't talking about the blade," replied Poule. "That little jewelled trinket is cursed. And I don't think the lad has any more idea about what it is—or what controls it—than we do. I'm just saying... have a care."

"I haven't forgotten that either. But I'd rather have him under my nose than out of my sight." He straightened up and glanced back to the men. "Time we moved off. I will send word later. Fare you well!"

Poule released the horse's bridle and raised his hand in salute. "And a successful barter for you with the pirates!"

* * *

CAPTAIN STRYKAR LED the way through the heavy iron-studded gates of the palazzo, his retinue and strange cargo following behind. Danamis stood at the porchway, hands on hips, in a dark red slashed doublet, hose and brown knee-length boots, his falchion hanging at the waist. The *rondelieri* made a good entrance, he would give them that, their helmets and shields shining in the mid-day sun. He was no soldier nor had he ever witnessed a land battle, but he knew how these *rondelieri* were employed. Advancing at the rear of spearmen and pole-arm men, they would peel off and make a run at the flanks of the enemy's spear formations, hacking their way in with sword and shield until the square would disintegrate from the attack, front and rear. They were renowned for their tenacity and endurance. His eyes fell to the pack mules with their black oilcloth bundles. It was going to be an interesting reunion with Strykar, that he knew. He had already sent Escalus down to the vault to bring up the bags of golden ducats, a pay-out that would leave him with next to nothing, and that would only cover him for the previous shipment of myrra that he had given over to the merfolk during the disastrous exchange.

Two groomsmen came running out to take hold of Strykar's mount and Danamis walked out to meet the captain as he swung out of his saddle, his armour jangling as his boots hit the dusty red clay of the courtyard. They embraced; Strykar, nearly a head taller, slapping the younger man on the back.

"Well met, my lord!" said Strykar, holding Danamis by the shoulders. "You look none the worse since last we met. How goes it now in Palestro?"

Danamis laughed and clapped the captain on his pauldron. "As well as can do for an admiral in the service of the king. Which is, to say, often leaving me wishing I was a pirate again!"

They heard the gate slam and Danamis's retainers lowering the great bar. Strykar turned and waved his hands towards the pack mules.

"And here is your shipment, Nico, safe and sound. Where do you wish it?"

Danamis chuckled nervously. "Excellent. Have your men bring it into the palace where my people will take care of it." His eyes settled on Timandra where she was standing with Acquel. "And I see you have brought us the Widow Pandarus as well. It is good to see her again."

Strykar gestured and Timandra came over to them, Acquel at her heels. Danamis smiled and bowed his head as he took her hands in his. "You are welcome again in Palestro, mistress. I hope you find much here to replenish your stock."

She inclined her head in return. "I am pleased that the saints have allowed me the favour of seeing Palestro and you again, my lord."

Danamis looked past her to a somewhat awkward looking man whose partially shaved head said he was a monk but whose garb told a different tale. "And who is this, Strykar?"

"This is... Acquel, a monk in search of some proper vestments." He laughed. "You know, the company lost the last one to an unfortunate illness."

Acquel smiled and bowed deeply. Danamis's eye did not fail to catch the dagger on his hip.

"Well met and welcome, Brother Acquel," said Danamis, his curiosity now piqued. "I trust you will find what you require here in Palestro. Perhaps even... some new clothes."

Acquel's eyes remained downcast. "Thank you, my lord— my admiral... sir."

Danamis looked to Strykar again. "We can billet your men in the outbuilding as last time. If that will be acceptable. I'll have water and wine brought out to them presently. We have quarters for Mistress Pandarus and Brother Acquel inside. My castellan will see to it."

Strykar nodded. "Most generous."

Danamis touched Strykar on the arm gently. "While the goods are unloaded, I think we should talk inside. A lot has happened in the last six months."

Acquel took a half step forward but Timandra pulled at his doublet, holding him back, and announced that she had to see to her goods. Danamis called to a retainer to help her, then ushered Strykar into the palazzo and the sunlit inner courtyard and arcade. Already a servant had laid out a platter of olives and breads, the wine being poured out into goblets. Another servant followed bearing a huge silver plate piled with roasted fowl and set it down upon the table near to the fountain and couches.

Danamis motioned for Strykar to seat himself. He did so, yet awkwardly in his armour.

"I can have my man help you get that harness off if you like," said Danamis.

Strykar shook his head. "Nay, no bother. I'd rather start on this food."

Danamis handed a goblet to Strykar and then picked up the other for himself. "And now my friend, I will raise my drink to you and the Black Rose. And then, I will tell you of events of late, and it is not altogether good news."

Strykar raised an eyebrow as he took a long swig of wine. He lowered the cup and reached for a chicken drumstick. "I'm listening."

Danamis told him of the voyage, the attack on the merfolk, and the aftermath. As the tale went on, Strykar's demeanour darkened. When Danamis finished, the mercenary sat back and stared at the fountain.

"So, the trade is over?"

"I do not know. I would like to try again at the next full moon but they may not show themselves."

Strykar nodded. "And so that brings us to the money, doesn't it?"

Danamis looked him in the eye. "It does. I can pay you for the last shipment. But not for the one you bring today."

"And you may not have a customer for it anymore."

"I won't lie to you, I don't know. They crave the leaf so perhaps they will come back. At least the fools didn't kill any of the mermen."

Strykar ran his hand along his square-cut beard. "Like you, I've got to pay my men."

"I can offer you a vessel—two—until I get the trade going again."

Strykar snorted. "Do I look like a fucking sailor?"

Danamis smiled and shook his head. "Well, I thought it was worth putting on the table."

"Aye, well, you and me go back a long way. I reckon you might have just enough credit—and I mean *just* enough— that we can work something out." He set down his goblet and held out his hand to the Palestrian. "And you're still the only admiral I know. Who knows when I'll need a boat?"

Danamis seized his hand tightly. "The Lord love you, my friend!"

"My lord." It was Escalus, standing at the pillars of the arcade. "I must needs speak with you." Danamis could see how large his eyes were, as if something terrible had just happened.

As Danamis reached his side, the castellan grabbed his upper arm and whispered into his ear. "Who else has a key to the strongbox you brought from the ship?"

Danamis scowled. "There are only two. You know that. What's happened?"

"The sacks inside the chest. They are filled with stones. There is no gold. *None.*"

Danamis took a step back, his ears beginning to ring. "Sweet God. That can't be. I loaded it myself on ship. I locked the chest."

Escalus's face was ashen. "When? When did you last see the gold?"

"Two days before we made port." And then his voice dropped even lower. "But I did not open it once afterwards."

"Two days at sea," hissed Escalus. "And you with the only key. Then how could someone have stolen it all? This is a new strongbox, is it not? I had not seen it before this last voyage."

A sick feeling flooded over Danamis. "It was given to me before the voyage. By Uncle Tetch."

"My lord, if this is Tetch's work, it's far more than thievery, it's a mutiny. And this is the first shot."

Ten

"You have a fine way of demonstrating hospitality, Captain Danamis." said Strykar, resigned to the fact that his trade deal was probably now stone-dead and the prospect of his treasure a fading fancy. "Do you want me to kill him for you?"

Danamis had taken the mercenary up to the mezzanine to gain some privacy. "If I find out it was him, I will kill him myself." He had finished the last of his wine, the base of the goblet he now tapped on the balcony, trying to contain a simmering rage. "I just don't understand why Tetch would do this. Makes no sense."

"Love of gold never makes any sense. It just is. I suggest you drag his arse here before he spends it all."

Danamis scanned the portico below for Escalus who had, inconveniently, made himself scarce. He had muttered something about "securing the cellars" and had left. That had been more than an hour ago, and now he had to deal with a mercenary who he was in debt to up to his neck, and Strykar's forty unpaid men were itching to get some coin or else take it in-kind from his house.

"No point in summoning him. If he's guilty he'll take to *Firedrake*. If he's not on her already. I had best lead a party to his house unannounced." He scraped the silver goblet along the railing. "The untrustworthy bastard."

Strykar folded his arms. "Shall my men come with you? I've got a vested interest in this after all."

Danamis nodded.

"These things are best handled with speed," said Strykar. "I counsel we move on him now. This very instant. If you're in agreement I will have the men prepare. We've got a few crossbowmen of our own."

Danamis looked at Strykar, decision finally taking hold. "Agreed, I will summon my men-at-arms."

HE HATED WEARING it, but going where he was going, the studded red velvet brigantine of plates was a prudent measure. He tugged at the padded arming doublet underneath to seat it properly on his shoulders as a retainer finished buckling the side straps. Another retainer reached around to secure his light woollen cloak. Danamis took the sword belt as it was handed to him and buckled it on himself. His tan leather gauntlets he pulled up over his white cambric shirtsleeves. *How could he have done such a thing? He was near enough blood.*

"My lord!" A retainer came into the loggia at a trot. "This just delivered at the gate." He held out a velvet pouch. "There's also some commotion outside, my lord. Shouting and such outside the wall."

Danamis opened the pouch. In it was an ornate iron key—a twin to his own and the third to the strongbox. He felt his face flush as he pulled out the parchment note that lay in the pouch with it.

Come outside nephew. The die is cast. Surrender yourself and the palazzo to me and your people will be left in peace.

Danamis let the note drop from his hand as he walked out into the courtyard to the sounds of the mob gathered beyond his gate. The noise was a rolling rumble of harsh cries, whoops, and laughter. He could hear the steady beat of a large drum underneath it all—*doom, doom, doom*—orchestrating the crowd beyond the wall.

His liveried house men stood about the courtyard, looking confused, unbelieving that the palazzo was under attack. Danamis sprinted to the small iron grating that was at head height in the great double oak gate. Already it was squeaking at the hinges from unknown hands pushing on it. He stood to the side then quickly put one eye to the opening. He saw hundreds of men filling the square, all armed, swords and glaives gleaming, and more were streaming in from the surrounding streets. They were seamen and soldiers alike.

My God. So many.

He took a step back as a brown jug shattered at the grating. Strykar was now at his side, buckling his sword belt.

"What's this then?" he said. "Has Tetch come to us instead to save us the trouble?"

Danamis nodded. "He's got at least three ship crews out there."

Strykar chanced a glance through the gate and then moved away. "It's been three months since I had a good scrap but I wish I had the rest of the company in here with me to even the odds. I don't know what you did to piss off this lot but you've got a rebellion on your hands."

Danamis looked around him, and half a dozen men-at-arms wearing his tabards of red and white stared back at him. He remembered Gregor's warning of two nights ago and he cursed himself. Cursed himself for his self-pity and for his wishful thinking that it would all work out for the best if he just let it be for a week or two. Now, he was betrayed.

A great trumpet blast sounded beyond the walls, and then another. Like a dying whirlwind, the cries of the mob subsided, leaving only a low rumble of voices without.

Danamis looked at Strykar who raised an eyebrow in reply.

"Captain Danamis!"

The voice of Giacomo Tetch bellowed out, echoing off of the tall façade of the palazzo. "Come now! Surrender yourself. We've all had enough of your ill-made plans and your trade with the fishmen." Danamis walked closer to the gate, silent. "Danamis! You've lost command. The Council has had enough. It's getting late in the day, boy, so let's make an end to this."

"You are a treacherous one-eyed son of a whore!" Danamis shouted out.

A rumble of laughter floated over the wall.

"Now be careful, boy! Where did your mother get to after she whelped *you*?"

More laughter. Danamis felt his heart hammering away.

Tetch spoke out again. "Look, you come out and surrender to us and we leave your household alone. And I know you've got some Black Rose soldiers in there too. We don't have no fight with them. They can go free as they please."

Strykar shot a glance through the grating. "The bastard is moving up a ship's cannon lashed on a handcart. This gate won't hold up after a few rounds from that. This is your house. What's your plan?"

Danamis was trying his best to think calmly as waves of red fury rushed over him. They could try and cut their way out, but in close confines, even the *rondelieri* would be overwhelmed by sheer numbers. They might reinforce the gate but there was now no time for that. He looked at Strykar. "I'm the one who has stepped in this turd. Take your men and get out while you can."

Strykar shook his head. "I trust that fucker about as much as a Naresis rug merchant. No, I'll get the chosen men into harness again. We can try and get out another way." He paused. "There is another way out of here, isn't there?"

Danamis's chin fell a little. "There was. But not anymore."

"There is, my lord!" A voice from behind them brought them both around. It was Escalus, striding towards them. He rapidly closed the distance between them and spoke in an urgent whisper. "Captain, you must take the old tunnel in the cellars that leads out to the culvert below us."

"My father bricked that up years ago," shot back Danamis.

Escalus shook his head. "No, listen to me. There is another portal down there that connects to it. Your father wanted everyone to think it had been walled up. Including Tetch."

Another trumpet blast sounded followed by Tetch's voice rising over the wall.

"My patience is running thin, boy! You might have noticed our little *falconet* out here. I've got it pointed at your gate, and I wouldn't bet a brass denari that it will last even two rounds!"

"My lord," said Escalus, "Gregorvero moved the *Grace* last night into the middle of the harbour. He's waiting for you there now. And I took the precaution last night of moving a few bags of ducats out there with him when he left. He says most of the fleet has gone over to Tetch but some crews are fighting it out. You'll need to go to the west side of the harbour and board longboats from there. You must go now!"

"Gregor didn't tell me a thing. That dear fat fool!"

"He did, my lord. You weren't listening."

Strykar had heard enough. "We can lead the way out," he said. "I'll get them assembled inside." And he was off, harness jangling.

Danamis grabbed Escalus by the shoulder. "Get the women out for me. Do you understand?"

Escalus nodded. "I will get them out safely. And the retainers."

"And join us by the same way down to the docks."

Escalus face was expressionless. "My lord, your father left me here to run this house as his castellan. And I will not surrender that responsibility."

"You'll be killed."

"I have no intention of being killed or captured. There's a lot about this palace you don't know about. Last night I took the liberty of sending the myrra down to the ship. I've hid the silver and jewels too. They'll never find them. Now go!"

There was an explosion as the cannon outside the gate let loose. The shot had struck where the gate met the stone wall and great splinters of wood splayed inwards as the top hinge was blown away.

"All of you! Into the house," cried Danamis.

In the hall, Escalus and Danamis manhandled the oak beam into place at the doors of the palazzo, dropping it into the iron brackets. Tetch's gunners were slow. They had not yet fired a second shot to take the gate down. Danamis turned to Escalus. "Get Kassia and Talia out of here."

Escalus nodded. "I will. And you will be back, captain. When they least expect it."

Danamis clapped him on the shoulder. "My father chose his castellan well."

"Thurio will guide you down to the tunnel. I showed him earlier." Escalus gestured to the trembling houseboy who stood near the pillared portico before picking up a sword belt from the hall table and buckling it on over his robes. The weapon was long and thin, a gentle curve all along its length; a Southlander's sword. "Fare you well, my lord!"

Strykar and his forty men had now arrived, and with them, Timandra and Acquel both looking bewildered. Danamis eyes turned to the marble staircase. The women were standing at the top, clutching a few belongings, the fear on their faces clear. He bounded up even as Escalus cried out again for him to get to the vaults.

"Escalus will take you away. You will be safe," he said, reaching out to pull his women to him. Their eyes shone with not just fear but anger besides. They both recoiled from his embrace.

"You are no man," hissed Kassia, practically spitting at him. "You run away but leave us to fend for ourselves."

Talia nodded, leapt forward, and shoved Danamis with all the force her little body could muster. "Coward! At least Tetch knows how to fight and lead men like a warrior! What do you think will happen to us now?"

He froze there on the steps, his mouth hanging open, bereft of any comforting words to impart. They were right.

Escalus was now beside him, pulling him away and down the steps. "For God's sake, my lord, go!"

Danamis threw one last glance to his courtesans, now forfeit along with his palace. He could not look them in the eye. He turned again at the bottom of the stairs, even as Escalus dragged him by the shoulders. The castellan wheeled him round and gripped him by both shoulders like a scolding parent. "Find what you have lost! Do you understand me? And then come back. Come back and defeat him."

Eleven

THE OLD BRICK-LINED tunnel, dug out and built when the palace had been constructed, ran straight as an arrow, gently sloping as it descended. It was wide enough for two abreast, barely that for armoured men. Timandra was behind a torch bearer—one of the house servants—and in front she could see Strykar, his round shield slung over his back, hunched over as he moved forward in the stinking darkness. She had left everything on her mule up in the stable, a gift to the shitting sailors who no doubt were bursting through the gates above right now. She cursed and felt to make sure she still had her near-bursting purse lashed to her hip. She glanced behind to Acquel, his eyes as big as plates as he splashed through the fetid drain water that puddled about their feet.

It grew brighter ahead, and then she was outside, practically pushed by Acquel into a milling mass of soldiers. They were in a cobbled street. Above them the red sandstone cliffs rose up to where the palazzo stood. The street, little more than an alley, was bordered by tall ramshackle houses, cheek by jowl, roofs bent with age and decay. As the small army of sweaty sword-and-buckler men poured forth from the old drain, Timandra heard the sound of slamming doors and shutters echoing around them.

"Now what, cousin?" said Timandra as she reached Strykar, who was pulling his shield around to his arm and drawing his sword.

"Where the hell is Danamis? You three!" he called out to the closest soldiers. "Form three files over there!" And then to the others, "Form up on those men, three columns! Move!"

Timandra stepped in front of him. "I've lost all my stock and my mules and you're planning on cutting our way out of here and down to the harbour?"

"Not now, cousin!" he snapped back. "I've lost a good piece of horseflesh worth twelve ducats so keep your mouth shut and get behind us."

She growled and turned to see Danamis sprint past, drawing his falchion as he reached the head of the fast-forming columns.

"I will lead you down to the ship!" he shouted.

Strykar pulled over a short soldier in a dented barbute, rusty mail coif and steel corselet. "Tiran. You know your way around Palestro, don't you?"

He nodded vigorously.

Strykar reached out and yanked another soldier. "You... and you! Tiran, take these two with you. Get out of the city by way of the gate we came in. Get back to the camp. Tell the lieutenant what has happened. Tell him if we have not returned by the morning he is to break camp and go to Maresto. He must go to Count Malvolio and tell him that Captain Tetch has taken over the Palestro fleet. Do you understand all that?"

Tiran nodded. "Aye, captain!"

Timandra's mouth fell open. "If we don't return by morning? You mean to say we are taking ship with Danamis?"

"Just keep the holy man close," he shot back. "That is your task."

They made their way down the winding streets at a trot, scattering chickens and sending townsfolk into their doorways and alleys. Timandra clutched her swinging purse with one hand as she ran. She could feel the sweat pouring down her as the heat of the day bore full on them. Danamis was leading them round and down and she prayed he was not lost in the maze of Palestro's worst neighbourhoods. Then, the view ahead became clear and she saw the harbour and dozens of ship's masts. They had emerged from the houses and down to the quayside, a long and wide run of great wooden planks laid along the stone harbour wall. The quay was practically empty and Timandra could see why. On the far side of the horseshoe-shaped harbour, hundreds of sailors and soldiers thronged. At least one vessel was burning alongside the dock. Of the great sailing ships, all but one were flying blood-red ensigns. The one remaining carrack that did not was taking a hail of arrows from the soldiers on the quay. Two longboats, stuffed with soldiers, were halfway between the dock and the carrack and were themselves taking arrows from the beleaguered ship.

Timandra ran to Strykar who had joined Danamis at the edge of the quay.

Danamis ran his hand back over his scalp. "My God. I've lost her."

The *Royal Grace*, sitting quiet out in the harbour, flew a red ensign from her mainmast. It rippled and dipped in the breeze, taunting them.

Strykar took a pace forward. "The *Grace*? Surely she's not gone over?"

Danamis said nothing. He was watching as two longboats appeared from around the stern of the ship, pulling hard towards them. A sailor stood up and waved wildly with both of his arms.

A smile broke out on Danamis's face. "They haven't gone over. Gregor is just buying himself some time."

They could see the other carrack starting to raise canvas.

"*Salamander* is fighting Tetch's men off," said Danamis, his face now animated at the chance of escape. "She's going to make a run for it but there's precious little wind to get behind her." He turned to Strykar. "I've got to get onto my ship. We'll thrash our way out of this, my friend!"

Strykar was taking in the scene, looking for other avenues of escape. He could see none. "I was not planning on a sea voyage this week, Nico."

Timandra stepped forward. "What? We're actually getting on that ship?"

Danamis had frozen, staring intently across the far side of the harbour, watching as a dozen or more men climbed the massive stone steps up to the tower of the chain.

"Shit. Hell and blazes. They're going to raise the chain at the harbour mouth." Danamis turned to Strykar. "But they need to do it from both towers. Look." And Danamis pointed to the large party of men that were now rounding the horseshoe, coming towards them. "They'll get into the tower and raise the chain at this end before we can pass over it. We cannot get under way that fast."

Strykar nodded. "I'll hold them off. You get aboard."

"I'll have no way of picking you up from the tower— unless you and your men jump from the parapet."

Strykar inclined his head. "Your credit is fast disappearing."

The two longboats had now reached them and a cheer from the sailors went up as they saw their captain on the quay.

Strykar grasped Danamis by the arm. "Take Mistress Pandarus and the monk with you. And pray there's some long rope up in that tower."

Danamis clapped the mercenary's shoulder. "God's speed. We'll hold steady for you if we can once we pass over the chain."

Timandra looked at Strykar, at a loss for words. Acquel took her hand and said, "There's nothing else for it, mistress."

Strykar's men had already formed a shield wall along the width of the quay. As soon as the longboats had pushed off with Danamis, Strykar ordered his men to fall back towards the tower. As he did so, his eyes alighted on two upright stone columns that stood along the dock. Two coils of cable were looped alongside.

Elded smiles on me today.

"You two! Fetch that rope there. Cut it away! All of it!"

They had more than a hundred feet to go to reach the tower. Strykar could see the Palestrian mutineers had rounded the quay and were closing fast, some armed with crossbows. The *rondelieri*, trained to harry the enemy on a battlefield that could change in an instant, found themselves back-pedalling fast to reach the tower. As Strykar mounted the tower steps he encountered his second piece of luck: the great wooden door was ajar. He looked behind him again. Tetch's men were nearly upon them and he could see them readying their polearms for a rush. He had to prevent them from gaining the tower. A quarrel whisked past him and shattered on the stones and he saw one of his men struck with another, the bolt protruding from his face.

He pushed the heavy oak door with the rim of his shield and leaned in. There was blur of silver and he instinctively dodged his head and raised the shield as the blade of a glaive slid past, scraping his buckler. Instantly, he stepped in, pressed his shield to the doorway, locking the haft of the glaive, and gave a high underhand thrust with his right arm straight into the throat of the soldier at the other end, one of two defenders in the tower. Another quarrel burrowed into the door as he pushed it open and the second defender was upon him. But Strykar's men were now up the steps, the last of them locking shields again as Tetch's soldiers piled in, thrusting and raining down their pole weapons. Strykar despatched his opponent with a feint and shield jab, chopping him down as he recovered from the shield rim stunning him.

The *rondelieri* poured into the large square room of the tower, a few falling at the doorway as the Palestrians tried to push in, their hafted weapons thrusting and jabbing. But slowly, the weight of the *rondelieri* pressing hard, the great door began to close. Thrusting through the space, a veteran was taking men down with precision thrusts while his comrade had dropped sword and shield to wrest polearms out of slippery hands. It was work done without word or command. The grunts and short cries of those struck were the only sound. In the centre of the room, mounted on the stone floor, was a great capstan wound around with a massive chain that snaked its way out a small round opening in the wall, down to the harbour mouth. At the far side of the room there was a wooden staircase that led to an upper level.

Strykar called to the men with the rope to follow him. They mounted the stairs and found themselves on an open platform, crenelated walls surrounding them at chest height. Strykar looked out into the harbour. He could see the *Grace*. She had not raised sail, but instead, was being towed by the two longboats, their crews straining under the load. Strykar knew he was no seaman but it looked like slow work to him. He looked over to the opposite tower. Like some monstrous serpent, rising out of the depths, he could see the black iron chain being pulled into the tower. He hoped for Danamis's sake that it would not raise all the way up to block the whole of the entrance.

"Secure the ropes to these stones—here... and here!" He turned to head back down the stairs and then paused. "And you two are the first to go down so you better use the right knot!" There was a trap to the stairway, held open with a hook; that would be their last defence. As he reached the main chamber again the sounds of his men straining filled the room. They were slowly losing the struggle. Sooner rather than later the weight of sheer numbers would tell and the door would be breached. So too, he knew that the retreat to the top level would be their most vulnerable time. He quickly counted who was left. It looked like he had lost at least seven.

"Come on, lads! Hold them! They're not going to let you walk out of here if you let them in!" Strykar leapt up the stairs and saw that the ropes were fastened, and when he peered over the parapet he could see the ship had nearly drawn up to them. He could almost reach out and grab the foremast spar that bobbed in front of him. It was time. Crashing down the stairs, he ordered six men at the rear to accompany him, sword and shields ready, at a hanging guard. The moment they took off the pressure, the door groaned inward a foot and a cheer went up from the outside.

"The rest of you... when I give the word, you make for the stairs and get on those ropes. Sheath your swords but leave your bucklers! And you lot"—he spoke now to the six—"you and I are going to fight them up the stairs. They can only get so many through that door so fast." And he had no idea how it was going to work. He hefted his sword and raised the rim of his shield. "Now!"

His men scrambled for the stairs, passing the rear guard who moved forward as the door opened wider. He could hear them pounding up the stairs behind him as he moved forward to lock his shield with the man on his left. They were hit with a wave, pushing them back as blows rained down on their shields and helms. Strykar took a glancing blow on his sallet from a glaive but shook it off and struck back with a wrist-snap blow of his own that took the arm off his attacker at the elbow. In seconds they were at the stairs. Strykar saw one of his men fall on the left. The huge capstan in the middle worked to their advantage as the enemy could only get two men through the gap either side. And then they were falling up the stairs, shields warding what they could, their armour the rest.

Two more fell on the stairs, stabbed in the thigh and belly. Strykar and the rest came through the top still flailing away and the captain put a boot into a face as his sword pommel knocked the iron hook away and dropped the trap door down. One of the *rondelieri* severed a flailing arm that kept the hatch from closing and Strykar stood on the door as it sounded to the crash of blades pounding away. He could see his men helping each other to balance on the crenelated parapet, scrabbling to grasp the thick ropes that led to an uncertain rescue. The hatch beneath Strykar's feet thumped and the hinges rattled, bolts jumping out.

"I can't keep them all day, you lot! Get over that wall!"

A *rondelieri* grinned at Strykar and joined him on the hatch, first throwing his shield down under his feet. The sound of splintering wood soon followed and the tip of a glaive shot upwards through the gap in the planks next to Strykar's left foot.

BELOW THEM, ON the deck of the *Grace*, Gregorvero was almost purple as he barked at the four men that were awkwardly wielding a mast spar to keep the ship from crashing into the tower with every swell of the sea. With each rising swell, they braced at the deck and rail and pushed off against the stone retaining wall, a gut-wrenching scraping noise carrying across the ship. Danamis craned his neck to see the *rondelieri* hanging—three or four at a time— down the ropes that dangled from the side of the tower.

Another one of Strykar's men was plucked by his crewmen from the fraying line and rolled onboard. Danamis heard a scream as one of the *rondelieri* fell from the top, crashing into the water and disappearing. Gregorvero had done his best to position the high fo'c'sle near the ropes but now a particularly heavy swell pushed it into the wall with a terrible cracking noise, splintering the carved railing. But more *rondelieri* were managing to scramble aboard, the weight of their armour forgotten in their urge to escape. Danamis ran to the larboard rail and looked astern. *Salamander* had her foremast topsail raised and her mainsail, but the awning over her sterncastle had been set ablaze by fire arrows. With hardly any wind, she was barely making headway and would soon be boarded.

Danamis knew if Tetch have been there to lead the mutineers, rather than tearing down the palazzo, he would stand little chance. Even so, a contingent of archers had appeared on the quayside off his stern quarter, bearing tallow torches and preparing to ignite their shafts. Between them, the sea and the tower would turn his ship into kindling or else the fire arrows would do the rest. And now he saw two longboats pulling towards him, rammed to the gunwales with soldiers.

On the roof of the tower, Strykar felt his foot nearly go through the weakening timber hatch and he pulled it up before it crashed downwards. Several bill heads and glaives were chewing the trap door to splinters like the claws and beak of some monstrous beast. He saw the last two of his surviving men bar one go over the parapet.

"Now, you!" he said to man next to him.

"We have to jump to the rope together, captain," he replied. "They might hesitate to decide who to strike first when they come through."

Strykar laughed. "Are you thinking like a Palestrian now? Very well, sheath your blade. And be quick or be dead."

The soldier nodded. Strykar nodded back as he slid his sword into his scabbard. They leapt from the hatch and scrambled for the parapet. The soldier had mounted the wall and he now reached to pull up Strykar who cried out as he strained to raise himself. The mutineers came through the hatchway, pausing only a moment, but then seeing the two men on the wall, bounded forward, pole arms forward to impale or push the *rondelieri*, Strykar's companion grabbed the rope and swung over the side. Styrkar did the same as a glaive struck the stone next to his arm while a sword blow knocked his sallet askew. He slid, feet dangling, but the weight of his harness was proving too much for his grip. He was no more than a few feet down when he looked up and saw a young pirate on the wall—no more than a beardless boy. He crouched and looked down at Strykar. He watched the lad stand on the parapet, single-edged falchion in his hand. Strykar felt his grip slip again, and he kicked to try and get his legs around the rope. The boy was smiling down at him. Smiling as he raised his blade and brought it down with a ringing clang upon the rope.

Strykar felt himself tumble, blue sky filling his vision as his stomach came up into his mouth. And then an explosion of light and agony. And then nothingness.

Twelve

"I WILL MISS you, sister."

Lucinda smiled and stroked her sibling's long blonde hair. "Silly thing, you know we are never *really* parted from one another."

Lavinia gently enveloped her sister's hand with hers. "It is not the same as sharing the same room, smelling your hair, or… holding your hand. That is what matters."

They were in a high-ceilinged bedchamber of the sprawling palace that adjoined the Ara monastery. It rose up in the shadow of the Temple Majoris, its myriad spires all clad in gold, shining like some huge crown set upon the brow of the stone mount upon which Livorna had been founded. Compared with the High Priest's palace, the far older Temple looked brutish and cold, all sharp angles and soulless columns of marble and grey stone. The chamber was welcoming, covered in rich velvet draperies and bright tapestries, a great four-poster feather bed and curtains against the far wall. Unlike the cold stone tiles that floored most of the receiving rooms in the palace, this chamber had polished inlaid oak floors, warm to the touch of bare feet.

Lucinda patted Lavinia's hand and rose, moving to a side table. She took a fig from a plate and carefully peeled it.

"You know you will be able to see further than me, and you will always know exactly where in Valdur I am. You just reach out, like you've always done."

Lavinia's face broke into a mischievous grin. "Has he spoken to you again?"

Lucinda raised a forefinger to her lips. "You mustn't mention him. You know that, my love."

Lavinia's perfect mouth pouted. "You always say that, and you never really tell me what he... what the message is." She turned to look out the large double-arched window. "And I don't understand why *you* were chosen. I can see farther."

Lucinda popped the fig into her mouth, took and peeled another as she chewed, and brought that to her sister. "It is not for us to ask such questions. It is enough that we are part of something so much greater. That we can use the gifts we have been given."

Lavinia's voice became little more than a soft exhalation. "The wound. Does it pain you? Will I have one soon?"

Lucinda's face grew dark and she swiftly grasped her sister's pointy chin. "You must never mention that. That is the rule." And as quickly she pulled her hand back and stroked the girl's hair. Her voice was quiet, reassuring. "It would endanger us both. They would not understand."

Lavinia nodded, for that was most definitely true. Their distinctiveness had always been a danger to themselves. People feared such things.

"Imagine what the Magister would make of such intelligence," Lucinda said, reaching for the veil and circlet upon the table. "It would put him into a difficult position." She arranged the white gossamer veil upon her sister's head, pleated a fold on either side, and gently placed the circlet upon it. "Now, do we have to go over again what you are to tell him about the monk's whereabouts?"

Lavinia pulled away slightly. "I don't like it when you treat me like a child. I know exactly what we will tell him." She paused. "But I remember you once told me that everyone would be told everything. When the time was right. Told the truth about the Lord's great purpose. Freed from the old lies."

Lucinda leaned over and touched Lavinia's shoulders as she spoke into her ear. "Yes, my love. That is still very much what will happen. But not until the time is right."

"Father did not believe what you told him. And now he's gone." Lavinia absently played with the veil about her shoulders. "Why would the others behave differently?"

Lucinda knelt next to her sister and grasped her hand. "They will. It will be very different when the time is right."

There was a hesitant knock upon the door. Lucinda gave her sister's hand one last squeeze and went to open it. A young maidservant curtsied in the doorway.

"The Magister is without and wishes to join you. May I send him in?"

"Tell him to come through."

Kodoris entered and made a brief sweeping bow. "My ladies. I trust that these accommodations have been comfortable? We often place guests in this part of the palace —pilgrims and such — and over time I like to think we have managed ourselves as a good hostelry. The Duke of Saivona stayed in these very apartments not two months gone by."

Lucinda laughed. "Magister, this is far better than we are accustomed to at Saint Dionei's. We might not wish to ever leave!"

Kodoris bowed his head. "And though I would have you stay as long as you desire, we all know that time is not with us. Shall we go out into the gardens on such a golden morning? It will make our business more pleasant."

When they passed through the red sandstone portico at the rear of the palace, they entered a world of carefully cultivated greenery and delicate yellow and orange fruits that hung over their heads. The branches that interlaced above them, as well as the hedges that bordered the garden, were fair alive with birdsong.

The hem of Kodoris's burgundy robes wafted in a warm gust that suddenly blew past. "It is always better to be in the outside air when needing to discuss heavy affairs. It opens the mind as well as the lungs."

The canonesses joined hands and walked at his side as they went deeper into the verdant bower, sun shafts piercing in a hundred places. Kodoris smiled. He felt a slight stirring in his aging loins as he looked on the sisters. So beautiful, almost too perfect. But, as a starling knows to leave untouched the most colourful caterpillar, so too was he wary of their strangeness, and their gifts.

"Something you told me at the priory has been weighing on me heavily," he said, slowing and stopping. "Lavinia, you said something about the greyrobe having discovered the conscience of Elded. What do you think he found?"

Lavinia's fingers played with the tissue of her veil. "It was so very faint. Just a fleeting moment that filled me with an image of the Lawgiver."

"And since… nothing more?"

Lavinia stared into the middle distance as she recalled what she had felt.

"It was something tangible. Something that the greyrobe held in his hand. And then the image was gone from my mind."

Lucinda looked at Kodoris. "Do you know what this might be? Some object?"

"I do not, mistress." And she knew he told the truth.

She nodded. "My sister has been challenged with this Seeking. We do not know why. It is almost as if…" She shook her head as if not quite believing herself. "Almost as if something is shielding him from the Sight. But Lavinia thinks she knows where he is or at least where he is bound."

Lavinia spoke up. "I have seen a town on the coast. Fishing boats and warships both. It is built upon a slope. Much like this place."

"Palestro," muttered Kodoris. "That must be where the mercenaries were going. That would make sense. The Black Rose is out of Maresto and Maresto is in alliance with the pirate fleet of Danamis."

"Then that will be my destination," said Lucinda. "Is Captain Flauros ready to ride out on the morrow?"

"He is. He has hand-picked five men to accompany him. You will be in safe hands."

Lucinda smiled again. "I'm sure we will be in no danger. We will merely be on pilgrimage to the shrines and temples along the way." She looped her arm in her sister's. "And Lavinia will be guiding me."

"And what of *your* art, mistress? What do your feelings tell you about his location, and who he is with? I am anxious to know whom he has spoken to."

"Magister," she replied, as if talking to a boy. "It is Lavinia who *sees* things from afar. I, on the other hand, compel people to *do* things."

Kodoris gave a little bow. "I remember, my good lady."

Lavinia patted her sister's hand. "She can see some things, some of the time, just not as far as I can. But she has other gifts."

Lucinda looked directly at Lavinia, her face expressionless. But Kodoris almost knew for sure that they were exchanging thoughts without words. Almost as if Lavinia had revealed too much.

Such beauty. And such coldness. But they were all he had. He had to get the greyrobe back before the truth could be sowed, and doubt take root.

* * *

A NIGHTINGALE SANG in the tree outside the open window. Lavinia sat up in bed, throwing off her coverlet. Her long hair tumbled about her shoulders as she rubbed a hand across her eyes. She pulled her chemise closer to her neck even though the air in the bedchamber was warm. She sat still for a moment, the dream playing again in her mind's eye, and then she reached over and shook her sleeping sister.

"Lucinda! Wake, please wake."

Lucinda opened her eyes and sat up. She was instantly alert and unperturbed by the awakening, blue eyes wide in the moonlit room. "Yes, sister. I am here."

"I have seen a large ship. A ship at sea. He is on it."

Lucinda reached out to Lavinia. "At sea? But how can you see him when before you could not?"

"I can't see the greyrobe but there are others talking about him. *Thinking* about him. They are on the ship. He must be with them too."

"But headed to where?"

Lavinia shook her head. "I can't tell! There's nothing to show me. Just endless ocean."

Lucinda stroked her gently curling locks. "Perhaps the mirror will reveal more. Shall we consult it now? Can you do that?"

The girl nodded. "Yes, let us go and sit at the window."

"In the moonlight."

"Where it works best." And Lavinia's teeth shone as she smiled in the darkness.

Silently, they slid out of the huge bed and padded over to the wide stone sill of the casement window. They saw that the moon was now low in the night sky but still pouring its rays strongly against the palace wall, and spilling into their chamber.

"I will retrieve the mirror," whispered Lavinia, and she moved quickly to the table, her chemise flowing out behind her. She returned in a heartbeat, clutching a flat black disc the size of a man's palm. It was polished jet, and as she sat next to her sister on the window ledge, she gently moved her fingers over its smooth surface. It shone like ice, reflecting the moon, but to Lavinia, it was like some deep dark well, black water glistening on the surface, and when she peered into it, she would always have to fight the feeling that she was falling.

She smiled at her sister. "It's pulling me again." And she brought it to within a foot of her face.

"Concentrate, sister!" whispered Lucinda. And as she watched, Lavinia's face was illuminated by a bluish glow; a light more colourful than that reflected by the pale disc of the moon. She watched as her sister's eyes widened, her pupils so huge that she looked like a cat. Lavinia's neck bent forward slightly and she leaned further into the mirror. Her eyes were fixed now, staring into the black vastness of the polished stone. Her breaths became more rapid and shallow.

"What do you see, sister?"

"It is a woman," hissed Lavinia, eyes not wavering and still hundreds of miles away. "She is not high-born and sits with others. She is upset. Upset that she has lost something. She does not want to go where they are going! Maresto or Perusia. Maresto or Perusia, she thinks."

Lucinda's hand reached forward but she dared not disturb her sister.

"Her heart is so very sad," Lavinia said quietly. "Acquel is more soldier than monk. Not a confessor. She needs him. He looks at her now with a different eye." The corners of her mouth drew up, revealing her teeth. "She must not encourage him. But he is a man. And he finds her... desirable."

"Maresto or Perusia?" Lucinda whispered.

Lavinia was still smiling, lost in the musings of Timandra Pandarus. "Should rejoin the Black Rose, she says. Before it's too late."

Lucinda's nails dug into Lavinia's wrist. The mirror wobbled. "Maresto or Perusia?"

Lavinia's mouth opened, her eyebrows raised in concern. "Captain Danamis decides. I can do nothing."

Lucinda reached out and took the mirror from Lavinia's hands. Lavinia drew a sharp breath and her eyes flickered as she beheld her sister once again. "He is there with this woman. On a ship of war."

Lucinda looked out of the window and across the shadow-laden gardens. "You will have to try again tomorrow, my love. You need to find out which city they sail to."

Lavinia saw that one of the four little half-moons on her wrist, left by Lucinda's grasp, was bleeding. She brushed her fingers over the wounds. "It is like I am looking through some great grey fog that has descended upon me."

Lucinda turned and embraced her. "Fear not, sister. We cannot see the greyrobe but we can see those around him. Those who care for him. They will lead us to him as the bee does to the flower."

Thirteen

DANAMIS SAT IN the near gloom of his airless stern cabin, a cramped space that even a short man would barely be able to stand up in. The small half-moon openings carved into the planks barely let in any of the rapidly dissipating sunlight. Elbows on his chart table, his head rested in his hands as he fought back tears.

One fucking ship. Half a crew.

He sucked in a long breath of frustration, tearing at his black sweaty curls as they slid through his fingers.

So goddamned blind.

A knock sounded on the cabin door. He sat up and ran a grubby sleeve across his face. "Come!"

It was one of the ship's boys, come to light the lanterns. He struck flint to the tinderbox and wordlessly brought light into the cabin as each tallow candle sputtered into life.

"Boy, tell the master I want to see him."

The lad put a thumb to his forehead and scuttled out the passageway. Danamis heard the unsteady tramp of boots in the adjoining cabin. The woollen curtain parted as Strykar scraped against the bulkhead that was obviously holding him upright. His arming doublet was stained with dried blood and rust.

"Julianus! You fool," Danamis gasped. "What the hell are you doing out of your berth?"

The mercenary grumbled something under his breath and touched at the rag wrapped around his head. "I got tired of puking my guts out. Don't know if it's my head or your goddamned ship."

"Get back to your rack. You ought to be dead by anyone's reckoning."

"Something must have broken my fall," he slurred.

"It was my deck."

Strykar coughed and then winced. "You bastard."

Danamis swore and moved to help him over to a bench. He reached for a mug of ale that was holding down the grubby chart on the table and shoved it into Strykar's hands.

"You were the last man off the tower. We managed to pull ourselves out past the chain and raise sail. *Salamander* blocked the exit behind us as she caught fire, but you bought us the time we needed."

"It's going to cost you." Strykar drained the cup and then pulled off his bandage, touching the purple egg on his forehead. "A lot."

Danamis looked down at his chart. "I've put us on a heading due south. Until I can decide where we should go. I don't want to chance Tetch intercepting us if we stand in sight of the coast."

Strykar raised his head. "South? Surely we sail west for Maresto. What else can you do? I've given orders for the company to return there, which they've undoubtedly done by now if Tetch hasn't had a go at them."

Danamis's pale grey eyes turned to the mercenary. "I am in your debt. I know that. But I will decide the course of my ship."

Strykar pushed back the little bench and rose unsteadily, nearly bumping his head on a beam. "It's your ship, my friend, but there's only one place we're headed and that's

Maresto. So let's not fuck around concerning that."

Danamis leaned back. "There's more I haven't told you yet. We managed to pick up a few of *Salamander's* men that jumped ship when she caught fire, including her captain. He tells an interesting tale."

"Not my worry, Danamis."

"Hear out Bassinio. I trust his word. We're going to sit tight here for the night so you've got the time."

"And you've got precious little. I'm going on deck to see how many men I've lost this day when we saved your skin." He swore and turned to make his way out, hands groping to fend off the beams and steady himself as the vessel rocked.

"Blessed saints! You can barely walk, you fool."

But Strykar had already gone. A few moments later Danamis heard a great cheer rise up from the main deck. Strykar had reunited with his men. Danamis slumped and reached out for the ale pot.

Three rapid raps on the bulkhead rattled the walls and Gregorvero entered. His perpetually reddened face now held a somewhat darker cast.

"Gregor, drop some canvas and let us drift for the night. Until I figure out where we're going." Danamis ran his hand over the chart again.

Gregorvero moved closer to the table, arms across his barrel chest. "We'll drift west."

"I know. But until I can decide which course we set for."

"Well you damned well better decide and the quicker the better!"

Danamis was on his feet, the bench crashing behind him and his finger pointing. "If you weren't my friend, I'd have you thrown over the side for that."

With a speed belying his bulk, Gregorvero seized Danamis's wrist and slammed his hand down onto the table. "If I wasn't your friend I would not have said it." He pointed at the golden signet upon Danamis's little finger. "Your father gave you that for a reason when he left these shores."

Danamis stood frozen, looking at the deeply scored band, the seawolf intaglio worn but still visible in the red carnelian stone. Gregorvero released him, pushing the hand away as he stepped back.

"And he did so because he wanted you to lead the fleet. Not Tetch."

Danamis leaned on the table. "I was not his first choice. You know that full well."

"Your brother died a good death. He was a good captain—and he was senior. But your father would not have named you had he not believed you were man enough to rule in his stead."

"He had to give me the command if he was to keep it in the family. Hardly an act of faith in me, was it? I despised him, you know. For what he did."

"That's in the past. But you can't just keep throwing gold at men to buy their loyalty. Truly loyal men need more than that."

Danamis nodded slowly. These were words he already knew to be true despite his worst nature. "I know I did not listen to you when I had the chance. I regret that now. You saw things more clearly than I did. You knew the storm was coming. You saw what Tetch was up to. And probably a long time ago."

"You were too busy wenching and drinking when not trying to buy your way out of trouble. Now that you're a pauper you'll have to think differently. And act differently. So stop your mewling and start making some decisions."

Gregorvero lifted Danamis's doublet off of a peg on the bulkhead and held it out. "And you could do worse than go out on deck and address what's left of your fleet. Tell them what they need to hear. A plan of battle."

Danamis took the doublet and pulled it on. "I'm making it up as I go along."

Gregorvero smiled. "Even the best of them do that." He paused. "Nico... you *know* in your heart what you want to do next. Trust the men to follow."

Danamis looked again at Gregorvero, his face lined with determination but tempered by shame for what he had and had not done in the months gone by. A place he could never revisit. "Aye," said Danamis. "I believe that I do. Ring the bell."

ACQUEL STOOD ON the sterncastle deck, gripping the railing tightly as he watched the sun melt into the endless horizon. The sea was calm but the gentle rolling of the ship still set his stomach to lurching and he swallowed hard. He had never before glimpsed the ocean except in his dreams. Nor had he ever set foot on a great ship. And today he had done both, just a few days since he had been in the bowels of that tomb. The life he had known was undone completely, his future a die to be cast. Elded's ghost would not be deterred. He knew that now.

For the first time since he had been on the run, he thought of his mother. Was she even now beating out the linen on the stones in the palace of Count Marsilius, High Steward of Livorna, proud of her son's pious work further on up the mount at the Ara? Or had the news of his flight and the false accusations of murder already spread and poisoned her ears and those around her? He realized then that she might even have drawn the wrath of the Temple down upon herself. Marsilius was nothing more than a creature of the High Priest and the Nine. He would do whatever they bid of him.

Above his head, the lateen sail on the mizzen sagged as the breeze died. All around him nothingness. Even the coastline had vanished, falling over the edge of the sea. He reached to the belt and pouch that still rode high up on the waist of his doublet. He opened it and pulled out the amulet. It was a reddish gold, the lapis stones now dark, almost purple in the fading light. The designs and engraving still stood out, their indentations blackened with the dust of the tomb. For an instant he was seized with an impulse to throw it into the deep. And then he smiled—more a grimace—as he knew it would never stay there. He lowered his head and put it around his neck, gently tucking it into his shirt. It was oddly warm upon his breastbone.

Five shirtless and barefoot sailors clamoured about the mast, shouting as they worked to haul down and furl the great piece of canvas, and as he watched he saw Timandra climbing up the stair to the deck. Her hair was wild and loose, the sleeves of her chemise rolled up high. And though she looked tired and worn out, to his eyes she was yet alluring. Acquel knew she had tended to Captain Strykar for hours after his fall. It had been a mad headlong flight once they had dragged the captain down off the fo'c'sle, arrows raining down upon them from the quayside. In the pandemonium he had found himself knocked over and nearly trampled by the sailors and soldiers as they ran across the deck. And then, they were out of the harbour and he somehow found himself being pulled to his feet and pushed forward to help bear Strykar down below with Timandra and two other *rondelieri*, not knowing whether the man was even alive.

"Mistress!" Acquel grasped her hand and covered it with his other.

"Stop calling me that. You know my name." She leaned over the rail and took a deep breath.

"How fares the captain?"

"Ah! He's more bear than man. It would take more than a drop off a tower to kill him. I dressed his head wound and he was well enough to curse me while I did it. I don't think we will have need of your service now, brother monk."

Acquel smiled. "I'm not a blackrobe. I don't have the ability to perform the rite of the extremis blessing."

She looked at him, her eyes gentle, almost forgiving. "Oh well. You are somewhat less use than I first thought. Let us hope no more of us have need of the rite."

"Do you know where we will go now? Will Danamis take us to Maresto?"

"That is not for me to say. This morning I never expected to be on a ship sailing into open waters. All I have left is this purse with some silver and a few ducats. Palestrian devils are probably dividing up what stock I had on the mules. Bastards."

"Where can Danamis go? Surely Maresto will give him aid?"

"I didn't think you'd be in a hurry to go there."

Acquel lowered his head and, seeing this, Timandra reached out and touched his wrist. "I am sorry. I did not mean to be so callous."

"I know that. We have all been thrown upside down this day. Strykar more than the rest of us!"

She smiled broadly and shook her head. "Aye, true enough."

Just beneath them, where the main deck began, the ship's bell began to ring out, a steady clanging to gather the crew. They looked at each other and moved from the stern to the forward rail. Below them they could see the *rondelieri* gathered in a circle around Strykar.

Timandra swore. "He's had his skull cracked and now he's up again after I told him to lie still."

Acquel's eyes quickly scanned the heads. By his count, there were just over 30 of the swordsmen remaining, the rest having fallen at Palestro. Most of the survivors had lost their great bucklers in the escape but a few still lay propped here and there or sitting on the four great wrought iron cannon that were lashed amidships pointing out over the railings. "At least he still lives."

Seamen came sliding down the ratlines from above and on the fo'c'sle another dozen sailors and bowmen gathered. Acquel's eyes moved rapidly from fo'c'sle to main deck and then to where he stood on the poop; he made it sixty-five men in all. This was all the admiral had left to his command. Leaning over, he saw the ship's master, a portly man, stride out from the stern cabin and pound down the small set of stairs to deck. Behind him was Danamis.

"Give ears to your commander!" bellowed Gregorvero and the raucous banter subsided like the sudden halt of a rain shower. A few coughs followed but no one spoke. The creak of rope and board echoed all around them while Danamis walked to the mainmast, a stout oak the thickness of two men, and placed a hand upon it, patting it soundly.

"This good ship! This fine vessel made finer by the stout hearts who sail in her!" Danamis's voice lifted high, reverberating off the fo'c'sle bulkheads and carrying across the deck from stem to stern. "As God is my witness, I give thanks to you all for your loyalty and your courage! Just as I curse the rank treachery of that bilge scum behind us in Palestro!"

There was a ripple of cheers and huzzahs from the pirates but the *rondelieri* stood quiet, arms folded, or leaning back upon the rails.

"Just tell us where we're going, you swarthy bastard," muttered Timandra.

Danamis walked around the mainmast. "We are not done with this. We are not content to let Giacomo Tetch have his way. And we are not alone. There are our comrades who could not escape. Brave *Salamander* was not the only ship who fought the mutineers. *Swiftsure* and *Bonadventura* resisted too and we may yet see their sails on the north horizon!"

The light had nearly faded away now, the sky purple. Danamis gestured up to men manning the fo'c'sle deck. "For your day's hard work I give you a reward..." And he whirled to raise his arms to the sterncastle. "A gold ducat for every man!"

A cry went up throughout *Royal Grace* and feet stamped upon the decks. "And the same to our brave *rondelieri* comrades who shed their blood with us!"

A few of the swordsmen nodded their heads and exchanged looks but this news was more soberly taken than by the sailors. Strykar seemed to glower in their midst.

Danamis looked down at his boots. His voice became softer. "And my brothers, a new day will bring a new course for us to sail." He looked up again, his eyes wide. "As the Lord Admiral of our king, it is to Perusia I must go. The king must be told of this terrible crime and betrayal. And there will I gain the ships and men to return and thrash the traitors! Long live the king!"

The cry, taken up by all, sounded across the ship. "Long live the king!"

Acquel watched as the *rondelieri* stopped their slouching and stood up straight. He saw Strykar push his way toward Danamis. But Gregorvero walked between him and Danamis and raised his voice high.

"Back to your stations! Set the first watch!"

Timandra swore and looked at Acquel as she leaned over the rail. "I damned well knew that's what it would be. There'll be one unholy fight now."

Next to her, Acquel overheard two seamen sniggering in a conspiracy. "By Elded's bollocks," said one to the other, "we're off with our begging bowl to Sempronius. God help us."

And Acquel now realized his reluctant adventure was taking yet another turn.

Below, Gregorvero reached for Strykar's arm. "Captain, we would urgently consult you. Now, please." And Danamis nodded to Strykar.

"You may have a battle on your hands sooner than you think," rasped the mercenary. "But I'll forbear it out of past loyalty and hear you out."

Gregorvero, his shoulders relaxing, took a step back. He gestured with a movement of his arm and a scowling Captain Strykar turned and headed for the stern cabin, cursing all the way.

Fourteen

STRYKAR'S EYES WIDENED as the man walked into the gloom and fug of the admiral's cramped cabin. In the light of the lantern that hung from an oak stanchion, he saw that half of the man's face was seared raw and weeping with fluid, the wound creeping down across his jaw and neck. He had been burned, and half the hair on his head was singed to frazzled stubble. An acrid smell wafted across the cabin.

"Bassinio," said Danamis. "This is Captain Strykar of the Company of the Black Rose."

Bassinio turned to Strykar and nodded. Strykar did the same.

"I want you to tell Captain Strykar what you have told me—from the beginning."

Bassinio cast his eyes to the table. "Give me a drink first."

Danamis poured him out some ale from the pot and placed the cup in his hands. Bassinio drank it one gulp and handed the cup back.

"They went aboard all the ships in the morning. Tetch's mates. They said that it was time to choose between Danamis and Tetch and that Tetch had the backing of the Decurions and of the temple priests. They didn't give much room for argument. I told them to get off of my ship and go to hell."

He gestured for the ale pot as he paused and swallowed hard. Danamis filled the cup again.

"Well, luckily my lads weren't having any of it. Tetch's men gave me a tongue lashing but they left in a hurry. I saw other vessels start hoisting the bloody ensign and I knew it had all started. I gave orders to take to arms and raise anchor because they would be coming back to try and take us. And the devil take them they were back with crossbowmen within one hour. I got *Salamander* under way with a tow but lost men as they rowed us out. It took us too long and they had managed to bring up a longboat alongside to board. We were almost to the mouth when they set us alight with fire arrows. I could see you alongside—at the west tower— and we pulled hard to make it over to you. I was up on the sterncastle trying to put out the fire when the enemy managed to board us amidships and rushed us. The whole stern awning was ablaze by then. And then it just collapsed on us. I managed to jump over the side with a few others."

"That's a hard run of it to be sure, captain," said Strykar. "And I am sorry you have lost your ship and your crew." He turned to Danamis and Gregorvero. "But that has bugger-all to do with you setting a course for Perusia."

"Bassinio," said Danamis, his voice low, "tell Captain Strykar what Tetch told you the night before."

Bassinio nodded. "I was at the alehouse with two other captains and their masters. Tetch comes in and we take a table in the room at the back. See, he wants to have a quiet word about the state of affairs, as he puts it. Well, after a few jacks he all but comes out against you, admiral. He says that he has been in negotiations with Torinia—Duke Ursino himself no less. Says that if Palestro signs a treaty with him, Torinia will give more ships and more men. And they don't give a rat's arse who Palestrians pirate from so long as it isn't Torinian ships."

Strykar didn't move. "You swear that is what he said was on offer? An alliance?"

Bassinio nodded again. "And he said that Maresto could go fuck themselves for all the use they were to Palestro."

Danamis put his hands on table and looked straight at Strykar. "And what do you think Duke Alonso would make of that?"

"All the more reason we sail there now to tell him."

"And how many warships does Maresto have in port?" countered Danamis. "Five? Two? We won't get the help we need there. Only the king has a big enough fleet—and a purse to match."

Strykar grumbled. "You don't know that for sure. It's still a gamble."

"There's more, Captain Strykar." It was Gregorvero, standing back against the stern bulkhead with his arms crossed. "When we ground against the chain tower in Palestro, the bow timbers took a pounding. We've got over a foot of seawater in the bilge and I can practically poke my finger in some of the seams."

Strykar covered his eyes and shook his head. "By all the fucking saints! So we are *sinking*? Is that what you're telling me now?"

Gregorvero pursed his lips. "Well, it's not getting any better. What I've told Captain Danamis is that if we raise full sail and increase speed—or if we run into a head-sea that pounds the bow—we'll take on water even faster. I've plugged the worst with strips of canvas but that just slows it a bit."

"What he's saying," said Danamis, "is that if we turn back and sail west for Maresto, we have to run the gauntlet of Palestro. We can't sail fast and we can't sail against the wind and wave. If we sail eastwards now, we have a following sea. And we stand a good chance of making it to a safe port."

Strykar shook his head as all the implications washed over him. "You have put me in the shit this time, Danamis," he said with a resigned sigh.

"I am the king's admiral. It's my duty to tell him what's happened in Palestro. With his aid I can put together a fleet to challenge Tetch. Hell, Tetch may find another mutiny on his hands if Sempronius declares him traitor to the kingdom."

Strykar raised a finger to Danamis. "So help me, Nicolo Danamis. If we don't end up at the bottom of the sea first, you will be paying me back in full chests of ducats in Perusia. I promise you that."

Danamis smiled thinly. "My banker in Perusia is at your disposal, old friend. And don't forget we have your myrra leaf below."

"Damned good it will do me now." He turned to Gregorvero. "Just get us there, master Gregor. Keep this pile of kindling together and get us there." He muttered under his breath and looked again at Danamis. "I'll go tell my men before they start trouble."

"I'll see your men are properly berthed," said Gregorvero, "and find them some more food." Strykar nodded and made to leave. He ducked his head down and left the cabin, bouncing off a bulkhead as the ship skittered on a wave crest. Damamis bent over his chart and exhaled heavily. He turned to Gregorvero.

"Well spoken. Both of you." He looked over to Bassinio, whose jaw was clearly pulsing, clenched in pain. "Bassinio, seek out the Widow Pandarus. She may be able to treat your wounds."

"Only if she has some *acqua vitalis* squirreled away," he said, before turning and shuffling out of the cabin.

"I did what you ordered me to," said Gregorvero, his voice tired, after Bassinio had gone. "But you should have told him the truth of it. He deserves that."

"What? And risk a mutiny by the *rondelieri*? I'll not take that chance."

"So... you lie to a friend and comrade? You had better hope he doesn't soon discover that we're not sinking."

Danamis pulled himself up straight, his head brushing the stone-hard oaken beams. "I will do what I must to get my fleet back. Anything. And I won't waste time lying-to out here. We must put on some sail through the night and make headway east."

Gregorvero stepped forward. "Risky," he said. "But I agree. There's little to be gained from standing still and drifting. Foremast mainsheet and spritsail only and I'll make sure the helmsmen damn well stay awake. Come daylight we can raise more canvas."

Danamis gripped his shoulder. "Good. Set sail and make course east."

Gregorvero returned a look of cold resolve. "Aye, captain. But, in future, don't lie to *me*."

OUTSIDE ON THE main deck, Strykar's men stood at his approach, gathering amidships from where they had been, whether sitting or sprawled out on the planks, sick from the rolling of the *Grace* or from the meal of black bread and smoked mackerel they had been given a few hours after their escape. Strykar beheld them in the light of the huge lantern that hung from the fo'c'sle. They were no men of the sea and nor was he. Many had never been on a boat before. He stepped into their midst, clapping the shoulder of one he knew well, Brognolo, a sergeant a fair bit older than he was. He looked from face to face—some young and beardless, others grizzled and well-lined, but all tired and streaked with sweat and salt spray. They had been chosen to enter Palestro first, to lead the way for the company in what should have been a routine trade. Then, that done, they were meant to partake of comfort and merriment, of good food, passable drink, and women with little virtue. Instead, they had fought for their lives, lost a quarter of their comrades and were now on a stinking and sinking ship of a pirate who had nothing left but his name.

"Well, here we are my lads," he said. "On the sea voyage you always wanted."

Those who weren't seasick laughed.

"It's been a close scrape today, I know. The Lord does that to us sometimes. Tests us and our faith." He moved amongst them. Looking them in their eyes, grasping a shoulder here and there. "But we fought off that rabble on the docks and we live to fight again."

"Will they bury the dead we left behind?" someone shouted.

"If there are still good men in Palestro then yes, they will. But I cannot promise you that. It is for us now to look to our front and where we are headed. All of you I chose because you can be trusted with my life. And because you're damned hard to kill." A ripple of laughter laced with fatigue rose around him.

"And I am telling you that we must journey to Perusia." A murmur ensued. "I have just been given news that cuts at the heart of Maresto. The traitor in Palestro who took our comrades this day also means to make war on Duke Alonso. In alliance with Torinia."

Strykar raised his hands for silence.

"That is the truth of it, my lads! Now...who do we serve? We serve Count Malvolio. And he serves Duke Alonso. And Duke Alonso serves Maresto."

"But why Perusia, captain?" It was Brognolo.

"Because sergeant, that is where the king is. And he has the gold and the men and the ships to put Admiral Danamis's arse back in Palestro. And that is what the Duke of Maresto would want."

Brognolo gave Strykar a smile. "I don't need to hear no more, sir. I am with you. We are still of the Black Rose even at sea."

"And what say the rest of you?" Strykar's eyes shifted from man to man. "What say my chosen men?"

A murmur ensued again followed by shouts of "Aye!" and "Perusia and the King!"

Strykar nodded in approval. "Good, my lads. The pirates say they will feed you below and give you a place to put your heads down. Get some rest tonight if you can. We do not know what the morning will bring." And he pulled Brognolo aside. "Make sure they all get billeted down properly. I will send the ship's master your way."

Brognolo grinned, half his teeth missing like the windows of a ruined manor house. "I could do with some grub after this day's work—even if it is ship's fare."

Strykar made his way aft, wobbling slightly, his head throbbing. He needed to eat and sleep. And to pray that the ship would make it to Perusia before sinking.

ACQUEL LAY IN a narrow hammock and blinked in the darkness of the fo'c'sle cabin. He was wedged in among *rondelieri* who snored and gurgled away in their fitful slumbers. It was as if he was back in his dormitory with the greyrobes and novices—only louder and smellier. He had somehow drifted off earlier but now was wide awake. He squeezed out of his berth and felt his way to the hatchway, outlined in light from the lantern that burned on the main deck.

He was not challenged as he made his way astern. He could see one great sail on the foremast filling with the light warm breeze that washed over the deck. The few sailors on watch paid him no heed, nor the helmsman on the whipstaff at the base of the sterncastle. He mounted the ladder that led up to the two cabins and went inside. A punched-tin lantern with a single candle was on the table and he could just make out the hulking figure of Captain Strykar rolled up in a berth rack. He was snoring softly. Timandra raised her head as he entered, pushing herself up into a sitting position from the mattress on the cabin floor.

"I can't sleep anymore," he whispered as he padded inside. She gestured for him to come to her and he sat down next to her, folding his long legs underneath himself, back against the bulkhead.

"Nor me," she said. "But not a problem for him."

Acquel tilted his head towards the captain. "He's going along then with the admiral? To Perusia?"

"I think it's a fool's errand but he has other concerns."

Acquel looked at her. "What do you mean?"

Timandra pulled up the thin coverlet she had over her and tucked her chin into it. "He's trying to think what Count Malvolio and the Duke would have wanted. He knows they want the alliance with Palestro to continue. With Tetch seizing the fleet that will now change."

"But why these pirates of Palestro?" he whispered. "What makes them so useful?"

"Maresto has few warships but a lot of wool merchants. Danamis's fleet gave protection to our shipping. They beat up the Southlander corsairs so badly they rarely come into coastal waters anymore. If Tetch gets his way with Torinia, Maresto will be exposed to Torinian extortion. Pay us or we take your ships. There is no love lost between those two houses."

Acquel's brow furrowed and he pointed to Strykar's sleeping form. "But... he's just a mercenary captain. That seems a concern far above his station in life."

Timandra smiled and shook her head. "Perhaps."

Acquel found it difficult to take his eyes from her cascading hair and her full lips. He put his hands on his knees and contemplated his feet instead. There was silence in the cabin except for the steady snuffling of Strykar and the unceasing creaking and rocking of the ship. After a short while Acquel ventured to speak again.

"Three days ago I was chased out of Livorna and nearly killed. Now I am on my way to the royal enclave—maybe even to see the king." He turned and looked into her eyes. She was watching him intently. "This is all happening for a reason. Can't you feel it?"

She could see the golden chain dangling around his neck, disappearing down into his shirt front. Her own eyes had witnessed what the remarkable jewel that he wore could do, and she had more than once thought about what other powers it might hold. And more to, why it had chosen Acquel—and now her and the Black Rose—to keep company with. She desperately wanted to believe that it was a holy miracle but a part of her held back, fearful that it represented something wholly different.

"I'm not sure that I can," she lied.

"Well, if I cannot rid myself of it then I will have to see where it takes me... for better or for ill."

She reached over and grasped his hand. Acquel squeezed hers in return.

"Maybe I can find someone who can tell me more," he said softly. "Someone in Perusia. Have you been there before?"

"I have. It is a great city." Her eyes settled upon the chain again. "Acquel, will you let me have a look at the amulet?"

He lowered his chin and lifted the chain over his head, pulling the strange pendant out of his shirt. As he offered it to her, he leaned in closer, dropping it into her palm. The urge to kiss her was overpowering him and his face moved towards hers. Timandra drew back as her hand folded around the amulet and Acquel, embarrassment flooding over him, pulled back too. She recovered from the awkwardness without even a twitch, ignoring what might have happened if she had noticed it at all.

Acquel watched as she held the amulet close, examining the writing in the guttering candlelight.

"It is beautiful, isn't it?" She turned it over. "I cannot read this old Valdurian script. But I might know someone who can."

"Someone in Perusia?"

Timandra nodded. "There's a chance. But I think we have to be very careful about who we share this secret with and how. Understand? So, do as Strykar bids you. Show it to no one and tell no one. I will think upon what we might be able to do." She handed it back to him.

"Seems I know too many secrets," Acquel said. "I discovered Elded's and now I won't be left alone."

"Don't say that. You *think* you saw something in the tomb. But you don't know the truth for certain."

Acquel shook his head. "You don't understand. I have seen Elded. In my dreams. And more than once now. He *is* merfolk. And they are trying to kill me for it."

He saw the look of reticence on her face and regretted his words. "I should go back now." He stood up, careful not to wake Strykar who had turned over, groaning in his sleep. "I hope you are able to rest, Timandra."

She smiled that he had finally called her by her name. "Fear nought. You are with the Black Rose now. We look after each other."

"For all you and I know, he will throw me back to the Ara if he is ordered to." Acquel gestured to the sleeping mercenary.

"Do not be so hasty to judge him."

"But he seems to have no other loyalty than to the Black Rose. No wife? No family? And you ask me to trust him with my life."

Timandra looked at him, her eyes scolding. "He lost his wife and all his children ten years ago. A raid over the border by a band of Torinian soldiers turned rogue. He has had no other woman since."

Acquel looked down. "I am sorry to speak so about your kin," he said quietly. "I will go now."

She grasped his hand and squeezed. "Fear not. All will be well."

But his words still ran through her mind. And with them all the doubt and worry that they conjured. The mystery of this monk persisted—and with it an unwanted ghost that hovered over all of them.

Fifteen

DANAMIS FELL INTO a slumber so deep and so dark that it seemed he dreamt for years on end.

He was a boy again, with his father on *Royal Grace*, sailing to Naresis to dictate terms to the corsairs. Something he always thought amusing since they themselves were supposed to be pirates. But the ship was far bigger than he remembered, the Sea of Valdur transmuted to purple wine, and his father slowly transfigured into a merman as he watched, horrified.

The dream shifted again. He was with Citala, the mer chieftain's daughter, looking into her eyes of deepest violet; fiery and unnatural. They were embracing, kissing. Her lips were warm when everything told him they should be cold. He desired her completely. They were in the sea together, sinking down deeper, entwined. But then he was drowning, water filling his nose and mouth, suffocating. He thrashed wildly and in doing so, he awoke.

Shaking his head like a dog that had just been kicked, he swung his legs out of his boxed wooden berth and grabbed his boots from the floor. It was full light. Gregorvero should have woken him earlier. He mumbled a curse as he laced up

his boots. With just one arm in a sleeve he bent his shoulders
down and barrelled out of the cabin.

IN THE FO'C'SLE, Acquel was being prodded into wakefulness
by the toe of a *rondelieri's* boot. All around him the soldiers
were rising, coughing and farting, and he could see a line
of men out the hatchway to the fore, all waiting to take
their easement out on the ship's prow. Sometime in the early
hours of the new day he had finally drifted off to sleep, and
now, he was one of the last to awake.

"Have a care, brother monk!" He was shouldered aside
by a short burly soldier, intent on getting out into the fresh
air. He hurriedly pulled on his doublet, damp with the
moist sea air, cinched up his hose and fastened his belt,
dagger and pouch. On the main deck the life of the *Royal
Grace* had begun anew. And though he had just arisen,
already he felt like superfluous baggage with no purpose
other than to keep out of others' way. Sailors were climbing
the rigging, hauling on lines. *Rondelieri*—sullen and bleary
in the main—hung about the gunwales staring out at the
endless azure water. Acquel saw that the mainsail and
mizzen sails had been set and the ship was moving faster,
the sheets snapping. He looked up astern and saw the ship's
master and Captain Danamis exchanging words, hands
gesticulating and arms pointing out to the west. He walked
across the deck, jostled by men intent on their duties, and
ascended the ladder up to the poop.

He approached Danamis who was staring intently out
over the rail, looking west.

"Good morrow, holy man," he said, not turning. "How
good are your eyes?"

"I'm not sure, my lord," he said. "Too many manuscripts
copied in bad light for too long, I think."

"There! Look along my arm."

That the hazy sky seemed to merge with the horizon did not help as Acquel squinted and shielded his eyes with his hand. But after he blinked a few times he saw them. Two sets of sails, close together, hardly more than mere specks but vessels nonetheless.

"Yes, I see them now. Two ships. Is it Tetch?"

Danamis gripped the railing with both hands. "Too early to tell."

"For my money," said Gregorvero, "I reckon they're Southlanders. But we're running broad now and making good speed to the east."

"Hell's teeth," cursed Danamis. "The good Lord is not looking kindly on me these past few days. Can you help with that, brother monk?"

Acquel bowed his head. "I fear not, my lord."

"Then we'll just have to trust to the winds." Danamis pushed himself off the railing. He took another long look at the distant vessels, hoping for one or the other to change course, if only to afford a clearer view. "Gregor, nudge us northeast by east. Get us closer to the coast."

"That'll be Torinian waters, you know."

"I do know. So what would they do if they saw this flagship? Attack us?"

Gregorvero shrugged.

"Just keep a sharp eye on those ships," said Danamis, stabbing a finger westward. "And pray they're not pursuing."

Gregorvero gave Acquel an almost apologetic look and then followed Danamis down the ladder. Acquel looked about him. Four cast iron swivel guns were spaced out on the stern railing and he suddenly imagined what it would be like to face the might of such weapons. If he had felt useless when he had first stepped out on deck, he felt now probably worse than that: he was the bearer of a curse.

Some time passed, in which worry gnawed at the monk and the crew of the *Royal Grace* grew more tense with the two vessels nearing; Danamis was back on the poop, looking out over the transom. In addition to the ship's master and the young monk, Strykar and Timandra Pandarus were there too. Over the larboard side, a dark undulating line on the horizon ran as far as the eye could see. The coastline of Valdur was again in view.

Strykar was staring out over the railing west and shaking his head as if he was seeing a phantasm. "Are you sure? Fucking Southlanders?"

Danamis was subdued. "Yes. We can tell by their rig."

And Strykar could clearly see that the two ships bearing down upon them carried three large red triangular sails. "We are truly being shit upon from on high. Can we outrun them?"

"No. But we can try and out-manouevre them," replied Danamis, "but we must prepare to fight if it comes to it. You should tell your men."

Strykar's laugh was bitter. "Well, you have barely thirty *rondelieri* who just happen to have left their shields back in Palestro." He jerked his thumb towards the Southlander ships. "And how many men do they have?"

"If they're hunting, it could be over a hundred and fifty per ship."

Strykar swore. "What is it, Admiral Danamis, that drives you to persecute me so?"

"Fate has been cruel to us both, I'll give you that. But I've got four sakers, ten falcons, and a dozen swivel guns on this ship. We can give them a belly full of stone shot. That will give them pause."

"But how many soldiers have you got left to fire them? Or

bowmen." Strykar turned to Acquel. "Brother monk, you had better start your prayers now, my boy!"

"We've got a few hours before they can catch up to us," said Danamis. "And maybe the wind will turn against them. But we will prepare now to be boarded. Gregor, get the nets up over the gunwales and break out the charges and shot for the guns."

Strykar looked at Gregorvero. "Is he mad? Boarded by over two hundred to our... Elded's beard! I don't know how many we've got left but it's barely enough for a tavern brawl."

"I've fought worse odds," replied Gregorvero, although he wasn't quite sure that was true. "We have the bows if your men can use them."

Strykar nodded. "They'll do what they have to."

Timandra pushed past Acquel and seized Strykar's forearm. "Cousin, if it comes to the worst, you won't let them take me." It was not a plea but an order.

Strykar looked at her. "They won't take either of us alive— if it comes to the worst."

From behind, Acquel spoke up, his voice sticking in his dry throat. "Lord Danamis, what can I do?"

Danamis turned, having forgotten the strange young monk who stood there, gormless and awkward. "Brother... Acquel? Good. You can shift the shot and powder charges."

"As will I," said Timandra. "Show me."

Danamis smiled. "Very well, Mistress Pandarus. I'll not refuse any aid this day."

The upper decks of the carrack were as chaotic as a fairground. The great red and white striped awning of the sterncastle pulsed in the breeze like some giant jellyfish as it came down, hauled on and stowed for fear of fire arrows. Thick rope netting crept up the sides of the *Grace* from castle to castle as half a dozen seamen sweated under block and tackle to erect the defences. Talis, the captain of the fo'c'sle, divided the remaining soldiers of the ship, both fore and aft crews, to either man the guns or take to their bows. Ramus, the commander of the *Grace's* sterncastle, had not been seen since the afternoon of the mutiny and so there was an answer to the mystery of Tetch's man with the key to the iron strongbox. Timandra, her long hair tied back in a kerchief and tucked up high like the turban of a silk merchant, lugged cast-iron breech chambers for the swivel guns. Men muttered oaths under their breath as she scuttled past, fearful of the presence of a woman on ship, their current predicament proof enough that her presence was an ill omen.

Acquel bore up as best he could, unused to clambering on a ship at sea, and an utter stranger to hefting hempen bags of grapeshot and stone balls half as big as a man's head. By the time he had made four trips to the cramped stores below, he was dripping with sweat, eyes stinging. The four great sakers on the main deck, six feet long, were loaded and primed inboard before being manhandled forward again through the cut-outs in the gunwales of the ship. Talis himself checked each breech and then locked in the chamber, first kissing his fingers and then touching the six-pound stone shot that nestled in the wrought-iron barrel. The black guns, pitted with blooms of orange-red rust, were then lashed down, ready for the touch of the smouldering linstock when the fateful time came upon them.

"How many more of these do you need?" Acquel asked Talis as he dropped the shot into its wicker basket with a dull thud.

"Don't need no more. We'll be lucky to get two shots off from these here guns before we're scrapping with the devils in the netting. Fetch more of the small shot for the falconets!"

Acquel blinked and wiped his eyes. Two shots if they were lucky? And all he had was his dagger in his belt. He did not know how much time had gone by. He poked his head through the boarding nets and tried to get a look astern past the bulk of the castle. He could just make out a Southlander corsair, its three blood-red lateen sails billowed out full in the wind—far closer than when he had seen it up on the top of the sterncastle, they were closing faster than he could have believed. Before he dived below again, he heard a cry from the crow's nest on the mainmast.

"Sail Ho! Master Gregorvero! Broad on the larboard beam!"

Acquel bolted up the ladder to the stern deck, two steps at a time. Danamis and Gregorvero were at the rail, squinting off into the distance towards the low grey line that was the Valdur coast.

"There they are!" said Danamis. "Two of them... and they're lateen rigged." His face split into a broad grin. "They're galleys. The king's galleys."

Gregorvero gripped a thick shroud of ratline rigging and focussed on the still distant vessels. "Aye, lateen rigs. But not so sure they are the king's. Still too far to tell."

Danamis clapped his sailing master on the back. "I will take that chance. I want you to steer for those vessels now and close up that distance."

"And if they're Torinian then we will be caught in the middle."

"I haven't met a Torinian yet who would turn down the chance to fight a Southland corsair. Let's go ahead and even the odds. And break out my battle standard—the *big* one. I want that to be seen by all parties."

Gregorvero pursed his thick lips and shook his head. "You've got bigger balls than me." He made for the ladder. "And you better had get your armour on. We will be in their range soon. And you," he said pointing to Acquel, "you better get below and find a helm and a sword, holy man or not!"

Acquel nodded and followed the master down. Danamis looked over the stern transom to see the red sails bearing down on them, close enough now that he could see the white spray thrown up in front of their bows as the long lean vessels cut the waves; close enough to recognise their flags. They were out of Darfan, the island kingdom a hundred miles to the south. A few moments later he felt the *Grace* heel over slightly as the turn north was made. He watched as, behind them, the corsairs followed suit, their sails buffeting as the wind now took them from abeam. The *Grace* gathered more speed now with a beam wind, just as the enemy did. He heard Gregorvero below, ordering sail to be let out more to take advantage of the wind coming over the larboard side. Overhead, one of his men, a canvas bag slung on his back, climbed the rigging to the mainmast crow's nest. A few minutes later, Danamis saw his standard unfurl and trail out fifteen feet off the mast, snapping like the tail of a serpent, red dolphin and falchion emblazoned on the brilliant white cloth.

He went down into his cabin, strapping into his brigantine coat of plates and cinching up his sword and scabbard. He always foreswore any helm, not out of vanity as was claimed, but so that his men could clearly see him in any fray. When he emerged on the landing and looked down to the main deck, he saw the *rondelieri* assembled, Strykar in their midst. Many carried strung bows and crossbows, quivers slung over their backs. These men were worth twice their number of Southland corsairs, thought Danamis, and if they did manage to get boarded he knew they would make a good accounting of it to the last man. Yet he was still hoping he knew his Darfan corsairs better than they knew themselves. An equal contest was not usually to their liking if past experience was anything to go by. He called down to Talis who was blowing on the saltpetre match of a linstock.

"Talis, time to have your gunners take their stations on the sterncastle! They will try and overtake us from the larboard side!" He knew full well if they could get close enough they would throw lines and grapnels.

Strykar looked up at Danamis on the rail, finely arrayed in red brigantine and knee boots. "Preening cockerel!" he said to the men around him, "But I'd expect no less of a Palestrian pirate!"

Slowly, but steadily, the space between the *Grace* and the corsairs shortened. So too, the sails of the ships ahead of them grew larger. Danamis heard Gregorvero's voice boom from the fo'c'sle.

"They are the royal galleys! By damn, you were right!"

Danamis now prayed that the galley captains would give aid when they saw his flag—and not turn about for port.

Timandra had tucked herself into one of the four corners of the fo'c'sle top, her palm worrying the pommel of her dagger. She too watched as the galleys came on, pennants waving. She heard movement at her side and turned to see Acquel joining her; an Acquel arrayed in a sallet helm and carrying a single-edged cleaving sword. He looked self-conscious and in spite of the fact that they were minutes from battle she allowed herself a smile. He had at least gotten what he had wished for in the encampment a few days before.

"I will stay with you," he said quietly, the lip of the helm sliding down to his eyebrows.

"And I with you, Brother Acquel."

The cries of the crew were growing louder now. Acquel looked over his shoulder to see the red sails of the Southlanders pulling even on the larboard side. The bow of the *Grace* hit a trough and the ship lurched down and to starboard, throwing Acquel off his feet. Timandra reached down and helped him steady. He grasped her shoulder as they arose together.

"Are you frightened?" he asked, pushing his sallet helm back up on his forehead.

She smiled at him. "Only if we lose. And Strykar isn't about to let that happen." She had been on the edge of battle before, in the baggage train, but never this close. And on ship there was nowhere to run when the tide of battle turned against you.

Ahead of them, the foremast mainsail billowed enough that Acquel could see the king's galleys bearing down but not yet close enough to engage. Two soldiers suddenly clambered up over the top ladder, pushed them aside, and swung the rearmost loaded falconet back towards the enemy. And nearly frozen, Acquel stood and watched as the game began in earnest.

ON THE STERNCASTLE, Danamis stoically observed the Darfan ships drawing nearer. On the closer vessel he could clearly see the crew jostling amidships and on their sterncastle, dressed in their outlandish loose baggy hose tied close at the knee, coloured sashes about their waists. The mouth of a single demi-culverin stuck out from a gap cut in the gunwale and he spied only two smaller swivel guns on their low fo'c'sle. That was some consolation, he thought. But the archers were a different matter. Already they were drawing back their wicked little horn bows on the fo'c'sle deck. A soft whooshing sound carried past his ear and a fletched shaft protruded from his mizzenmast four feet over this head.

"They're ranging us!" shouted Gregorvero. Danamis looked over the rail, down to his main deck. His two sakers stood primed and ready, the gunners crouched and hugging their iron monsters. A pace behind, twenty-five of Strykar's men stood ready with bows, waiting for the target to come up alongside them. Danamis turned to gauge the distance again and then shot a look at the fo'c'sle captain standing near the transom with a dozen of his archers. "Talis, give them a volley."

A moment later a cloud of iron-barbed shafts arced out and down to the Darfan lead ship, which sat lower than they, some finding their mark on the fo'c'sle and others striking men down amidships. This was answered instantly by the Southlanders as a staggered volley hit the sterncastle of the *Grace*, arrows snapping and biting into the railings. One pinged off a helm, stunning the Palestrian, and then bounced off the brigantine of his comrade. There was less than thirty feet between the vessels now. And as the Darfan ship pulled nearly level on the windward side, the sails of the *Grace* sagged as their wind was stolen. Gregorvero ordered starboard rudder to pull away and the *Grace* recovered like a stumbling stag. Before the Darfans could fire their gun, the *Grace's* first saker on the main deck thundered, sending its large stone shot crashing into the railings of the enemy; it shattered, the shards ploughing down a score of the tightly packed Darfan boarders. Arrows were now flying between the vessels at will. Danamis felt a shaft strike his brigantine and he instinctively doubled up. But it had been spent and merely deflected off the armour. Others weren't so lucky and several crew were on the decks either shot dead through the head or writhing with arrows in their thighs or arms.

Danamis felt his ship go into a turn as Gregorvero's tacking manoeuvre began and Talis fired the two transom-mounted falconets. But the Darfans' swivel guns answered immediately. There was a sound of splintering wood and a cloud of black and golden splinters as the elaborate painted stern railing exploded. The soldiers scrambled for another loaded breech chamber and swapped out the spent ones. Danamis caught a glimpse of a giant corsair below them perched on the gunwale, hefting an iron grapnel and line. They were minutes from sinking their teeth into him.

* * *

STANDING NEARLY FROZEN still in the fo'c'sle, Acquel's whole body twitched as one of the swivel pieces went off near him, sending out a cloud of acrid white smoke. Timandra stepped back and pressed in close to him. She turned and looked up into his face.

"If we are boarded… I will need to tell you something. In case I die."

Acquel took her hand. "Do not say such things." A sound like wasps streaking over their heads made him look up. The sail had just had a hundred small holes torn into it.

She grabbed his doublet and pulled him closer, her eyes drilling into his. "You must needs hear my confession. *Swear* you will do it."

Acquel nodded. "I will."

The smoke cloud blew off the fo'c'sle and Acquel heard a gunner cry out. Looking over the railing he saw a galley ship pass them, the most amazing sight he had ever seen. It was under power of sail only, its many oars raised and locked along the hull. A huge square battle standard mounted on the trailing edge of the lateen sail carried the twin rampant griffons of Valdur, gold upon red. Impossibly long and sleek, to Acquel the galley appeared powerful and delicate at the same time. As it passed less than a hundred feet off their bow, he saw it had a large gun strapped to the fighting platform of its prow. A tongue of fire flashed out, followed a second later by a massive roar. The galley had joined the fight against the Southlanders. Timandra was half leaning out over the fo'c'sle to see the spectacle and Acquel moved to join her, heedless of the occasional whizzing arrow shaft. A second galley followed in the wake of the first and Acquel could see dozens of men crowded onto the broad platform at the bow, their bills and helms flashing in the sunlight.

* * *

From his vantage, Danamis saw the round from the galley cut across the deck of the Southlander, ripping through rigging and sails before slamming into the low sterncastle and destroying ladder and deck. A moment later the vessel turned hard to starboard and fell off, passing into the foaming wake of the *Grace*. A ragged cry went up from his men as the second Southlander followed the first. Danamis allowed himself a smile. He waved a salute to the commander of the Valdurian galley who was standing tall on the stern platform as it glided past. The captain made a sweeping bow from the railing, his beret in his hand.

Danamis and his men gathered at the railing, watching as the two Darfan ships went close-hauled and beat to the south. He liked to think he knew his Darfan captains; don't risk a fight unless the odds are with you. Meanwhile, both galleys had tacked into a turn and were lessening sail.

"Two dead, my lord and four wounded," said Talis as he approached across the deck. "We're bringing them down to the orlop, but we don't have no chirugeon anymore."

Danamis nodded. It was a reckoning that could have been far worse and one he could live with. "Go see if the woman and the monk can attend to them." He bounded down the ladder to the main deck and found Gregorvero near the helm. The huge man came upon Danamis and seized him by both arms.

"I reckon that monk in the fo'c'sle had a few words!" he laughed as the sweat poured down his jowls.

Danamis clapped him on the shoulder in return. "Aye, Gregor, we deserved a little mercy this day, I think. And now I want to have a goodly conversation with our friends on the galleys."

"We'll drop sail and give the lads a drink! You there! Get to it—foremast and main!"

"And what about my bowmen who've done you good service this afternoon?" barked Strykar as he approached across the deck, swinging his sallet by the strap. "By Elded's beard, you're getting your money's worth out of us, Danamis."

Danamis bowed to the mercenary. "And as always, my friend, I am ever grateful."

"Even if your purse is ever empty."

THE SEA WAS as glass, barely a ripple though they were nearly twenty miles out. The chase had taken them north by northeast to waters Danamis knew well. In the distance, several miles further south, he could see the hulking form of Nod's Rock in the sea haze, appearing like some squashed sugarloaf. For an instant the debacle of the last trade with the mermen filled his mind's eye. But then a cheer went up as the captain of the lead galley was rowed over in a little double-ended boat. As the rowers held the craft steady, the little man clambered up the rope ladder amidships and onto the deck of the *Grace*.

Danamis and Gregorvero both gave a bow which was returned with a brief flourish by the galley captain, a silver pomander in his hand.

"Captain Alandris," said Danamis. "It has been some time since last we met but your arrival was heaven sent."

The commander adjusted his fine emerald-green silken cloak which he wore twisted about his arm and shoulder. And like most galley captains that Danamis knew, Alandris had been wealthy before he took service in the king's fleet, for galley captains invariably paid the king to get their ship and command. "Admiral Danamis, fortune brings us together it seems. And none too soon for you. Where is the rest of your fleet? Or have you taken to being a lone raider these days?"

Danamis gave him a smile. "I have urgent business with the king and am on way to Perusia."

Alandris nodded and glanced around at the lean complement of sailors and soldiers, far too small for a carrack of war. His eyes rested briefly on the *rondelieri* standing across the deck, their commander at the main mast, arms folded across his chest and a look of disdain on his face.

"Recruitment trouble in Palestro these days?"

The smell from the galley upwind of them had now made its way to the decks of the *Grace*. A hundred rowers on the benches in the summer heat made for a miasma that was a weapon in its own right. Danamis looked down to the pomander briefly, one no doubt filled with lambsmint or something equally potent to ward off the stink. He rubbed his forefinger under his nose and directed his gaze towards the overcrowded galley.

"Recruitment?" said Danamis, grinning. "I think maybe you've forgotten just how many men you need for your galleys. But, then again, recruitment isn't a problem when you have men willing to work off their debts or get their sentences commuted. I imagine you wear them out rather quickly."

Alandris smiled, annoyed. "Perhaps you are right, Admiral. A poor comparison. But you were damned lucky we spotted you as we came out of Torinia. And we are now bound for Perusia. If you are willing to make a short stop at Telos while we replenish before we enter Blasius Bay, then we would be glad for the company."

A second small boat had arrived at the side of the *Grace*, bearing the other galley captain. Danamis watched as the smug Perusian beamed and waved up at them, obviously overjoyed that he had had a hand in rescuing the king's pirate admiral from certain destruction.

Danamis nodded. "We would welcome that. When your comrade arrives let us repair to my cabin to take some wine. I would hear what news you both have to tell of the city."

* * *

BELOW DECKS, TIMANDRA and Acquel worked in the sputtering light of two candles as they tended to the wounded. For all her skill with herbs, she found the chirurgeon's chest had none, not even hemlock to numb pain. Talis had scrounged a bottle of *acqua vitalis* and this she directed Acquel to share among the men that were sensible enough to drink as well as poor Captain Bassinio who lay there too, still in agony of his burns. Two of the crew would live if the arrow wounds did not rot but two others had arrow heads so deep she would not likely be able to dig them out. Their fate was in Saint Elded's hands and those of God.

"Hold him down by his shoulders," she told Acquel as they knelt over one of the soldiers who stood a chance of surviving. As she dug into the wound with a small knife she had heated, the man, barely conscious and dripping with sweat, screamed out. Acquel pressed him down onto the reeking mat and watched while Timandra dug her thumb and forefinger into the wound. The soldier's head rolled to the side as he passed out and Acquel clearly heard the sucking sound as she prised out a small triangle of iron from the thigh along with what was left of the shaft.

Timandra wiped her forehead with her arm and poured a bit of *acqua vitalis* into the wound. Acquel looked at her. "I am ashamed, Timandra."

She paused. "Ashamed? No need to feel that for being afraid. I'm surprised we're even still here."

He leaned back on his haunches, shoulders hunched. "No. I mean I am ashamed because I was... excited. Excited by everything. I think I would have killed a corsair myself given the chance. That is called bloodlust. A sin."

Timandra's mouth opened to reply but words would not come, for his admission had not been what she expected. She looked down and went back to work. "It is over now," she said quietly. "Think no more of it."

As THE BATTERED carrack and two galleys bobbed together in the gentle seas, half a mile away three mermaids kept watch.

Do we venture closer still? asked one, her long webbed fingers gently treading the surface of the water, her mind in wordless conversation with the others.

Citala kept staring at the ships, her thoughts a bitter swirl of confusion, curiosity, and anger. Anger that she held towards herself. Anger for ever agreeing to help her father negotiate with the landsmen. And anger for the fascination she had for these creatures. A fascination where most of her people held fear. She plumbed her soul to try and fathom why such curiosity had rooted itself so firmly but no revelation ever came. And, only half-admitted, there dwelt inside her an abiding interest, maybe even the seed of an obsession, for one landsman in particular. She gave a rapid kick, her naked torso rising up from the placid surface, her chin held high and almond-shaped eyes squinting against the sun.

No, she replied. *I know who they are. And who is there among them.*

Sixteen

TWO HUNDRED MALE voices soared a hundred feet up to the massive painted ceiling of the Temple Majoris, richly harmonious and perhaps slightly the purer for Brother Acquel's voice was not amongst them. They sang a song of devotion to Saint Dionei, for today was her day upon the One Faith's calendar. She who had seen what others had not and who had recognized one among the followers of Elded was not what he appeared to be. Twelve great cylindrical columns rose up on either side of the stone temple, itself a perfect square, the whole of its length. At one end, two giant oak doors, sheathed in hammered copper plate that in the morning sun shone like fire, gave way to the tiled centre aisle. At the opposite end, the altar rose up on a tier of white marble reached by seven steps. And high above this hung the symbol of the One Faith: a golden disc twelve feet wide surrounded by seven long rays, and between each, a smaller tongue of flame. One ray for each of Elded's commandments.

Magister Kodoris, from his personal nave opposite the choir, surveyed the hundreds in attendance as they watched the High Priest walk up the altar dais in his long purple robes, flat-topped mitre balanced on his head. Behind him two dozen blackrobes arrayed themselves. And as Brachus raised both arms towards the golden sun, all blessed themselves in unison: fingers to forehead and then centre breast. Kodoris did the same and looked down to Lavinia at his side. She was smiling, the joy of devotion emanating from her alabaster face.

Brachus, in his halting reedy croak, began to intone Elded's Prime, the most holy of prayers. It was barely audible from even where Kodoris stood but all knew the words just the same. Lavinia's sweet voice drowned out Brachus and Kodoris smiled in spite of all his burdens. As the prayer ended, all the greyrobes and whiterobes burst into a new hymn and the great temple was a swirl of sound as the long trumpets accompanied in a fanfare from the gallery high over their heads.

Lavinia arranged her blue satin veil over her shoulders and then touched the capacious sleeve of Kodoris's woollen robe. "Is it not wondrous, Magister? It climbs to the heavens on invisible wings."

Kodoris reached over and covered her hand with his own. "It is indeed, my dear," he whispered. *Despite Brachus*, he thought to himself. As the chorus ended and the last peals of the trumpets echoed, final prayers were sung. Another blessing, and then Brachus was assisted down the steps, teetering dramatically as blackrobes steadied him in his excessive curled-toe slippers.

They watched as the High Priest and his contingent of blackrobes processed down the mosaic aisle and out the towering doors. Then followed the nobility of Livorna, the wealthier merchants, and the villa owners. Lastly, the lowly filed out: artisans, shopkeepers, and peasants from outlying farms miles distant. A day ago he had instructed the whiterobes to clear the broken roof tiles that littered the narrow winding streets up to the Ara plateau so that those trudging up the hill or being borne in litters would not be bothered by the recent memory of the tremors that had shaken the city. And now, as they went their way through the great arch in the plaza outside the Temple, back down into the lopsided and precariously perched city, they could look forward to an afternoon of delights as the Feast of Saint Dionei began in earnest.

A roast ox in the marketplace, jugglers, minstrels, harlequins, and so much wine that it would flow from the gutters by nightfall. Games aplenty for young and old, tricks, treats and sleight of hand, and an eagerly anticipated time for the pickpocket gangs of the low town. His memory began to pull him back into his own past. He remembered the feast days of his boyhood and the excitement that spread through Livorna like a town freed from the iron grip of a siege. He remembered how the men would scramble and kick the decorated air-filled cow's stomach from the Ara down to the city gates, each seeking to be the one to give the final kick that would send the inflated effigy of the Deceiver out of the gates. Always a few heads cracked and broken legs in those days. Far more tame now, he mused. And a wave of regret for times gone by filled his stoic heart, a yearning that somehow took him by surprise. For he could nevermore celebrate as he once did now that every day began with the memory of Saint Elded's shattered tomb and what lay within. As he watched the tottering High Priest reach the copper-clad doors, he keenly felt the burden of his terrible secret—and the burden of Brachus. He alone had to do what needed to be done.

Kodoris gestured to Lavinia for them to take their leave and he guided her around a column and down a side aisle of the cavernous place. The north side of the Temple Majoris was always cool to the point of cold, even in high summer, and the tall thin windows did little to illuminate the corridor. They walked for a few moments in silence and then Lavinia said, "Magister, tell me about the old faith, before the coming of Elded and his brethren. Who were the old gods?"

Kodoris clasped his hands behind his back and raised an eyebrow. "That is rather an unusual question to pose to a monk. What has prompted such a thought, my dear?"

Lavinia looked at him, almost mischievously he thought. "Lucinda sometimes talks of such things. Of the ancient days."

"To frighten you, child?"

"No, Magister," she said, grinning at his ignorance. "She sometimes tells me stories of the ancients, at night before we sleep."

"Let me show you something," said Kodoris, placing an arm around her shoulders as he guided her to the beginning of a passage that connected the Temple to the maze of the Ara monastery. They stopped at the portal and Kodoris pointed up to the archway over it. Here the stonemasons had carved marvellous things. Sinuous grapevines and acanthus wound their way up on either side and continued towards the keystone. A round window in the west wall illuminated the entranceway.

"There… do you see the man peeking through the grape leaves? Not quite a man really."

Lavinia craned her neck and searched out the figure. "Yes! I see it. He looks angry—or frightened? What a strange face and ears he has."

Kodoris nodded. "He is a forest god. Look at the keystone. There is Saint Elded, spreading the word of the One Faith. The forest god is hiding… and you are right. He is afraid."

Lavinia's eyes scanned the arch and suddenly she laughed, like a child playing a game. "I have found another over here! And this one is slinking away."

"There are actually five in there if you look hard enough."

She turned to him. "Lucinda says the gods were in the rocks and trees then. That people sacrificed children to them every moon."

Kodoris was growing curious. "Your sister tells you of such things? "

Lavinia nodded and, again, that strange smile appeared on her lips.

"The old gods were evil and caused men to do terrible things," Kodoris said.

"Was Berithas a forest god?"

Kodoris felt a chill as the light around them slowly faded as a cloud passed outside. "The Deceiver? We think of him as less than a god but more than a spirit. A demon who took corporeal form."

Lavinia passed her hand over the rough carved column of the doorway. "Lucinda says that when the old gods were no longer worshipped they diminished and became demons."

Kodoris cleared his throat. "Your sister tells you interesting things. You should not trouble yourself with such thoughts. We don't sacrifice people anymore."

Lavinia looked back at him, her blue eyes piercing. "Don't we?" And her lips curled slightly again as they shared their little secret of the tomb.

Kodoris met her gaze. "We should return to the palace now," he said tersely, fighting back the urge to shake her. "I would hear of your sister's progress if you have word of it."

"Yes, there is word. I have sent them to Perusia for the one you seek. That is where he is going."

Kodoris started, thunderstruck that she had not revealed this earlier. "Perusia? Are you certain? But why there?" Instantly his mind was a whirl of motives and fears. Was the boy going to tell the royal court what had happened to him? Reveal the truth he had discovered?

Lavinia grasped her taffeta skirts and walked ahead into the dimly lit corridor. "Come, Magister," she called back, "and I will tell you what I have seen."

* * *

FIRST, I WILL pull out his teeth...

Captain Flauros let go his reins and flexed his gloved hands as he mused about finding the renegade greyrobe. It was enraging that he had to leave the Ara to go on this mad quest for a murderous monk, but more so because he had let the greyrobe slip through his grasp the first time. The whole situation was dire enough, but then to learn from Kodoris that four of his men had deserted the guard and bolted, well that was simply infuriating. He had known them—hand picked them when the Magister had asked for an escort. Kodoris assumed they must have found gold in the crypt and then decided to spend their good fortune in parts unknown, slipping away from the Ara under the cloak of night. After such a failure of oversight as that, he was beginning to wonder how much longer Kodoris would keep him in command.

Around his small party the din of a thousand chirping crickets in the high grass nearly drowned out the clop of hooves. They were deep in the north of the Duchy of Torinia in the exact centre of Valdur, along the main road that led a circuitous path eastwards towards Perusia. The terrain was relatively easy riding, gentle rolling hills and meadows, villas and smallholdings. As the road passed through the larger villages and towns of this part of the duchy, Flauros set the pace so that they could reach an inn or hostel before each night descended. He picked up the reins again and watched the woman in front of him as she rode, her long dark red cloak spilling around the saddle of her mount. *Beautiful creature, but a monstrous bitch.*

He wasn't comfortable without his helm. Or his breastplate for that matter. But she had said they must look the part of her retainers. So the crimson satin sashes and armour went, and now he and his men had brimless felt toques perched on their heads. *Elded's balls,* he thought. *We damn well are her retainers since Kodoris ordered me to do whatever she asks.* At least he still had his steel buckled at his hip. He had chosen his five men carefully. Tobias and Elkan were sharp blades and could think clearly on their own. That was needed if anything happened to him. The other three were chiefly muscle. That was so nothing would happen.

They rode at a measured pace. He might have to urge them into a trot in another hour for he wasn't quite sure how many miles they were from Cameri and it was already mid-afternoon. Tobias and Elkan were deep in quiet conversation behind him. At the rear rode Timus and Relan. He could hear them sharing jokes, hushed tones punctuated by laughter. Out in front rode Demedrias, as big as a wall and about as bright as one. But he could stop a charging boar with a single punch. For two days he had been making cow-eyes at the canoness, who refused to even acknowledge his presence, never mind his lingering glances. But who could blame the fat-necked fool? She had the kind of cold beauty that would stop men in their tracks—and she had done so these past few days on the road as peasants, peddlers, and noble folk alike swivelled their heads when she passed.

How she could think the monk was in Palestro one moment and then in Perusia over a hundred miles away, he did not know. Nor was he certain he wanted to. At least they hadn't wasted too much time on the road south before turning east for Torinia. But Perusia was far bigger than Palestro and being the royal enclave their hunt might draw more attention than he wanted.

Flauros gave a gentle kick to his horse and moved up to ride at Lucinda's side. She turned and smiled as he drew knee to knee.

"And how is our progress this afternoon, Captain?"

Flauros noticed how her face was barely perspiring or

even flushed despite the heat. "We may have to increase our pace a little to make Cameri at a reasonable hour. Nothing too demanding though."

"I find your skill for judging time and distance most extraordinary." She smiled again, her eyes teasing. "The Magister told me you were a soldier of remarkable abilities. He might have added handsome too."

Flauros grinned at her flattery. He wanted her, of course. But even if that were possible it would lead to unnecessary complications. "I do not think there is any chance of getting lost in the countryside, my lady, when we have a Seeker with us. I'm sure *you* always know exactly where we are. As for me, I'm usually just a lucky guesser."

She pushed off her right shoulder the white linen veil that shielded her head and neck, exposing her long golden locks. "I know the measure of men," she said, her tone jaded, "and you sell yourself a bit short, Captain."

"May I ask you a question, my lady? I am curious as to why this one greyrobe is being chased down while the others who escaped with him seem to have been all but forgotten. Does that not seem odd to you?"

Lucinda tilted her head to contemplate a reply but kept her eyes on the road ahead. She knew that Kodoris had lied to Flauros, the poor fool swallowing whole the Magister's elaborate concoction. "I don't think it is so strange. Did not the Magister say that Brother Acquel was the leader? Perhaps we may find all of them still together."

Flauros shook his head. "Not likely, my lady. When we cornered him last week on the road south of Livorna, he was alone. I am in no doubt of that."

"Ah, then perhaps they did separate shortly after making their escape. Given their circumstances that would have been the wiser course, I suppose." She turned and looked at him again, her eyes probing.

"I would not hazard a guess at what four young monks might conspire to after they murdered their brethren. I find it... bothersome. Bothersome that we have seen or heard nothing of these other monks in Livorna or the countryside. Just doesn't sit well in my mind, my lady." Flauros bowed his head to her. "But I give way to your wisdom and that of the Magister in such matters. My task is but to look after your safety and comfort."

Lucinda smiled broadly at him. "Captain, in that you are most trusted and I am in your debt."

Flauros nodded again. He knew she was hiding things. Things that Kodoris had told her and God knows what else that her special arts—damned witchcraft more like—allowed her to see. He looked ahead and recognised where he was: an old red-tiled villa on the right that had fallen into decay, roof collapsed, told him that Cameri was perhaps a further two hours ride. More than enough time to refresh themselves.

"My lady, we are making good time after all. I know of a stone temple just ahead said to be the oldest in Valdur. Would you not like to visit and take some rest while we have the time? We can water the horses and still make the town by nightfall."

She turned her long neck to face him again and nodded pleasantly. "In these matters, Captain Flauros, I am at your disposal!"

He kicked his horse and shot ahead up the road to tell Demedrias to look for the next crossroads and a small trail that would lead off to the left.

WHEN THEY REACHED the ancient temple, Lucinda dismounted effortlessly before Flauros could assist her. "What charming disarray!" she said. Large rectangular grey blocks of stone lay strewn around the overgrown grass, as one side of the temple had collapsed long ago. Only two walls and the tiny bell tower remained.

The soldiers had all dismounted and were leading their horses to the cool of the nearby trees. Flauros could not take his eyes from her adventurous garb. She was half lady of the court and half huntress. Her long dress was divided front and back and as she walked one could clearly see the hose she wore underneath. No slippers on her feet but instead soft doeskin boots that climbed to her knees. She was dressed for the pursuit. And he noticed that Demedrias was staring again at the canoness like some besotted youth. He shook his head and smiled. Hope against hope.

"Timus! There's a well over by the temple. Draw some water and see if it is still sweet." The large cypress grove beyond the temple wafted its beautiful scent through the clearing. He inhaled deeply and arched his back.

"You say this is the oldest temple in the land?" remarked Lucinda, strolling towards him. "Pity it has fallen into ruin. Not an indication of the devoutness of the local people I would hope."

Flauros shrugged. "Don't have any idea of that, my lady. Nor is it my concern. But it is a good place to stretch the legs and take some water. I will get Timus to fetch some for your horse."

She nodded her thanks. "And I will take my necessary, Captain, if I may." And she turned and walked off towards the cypress trees, her skirts held off her ankles in either hand.

THE SOLDIERS HAD spread out to tie off the horses, relieve themselves and to fetch water. Relan was already spread-eagled on a mossy patch that lay in the shadow of the grove. A few yards into the trees, Demedrias had finished shaking his member of its last few drops as the corner of his eye caught a glimpse of red. It was Lucinda making her way deeper into the grove. He hurriedly laced his hose and moved quietly to follow her, his boots sinking into the spongy undergrowth. She was moving carefully, warding off low branches as she made her progress deeper in. She stopped and Demedrias moved behind a tree and stood motionless, his small deep-set eyes locked on her. His mouth opened slightly as she pulled down her hose, hiked up her skirts, and squatted down. He wanted her. More, too, he knew she wanted him. He could feel himself becoming aroused as he stared, and before he knew it, he was creeping towards her.

He was a few feet behind when she became aware of him, half turning to face the intruder. She gave a low gasp and then pulled up her hose. "You oaf! Turn around this instant!"

Demedrias flexed his hands, and for a moment, indecision gripped him. If he could only have her just this once it would be worth it. And he would ride on alone, make a run for it and sign on with a good company of *aventura*. Fuck the Temple guard. In her anger she was even more beautiful than ever—and more than he could bear. Lucinda took a step back and her eyes bored into him.

Her voice was quiet and measured, but laced with ice. "Turn around now, you fool. Or I shall have Flauros kill you here and now."

His left hand reached up and he pulled off his felt hat, crushing it in his hand. "No disrespect, my lady! But no one need know."

Lucinda concentrated, locking her eyes onto his, and pushed into his mind. And as she did this he was upon her, one meaty hand over her mouth. She clamped her hands onto his doublet to fend him off as he bore down on her, his weight pushing her to the peaty floor of the grove. She tried to hold him off even as she felt him ripping at her hose, pulling them down her thighs. She tried reaching for the slim dagger she wore in her narrow leather girdle but he caught that movement and pinned her hand. He was talking softly, telling her to be still even as she pushed deeper into his mind. But to no avail. His lust was overwhelming, a shield to her influence.

In desperation, she bit into the forearm that was pinning her shoulder down. Demedrias grunted, lifted his meaty hand from her, and then ripped the neckline of her dress, exposing her breasts. She was losing, her concentration crumbling. Now fear filled her as she felt him stabbing at her loins. He was too powerful for her and too simple of mind for her to dominate. But she suddenly felt him hesitate as he looked at her collarbone, and her wound.

"What? A harlot's mark!" he whispered, half to himself. Lucinda gasped as he entered her, the scream in her throat stifled by his hand. But someone else spoke. Demedrias pulled back as the livid lips of the wound between her collarbone and breast seemed to part, to move. And to utter words.

Hadrothna vog! Hadrothna vog!

The voice was neither man nor woman. It was a strange mix of both, lilting, almost musical.

Arbora Vitalis! Arbora Vitalis!

Demedrias's eyes grew large as the horror spoke but as he tried to push himself off of the canoness he felt her hands seize his doublet and hold him fast. And just as quickly, he felt his body weaken, his thighs and biceps shaking, twitching. It was as if his life was pouring out like the sands of an hourglass. He fell upon her, gasping for breath, his heart pumping ever faster. The voice changed to the Valdurian tongue.

Drink him, drink him, my daughter!

His prick felt as if it was in a vise. His head swam as everything began to swirl around him, his stomach sick. He lay his head on her shoulder for he no longer could hold it up, nor could he summon the will to scream. The last thing he saw as his eyes rolled up into his skull, the flesh on his face tightening and pulling, was the quivering lips of the ghastly mouth as it sang.

Hadrothna vog!

Demedrias shrank and shrivelled upon her body, his clothes draping her. Soon there was nothing left of him except a caul-like blanket of translucent skin, every last bone dissolved to nothing. His scabbarded sword and belt slipped down over her thigh and tumbled onto the soft earth.

Lucinda shoved the grisly bundle off of her and sat up, breathing heavily. She felt strong and vibrant despite the violation. Whole. The wound had shut, silent now, and she pulled up the neckline of her dress. "Thank you," she whispered. "You will guide me and I will follow." She stood up and arranged her hose and her dress, moving a clasp from her cloak to secure and conceal the rip in her dress. She took a deep breath and smoothed her long hair with both hands, arranging it around her shoulders. Retrieving her veil and circlet this too she put back on. She looked down at the pile of skin and clothes at her feet and gave it a little kick with the toe of her boot.

"Bastard." Anger welled up inside her even as she felt new strength course through her veins. Anger for failing to defend herself and her honour. She was no maid and had not been for years, but she had never been ravished and violated. He had saved her though, and the ravisher had become the ravished. She wet her lips and stepped away from the spot, making her way back to the temple ruin.

As she stepped into the clearing, Flauros came towards her, almost at a run.

"My lady, we were beginning to think you had gotten yourself lost." He reached her and his quick eye settled on her garment, mud-stained and dishevelled. "Are you unwell?"

"Unwell? I just fended off one of your men. That large beast."

Flauros blanched and stuttered a reply. "Demedrias? He attacked you?"

"Pushed me to the ground but I kneed his cods and he stumbled off." Lucinda didn't wait for his reply but stormed towards her horse. Flauros hurried after her and tugged at her elbow but she brushed him off.

"Are you... *hurt*, my lady?"

She turned to him. "Thank the saints, no I am not. But I expected you to know the mettle of your men, Captain."

Flauros dipped his head. "I am most sorry, Lady della Rovera. We will catch him. He won't get far on foot." He shouted to his men who were readying to resume the ride. "Tobias! Get the others and find Demedrias! He has attacked the canoness. No, you dolt! Mount up and find him!" Flauros could feel his face reddening. If she shared this with Kodoris later he would be flayed.

Lucinda put foot to stirrup and swung up into the saddle. "I will join them. But we shall not waste too much time on looking for that miserable creature. We must get back on the road and to Cameri by nightfall. Let the wolves take him tonight if we do not!"

Flauros bowed again. "As you wish, my lady." He untied his mount and threw the reins over its head. He watched her as she jerked her reins and followed Tobias, Elkan and the others. Flauros slowly shook his head, slightly in awe of her resolve. Any other woman would have been a quivering wreck. But there was something more in her demeanour, he thought as they swung past the ruins of the temple. Something that was not quite right.

Seventeen

GREGORVERO LOOKED UP from the small oaken coffer, wearing an expression like a starving peasant contemplating his last two crusts of bread. He pushed a meagre stack of silver lire across the table towards Danamis.

"Here. That should get you a new set of clothes to see the king in. Don't reckon it will go as far as new shoes though."

Danamis palmed the coins. "It will have to do. Better we use what's left to get the ship refitted and to find more crew. At least we've paid the men for now—and kept the *rondelieri* reasonably happy."

"Not all of them," grumbled Strykar from his bench. "There's a sizeable hole in my ledger book under your name, my friend." They were huddled together in the stern cabin, the *Grace* now safely tucked into one of the ancient docks that stretched like long wooden fingers out into the harbour of Perusia. The trip there had been uneventful, refreshingly so, and it took them just two days sailing to reach the royal enclave. But the galley captains that escorted the battered carrack had now had more than enough time to puzzle out Danamis's predicament. Indeed, they had fairly guessed at it from the outset. Captain Nicolo Danamis would never have ventured out across the Sea of Valdur in just *one* ship unless he had to. Danamis had danced around the tale of the hasty departure from Palestro and the word mutiny never passed his lips. But he was no fool and he knew that soon the rumours would fly, starting in the crammed stinking harbour taverns. And once word came from Palestro, all in Perusia would know what had happened to him.

"I always pay my debts, Julianus. And to my friends first. And I promise to get you and your men back to Maresto."

Strykar took a swig of sharp Milvornan wine from his cracked wooden cup. "I don't doubt your intentions, Nico. Just your means. And now I have to find lodgings in town for a gang of ill-tempered *aventuri*. Lodgings that would be willing to take them in, that is."

Danamis gripped his wine cup with both hands, grinding it into the scored tabletop. "The king will help me. First, he'll declare Tetch an outlaw. Then, I'll convince him to loan me the ships and men I need. We can lure the bastard out into open waters and then take him."

Strykar nodded. "Easy enough then. So what is your plan, admiral?"

"Gregor and Bassinio will get the Perusian shipwrights in to make repairs and they'll set about recruiting for the voyage back." Gregorvero gave a silent nod of confidence.

Strykar laughed derisively. "Interesting how this washtub is still afloat even after a few days at sea. Did you think you would put that one past me? But do go on."

Danamis ignored the remark and pressed on. "First I will go to the tailor—"

"Yes, a tactical priority—cunning too." Strykar was smiling broadly. "The barber next I assume?"

Danamis leaned towards the mercenary. "Yes! You think I can go begging to the king—or my *banker*—"

"First priority," interjected Strykar, raising a finger.

"Or my banker," repeated Danamis, "looking like some bilge rat. If I do not look like the king's admiral then I am not the king's admiral and my chances will be next to nothing. And before I seek an audience, I will find an old merchant adventurer and friend of my father—Piero Polo. He runs the greatest trading house in the land and nothing escapes his ears. I just pray he's here and not out at sea."

Strykar drained the last of his wine. "I have not met the king but from what I've heard tell he is not terribly interested in anything unless it be hunting, eating, or drinking. And maybe women at the bottom of that list."

"And Polo can tell me what is his latest amusement—or vexation. We need that intelligence before going to the palace."

"We?"

"You don't expect me to arrive unescorted like some pedlar going door to door? I would ask you and your men to come to the palace gates. I will bring some of my men too."

Strykar smiled again and shook his head. "You do have some balls, Nico."

Danamis looked hard at Strykar. "That is what *I* propose. And now you can tell me what it is about this monk you keep within an arm's reach all the time. A personal confessor? And he's hardly dressed for his role in life."

The smile on Strykar's face evaporated. His eyes drifted to the cabin doorway then came back to settle on Danamis. "Aye. Him. Well... he near enough fell out of the sky a week ago." He absently ran his hand over the bump on his head and winced. "We damn near rode him down on the road near Livorna. He was being chased by the Temple guard. We got to him first and then I refused to give him over. Mainly to piss them off. So now... he's with the Black Rose."

"Heart-warming. He must have a treasure horde somewhere no doubt?"

Strykar started forward, indignant. "What? You think me *that* mercenary?" He paused, frowning. "Bah! You know what I mean. Self-interested."

"So why did you save him then?" said Danamis, glancing over to Gregorvero.

Strykar was gnawing the inside of his lower lip, weighing up whether to mention the amulet. "He is accused of murdering some blackrobes. He's no killer to my eyes and I told that trumped-up captain of the guard to fuck off back to the Temple."

"So you risk angering the High Priest and his Magister over this monk and potentially embarrassing the Duke of Maresto? I am sorry, my brother, but that story has a whiff of fish about it."

"You should hear *his* story," replied Strykar, his voice quiet.

"Go on, then." Danamis refilled Strykar's cup with the raffia jug from the table.

"First, you must swear to me you will tell no one about this. You too, Master Gregor. Not a word. Upon your lives not a blessed word."

They did so, and Strykar told them.

ACQUEL STOOD AT the fo'c'sle railings, arms leaning over the side that faced the dock. Timandra stood next to him, watching the bustle of the quayside: porters heaving bundles, cranes squeaking as their pulleys strained to offload cargo, and a myriad of little boats scuttling between larger vessels as they delivered and took away passengers and provisions. He had not left the ship since their arrival the previous day. And though he wore no leg irons he was just as much a prisoner of the *aventuri* as he had been over a week ago. But even if Strykar would have personally rowed him ashore, where could he go? He was utterly alone, marooned in a world that offered no answers.

Timandra had unwrapped her headdress and wore it as a silken veil. She had been silent for some time, even though they stood side by side, shoulders touching.

"You have been here many times?" asked Acquel.

She turned to look at him, a wan smile on her lips. "Twice before. And I wish we were not here again. We ought to be in Maresto. But now that pirate has cozened my cousin into helping save his arse. That's the loyalty of friendship—or half-friendship."

Acquel looked down at the lapping waters of the battered wooden dock, rubbish and flotsam bobbing on the surface. "Do you think the king will help him?"

Timandra chuckled quietly. "Well if he doesn't that's the end of his quest for revenge. And we'll be stuck here in Perusia penniless. He damned well better help."

Acquel gestured downriver. "And that is the palace?"

Timandra looked and nodded. The great outer wall of the king's palace began near the water, its crenelated battlements soaring up fifty feet; the walls stretched inland for half a mile. Acquel could just make out the high red stone towers of the castle itself, four-square and each capped in copper roof plates, now long covered in verdigris that oozed down the dark stones. From several of the towers he could just discern the flapping royal standards of Valdur: deep blood-red, the golden griffons emblazoned on them nothing more than yellow blots.

"And does he keep an army in there with him?"

"He maintains a guard of a few thousand I believe. But it's the duty of the dukes and stewards to support him with armies when he demands. But he hasn't asked for years and the aristocracy now just squabbles amongst themselves. Still, more work and money for the Black Rose...."

Acquel's gaze turned to the right, beyond the town with its bleached sandstone buildings and high-rising towers stacked tightly one to another, and over to the tall green hills beyond. "The king rules Perusia directly. But nowhere else in Valdur. I've never understood that. But we're simple up in Livorna so maybe there's more to it."

"You're looking at the answer to that," said Timandra. "Those hills hold the royal mines. All the gold in Valdur comes from there and virtually none anywhere else. That's why the kings rule this enclave directly. It's the source of Valdur's wealth, and Sempronius sprinkles enough gold around the land to keep all the wolves happy, and away from his throat." A flock of jeering gulls descended across the docks and made for the cobbled square and stone fountain just beyond, scattering some foraging pigeons.

Acquel reached over and covered her hand in his. "Are you still going to help me? To learn about the amulet?"

"I told you I would. And if we're given half a chance maybe we can slip away and do so." She became aware of their stacked hands and drew away her left. "There is someone I know... a very learned man. I think he may be able to read the script. Have you tried again?"

Acquel shook his head. "I tried. But I don't recognize the script and we have not learned anything other than the Middle tongue. Ancient Valdurian is only known by the older blackrobes—if that is even what it is. Who is this man you know?"

Timandra turned to sit on a barrel next to her on the fo'c'sle deck. "Well, he is what is called an oculist. He crafts spectacles and is an expert at working with glass. But he also has a library and his shop has books everywhere. I do not read well at all, enough to keep my accounts, but these books he has are the most wonderful things." She smiled up at Acquel. "So much knowledge if one has the key. If anyone can help you, it will be him."

"*If* he will help us. I cannot pay him."

"Stop building walls before we've even begun. I've bought spectacles from him to sell on in Maresto. He knows me. He only need translate what the amulet says. How big a task is that?"

Acquel stooped down at her feet. "Timandra, you have to convince Strykar to let us go. Let him send some men with us if he must. But we've got to get off here."

She looked up into his unshaven face, more rugged—even more confident—than when they had first met. "I will speak with him. If anything, he will want answers too about what it is you bear."

They heard voices below them on the ladder and turned to see Danamis ascending to the deck. Acquel bounced up from his awkward position as Timandra stood at his approach.

He smiled as he walked toward the pair, a slightly mischievous look on his face. "I trust I'm not interrupting anything sacred, Timandra Pandarus. A confession perhaps?"

Timandra eyes flashed a moment but her voice was sweet. "No, my lord. We were only just now speaking of the royal palace and the wonders of Perusia. Wonders that we both hope to see. Soon." She thought Danamis was vain, impulsive, and by all accounts, a poor judge of men. But she, like Acquel, was chained to the fortunes of the *Royal Grace* for the foreseeable future. And she resented it with all her heart.

"Strykar is preparing his men to go into the city to find lodgings," said Danamis. "Perhaps you might go with him. I would have words with Brother Acquel."

"Perhaps I will," replied Timandra. "But Brother Acquel is in my charge. If I go, he's coming with me." Acquel smiled self-consciously and rubbed at his ear.

Danamis pursed his lips. "Of course. If Strykar allows it I have no say. I merely wanted to ask Acquel about the amulet."

Acquel and Timandra blanched. "You know about that?" gasped the monk, unconsciously grasping at the jewel in his shirt.

"Strykar told me what has happened to you. I have sworn to keep your secret but I would ask that you show me this thing."

Timandra closed the space between her and Danamis. "That is most unwise, my lord. Not here." The fo'c'sle was empty of seamen for the moment but still, thought Timandra, this was dire news indeed.

Acquel's voice was quiet and confident. "No, Timandra. I will show him if he asks." Timandra sputtered her objection but Acquel raised his hand. "Perhaps he can help me too."

Timandra's jaw went slack. Every new person that shared the secret of that jewel put him in further danger. Acquel moved close to Danamis, reached into his shirt, and pulled forth the pendant on the chain. He held it between his fingers as Danamis leaned in to examine it, his eyes unreadable.

He looked up at Acquel. "From the very tomb. And it... stays with you alone?"

Acquel nodded.

Danamis glanced at Timandra, and she could tell he was debating with himself whether to say more or bide his time until she was gone. But he turned his attention back to Acquel, his face now keenly serious.

"You saw him?" he whispered. "You saw him and you are certain he was merfolk?"

Acquel nodded again, suddenly reliving the scene in his mind's eye. Danamis reached out and grasped Acquel's arm. "Brother Acquel, I have had dreams of late. Confusing dreams that concern the mer."

Timandra now stepped in to hear him better.

"Damn you, woman!" spat Danamis. "Am I not allowed to speak in confidence to a holy man?"

Timandra fixed her green eyes upon his. "Since when did you need the services of a holy man? We all share his secret and there will be no others amongst us."

Danamis opened his mouth again to tongue lash her, but quickly lowered his head and sighed. "If truth be told I am plagued by dreams of merfolk."

"As am I," said Acquel.

Danamis's eyes widened. "Then you know of what I speak. I do not know if it is because I desire to resurrect the myrra trade, or if something is going to happen to me. With them. Is it a foretelling?"

Acquel spoke slowly as he recalled his dreams. He spoke of Elded and the children and of the mer in ancient times. He told Danamis how the two peoples seemed to live together as one, in peace.

"My dreams tell me the mer will drown me. Just as the priests tell us," said Danamis.

"What are they like? You have been with them. In my dreams they are like men and unlike men at the same time."

Danamis nodded. "They are manlike to be sure. But there is much about them which is not human." He paused to gather his thoughts. "They do not see the world as we do. The men are ugly to behold but their womenfolk are more comely."

"They seem so real when I see them in my dreams," said Acquel.

Timandra suddenly felt a stranger among them. She could see how intently Acquel had latched onto Danamis as both of them tried to make sense of what they had experienced.

"Do they breathe under the sea as fish do?" asked Acquel.

Danamis shrugged. "I do not know. They must. How else could they delve so deep and so long?"

Acquel looked squarely at Danamis. "Captain, I must see the merfolk for myself. Why else would the Saint be sending me these visions?"

"I would see them again too but for wholly selfish reasons, I confess. But they have fled to their lairs under the waves and I do not think I will find them again."

"You must. For both our sakes." Acquel reached around his neck with both hands and removed the amulet. "If you do not believe that the blessed Saint himself is behind all this then I ask you to take the amulet."

Timandra pushed in. "Acquel, no!"

"You know what will happen, Timandra. He must see too." And Acquel put the amulet over Danamis's head even as the pirate sputtered his protests.

"Do not give this thing to me!"

Acquel pressed his hand to the amulet as it lay on the captain's chest. "I *can't* give it to you. You will see." He put an arm around Timandra's shoulders. "Captain, go back to your cabin. Then you will understand."

Danamis started to reply, closed his mouth, gave a last look of puzzlement to the monk, and turned away. As he descended the fo'c'sle he felt the eyes of his much diminished crew upon him. He walked across the deck to return to the stern cabin and to tell Strykar of his conversation. The amulet seemed so light as to be insignificant and as he stepped into the cabin his hand went to clasp it, and it was gone.

ON THE OTHER side of the royal city, at the great south gate, awash in silk banners of red and gold, a tall liveried retainer lifted his noblewoman from the saddle while traders and townspeople gawped. She had slumped over as if dead and nearly tumbled just as they had passed beneath the enormous iron portcullis. The woman's other retainers clustered around her nervously, facing outwards and pushing away two gawping merchants who drew too near. The tall retainer held her up and rearranged her headdress that had fallen over her face. And then she recovered from her swoon, awaking in his burly arms. Her eyes fluttered rapidly and she recognised the face close to hers.

"Ah, Captain Flauros," she said, smiling as her pale cheeks became slightly less pale. "I am returned, and the one we seek is here."

Eighteen

"You LOOK A right fop." Strykar took a step back from Danamis, shaking his head in feigned disgust.

Danamis frowned and looked down at his new clothes. "What are you talking about? So the sleeves are puffed, that's the style."

"You've stuffed your codpiece."

"Fuck off! I have not." Danamis tugged at the pleats of his short fine woollen robe, black and sleeveless so that the rich satin of his russet doublet could be seen.

They stood on a busy street of high houses and balconies in the quarter of the city where the wealthiest commoners lived alongside lesser nobility who had fallen on harder times. It was a neighbourhood of impeccable taste and fashion, and Strykar felt distinctly out of place. He looked past Danamis and up at the villa of Piero Polo. It was every bit as grand as Danamis's house in Palestro and at least as large. He reckoned the glass panes in the enormous rectangular windows of the house, three floors worth, would have alone cost a fortune.

"I will leave you to your meeting, then," he said, suppressing a chuckle over the little felt hat that perched on the pirate's immaculate black ringlets, glistening with olive oil. "You can meet me down the road at that tavern where we left the lads."

"Very well. A few hours then."

Strykar raised a forefinger. "And then to your banker."

Danamis clenched his jaw, put hand to sword pommel and made for the doorway to the merchant's house. He had earlier sent a messenger from the ship to announce his arrival and, luckily, Polo had returned two weeks ago from across the eastern sea. More importantly, he had sent back word of his joy of the arrival of Nicolo Danamis and his desire to see him forthwith.

The household retainers that greeted him bowed and led him into the cool of the high-ceilinged villa, its salmon-coloured walls and golden trim giving the halls an exuberant lightness. He was led past the great receiving rooms of the ground floor and taken up to the apartments of the merchant adventurer and fabled explorer. It would be an informal and very private audience. As Danamis reached the top of the marble stair he was greeted by two huge wolfhounds, their tongues lolling. They amiably followed a few paces behind him as he walked with the houseboys down the painting-lined corridor and to a doorway with an intricate carved lintel in the old style: all angles and egg-and-dart friezes.

"Come in! Come in! King's Admiral Nicolo Danamis!" The voice was deep and powerful beyond the half-opened door. Piero Polo was standing in the centre of a large anteroom to his personal closet, a massive fireplace at this back. He was wearing a long green velvet robe that reached his ankles, long-toed red slippers peeking out from underneath. Danamis approached, spread his arms and gave a deep bow. But Polo rushed forward and enveloped him in an embrace of friendship, and in an instant all of Danamis's worries dissipated in the genuine warmth of the man.

"What brings you to Perusia, my boy? Have you cleansed the southern sea of every last Southland corsair?"

Danamis looked into a face he had not seen for two years. A little more lined perhaps but the same large, slightly protruding hazel eyes, the high noble brow, aquiline nose and clean-shaven square chin that he remembered well. He tried not to look sheepish as he answered.

"In truth, my lord, I have fallen on ill fortune and calamity. I need your advice."

Polo frowned. "And you've come all the way from Palestro to seek me out. That does sound serious. And that calls for some wine." He clapped his hands twice and his retainer appeared from the corridor outside.

"Fetch us wine. None of that Milvornan rubbish, mind you. Bring up that Colonna *zorzalis* I just brought back." He ushered Danamis into his chamber; a modest canopied bed in one corner, the remainder of the room filled with shelves of books and curiosities, and a long table near the windows covered in maps. He beckoned for Danamis to seat himself in one of the two high-backed and throne-like chairs.

They sat and Polo leaned back and crossed his legs and bade Danamis to tell him what had happened. Danamis didn't wait for the wine to delve into the particulars. He was relieved to be with someone who might understand—even offer real help—and it loosened his tongue mightily. He told of the myrra trade (but Polo knew about that going on) and of Tetch's mutiny having stirred up the fleet for weeks if not months. He recounted how they cut themselves out of Palestro with but one ship and how only by the luck of the royal galleys stumbling on them they avoided defeat by corsairs. The sole detail he left out was what he had just learned from Strykar. The astonishing tale of the monk and former thief who was now cursed by Saint Elded. Or chosen by him. That he had sworn to keep secret and with good reason.

Piero Polo sat with his hand in front of his mouth as Danamis relayed the sorry story. Having finished his tale Danamis now felt a deep sense of shame as the retelling only made his failings more manifest. The retainers came in with wine and Danamis paused as the drink was poured for them into silver goblets. When the servants had departed, Polo took a sip and spoke.

"That the world has sunk so low as to see this level of treachery by one so close. Nearly blood even. I am heartily sorry to hear your tale. I don't think I have to ask whether you mean to take the fight back to him."

Danamis fingered his goblet and took a long swallow of the light, slightly sweet red wine. "My lord Piero, I have but one ship left and half a crew. If my father's bank does not see its way to lending then I fear I am done for. And without the aid of the king there will be no other ships and crews."

Polo leaned forward, caressing his cup. "The king? Well, the fates are truly aligned against you I fear. His concerns are elsewhere in the next month. Have you not heard of the great delegation arriving?"

"What delegation? Ambassadors? From where?"

"He is hosting the Sinaens and this is the first time they will have set foot on these shores. Not their proxies. They themselves. They will leave half the delegation here. Surely you saw their great ship when you sailed up the bay?"

Danamis shook his head slowly. "We did not."

"What? As long as two great caravels and with four masts. My boy, you have been far too long playing in that lake of yours you call the Sea of Valdur. There is far more happening across the *Mare Infinitum*—which I myself have shown is nothing of the sort. Do you not keep up with any intelligence from Perusia or Milvorna?"

Danamis sank a little. "Not of late, my lord."

"Much has happened. The kingdom of Partha has now sworn fealty to the Silk Emperor and I suspect that neighbouring Scythiana will eventually follow suit. That gives the Sinaens a direct sea route to Valdur; they are formidable sailors and shipwrights."

Danamis set his cup on the table and ran his hand across his damp brow. "Palestro will be the last of the king's concerns now."

Polo nodded. "I'm afraid so. He plans a great tournament and a feast, and will lead the hunt in the royal wood himself. All in the coming days."

"Then I am finished."

Polo placed a hand on Danamis's knee. "Hold on there. That is not the scion of Valerian that I have known these past ten years. If you want Palestro back you will have to be cunning—and be willing to fight for it."

"Then what is your counsel?"

"You must seek an audience with the king immediately. It is your duty as his admiral to report the seizure of the Palestrian fleet. That is your first task. And you must make it clear to him that treason unpunished only encourages further treason elsewhere. That should get his attention—and more importantly, that of the king's chamberlain, Raganus. How many ships would you need to take on Tetch?"

Danamis thought about this. It depended on how many of his fleet were still loyal to him. He knew that some ships and crews had resisted the mutiny. "With six ships, including the *Grace*, if I can lure him out of Palestro—or catch him on the sea—I can defeat him."

Polo nodded his leonine head and tapped his goblet. "Hmm. You might scrape together six but the Perusian fleet has only galleys. We might find a caravel or carrack for hire in Colonna, with a good crew of mercenaries..."

"There is one problem though," said Danamis. "Tetch might have entered into an alliance with Torinia. Which means that shit Duke Ursino could come to aid him."

"True. But your bigger problem is getting the king to open his purse. I do not have the sums required to give you a fleet, would that I could. You will have to convince him to support your house."

The abrupt sound of a creaking bedframe made Danamis twist about in his chair.

A woman was waking and extricating herself from the sheets. She sat up, naked, the colour of pale ochre, and smoothed back her long black hair. Danamis looked over at Polo who in return gave a small grin.

"I forgot she was still there, Nico. My apologies. But have no fear, she does not speak Valdurian." Polo spoke to her in a foreign tongue and she quietly stood, wrapped herself in a sheet and padded out of the room. Her eyes seemed to drill into Danamis as she passed him.

"She is from the East?" said Danamis. "Sinaen?"

Polo nodded.

"So you are an ambassador of sorts as well, my lord."

"They're an interesting people... in many ways." He picked up a map from the pile on the table before him. "So much has changed in the world since I was a younger man, Nico. And we here, in the middle of these petty squabbling principalities—Torinia and Maresto, Milvorna and Colonna—we forget that the world beyond Valdur is growing, changing. I have seen this with my own eyes."

"My supper plate has enough upon it without worrying about Partha or any other land over the sea. My world is here and it has shattered like weak crystal in just a week."

"Nico, you must regain what was yours. And that means you will have to muster every last ounce of charm to sway Sempronius. Appeal to *his* interests, not yours. If I find an opportunity to intervene with the king's ministers in the next week, I will do so. Be strong and trust in God!"

Danamis managed a smile. "I will, my lord."

Piero Polo placed his hands on the ornate arms of the armchair and stood. Danamis, a little taken aback, followed suit, not sure if the audience was at an end or if the great traveller was just stretching. Polo stepped away from the table and chairs and rearranged his wide-sleeved gown.

"Oh, and one other matter, my boy. Giacomo Tetch must know you're alive. And he's probably guessed already that you've come here to get ships and men. He won't be waiting for that. If I were you I'd keep a sharp watch. It's cheaper and less trouble for an assassin to deal with you rather than fighting a pitched battle at sea. Actually, the same advice applies to you, *if* you had the money for an assassin." And he barked out a laugh as he clapped Danamis's shoulder.

As Danamis stood in the wide cobbled street again, looking up at the edifice he had just departed, he was not quite sure if anything had been gained at all. Still, it was better than walking into the palace blind. He sidestepped a gang of screeching boys who ran past, headed down to the market stalls at the bottom of the row. For an instant he was transported back to his own boyhood, to the days of teasing fishermen down on the docks and stealing pies. And just as suddenly he was back, standing there in his fine clothes and near empty purse, his head spinning with worry. It was time to see the bankers and to negotiate a golden thread to keep his hopes alive.

Nineteen

Two hours later, Danamis entered the tavern at the sign of the golden bowl, where he had agreed to meet Strykar and his men. It was a long and low room that seemed to go on forever, and now, in late afternoon, was near to bursting with drunken merchants, chattering moneylenders, seamen, guildsmen, apprentices, and not a few whores. To Danamis, it almost looked like the orlop deck of some vast ship: cramped, dark, and reeking. The light provided by the few windows was meagre at best and the fat tallow candles melted to the heavy plank tables barely illuminated the sea of sweaty faces that guffawed and yelled across to their companions. His eyes sought out Strykar as he pushed past topers, each staring him down for his insolence in daring to disturb their revelry. He was sweating underneath doublet and woollen robe, the necessary accoutrements of doing business in Perusia. That business had now nearly run its course. So heavy was his heart as he waded deep into the tavern that the sight of a full wine jug on a table filled him with a resigned kind of joy, an anticipation of the forgetfulness that drink would bring. A raised cup of cheap wine would be his fist of defiance to Fortune who had turned on him so suddenly.

Near the back of the room and near to the open door to the courtyard, he spied Strykar at a table with two other *aventuri*, a large blue earthenware jug between them. He saw that one of them was Brognolo, Strykar's grizzled sergeant, and the two were in deep conversation, voices low. Danamis glanced quickly around him and slid onto the bench opposite Strykar. He pulled his hat off his head and leaned on his elbows. Strykar eased himself back on his bench.

"Brognolo, wait outside with the others. Better yet, get back to the hostel and see that the others haven't ripped it apart yet. I'll return presently."

Brognolo gave a curt nod and wordlessly signalled the others to get up.

Strykar pushed Brognolo's half-filled cup over to Danamis. "I would say from the look on your face that you could use a drink—or a woman. Or both."

Danamis's fingers closed around the earthenware cup and he swirled it a little before raising it to his lips.

"But," continued Strykar, "I trust you found out what you needed to know?"

"I found out that our arrival here is not the biggest news in Perusia this week. I'll be lucky if the king even bothers to see me himself."

Strykar hunched over his wine. "What? Even though you've managed to lose an entire fleet?"

Danamis gave the mercenary a basilisk's glare. "The ambassador of the Silk Empire arrived here just before we did."

Strykar shrugged and pulled a face. "So what? Probably a delegation from somewhere or other every fucking week."

"You don't know our king like I do. It's going to be feasting and games for a week—or two weeks. The whole blasted court will be in knots trying to impress the Sinaens. I won't even get a look-in."

Strykar dragged the wine jug across the table and refilled Danamis's cup and then his own. "You must demand an audience," he said. "The king has no guarantees about what Tetch will do now with Palestro."

"We've had an unusual alliance, you and I, these past two years."

"Pah! Unusual? Like a bad marriage more like. And it's one that I can't walk away from."

"Maybe you can now. I am sorry that I dragged you into all of this. Should not have happened. But God knows, I wouldn't have been able to cut us out of Palestro without you and your men at the tower. I am grateful for that."

"And the corsairs?"

Danamis gave a weak smile. "And the corsairs."

"I appreciate that," said Strykar, his voice low. "Especially for the men I left behind at Palestro. But this is the life we've chosen. I just wish you had some better choices now." Danamis reached inside his doublet and pulled out a piece of folded parchment. He slid it across the damp table.

"What's this then?"

"I have just come from my father's moneylending house. That is a letter of credit made out to you alone. It gives you access to one thousand ducats. You are free to take them when you choose."

Strykar broke the wax seal and opened the parchment. His face split into a grin. "You have done well by me, brother!" He hastily refolded the paper and pushed it into his grease-stained leather doublet. "Seems like you underestimated your powers of persuasion."

"They would not give me my father's gold. It was not left to me—or anyone else, so it appears."

Strykar tapped his breast where the parchment now lay. "Then, how? You took all your own gold?"

Danamis looked down into his wine cup, empty once

again. "No. I have no gold in their vaults. I had to give them ownership of the *Grace*."

"Blood of the saints! You gave them your ship?"

"Could have been worse. At least they will let me captain it."

Strykar, who rarely ever felt a twinge of guilt, was now feeling the stirrings of a conscience somewhere deep inside him. "Shit—Nico, my friend—that is sore hard news." He could feel the thick parchment poking against his breast. He reached over, grasped the blue jug and poured out another measure for Danamis. There was silence between them even though the tavern roiled with good cheer and bawdiness. After a few moments, Strykar gave a low rumble.

"I remember when I was a lad. My mother would tell me stories from the holy book. There was one about a righteous man who lost everything. All his wealth, his family, his respect, taken away by God. And he did not know why he was tested so. But you see, God does not need a reason."

Danamis looked at Strykar, his eyebrows raised. "Are you trying to cheer me up?"

"Bah! I'm just saying that sometimes the only thing to do is to be mean enough to keep on living, despite the shit from God, and not give in. Besides, that there cove in the story held firm and got back his wealth and his health."

Danamis nodded and wrapped both hands tightly around his cup. "That monk of yours and the tale he tells—do you believe what he saw? Can it be true? What that little trinket can do surely lends credence to what he claims he saw."

Strykar answered in a whisper. "Do not talk of such things here. But, in truth, I do not know. I only know what I saw—what you have now seen—and that I cannot explain."

"But if it is true... my God if it is true, then what does it mean for all of us? That all we were taught is a lie?"

Strykar shook his head slowly. "I am long past caring about such things as the ways of the Faith."

Danamis looked at him, an expression of deep sadness and resignation both. Strykar cleared his throat. "Aye, well, time I went back to the men. And you will want to get back to the ship I expect. Fear not, the king will see you. He'd be a fool not to give you aid."

Danamis chuckled. "Like I told you. You haven't met him."

Strykar stood up. "Let's be off."

"I'm staying to finish this jug."

Strykar began to protest, paused, and then pushed the jug over to Danamis. "I will come by the ship tonight."

When Strykar had left, Danamis sloshed more wine into his cup and studied the men around him. It was a curious mix but Perusia was a curious place. It was as if everyone from the known world ended up here eventually, thrown into the hurly-burly of the royal enclave. At the table across from him, four artisans played at cards. One had a small monkey perched on his head, chattering as if to provide advice. Danamis looked towards the bar where a very drunken patron was fondling a whore, his unshaven face buried into her neck behind her ear. Her hand was buried in his belt purse. Feeling his bladder beckon, Danamis stood up and made a move to the rear door.

He stepped into a largish courtyard, open to the sky but enclosed by buildings on all four sides and laid with uneven paving slabs. At one side was a long stone latrine with a pump at one end to sluice it out. Two men stood over it now, swaying as they pissed. He walked to the far end, yanked his sword belt around to clear his hilt, and started to unlace the points securing his codpiece on one side. The two pissing downstream shared a laugh and stepped back, weaving a bit as they returned to the tavern. Danamis felt warm, the wine filling his head. As he relieved himself, his mind drifted to other times when he had riches and women. What had happened to Kassia and Talia? Were they part of Tetch's stable or had Escalus saved them? It all seemed an age ago. Behind him, he heard the latch of the door to the tavern make a metallic clink. He stuffed himself back into his braes and threaded a lace back into his codpiece.

A moment later he was shoved forward by a blow to his right shoulder, sending his face into the stuccoed wall and crashing his shins into the stone trough. At the same instant, he felt a sharp pain spread across his left ribcage. Even as his left arm flailed behind him to strike back, he knew he had been knifed. The blade had skidded over his rib, cutting into flesh and muscle, but it had not gone into his back. The choice of a full woollen *cioppa* with a dozen heavy pleats had disguised the target and the assassin had misjudged his thrust.

As Danamis turned, a cry on his lips, he heard the assassin's blade ring as it landed on the paving stones—it had been caught in his robe. He looked at the man: nondescript with short black hair. He could have been anyone. The man bounded backwards as Danamis lashed out, and moved to draw his sword. As he drew his falchion from the scabbard, he kept the hilt high and caught a full-speed side-cut aimed at his head. He was nearly off balance but even so, as his opponent's blade clanged and ran down his falchion, he managed to convert his guard into a downright blow at the man. But this creature was no bumbler, despite his first misjudgement. He was an adept. He recovered fast, blocking Danamis's cut as he side-stepped and then throwing another blow of his own. Danamis pushed the hilt of his sword across to his left side and just managed to ward the blow. He back-stepped furiously to give himself some distance. That was when he saw the second assassin moving forward, sword in hand.

Danamis felt as if he had a stitch in his side but the spreading dampness inside his doublet was a reminder that it was more than that. He held out his sword and began to move to his left to keep the other from flanking him.

"Bastards! Who sent you?"

Neither man was in the mood for conversation and they remained expressionless, stepping towards him, sword legs forward and rear closing, keeping their balance as they prepared to attack again. Danamis could not for the life of him understand why in a crowded tavern no one else had the urge to piss at that moment. He moved his falchion to the centre and gripped the pommel with his left hand. His wound would slow him in another minute or two and they would finish him with a joint rush forward. That meant no time to hesitate. He gave a stamp with his right foot forward, a feint, and then sprang forward off his rear leg at the first assassin. The man raised his blade as Danamis's falchion swung down. Danamis moved past the man to keep his comrade behind. Danamis's blow, intentionally slow, was blocked and his sword driven down. Danamis slipped his sword by bending his wrists, and gave a mighty backhand as he pulled the blade up again. A spray of bright red spattered him as the top third of his falchion's back edge, keenly sharp, cut across the man's neck. The assassin's eyes went large and his left hand grabbed at his throat.

The other was on Danamis without pause. An awkward block by Danamis and the man's blade bounced off and struck him on his bicep on the flat. Not as painful as the searing bite in his side. The wine and blood loss was making him light-headed. He raised his sword again as another blow fell. He blocked it, but it was converted into another blow at his other side. Danamis staggered back. The man came forward, faked an overhand blow and then shot forward a thrust to his gut. Danamis parried but as he twisted away, a paroxysm of agony made him nearly buckle. This opponent looked much like the other, who now lay writhing on the stones. Short hair, black doublet and cloak, dark green hose, fine, almost delicate featured face and small eyes.

Behind them, the crash of wood and clattering ironmongery sounded as the door was finally gained by those on the other side.

"Danamis!"

Strykar stepped through and took in the scene. He roared and rushed forward, not even taking the time to draw his weapon. The assassin shot past Danamis and made for an open door on the opposite side of the courtyard. Fleeter than the heavy-footed *rondelieri*, the assassin was gone before Strykar had made it even halfway there. Danamis sank to his knees, and seeing Danamis fall, Strykar turned back to help.

"Elded's balls! You're a bloody mess." He lifted Danamis off the flagstones as the pirate managed to throw an arm around the mercenary's neck.

"Who sent them!" rasped Danamis. "Ask who sent them! Set me down."

The courtyard was fast filling with patrons all jabbering away and beginning to crowd around. Strykar leaned over the grey-faced man, blood pooling about his gory neck and shoulders. He was gurgling still, just. Strykar pulled him up by his hair.

"You heard him. Who paid you?"

The man's eyes rolled upwards, bubbles frothing across his throat. Strykar dropped his head back to the flagstones with a sickening crack and turned back to Danamis.

"Well, looks like you fucking well cut his throat. He's not telling anyone anything."

The landlord came forward, shoving the ogling crowd away. "What's all this, then!"

Strykar had an arm around Danamis's waist, raising him up. "What's all this? Your fucking drinking hole is a nest of assassins!" He gestured down to the dead man. "Do you know him?"

The landlord blanched and shook his head. Strykar swore under his breath. "You better get this filth taken away."

Danamis somehow managed to hold himself up, his legs weak but his sword still in his fist. "Strykar, get me back to the ship."

And the tavern crowd parted, silently, and let them pass.

Twenty

LYING WEDGED IN the tight berth in his cabin, Danamis managed to push himself up onto his elbows. The high-sided wooden bed reminded him of a coffin. He winced as pain seared his left side. Timandra stepped back and put her hands on her hips.

"If you move around too much, Captain, you will ruin my beautiful needlework. And stop playing with the bandaging!"

"Seems you can't even have a piss safely in this city anymore," Danamis mumbled. He had passed a bad night, the wound throbbing. When Strykar had dragged him back to the ship, Timandra had cleaned him and stitched him, first pouring on some *acqua vitalis* to prevent rot setting in. She had told him he better pray that the blade had not been poisoned as any assassin worth his salt would have taken that precaution to ensure a kill. But he had been lucky. The dagger had sawn him straight across a rib, cutting into skin and muscle but no deeper. The bleeding had stopped thanks to Strykar tying a waist sash about him during their awkward journey back to the docks. He had yanked it from a merchant's window sill and thrown him a few coins with a growl. The man had not argued.

Timandra looked over to Strykar and Gregorvero. "He'll be stiff as an old man for a few days and you ought to have one of your crew find a cookshop and get him some meat. He's lost blood and a good chunk of roast would do him good."

Strykar nodded. This latest turn of events had changed the situation somewhat and he calculated that he should keep some of his men on the *Grace* for protection. Danamis's crew was small and recruitment had only just started. And Danamis, he thought, had lost a lot of his pride in the last few days. Now he was quieter and more reflective, each new travail sobering him further.

"How could Tetch have gotten his men here so quickly?" said Strykar. "It is as if they had wings."

Danamis shook his head. "They could have followed close behind us by ship. More likely overland through Torinia. It is possible."

Strykar scratched his beard. "Aye, reckon that they could have. Hard ride, but possible. What about any other enemies in Perusia? Any unpaid debts?"

"No. Nothing. And the only person I've met with is Piero Polo."

"And you trust him? Maybe he has some unfinished business with you you're not aware of."

"I couldn't believe that for an instant. He's an honourable man. I've known him for years, for God's sake. A confidant of my father."

Strykar smiled. "What? Like Giacomo Tetch?"

Danamis's chin dropped to his chest as he sighed. "That's right. Stick it in again, my friend."

"You cannot trust anyone anymore, Nico. And whoever it is, if they've tried once to kill you, they will try again. You need to find out where you stand with the king—and damned quick."

Danamis looked up again at Strykar. "Why did you come back for me?"

Strykar laughed. "I got to thinking as I was walking back. You looked like you were about to sink a gallon of stale Milvornan on your own and I thought, given the circumstances, that probably was not in your best interest."

"Thank you, for saving my life."

"I always said you were a good risk. A successful mercenary has to have an eye for that sort of thing. And well, damn…" He was about to mention how moved he was (and surprised) that Danamis had mortgaged his ship to pay his debt, but then thought better of saying that with the others present. "We've shared adventure before—good and bad, haven't we?"

"Ah yes, never was there a more loyal friend, cousin," jibed Timandra. "I will stay on ship to tend to the captain— along with Brother Acquel—if you allow."

Strykar nodded. "I'd have all of us stay on ship but for the fact that the lads hate it below deck. But I'll leave a few here to stand guard and relieve them tomorrow with another lot. And Master Gregorvero, you had better keep a watchful eye on any new men you sign up."

Gregorvero bristled. "Don't tell me how to run my ship, *aventura.*"

Strykar threw up his hands. "Just pointing out the obvious—as an *aventura.* But even a fool would recognize we're all on our own here." And he stepped out of the cabin.

Danamis swung his legs over the side of his berth. "Strykar means well, Gregor. And we can't be too careful now. Mistress Timandra, if you would kindly hand me my shirt…"

"Aye, well he's a swaggerer just the same. Apologies to you mistress, I know he's kin."

"You left out braggart," she said as she put away what was left of the medicines into a little casket. She nodded to Danamis and left.

"Nico, we've got about a week's worth of work on the fo'c'sle and bow, but we've secured stores and timber. Bassinio's finding us some good hands who want to sign on despite the fact that his face looks like a shank of overdone pork. Seems there are plenty about looking for vessels to ship on. But I'd give my right hand to have some proper soldiers lent to us by the king... if you can convince him."

"My next mission, my friend. Assuming I can stand up straight anytime soon."

ACQUEL STOOD AMIDSHIPS at the railing, trying to avoid getting in the way of the seamen who cursed at him as they went about their business of resurrecting the *Royal Grace* after the battering at Palestro and the attack by the Darfan corsairs. He smiled at the sight of Timandra emerging from the stern, and as she came down the stairs to the main deck, he suppressed a tiny thrill of anticipation. Immediately, he felt self-conscious and foolish and the smile evaporated.

"Mistress Timandra, how fares the captain today?"

"He's damned lucky that his attacker was poor at his trade. The wound looks clean but one never knows with such things. We'll be staying aboard for now so that I can dress the wound again later."

Acquel found himself staring at her lips as she spoke. "Staying aboard? God knows they've had enough of me here. Not earning my keep."

She scowled. "Let them think what they want. Dressed as you are they don't know that you are a monk trying to save all their miserable souls."

"You're still trying to get me to put on the grey again, aren't you?"

Her gaze went to the magnificent city that spread before them, its gilded towers and domes sparkling in the sun.

"I'm trying to remember what it was like back in the Black Rose, when I had a business and a purpose. Before all of this happened... And before you arrived." She glanced at the chain around his neck. "I wonder where Poule and the rest of them are now? Do you think they made it back to Maresto?"

"God willing they have by now."

Around them the cries of bargemen and dockworkers echoed off the warehouses beyond. A loaded carrack, its deck heaving with bales, eased its way off the wharf opposite them. "We are surrounded by people, Acquel— thousands more out there in the city. But I've never felt so alone. Yesterday I suggested to Strykar that he should send a messenger overland to Maresto to let Count Malvolio know what has happened to us. A good rider could get back there in a few days."

"And did he?"

"Did he? He said I was a sutler's widow, not a field commander, and told me to keep my mouth shut." She laughed. "And then he wrote out the letter and arranged a courier at a counting house!"

"You *are* a field commander, Timandra. To me anyway." She tapped him on his forearm as Strykar appeared on the docks, walking alongside an elegantly dressed young man; a man of some importance or, more likely to Timandra's eye, a man in the service of someone of importance. The man extended a red brocade-swathed arm holding a small beige packet. Strykar took it (a little hesitantly she thought) and the man (even taller in his high felt toque) gave a court bow and turned on the low heels of his long-toed shoes.

Strykar stared at the packet a moment then looked back after the messenger who had already disappeared into the throng of the fountain square. He then briskly strode to the ship and pounded up the gangplank. He was still studying the packet as he ascended the stairs up to Danamis's cabin.

"Let's go see what that is all about, shall we?" Timandra pulled Acquel by the hand (he did not resist) and they crossed the deck aft.

"I don't think they will want to be interrupted," said Acquel as they mounted the stairs.

"Then they can tell us to leave," said Timandra. She knocked and strode into the cabin without waiting for a response. Acquel followed, hands folded in front of him. Danamis abruptly stopped reading aloud from a parchment that dangled three large wax seals and ribbons.

"The king?" asked Timandra.

Strykar swore an oath and raised his hands. "Woman! Must you have your nose in everything?"

Danamis winced as he shifted his weight on the bench. "Let them both hear. They'll find out soon enough anyway." And he raised the parchment and read aloud.

"'Greeting unto Lord Nicolo Danamis, Admiral of the King's navy in Palestro and knight of the illustrious order of the Silver Boar...'"

"Really?" interrupted Strykar.

Danamis gave a sheepish grin and stuck out his chin before carrying on. "'You are summoned to appear at court, midday on the morrow, by the order of his Excellency the Baron Raganus, Lord Chamberlain of the kingdom of Valdur. It is requested that you be accompanied by Captain Julianus Strykar, commander of *rondelieri* of the Company of the Black Rose. This letter is proof to grant passage to the palace to you and your party.'"

Danamis put the letter down on the table and placed his hand on his wounded side, his breath hissing between clenched teeth. "It seems I am not destined to get much time to recover my strength before facing our king. But at least he will see me."

"They must have known you were here within hours of

dropping anchor," said Strykar. "But how did they know I was here too? Goddamned spies everywhere. I suppose that fracas at the tavern has spread the news even further."

"And they undoubtedly know that Tetch is now in control of Palestro." Danamis shook his head. "I should have sought an audience as soon as we made land. God knows what they are thinking—or planning."

"It's worse than that," said Strykar. "You need another new suit of clothes after yesterday."

Timandra spoke up. "It says 'your party'. Who else will go?"

"I need an escort, twenty to thirty men. And I will need my standard carried aloft."

"And a mount, I dare say," added Strykar.

"Then I will help get you ready for tomorrow," said Timandra. "We need to get you fed and watered and we'll have to dress that wound again twice before you leave. You should be lying down too, not hunched over on that bench."

Danamis's laugh turned into a pained cough. "Very well, I surrender to your ministrations." And he gestured to Acquel. "And those of the Faith."

Once outside, Timandra turned to Acquel, a sly look on her tanned face. "And when they are off to the palace, you and I will go and see the master oculist and try to get some answers to our little mystery!"

Acquel nodded obediently but a large part of him was not sure he wanted that mystery solved.

CAPTAIN FLAUROS WAS barely breathing as he peered through the crack in the door. He stood transfixed, both fascinated and horrified by what his eyes were drinking in. Lucinda della Rovera was seated in a high-backed chair, bolt upright and rigid. He could see her eyes moving rapidly as if she was following someone or something across the room, but he knew she was alone. Her lips were moving as if in conversation, but there were no audible words. The Magister said she was favoured of the Lord, a holder of a special gift—a *profetessa* possessed of far-sight. He was not so sure. Everything he had witnessed smacked of witchcraft, plain and simple. He was enthralled by the possibility of it.

She had led him and his men to Perusia based solely on a whim, he thought. There was no intelligence that the greyrobe was there. He knew that her sister was somehow guiding her, and that must be who she was communing with as he watched her mummery. But equally, she herself could not apparently find the monk. This begged the question: what could she do? Now they were in Perusia, ensconced in the apartments of the grand priory. No one, not even the abbot himself, questioned their purpose. Why shouldn't an aristocratic canoness go on pilgrimage to the royal enclave? He was tiring of playing the servant though. She was clever; giving him orders one minute and playing the teasing beauty the next. He distrusted her and burned for her in the same instant. Flauros wiped a hand across his mouth, took a few steps back, and knocked forcefully upon the door.

He waited for what seemed an age. And then she beckoned, her voice faltering. He pushed open the door and walked into the chamber, richly adorned with dark blue velvet curtains covered in little golden suns.

"Captain. You have need of me?" She had resumed her natural pose, her delicate hands resting on both arms of the large ornate chair.

Flauros gave a barely detectable bow. "My lady, I was hoping you would be able to give some... guidance of where we begin our search tomorrow."

She smiled. "I have told you they came by ship, and now I have further news. They are still on it, though it be here in the port."

"With respect, my lady, there are hundreds of vessels in Perusia on any given day. That is not much to go on."

"I have more. The ship flies a special flag. It is a sword and dolphin entwined—they are red upon a white banner."

Flauros now broke into a smile. "My lady, that is a help indeed, but it will take time to cover the harbour—and we must also hope that their flag flies still at the mast."

She scowled. "Have not you yourself seen this monk with your own eyes? Surely you would recognise him when you see him again. I have now enabled you to narrow your search."

He bowed his head. *If pigs could fly.* He had only ever glimpsed the greyrobe covered in mud and lying on the roadside. And it would take a few days to find the ship she spoke of, maybe less if they dared ask who flew such a flag. But *he* did not want more attention drawn to their hunt. "My men and I will set out to the docks in the morning. Will you accompany us, my lady?"

She folded her hands in her lap and gave him a pleasant look, almost affectionate, and all composure regained. "I would very much enjoy a visit to the harbour, Captain Flauros. We are *fishing* after all, are we not?"

Flauros turned to leave, paused, and turned back to face Lucinda again. "I'm still bothered by the way Demedrius vanished like he did. On foot, he should not have gone far—and he's a dolt besides. Probably wouldn't have the sense to climb a tree. But he disappeared like a will o' the wisp after attacking you. Don't you think it strange?"

Lucinda's face was a mask of blank charm. A few moments passed and then she replied. "I think it likely he was set upon by wolves—and devoured. For me, the matter is at a close."

Flauros bowed and smiled broadly. "My lady, something tells me that Demedrius would stand a better chance against a pack of famished Valdurian wolves than against you. But... yes, I suppose that was his likely fate."

And only then did Lucinda give the barest twist of a smile, a tiny crinkle at the corners of her eyes.

Twenty-One

IT WAS THE music of the soldier on the move: the rhythmic clanking of metal harness and plate as the armed party marched along the smooth cobblestones of the road leading up to the palace gate. In the vanguard stepped ten of Danamis's soldiers, in three files, their barbute helms polished but dented. The lead man hefted the Danamis dolphin and falchion standard on a pole the height of two halberds. Next followed four of Strykar's men, *sans* round shields but nevertheless gleaming in their breastplates and chainmail, their swords swinging at their hips. Behind this bodyguard rode Danamis and Strykar on proud but elderly stallions, hired at a shameful price and tacked-out in worn leathers and caparisoned in threadbare ancient parade velvets that gave them the look of mangy dogs. Danamis wore his red studded brigantine (despite his wound), his new boots and a great felt cap and brooch. He also wore a new woollen robe, dark blue with golden trim, to replace the bloodied and holed one that had helped foil the attempt on his life. Strykar rode along next to him, right hand on the hilt of his sword, an ornate silver sallet helm perched squarely on his square head. Their rearguard — such as it was, comprising a further twelve of Strykar's men—loped behind with occasional lewd gestures towards the braying apprentices and street children who capered alongside. Strykar had been reluctant to take any more in the escort—despite Danamis's bruised honour—for fear of leaving the ship and those who remained behind exposed to attack. Just from whom he wasn't sure, but nevertheless, it was clear that the *Royal Grace* and her commander had drawn enemies in Perusia already.

The little procession was poor by the standard of the week in Perusia. The Sinaens, humourless but imposing in their yards of bright silks and bizarre headwear, had already made their stately progress through the city and to the palace environs. And there were few taunts from the local boys as the visitors made their way up the streets under their stupendous dagged awnings and parasols, their armed escort of two hundred glaive-wielding soldiers marching in uniform step, black enamelled armour clacking like the sound of a thousand giant lobsters. The dukes of Milvorna and Colonna and their entourages also had arrived and made their way to the palace, each procession in turn stirring up the crowds as retainers flung sweetmeats and small silver coins into the throng.

As the townspeople, visitors, and swelling population of cutpurses knew, this was all just the preliminaries to the real festivities: galley races in the bay and a grand tournament of tilting at the barrier and foot combat in the lists. The latter would be seen by a lucky hundred townsmen chosen by lottery. For two weeks a feverish off-street market had been spinning up for tickets, both genuine and counterfeit. Banners and garlands hung between the tall houses on Perusia's narrow streets and the city had a feel more like All Saints' Day than of an ambassadorial mission. The city had swelled as outlying towns had practically emptied to come and see the spectacle. Few could remember a more exotic group of foreigners coming to Valdur's shores, or from such a vast empire and from so far.

Strykar gobbed a ball of phlegm at a particularly annoying boy who was trotting alongside, eliciting a curse and sending the lad diving off into the crowd. "I doubt this is what you expected, Admiral. But the best I could finance on short notice."

Danamis choked-up on his reins slightly, his eyes moving to the open windows above them either side. "I am more worried now about a goose-fletched quarrel being buried in my back than looking like a Goddamned fool."

Strykar laughed. "At least we would gather some sympathy from the Perusians. I feel like some country clown expecting a seat at the groaning board when it's bloody more likely we'll get scraps under the table."

Danamis inclined his head towards his companion. "I'd be less worried about food and more about getting arrested for not announcing our arrival earlier. I'm still wondering what I'm going to tell him."

"Well, you best quicken the pace of your cleverness, my friend. We're practically at the gates."

As Danamis well knew, very little came as a surprise to the palace and the captain of the guard and his men were already standing outside the massive studded oak doors to the gatehouse, the portcullis standing ratcheted and raised. The gates were bracketed by two vast scarlet gonfalons suspended from the parapets, their golden griffons rampant and nobly posed. Danamis raised a gloved hand to his brow in a salute which was graciously returned by the officer. The two great doors slowly opened inwards, screeching a coarse-sounding welcome to the curious-looking party. They passed inside the gatehouse and outer walls to find themselves in a middle terrace, looking upon the smaller inner wall, the royal temple, and the palace within.

"My lord Danamis," said the captain, his voice echoing off the russet stone walls, "if you would be so kind as to dismount here, my men will take your horses. Your retinue can remain here and we will see that they are refreshed."

Danamis nodded and raised an eyebrow at Strykar. He threw his right leg back over the cruppers of his mount and stepped lightly down to the pavement, his teeth clenched in pain. Strykar dismounted, patted the neck of his temporary ride, and joined Danamis as they followed the captain up to the inner gatehouse. Once inside, they were joined by another party of liveried guardsmen who led them into the inner ward of the palace grounds and to the residence. The castle was ancient, but Sempronius and his father had put much effort and money into making the residence as splendid as any great ducal estate. It was a fortress on the outside but within, an explosion of carved wood and marble, gilding and brocaded hangings. Soon they found themselves walking along a high-ceilinged corridor, three guards and the captain in front of them and three more behind, and all bearing tasselled halberds.

As they walked nothing was said. Only the clanking of armour and jangle of harness sounded as they passed great murals of ancient battles, depictions of Saint Elded preaching, the occasional alabaster statue of a naked nymph or bearded warrior, and dripping marble fountains set into dark corners. Danamis glanced up to see the entire ceiling carved in plasterwork of acanthus, oak, and pinecones with the twin griffons upon shields painted at each end of every segment of corridor. He heard a scratching of running claws on the tiled floor, and turned to see a cockatrice the size of a large goat approaching from behind. It sidled up and kept pace with them, its talons slipping on the smooth tiles and only its serpent body and long tail keeping it stable. It angled its head and blinked a beady red eye at Danamis, coxcomb shaking. Danamis saw that it wore a golden collar and a medallion which jingled as it shook itself as if it were a dog. It angled its head again, clacked its beak and squawked raucously before running on ahead. The captain of the guard gave its tail a gentle whack with the haft of his halberd as it shot past him.

"I hate those things," mumbled Strykar as he walked, his hand on hilt. "Shouldn't be allowed inside."

The party turned into a large square hall lavishly draped with embroidered tapestries that rose up three times the height of a man. He could smell the dank and dust of years on them and the room was close and stuffy despite its height. *Hunting scenes,* thought Danamis, snorting in derision, knowing well the king's excessive interest in sport at the expense of just about everything else. Strykar pointed to a large fresh white turd on the floor where the cockatrice had paused before heading down another branching hall.

The captain of the guard stepped forward and knocked three times on the great rectangular doors that Danamis knew from past visits led to the throne room. The doors opened with nary a squeak and he motioned Danamis and Strykar forward. The chamber was lit by tall windows on one side, a great chandelier overhead and wall sconces on the far wall. On either side thick draperies of rich velvet and satin brocades, bright blue and red, brightened the chamber further. As he entered the room, Danamis could see that the throne on the canopied dais was empty. Instead, to the left, his folded hands lost in the voluminous sleeves of his black houppelande gown, stood Baron Raganus, the king's chamberlain.

"Lord Danamis and Captain Strykar, welcome. It is good of you to finally pay your respects at the palace."

Danamis bowed curtly, his ears burning at the slight. "My lord. Our journey here has been an unlucky one and an attempt on my life has delayed our arrival further."

"Ah, yes. I had heard about that but was not sure if it was dockside rumour. But clearly, you have survived. And looking reasonably well, it seems."

"A knife wound. But short of the mark."

Raganus's eyes widened. "I was unaware you had been injured. I am glad you are well." Danamis looked at the relic standing in front of him and smiled. Raganus dressed thirty years in the past, his grey hair cropped in a bowl cut and slicked with duck grease and scented olive oil.

"I was expecting an audience with his majesty," said Danamis, his voice conveying polite dismay.

"Were you? I seem to remember dictating the summons myself. It was a summons to court—not necessarily to see the king."

"That's rather disappointing," said Strykar. "The admiral has undergone great trouble in coming here."

"We *know* why you have come to Perusia. The fleet has mutinied and you were forced to make a run for it." Danamis was silent. Raganus smiled smugly. "We do have our means of gaining intelligence. Quickly too, I might say."

"It is true," replied Danamis. "Giacomo Tetch has seized the fleet. But not without a fight."

Raganus nodded. "Seized? Or offered command?"

"Offered command? By whom?" Danamis snapped. "I am the king's admiral in Palestro. No man has the right to take that away other than the king."

Raganus slowly paced the chamber as he played with his chain of office. "You are right in that. And I suppose you are here to ask for men and ships to get Palestro back?"

Danamis slowly wheeled to follow the perambulating toad as he made his way across the mosaic tiles. "It is as much a slight to Sempronius that Tetch has seized the fleet. And an encouragement to others to challenge the king's word. It must not stand."

Raganus turned and faced Danamis. "The king and his councillors must first establish what happened. To find out where loyalties lie. To ferret out the facts of the situation."

Danamis's anger welled. "Do you doubt my loyalty to the king? My service to the crown?"

"The king does not doubt your loyalty in the slightest, Nicolo Danamis." It was a voice from across the room. All turned to see the heavy draperies part and Sempronius II enter the chamber, a mischievous grin on his wide, thin-lipped mouth. The captain of the guard belatedly banged the haft of his halberd on the floor and Raganus bowed low, both arms held wide. Danamis and Strykar, taken aback, made hurried awkward obeisance and Danamis gave a flourish as he doffed his cap.

"I sometimes let Raganus go too far in playing the cat's-paw. But the chamberlain must do his duty and generally he does a good job of it."

The baron bowed again, slightly unsure whether he had been insulted or not.

The king grasped the facings of his cloth-of-gold gown and stepped up onto the dais. He was an unassuming man for one who was king, of no great height or build, long black hair streaked now with grey. His eyes were large, perhaps too large for his face, his nose round and just shy of bulbous. He moved to the blackwood throne, gilded and upholstered in dark shades of velvet fabric, and plopped down without grace or ceremony. Danamis noticed that the sole of one of his bright red shoes was holed.

"I thought it better we meet outside a public audience. You do understand… given what has happened of late. Better for you I should think." The king extended his right hand and Danamis approached, stepped up onto the dais and then knelt on one knee. He kissed the hand and ring with the royal seal and then stepped back.

"I am grateful, my liege, that you have afforded me the honour."

"Well, the timing of your difficulties could have been better, Danamis. What with the arrival of the Sinaens and all. I've just been *drowning* in the planning. You wouldn't believe the details. Or, maybe you would… I mean, as a commander of men."

Two of the palace guard now flanked the throne, staring straight ahead as Danamis took another pace backwards and formulated his response.

"Sire, I would not deign to tell you what your councillors have undoubtedly already told you. It is true that Giacomo Tetch has seized the fleet. But not without a fight and not unopposed even now I am sure. With your help, I propose to sail back to Palestro and defeat him."

The king leaned forward, his hands resting on his thighs. "Yes, troubling tidings, Lord Danamis, troubling indeed. And, I am told, there was an attempt on your life since your arrival in Perusia?"

"That is also true, sire. And I suspect that too was Tetch's doing."

"He appears to have a long reach. Ah, family squabbles are the saddest of all."

Danamis bristled. "With respect, sire. He is not actually my uncle."

Sempronius raised a hand in weak supplication. "Oh, of course. It's just that I remember your father held him a close friend and advisor—like a brother."

"His loyalty was skin deep."

"Yes, apparently so…" The king wrinkled his nose. "My lad, all this curious trade with the fishmen… seems to have stirred things up with the common folk. Not to mention the priests. You know, I did tell your father that this myrra trade with the heathen was ill-advised. But I recognised his need to raise revenue in abeyance of his former activities on the high seas. Now it appears to have borne bad fruit."

Danamis could feel the ground starting to open up at his feet. "Be that as it may, sire, this mutiny by Tetch is an attack on your house through me."

The king sat back. "Is it really? Raganus, has Tetch renounced allegiance?"

The baron glanced at Danamis and bowed his head to the king. "We have heard nothing from him, sire."

Sempronius opened his hands expansively. "Well, you see Lord Danamis, we are not in possession of all of the facts yet, are we?"

Danamis could hear Strykar behind him clearing his throat in annoyance. He shifted his weight onto his other leg, hand on sword pommel. "My liege, are you saying you will not help your admiral of the southern fleet?"

The king narrowed his eyes. "I did *not* say anything of the sort, Lord Danamis. And your impatience marks you as somewhat impetuous—and insubordinate."

Danamis bowed. "I apologise, sire, if I have given offence."

"We will take the matter under consideration. But this week I have more pressing matters with these very odd Sinaens. So many details to deal with. And they have so many blasted questions about everything. The feast alone will cost me thousands! At least we will have some good sport though."

Danamis felt his shoulders sag. "If your majesty requires further details I will of course divulge them."

The king waved his hand. "Yes, yes, Raganus will meet with you if we need to know anything more. But you will attend the tournament of course, no? And Captain Strykar, yes I see you standing back there. I would be most pleased if you would enter the lists yourself. I'm sure your brother would approve, even though he is not coming." Danamis gave a half turn in surprise but stopped so as not to turn his back on the king. Strykar moved alongside Danamis and bowed. Sempronius smiled. "Oh, I'm sorry. He hasn't told you of his family connections?"

Danamis looked at Strykar whose cheeks and nose were now flushed scarlet.

"Captain Strykar here is the brother of the Duke of Maresto."

"Half-brother," Strykar whispered.

"And let us not forget the stag hunt. I am so looking forward to that tomorrow," the king said. "I am told that in the Silk Empire they don't even have stags. Can you believe that?"

"I was not aware of that, sire." Danamis's tone was weary.

"I will certainly expect both of you there for that," replied the king. "I will have the invitation sent to your ship by the end of the day. Raganus?"

"It will be done, sire!"

"Excellent! Now, I must return to the arrangements for the feast and the tournament... and all the other *details*." He shook his head and stood. Everyone bowed and the king smiled amiably. "Very good. Raganus, see our honoured guests out of the palace."

As the captain of the palace guard led them back down the long corridor at what seemed a double-quick pace, Danamis turned and looked at Strykar.

"You never told me."

"It wasn't an important detail. My father never acknowledged me."

Danamis shook his head. "The Duke of Maresto. Elded's bollocks." He paused and then looked back at the mercenary. "What do you think the chances are the king will help me?"

Strykar kept looking ahead, his armour jangling each step he took. "About the same as me avoiding the stag hunt."

GIACOMO TETCH ITCHED the whiskers on his throat and clicked his tongue. "Not looking down your nose at folks anymore, are you Master Escalus?" He put his hands on his hips and ambled about the loggia of what had been Danamis's villa.

Escalus stood unsteadily, supported by two of Tetch's men, bloody drool pouring down his chin from lips that were swollen purple as an overripe plum. One eye was puffed shut and as his head sagged down one of the pirates jerked him up by his long dank hair. Tetch reached down to the side of the marble fountain and picked up the long thin curving blade of a Southland sword. He hefted it and tossed it from one hand to another.

"Very light. And fast too, I imagine."

"And he spitted poor Donato and Biaggi before we could disarm him," mumbled one of the men next to Tetch.

Tetch turned to the man. "Ramus, what did you say he was doing when you found him at the gate?"

"He put two bitches on a horse and was giving them instructions or some such. When he saw us coming he sent them off at a gallop and turned to take us on."

Tetch clicked his tongue again. "La, la, la. Now I wonder who *they* were and why you thought they wouldn't be happy here anymore."

Ramus chuckled and Tetch reached for a silver goblet. "You know, Escalus, my men have searched every corner— every cranny—of this place and we have yet to find a single piece of treasure. All that treasure of House Danamis." He raised up his cup. "However, we do find hundreds of casks of passable wine in the cellars. Not much Milvornan, mind you, but passable. So that is some consolation."

Escalus's swollen lips moved. His voice was barely a rasp. "There is no treasure anymore. What was left he took."

"I am inclined to believe you. My men have beaten you half to death already for no answers and I suppose I've got the lion's share anyway."

Escalus raised his head. "You have nothing. You are without loyalty... or honour."

Tetch smiled a black-toothed grin and lashed out, slapping him with an open palm. "Honour? That boy ran with his tail tucked firmly between his little bollocks. I've been eating his table scraps for six years but not anymore."

Another soldier came into the loggia, his face red with exertion. "Captain, there's a another message here from Perusia, by way of the Palestro prelate."

Tetch held out his hand and the took the tiny rolled scroll. Even with his vision now blurred, Escalus could see that it was a pigeon-borne scroll, tightly curled. And his heart sank further as he realised that the temple priests were providing intelligence to Tetch. He watched as Tetch moved his lips to sound out the writing, his eyes screwed up and his nose practically touching the paper.

"Goddamn fools!" Tetch's fist crushed the note into a little wad and it fell to the tiles. He turned to Ramus. "They bungled it! He even met with the king today, the little bugger." He shook his head and swore.

Escalus began to cough, his chest convulsing. The cough slowly became a laugh. "The boy... not so weak as you think... he'll be back to slit your throat. I swear it."

The smile returned to Tetch's face, his one eye blinking rapidly for a moment. "I will *never* understand why Valerian Danamis brought you back from that Southland hole... Naresis, wasn't it?" He turned to Ramus. "Get down to the docks. The squadron sails tomorrow. Tell the others!" He turned his attention back to Escalus. "Sometimes there's no point in others doing your own work, is there? Now what was you and me wagging our chins about before?" He ran his thumb down the sword he still held.

Escalus spat a bloodied spray towards Tetch. "Your miserable lack of loyalty... and honour!"

Tetch wiped his doublet and nodded. "Yes, honour. Do you know what they say is the worst dishonour a man can suffer? I mean... other than having his balls cut off."

Escalus gave one last effort to throw off the arms of his captors. His head jutted forward as he made for Tetch but, strength all but gone, he crumpled.

"It's being killed with his own sword." His right arm drew back and with a rapid thrust he drove the blade through Escalus's belly and felt it bite between the back ribs and then push out the other side. "My greetings to your Southlander comrades in hell."

Twenty-Two

TIMANDRA FASTENED THE grey cloak she had liberated from the captain's cabin about Acquel's neck and freed up the hood at the back. She had already placed a shawl over her neck and shoulders as they prepared to make their unannounced trip ashore.

Danamis and Strykar had been gone for an hour and Timandra judged that if they were to have a moment to find the oculist, then it would have to be now. They loitered at the larboard rail near the sterncastle steps as Timandra carefully watched masters Bassinio and Gregorvero deep in conversation up in the fo'c'sle. They were arguing about the carpenter's work again and Gregorvero was in favour of letting the work pass as was while Bassinio demanded perfection. There were two sailors now stationed at the gangplank leading to the dock. A third—a *rondelieri*—had just gone to the fo'c'sle to relieve himself. The chances that Danamis's men would stop them were small and she knew it was now or never.

She yanked Acquel's forearm and the two calmly walked to the gangway and ascended the short step over the low railing. Timandra had just put one foot over when one of the sailors reached out and held her.

"Where are you off to, then?"

Timandra turned to him, her face stern. "Off to buy food since you lot don't seem to know what food is."

He smiled and grinned at his companion. "Well, little mistress, by all means. Piss off. But bring me back some pig!"

Acquel tutted and followed Timandra down the gangplank. They were soon striding across the wooden dock and ascending the stone steps leading to the pier side and the piazza beyond. As they entered the warren of lanes, Acquel pulled up the hood of his cloak and Timandra placed her shawl over her head. The streets, narrow as they were, were heaving with people, many pouring out from the main thoroughfare that led through the centre of the seaport up to the palace. Timandra and Acquel fought the flow of rough humanity as they made their way towards Guildsmens' Row. They were briefly spun around at one point by the press of bodies, so Acquel took the lead as Timandra gripped his shoulder and shouted directions into his ear.

They turned left and then right at a large tavern and straight into a group of drunken revellers who were singing and dancing their way past. A surge of Perusians, men and women both, pushed them to the side and Acquel found himself with Timandra between him and the wall of a house, their bodies close. She was laughing at the ludicrousness of their situation—the first true laugh he ever heard from her—and he too broke into a wide grin. As she looked up at him, cheeks red, her green eyes glistening, he found he was lowering his face to hers. He cupped her face in his hands as kissed her mouth. He felt her lips pushing his as she returned the kiss but in an instant, so too, he felt her hands pushing away his chest. For another instant, the kiss continued, lingered, and then she broke away. She looked down, pulling one end of the shawl closer about her.

"Who will hear your confession now? Or mine," she said softly.

"Timandra... I am sorry." He leaned in again and she gently placed two fingers on his mouth.

"No," she whispered. "It cannot be."

Acquel pulled back, the crowd now thinning behind him. "But why? Because I am a monk? I have not taken final vows, you know that!"

"No, it is because... It is not for me."

Acquel's brow creased. "I do not understand."

But Timandra had regained her steely edge. "We must go—now!" She pushed past, snatching his hand, and led the way.

They approached the Row from a stinking alley full of hissing cats, emerging at the opposite end. Timandra looked about her trying to remember where the shop was. She saw an oversized breastplate and helm hanging over a door—an armourer she had visited last time—and now remembered where the premises of the oculist lay.

Timandra was practically dragging him now, Acquel's head spinning with choked desire and the urgency of their mission. She scanned the shop fronts, doorways, and the hanging shingles of the craftsmen. After a few anxious moments she finally saw it and turned to him. "There!"

Acquel looked to see a pair of round spectacles fit for a giant hanging over an archway. He had seen a few of the monks wearing these devices fashioned of crystal and horn that gave them goggle-eyes like some monstrous frog.

She turned to him just as they were about to enter the doorway to the grey stone building. "Keep your hood up," she said, looking him in the eye. "And do not let on you are a monk or where you found the amulet. I will do the talking. Understood?"

Acquel nodded. "I will follow your lead."

They entered and found themselves in a room filled, ingeniously, with natural light. Two large workbenches stood in the front room and at one a man laboured with a small knife over the horn he was carving to fashion rims for lenses. Acquel looked up to see how skylights had been cut into the roof two floors above. The sunlight poured down and filled the workshop.

The young man looked up from his work. "Yes? What do you require, sir?"

Timandra spoke up. "We are looking for the master. He may remember me."

The apprentice gave a look of annoyance and hopped down from the stool he was perched upon. "Wait here."

He returned with an older and shorter man wearing a grey gown and a tight-fitting leather skull cap that covered his ears. Acquel marvelled at the round glass device that was strapped to his right eye with satin tapes tied about his head. The man slowly lifted the lens off and scratched at his thin grey moustache. "Do I know you both?"

"I am a trader for one of the free companies in Maresto," said Timandra. "You may remember that I have bought merchandise from you in the past."

The man took a few steps closer and shook his head. "No, can't say as I remember either of you. What is it you want. More stock?"

Timandra smiled. "Not this time. We were hoping you might assist with a translation we are puzzling over. I remember your knowledge of old Valdurian when you showed me your library."

The old man squinted at her. "Ah, now perhaps I do remember. Company of the Black Rose? Yes?"

"May we take a few minutes to show you something we have found... while on the march in Maresto?"

"What? A book?" The oculist impatiently gestured to his apprentice to return to his work. "I have little time to translate something of that length."

"No," said Timandra. "It is an artefact that has some writing on it. Maybe old Valdurian. We found it when clearing the ground for our camp. May we show you?"

Ever a curious man, the oculist looked at Acquel for a moment, assumed he was a mercenary, and then turned back to Timandra. "Well, I may be interested in seeing what you've found. But it will cost you. I'm a busy man."

"Agreed."

"Then come back here with me, into the rear workshop. And don't touch anything."

Acquel followed Timandra into the next room where more work tables were arrayed with panes of glass, polishing stones, and strange delicate metal tools that Acquel could only assume were for working the raw crystal into lenses. Like the front room, it too was lit by skylights supplemented with lamps on the table where the master himself had been busy.

"It is so wonderfully bright in here, as if one were out of doors," remarked Acquel as he followed the oculist to the rearmost work table.

The oculist cleared some documents away and plopped down a leather-bound book upon the table. "Mirrors. The proper placement of mirrored glass above reflects the sun's rays down here. I would have gone blind otherwise."

Timandra gestured to Acquel to take off the amulet. He did so and handed it to her, his heart filled with apprehension as to whether any of this was a good thing. Timandra took it from him and turned to the oculist.

"It is a piece of jewellery. An amulet of sorts." She placed it into his outstretched palm.

"Hmm. Yes, rather ancient..." He moved to another table and retrieved a lamp, bringing it back to where Acquel and Timandra stood. He looked again at the amulet, turning it over. He then sat on a stool and pulled down his magnifying lens over his right eye.

"You are right. Old Valdurian... but a very unusual script. A charming piece of lapidary skill—if a little crude." He paused and reached for a piece of parchment and drew a quill from the marble inkpot that sat at the corner of the cluttered table. "This script is most often seen engraved on old stones of worship around the kingdom. Places where they eventually built temples."

He began muttering to himself and then scribbling as he turned the amulet in his hand to catch more light. "Yes, it's devotional. You've noticed the sunburst symbol of the Faith?" He paused again and then turned around to face the pair. "Neither of you know what you have here. The script around the sunburst says: 'Eldred had me made.'"

Acquel looked at Timandra who did her best to look unimpressed. "And the rest?"

The oculist lowered the amulet. "This is clearly a relic of importance—and value. And it will cost you some coin to learn the rest, I'm afraid."

Timandra pursed her lips and reached into her belt purse. She pulled out five pieces of silver and held them out. The oculist tilted his head and raised his eyebrows in disappointment. Timandra dug again into her purse and pulled out a gold ducat. The oculist nodded and motioned for her to place the money on the table. He then turned his back and bent over the amulet again. He quickly picked up the quill and began writing.

"The reverse of this medallion carries the seven commandments of the blessed Saint Elded." He recited haltingly as he copied these down on the parchment.

"There is no God... but the Lord your Creator... You shall give thanks to the Lord in the Temple on the first day of the new moon... You shall not steal nor shall you fornicate. I am writing these down but I am sure you know them all, even if you don't follow them." He chuckled to himself and continued writing. Then he went quiet, the quill motionless in his hand. "But there are ten here," he whispered. He then started writing again, his head shaking in either dismay or surprise. He looked up quickly and leaned over on his seat to see where his apprentice was. He looked at Timandra, distrust sweeping across his face. The magnifier made one eye look a third larger than the other and Timandra was repulsed.

"There are *ten* commandments here!" he hissed at her. He turned and read the amulet, his voice suddenly becoming tight and strangled with his rising agitation. "The eighth says, 'He who serves in the Temple of the Lord is no higher than he who worships there. Beware false prophets.' The ninth—my God. 'Treat the Children of the Sea as you would treat one another; they are your Brothers and Sisters.'" He looked at Timandra and Acquel, his face changing again as the import of his words sank into his mind. "This is rank heresy! Where did you find this?"

Acquel felt his body go tense as the words filled his ears. Timandra grabbed the oculist by the shoulder and gave him a shake. "Tell us the tenth, damn you!"

The old man gave her a look of fear and anger mixed. He held the amulet up to his eye again. "The tenth," he whispered. "The tenth says, 'The union of Man and Mer is blessed in the eyes of the Lord.'"

Timandra took a step back. Acquel put a hand on her shoulder. "Timandra, we should leave. Now."

"First, he finishes writing it down," said Timandra, spinning the oculist on his stool. "Pick up that quill!"

"It's heresy!" he shot back. "Vile heresy. Take this away and get out of here! I could burn for helping translate this thing!"

Acquel reached under his cloak and slowly pulled his dagger out of his scabbard. He sidestepped Timandra and in an instant had its point placed at the neck of the oculist. "Do as she says!"

The old man reached again for the quill, dipped it into the well, and then scribbled again upon the parchment. "This will come to no good. I beg you to melt it down once you leave here." He threw the quill down. "There. Now get out." He pushed Acquel's arm away. And then he grasped Timandra's arm as his other hand whipped off the magnifier. His face was a mask of outright fear as panic gripped the old man. "Don't tell anyone I did this! I beg you!"

Acquel picked up the parchment and read the hastily scrawled words.

"Is it what he spoke?" asked Timandra. Acquel nodded, the implication of it washing over him again and again. "Yes."

Timandra snatched the amulet from him and gave it to Acquel. "And you would be wise to take the same advice. Tell no one we were here."

The oculist nodded and fair leapt off the stool. He ran to the back stairs, back hunched, and turned before he ascended. "Go! Now, damn you!"

Acquel took Timandra by the elbow as he crumpled the parchment in his fist. "We have to get back." She pulled up her shawl and strode rapidly from the house with Acquel right behind. They entered the crowded street and began diving and pushing between the townsfolk, working their way back to the quay.

They crossed the teeming piazza and walked briskly down the wide stone stairs that led to the tangle of wooden docks and back to the ship's berth. Suddenly, Timandra stopped and Acquel saw her head bow. He placed an arm around her shoulders and reached over and lifted her chin. Her eyes were moist but no tears fell.

"Sweet God, what have you found, Acquel? What you saw in the tomb... your dreams... the merfolk. Now this. What have you done. What have *I* done?"

Acquel felt a strange calmness fill him. "It is Elded's will. And his spirit is showing us this for a reason. I have to let him guide me. Guide me wherever it leads. I have nowhere I can run."

She looked up at him, his rough unshaven face suddenly looking older than a week ago when she had fed and clothed a young and frightened holy man; a holy man that doubted himself. "I am not sure I can follow you there. The Temple is hunting you. Now we know why. They will kill all of us. Just as they killed those other monks in the tomb." She grabbed his arm. "We mustn't tell Strykar! Nor Danamis."

"Very well. We keep the secret between us for now. Until I think of what to do next."

Timandra nodded. "Maresto. We will be safe there."

A cold, salt-laden breeze suddenly blew up from the bay and whipped across the quay, rattling mast lines and sails and tipping over stacked wicker crates on the dock. Acquel pulled her into an embrace, his cloak billowing, but she was limp in his arms.

KODORIS TAPPED AT his thigh with the flat of his palm. Repeatedly. She was late. They had arranged to meet in the gardens at the hour but time had moved on and Lavinia had not appeared, and he felt his skull was ready to burst with worry. Lucinda had not yet found and captured the young greyrobe and every passing day meant he could be spreading the word of what he had seen. Bad enough he had made it by ship to Perusia but why there if not to alert the king or the prelate? And why did she have so much trouble in seeing him when she could easily find others?

Brachus seemed to be more doddering and feeble-minded with each passing day. He had not even asked for further reports on the search. That was because he had forgotten the entire incident. It was only a matter of time before he would need to be replaced by one of the Nine. And thanks to his arm-twisting, he was now one of that number. He did not want to engage in that struggle without first ending the problem of Brother Acquel once and for all. But more than that, his little chats with the canoness had begun to unsettle him.

It had really only begun to sink in a few days previous just how peculiar a young woman she was. Perhaps no surprise for someone possessing the gift that she did. At times naïve, at others playful and almost lascivious, she teased and tantalised without really understanding what she was saying. And all this casual talk of her sister's interest in the days of Elded and the disciples. Random snippets of the sisters' conversation about Belial and the old gods, the missions of the early saints to stamp out the old ways, the worship of *trees*. The sacrifice of children. Why?

He adjusted his white leather belt and scanned the apartments of the palace cloister. He saw her staring out of a window. Not looking at him, but out into the distance. He suppressed an oath and stormed back inside. It took a chamber girl to get inside the apartments. Kodoris approached to find her still at the window, pale, her face frozen into an expression of intense concentration. He reached out and touched her shoulder. She collapsed at his feet. Kodoris cried out in alarm and lifted her up, carrying her over to the bed.

"You there! Fetch me some wine! Quickly!" The servant had stuffed her apron in her mouth but now turned and ran from the room.

"Lavinia, can you hear me?" Kodoris propped her head up with pillows. She was breathing but seemed as if asleep even though her eyes were still open. "Lavinia, girl!"

She made a sound in her throat and her eyes slowly came

back into focus. Her eyes closed and then opened again. She turned her head slightly towards Kodoris.

"Magister. I have been away."

Kodoris nodded earnestly. "Yes, my lady, you have. What have you seen?"

"I was preparing to come down to meet you when I had a vision. Very strong. I have seen the monk and the woman in Perusia."

Kodoris snapped his fingers as the servant returned, beckoning her over. He took the cup and offered it to Lavinia. She delicately took it in both hands and sipped, Kodoris supporting her golden head. She leaned back.

"It was odd. I was not even using the scrying mirror. It just washed over me and I was there." She tried to push herself up on her elbows. "They *did* take something from the tomb. Something small with writing." Her eyes shut as if the effort of memory was too much.

Kodoris grasped her wrist and tightened his grip. "What did they find? Think! Concentrate."

Her eyes fluttered open again. "There are *ten* commandments here! Heresy! You must go—now!"

Kodoris leaned in close to her. "Where? Where are they now?

Her voice hesitated, and she stared upwards at the canopy as if she saw with her mind's eye. "The Lawgiver's words. His commandments to us all. That which was lost."

Kodoris lifted her head and helped her to more wine. She coughed. "Where are they?" he demanded. "Look!"

Lavinia sat up, red wine dripping down the corners of her mouth and chin onto her chemise. She turned and looked up at the Magister.

"The craftsman. A master. The man... who makes spectacles."

Kodoris put both hands on her shoulders and looked

at her, his dark brown eyes burning into hers. "You must contact Lucinda and tell her. You must do it now."

She smiled strangely at him and put a hand on his. "Have I pleased you, Magister?"

Kodoris felt himself go cold. *Ten commandments*.

Twenty-Three

STRYKAR JAMMED THE butt of his hunting spear into his right stirrup and slid his grip down the shaft. "Fucking useless thing," he grumbled, as his horse ambled through the broken terrain and laurel bushes of the royal forest.

"It was afforded you as an honour," said Danamis, riding alongside and concentrating hard to keep control of the royal destrier atop which he was perched. The beast, to Danamis's dismay, kept snorting and ducking its head with obvious annoyance.

"An honour I could have done without," Strykar replied.

The sun beat down strongly but in the cool of the forest canopy it was comfortable, almost dank. Somewhere far ahead they could hear the barking of the greyhounds as they pursued their quarry deep into the oak and beech wood. They were well back from the main hunting party. Behind them came the royal household with pack mules laden with the moveable feast and a few of the more bored noblemen who rode even slower than Danamis, chatting all the while. In front, and just within view, they could see a cluster of riders: the dukes of Colonna and Milvorna and their retinues, and the Sinaen ambassador and his two councillors plus their guards. The latter walked on foot, clad in their enamelled black armour and leading the mounts of their lord. Each bore a nine-foot spear with a wicked-looking leaf-shaped blade, a red horsehair tassel just where the head attached to the pole. The ambassador cradled a red parasol against his shoulder as he rode, he and his advisors resplendent in their shining silk robes of many colours and sinuous designs. And just in front of them, Sempronius and his men trotted along, their voices bellowing among the trees.

"Your monk and the widow were rather quiet this morning before we left the ship," said Danamis as he watched the ambassador's parasol bounce off the dangling branches.

Strykar nodded. "Aye, but I expect they've had enough of sitting tight, waiting for God knows what to happen. We ought to be back in Maresto."

"I need more time with the king," replied Danamis. "To work on his sense of honour and loyalty."

Strykar shook his head. "For a pirate you are truly an optimist when you ought to be an opportunist."

The lead huntsmen sounded the horn; a long baleful note, followed by the baying of the hounds.

"About fucking time," said Strykar. "Give me three men and crossbows and we would have had venison on the plate an hour ago."

Danamis laughed as he ducked a low branch that his mount had guided him under, likely quite intentionally. "I think you're missing the point of the hunt, my friend. Let's ride ahead and catch them up."

Strykar lifted his reins and pulled out in front while Danamis followed, crashing past rhododendron thickets ten feet high. They overtook the dukes and their men and Danamis found it difficult to take his eyes from the Sinaens, their looks and clothing wholly strange in Valdur. Up ahead they could clearly see the king and his party, halted in a small clearing. The hounds were close by, and green-clad huntsmen were running back to report to the king.

The two rode into the clearing but held back from the king and his bodyguard. Sempronius, his flabby cheeks flushed bright red with excitement, spotted their arrival.

"Lord Danamis! Captain Strykar! Come, join Captain Polo and myself. We are about to go in for the capture, gentlemen."

Danamis bowed to the king and acknowledged Piero Polo with a nod.

"Glad to see that you are well enough to ride with us today, Danamis," said Polo, a broad smile on his face. "I knew you were fashioned of sterner stuff, my lad!"

"Indeed," echoed the king. "we are well pleased and happy that Lord Danamis survived such a foul attack." He tilted back the weighty coils of the elaborate felted wool chaperon that wound about his head and neck.

"I thank you for your concern, sire," said Danamis. "It was but a scratch."

The king turned in the saddle to look for the rest of the hunting party. "Not really joining in the spirit of things, these Sinae," the king grumbled. "My dukes are not much better. But my lord Xiang Liu Bo looks positively bored."

Piero Polo leaned over towards the king. "He *is* a *bo,* sire. What we would call a count here. And I don't believe he has hunted before."

The king made a face. "Never smiles either. None of them do. But at least he speaks some Valdurian."

"I am sure they are enjoying the sport, sire. Have no concern." Polo turned his mount around. "I shall suggest they join you, sire. Yes?"

The king nodded, obviously annoyed with the affair. "Yes, do ask them to close up the ground. We can't keep our great stag waiting."

As the others finally joined them in the glade, Danamis and Strykar set off and the entire group rode on to where the kennelmen and dogs had the animal penned in. They soon entered another clearing with few trees, but many laurel bushes and a large granite outcropping rising up from the forest floor. At its base, a thicket of laurel on either side, a massive red stag pawed the ground, snorting, head lowered and its rack of horns shaking with defiance. It was a giant, nearly as tall as a man at the shoulder and with an array of antlers that towered and spread like some monstrous bony claw. The greyhounds, mouths foaming, were being restrained from pouncing on the creature as the royal party came forward.

The king whooped and threw up a gloved hand. "By almighty God, it is a prodigious fine beast!" The Duke of Milvorna edged his horse close to the king's, as did the Duke of Colonna. Danamis knew little of the protocol of the hunt but he did remember that someone would be nominated by the king himself to dispatch the stag should he not wish to do so himself. The dukes both added their praise of the animal and urged the king to claim the honour of the kill. The king raised himself in his stirrups and looked around the hunting party, a playful look in his eyes.

"My lord ambassador," he called, "would you do us the honour of slaying the beast?"

Danamis smiled to himself. The right thing to do, for form's sake. But he doubted the delicate Sinaen would have either the skill or the will to wield a hunting sword or a spear. Strykar hung back, knowing that he had intentionally been handed a spear and afraid that the honour might go to him next.

But it was Xiang Liu who spoke up. "I am most humbled to be offered this great honour, your majesty," he said, in accented Valdurian. "And I accept."

Danamis smirked and even Piero Polo raised his eyebrows. But rather than dismounting, Xiang barked an order to one of his guards and gestured to the stag. The soldier bowed and strode across the clearing towards the creature where it stood its ground, stamping its hoof. The kennelmen whistled and shouted for their animals and the Sinaen took their place, moving towards the huge beast, his spear balanced in both hands. The king frowned and looked over to Polo who appeared just as surprised.

The Sinaen guard went into a slight crouch and extended his spear, lightly rapping the antlers. The stag brought its front legs up and then rammed forward. The Sinaen jumped backwards and spun his spear about, flourishing it in a series of rapid arcs as it twisted through both his hands. He paused and then lunged forward, carving off a section of antlers before pulling back his leg. The stag lowered its head and charged again. The Sinaen rapped it square on its forehead with the flat and then lopped off a section of horn on the right. The creature shook itself again, a spray of snot flying around it, and rose up on its hind legs in defiance and rage. The Sinaen, as fast as any man Danamis had seen in his life, gave another whirl of his spear at full arm's length, stepped in, and shot a straight thrust into the stag's chest, burying the spearhead full up to its tassel. The hart fell forward, crumpled onto its front legs and slowly rolled to its side. The Sinaen had withdrawn his weapon before it hit the ground.

There was a long and awkward silence in the clearing. The king motioned sternly to the master of the hunt who in turn signalled the horn. A blast sounded announcing the death. Danamis fidgeted in the saddle and looked at Strykar who seemed to be suppressing a belly laugh. The king began to applaud, a muffled lonely sound for his thick leather gloves. But he was quickly joined by the dukes and the others and a few cries of "Bravo!" burst forth.

"Well thrust, my dear Count! Your man is an excellent spearman." The king turned his horse to face the ambassador. Xiang in turn gave a bow of his head under his parasol. The king turned again to the hunt master. "Undo the beast and reward the hounds!"

The party returned to the first clearing to find tables assembled and draped in fine brocades; a sumptuous spread of smoked hams, cheeses, quail eggs, roast pheasants and silver ewers of wine. The king sat at table with the ambassador and the dukes while Danamis and Strykar hovered at the fringe with some of the lesser nobles. The master of the hunt returned with a silver charger bearing the slashed heart of the stag and all applauded as he knelt before the king before bearing it away.

"Watching that Sinaen dispatch the beast was worth the wait, I do confess," whispered Strykar as he eyed the food and drink. "But that is one less trophy mount for the king, I'm afraid." A retainer approached and offered them both a cup of wine. Danamis rubbed his side.

"I could have done without being rattled for half the morning on horseback," he muttered. "Probably have opened the wound again."

"Bah, the widow will stitch you up on ship. You had better think about getting the king's ear while you have the chance."

Danamis nodded. "Yes, but not here." He took a long swig of wine.

The musicians had finally caught up with the hunt and now began serenading the party with lute, flute, and shawm. Strykar had managed to liberate half a pheasant and found a tree to lean against while he ate. Danamis watched Piero Polo as he walked amongst the king's guests, the most famous man in the kingdom, laughing with the noblemen in attendance. Was Strykar right to distrust him? Had he ordered the assassins? That Tetch could track him so quickly seemed unlikely. But what motive would Polo have for doing away with him?

Danamis became aware of the greyhounds, still out in the woods. Their barking had suddenly intensified and he thought perhaps they were fighting over the scraps. But the master of the hunt suddenly dashed across the clearing and bowed low to the king. He was breathing heavily, eyes large and shaking as if he had been chased by a bear.

"Sire, the hounds have cornered something! We're keeping it at bay but, it is not…"

The king dropped his napkin on the table. "It's not what? What *is* it then?"

"Sire, it appears to be a satyr."

The king stood up and the rest with him, though it was not clear as to why the sovereign had risen.

"By all the Saints. A satyr has not been sighted in this forest since I was a boy. Take me!"

The table was in an uproar as the dukes rushed after the king and his bodyguard, who were already halfway across the clearing and into the woods. The Sinaens looked confused and began exchanging words while Polo tried to explain what was happening.

Danamis ran to Strykar who had just tossed the pheasant to the ground. "We must follow!"

No one had bothered to remount, all made a pell-mell dash into the trees and towards the sounds of vicious barking. They did not need to go far, for the satyr had been cornered at the same granite outcrop as the stag. Danamis looked and saw a crouching figure, backed up against the lichen covered rocks, its dark waxy face a pitiful mask of fear as it recoiled from the snarling greyhounds. The satyr had backed itself up against the outcrop as far as it could go, its hooves scrabbling for purchase on the crumbling stones. Its large head of thick black curls, two curling horns rising from the top, twisted about as it saw the new arrivals. Danamis watched as the creature's face changed from terror to anger. It had probably never been trapped before. Now it found itself surrounded by soldiers and dogs. Did it blame itself for wandering too close to the domain of men?

Two of the king's bodyguard raised crossbows and took aim but the king raised his hand to stay them from shooting. Danamis edged a little closer, Strykar alongside.

"I've never even glimpsed one of these creatures before," he whispered.

Strykar nodded. "I did, once, in the forests of Ivrea. They are fleet of foot. So why was this bugger stealing through the forest and how did he get himself caught?"

The satyr's visage melted again into one of abject fear. To Danamis, it seemed almost childlike in its swirling frustrations. It turned again as more arrived. The Sinaens and Captain Polo entered the clearing, and even the ambassador was gaping at what he saw. The satyr tilted its head, seemingly in bemusement, at the ambassador's party. It suddenly made a move to the side, but a black greyhound lunged and snapped, the huntsman straining to keep it in check upon its lead. The satyr recoiled.

"Who are you, beast-man, to come into the royal wood?" shouted Sempronius. "What is your business here?"

The satyr tucked an ear into its shoulder at the voice of the king.

"Damn you! Can you not speak?"

The Duke of Milvorna spoke up from where he stood near to the king. "Make him sing, sire! Sing for his life and his liberty!"

Sempronius smiled and nodded. "An excellent suggestion, your Grace." He put his hands on his hips and stood square as he turned back to the satyr, its brown chest glistening with sweat. "You heard him! Sing us a song and entertain us. I know you know our tongue."

The satyr gave the king a cold stare, its mask changing to one of defiance.

The king tapped the elbow of one of the crossbowmen. The man walked forward and brought the bow up to his shoulder. This elicited such a cry of frustrated anguish from the creature that the assembled nobles exchanged worried glances. It was unnaturally loud, reverberating through the ancient oaks. Sempronius was not deterred.

"Sing! I command you!"

The satyr looked around itself, at all of the noblemen. For an instant, his eyes seemed to settle upon Danamis, almost as if it recognized him. Danamis felt his shoulders tense. But the satyr moved its dark eyes elsewhere, to the rolling canopy of green over its head. It seemed as if it was giving up its anger, submitting to fate. A few seconds later it opened its mouth and the most pitch perfect, aching melody poured from its throat. It was a sad strange song that none there had ever heard, the words sounded in clear Valdurian but with a trilling lilt that echoed across the clearing. It was a song of the forest, of the reign of nature unbound. Danamis watched the alarm on the king as they heard the creature evoke names not spoken except in hushed tones, the names of the banished pantheon: Belial, Beleth, and Andras.

But the melody itself was haunting and beautiful and all there stood transfixed, enchanted by the song but also frightened by the pagan flood of emotion. The song rose and fell and the satyr fell into silence. The greyhounds barely whimpered. Not even a bird could be heard. The king appeared frozen in confusion; amazed and alarmed in the same instance. The crossbowman lowered his weapon and looked at the king.

Sempronius lifted his arm and gestured. "Begone! I give you your freedom!"

The huntsmen backed off with their hounds, giving the creature space. It blinked a few times and then hesitantly edged sideways along the outcrop and away from the hunting party. Then it leapt like a deer and plunged into a thicket of greenery as the dogs strained and barked. For a moment, no one spoke. Danamis and Strykar exchanged looks and Strykar raised his eyebrows. Someone laughed and then, like a small stream widening to become a river, others shared the laugh. Even the king broke into a smile.

A voice sounded, crisp and booming, and all looked up to see the satyr perched on the very top of the rocky outcrop, looking down on them. It held out a hairy arm, its extended finger singling out the king.

"Men of Valdur! War is coming! A war to swallow all your lands!"

Both crossbowmen raised their weapons high but the king raised his hand, his face set hard. The satyr jabbed the air.

"And you, mighty king of Valdur... you will not live to see its end!"

The king brought his arm down sharply and both bows snapped. One quarrel bounced off the top of the outcrop, the other sailed past where the satyr had stood an instant before. It was gone. And for the second time, there was silence in the clearing.

"AYE, WELL," said Strykar, "at least we didn't have to suffer any more of the nobility after that little entertainment." They had returned their horses to the grooms and were walking back through the palace, following the main corridor down towards the outer courtyard. Danamis didn't reply. He knew that his chance to speak with the king was now ruined and it only remained for him to return to the ship and hope for an audience on the morrow. As they entered the great open courtyard and its raised fountain of carved stone, they saw the chamberlain and two soldiers waiting for them.

"My lords," said Raganus, as they emerged into the open, "you were not planning on taking your leave just yet, I trust."

Danamis stopped in front of him. "It seemed a safe assumption that the festivities were at a close."

"And any word of which would be best left unsaid outside the palace. Wouldn't you agree?"

"I would. But many people witnessed it—including our Sinaen guests."

Raganus smirked. "That is not your concern. But we have other matters to discuss before you leave today. My men will escort Captain Strykar to the gatehouse."

Strykar moved a hand to his hilt and looked at Danamis.

"Do what he says," Danamis told him, his voice quiet. "I will meet you at the gate."

Raganus led Danamis back to the residence and its chequered tile floors and ugly tapestries. They entered a doorway off one of the corridors and entered a room packed with stacks of books and rolls of parchment, all piled on heavy refectory tables, much too large for the size of the chamber.

Raganus shut the door while the soldiers remained outside. "Lord Danamis, there is unfinished business I know you are anxious to resolve. I am directed by the king to discuss this now."

Danamis folded his arms. "Here? Now?"

"It is as good a place as any."

"And the king is not to see me?"

Raganus attempted a look of sympathy. "Alas, he is not now. Particularly in light of what you witnessed this afternoon. But we have discussed his views at length prior."

"So tell me."

"The king believes the status of the Palestro fleet is secure.

You and Captain Tetch must work out your disagreements between yourselves. It is not the king's concern except that he have allegiance and the service of the fleet."

Danamis felt his anger well up anew, his throat tightening. "You don't even know that you have Tetch's allegiance!"

Raganus smiled. "But we do, Lord Danamis. He delivered a chest of gold coin to the palace yesterday along with a letter addressing the situation."

Danamis closed the distance between him and the old man. "You're saying Tetch is here in Perusia?"

"I don't believe that he is. Nevertheless, the treasure—a gift to the king—was delivered by his messengers. The High Prelate of Perusia and his priests."

Danamis could ill conceal his dismay. The priesthood had helped Tetch? He looked out across the room and the years of records, treaties, and agreements it held on its shelves and groaning tables. His father's bargain with the House of Sempronius was probably buried under the dust here too.

"My lord Danamis, it's best that you seek some negotiation with Tetch. Return to Palestro." Raganus tried an accommodating smile but it ended up looking like he'd chewed a lemon. "Or... else, seek your fortune in some other place. You're still a young man, a seasoned sailor and commander. I understand that Captain Polo is putting together another expedition to the east."

Danamis looked hard at the baron but could hardly focus his thoughts to respond to the patronizing toad. Anger burned in his belly but the wind had fled his sails. He nodded slowly.

"It appears I have much to consider. So... I shall take my leave of you, Baron. And the hospitality of the king."

But even as he entered the gatehouse and left the palace behind, flanked by guardsmen, Nicolo Danamis was contemplating one last desperate throw of the dice.

Twenty-Four

LUCINDA DELLA ROVERA, canoness of St. Dionei, walked softly into the workroom of the oculist, gently holding the waist of her dress in both hands to raise its delicate hem from the floor. Captain Flauros was barely two paces behind. Three of his men remained at the door of the shop to discourage any further customers, though this was unlikely as Perusians were now gathering like moths to a candle in the central piazza to learn their luck in the royal lottery. The fourth guardsman, Tobias, he had sent to the harbour to keep close eye for the carrack they had been searching for; one captained by the infamous pirate and so-called admiral of Palestro, it had turned out. It was a discovery that worried him and the canoness both, for it was no mere merchant captain that the young monk had joined with.

The oculist looked up from his table as Lucinda entered and he dropped his tools and raised his eyepiece when he saw it was a woman—a woman of quality. He scrambled down from his seat and met her halfway, giving a smile and a bow while pulling the grease-stained brown leather coif from his bald head.

"Dear lady," he oozed. "What is it that you require? Sure one as young and beautiful as you has no need of spectacles. An aged father perhaps?"

Lucinda's smile widened further. "No, sir. I am here to obtain some intelligence from you."

The oculist's eyes now settled on Flauros, stone-faced, standing behind her. He laughed nervously and proffered her a chair near the table. "What could I possibly have of interest to you?"

"You saw a man and a woman here. The man may have had the appearance of a cleric. They showed you a piece of jewellery. A medallion perhaps?"

The colour drained from the oculist's face as he begin to stutter like some simpleton. "No... no clerics have visited, my lady."

She extended her hand, the smile still fixed on her lips. "Please take a seat, sir. Tell me what you know."

The oculist dropped down hard into the chair. "Many people come here every day. I cannot remember everyone!" he protested, hands starting to tremble.

Flauros slowly walked around the side of the room to take a station behind the oculist. Lucinda shook her head and moved to the work table, absently picking up a grinding tool and a small hand mirror.

"They showed you something very, very old, I think. Something they didn't understand." She held the mirror out in front of the oculist's face. "But *you* understood, didn't you? When you saw it."

The man ran a trembling hand across his mouth. "I told them to throw it away! I swear it! Has the prelate sent you? I did not know it was heresy that they carried."

Lucinda placed the mirror gently back upon the table, but the smile had now left her face. "Tell me what it was."

"It was a token... an amulet of sorts. Covered in old script.

Very old, as you say."

Lucinda put a hand on the oculist's shoulder and she felt him flinch. "You have nothing to fear. Just tell me what it said."

"Indecipherable," he mumbled.

From behind, Flauros rested a gloved hand lightly on top of the little man's head and gave it a gentle pat. "My lady?"

Lucinda raised her eyebrows. "Flauros... have patience." She turned her gaze back to the oculist. The words came from her mouth slowly and softly but encased in steel. "Tell... me... what it said."

Flauros noticed that her eyes were not blinking as she looked at the little man. They were boring into the object of her regard like a shipwright's drill. The oculist went rigid, his head twitching as if some fly was buzzing his face. His throat made a gurgling noise as if his mind was fighting for words. And then it all came tumbling out.

"Heresy. New commandments of the Saint. Ten commandments not seven! Beware false prophets! Treat the children of the sea as you would one another!" His head fell down and she seized his chin and pulled him up again.

"Write them down. Write all of it!" She motioned for Flauros to fetch the quill and paper.

The oculist sobbed. "I can't... can't remember!"

She clapped both hands on either side of his head, her face close to his. "You will remember!"

Flauros raised him by the scruff of his doublet and set him in front of the paper, the quill extended. The oculist was as if drunk, head lolling, but he wrote rapidly. Lucinda watched as he scratched ten lines of text deeply into the parchment, the goose quill squeaking. She stepped back and Flauros pushed the oculist back into the chair.

"Lastly, sir," said Lucinda, "look at me!"

The oculist raised his head, his mouth quivering.

"Who else knows? Your apprentices? Friends? Who?"

"Not a soul! I swear it! No one knows!"

She concentrated on him, digging deeper into his mind, delving past the fear that poured from him. He began to gibber, his eyes losing focus and rolling up. She broke her gaze.

"Good," she said.

She picked up a long workman's knife, the sort using for carving horn and wood. She placed it in his right hand. "Now you must save the Faith from heresy." Again she looked at him, eyes wide and unmoving. And again, the oculist went rigid, his hunched form sitting up straight in the chair. Flauros watched in wonder at her skill, and admiration. His lips parted slightly in anticipation of what she could accomplish.

His hand shaking, eyes locked onto Lucinda's, the oculist raised the knife to his throat. It lay there, motionless for a moment or two, and then pressed deep against his neck. Lucinda, never breaking her gaze, moved back a few steps. The oculist's eyes went wide as he looked past her into the middle distance, into nothingness. He quickly drew the blade across his flesh. A fountain erupted, spattering his chest and the chair. The oculist slumped forward, blood dripping around him onto the wooden floor, the knife still locked in his grasp.

Lucinda seized the parchment and scanned it rapidly. Flauros thought, just for a moment, he detected something in her face he had not seen before. Amusement.

"My lady!" he called.

She turned to him.

"I too now know that secret," he said, the trace of a teasing smile on his face. "Would you give me the same medicine?"

"Oh, Flauros!" she said, dismissing his concern. "You and I are of the same mind—and heart. We shall do great things together."

Flauros stepped around the crumpled body. "The greyrobe didn't kill the other monks, did he? He found out this—

maybe something more besides. That's why Kodoris wants him found, and found without a fuss."

Again, a curious half-smile crossed her features. "What are you saying, captain?"

"Kodoris had them killed. And four of my men went missing before another day had passed."

She folded her hands in front of her, opal-blue eyes staring into his. "And what if I was to tell you that your surmise is correct?"

Flauros nodded. "I never believed you were doing just Kodoris's bidding in all this. There's more to this quest than that."

She smiled at him and extended a lithe arm for him to take. Flauros kept his gaze upon her as he slowly closed the distance between them. Lucinda's long-fingered hand slipped in over his forearm and she squeezed.

"Bring me inside, my lady." His words were spoken like a lover's plea, honeyed, but demanding. "Share all of this truth you possess. Let me be your sword."

She reached up and stroked his bearded cheek playfully. "We shall see, Flauros. We shall see."

THE HARBOURMASTER'S LADS strolled along the mole with torches, lighting the braziers as darkness fell on Perusia. Groups of men came and went: fisherfolk, sailors, lightermen, most heading to the hostelries and taverns that littered the quayside streets. Acquel and Timandra stood in the fo'c'sle, both wrapped in cloaks to stave off the chill damp air blowing up from the bay. They had shared little of their thoughts the remainder of the day. They had, however, spoken with Strykar since the return from the palace. The latter had arrived back with Danamis in a terrible state, and they had seen the dark despair written on the face of the pirate. Strykar had told them of the king's refusal to offer aid. It was now back to Maresto and, for Danamis at least, an uncertain future.

"I for one won't be sad about leaving," said Timandra, leaning over the railings. "Even if the admiral didn't get what he wanted."

"I feel for him," said Acquel quietly as he looked out into the sea of masts in the last purple light of the dying day.

"We don't have any business being here. Never did. It was just blasted luck."

"But I have found some answers here," replied Acquel. "Not comforting ones, but answers nonetheless." He suddenly remembered their brief embrace earlier that day. He found it difficult to understand how she had buried that so quickly.

"Well, Strykar says we sail in the morning, ready or not. Danamis is determined to get out to sea."

Acquel nodded. He had watched them late in the afternoon loading wine barrels into the hold and taking on more provisions. So too, had he observed Gregorvero and Bassinio putting the new men through hell as they instructed them in the traditions of the *Royal Grace*. Bassinio in particular had become a harsh taskmaster since his maiming, half his face a mass of pink and white scabs, his head shaven. His eyes moved to the deck and railings that had been mauled in the escape from Palestro and the duel with the Southland corsairs. All as if never damaged, the new dark green paint still smelling of oils. Now most of the crew were below deck, eating or making final preparations for the voyage. Below where he stood, on the main deck, a few of the pirates joked and conversed while a contingent stood guard at the gangplank amidships. A light appeared across from him on the sterncastle. Someone had lit the great lantern at the rail. He watched as Master Gregorvero came down the steps to the main deck and ambled to the gunwales, staring out at the beacons blazing on the mole.

"We should go down now," said Acquel.

Timandra brushed back red locks from her face. "Yes, I'm growing cold."

Acquel let her leave the fo'c'sle first and he followed down the staircase and then again down to the main deck.

Timandra turned back to him. "I will go in and see how Strykar fares. Probably ought to tend to Captain Danamis's wound too. Will you come?"

Acquel forced a smile. "Yes, I will join you shortly."

Timandra touched his arm and moved off towards the stern stairs. Acquel sighed and walked over to Gregorvero, who was staring off over the quayside, obviously in a contemplative mood. He gave a greeting which was not returned until he repeated himself.

"Ah, young monk," Gregorvero said, almost as if he'd been dozing. Acquel had not heard him use that phrase before. He was always being shouted at as "brother monk" or "useless", but never that. The master kept staring out and Acquel followed his gaze. A large gang of seamen were ambling and laughing across the quay just before where the piazza began. And closer, standing around one of the flaming braziers, was another group, closely clustered and unmoving. It was these that Gregorvero was observing. And as Acquel started watching them, so too did he feel the amulet weighing against his chest, growing warmer. He reached inside his doublet and shirt and grasped it. It felt as if it had been lying in strong sunlight, not too hot to hold, but warmer than his body. And then he became aware of a sensation in his mind, not particularly sinister, but it was as if he was being observed.

"Come with me for a walk," said Gregorvero. "It is a fine night and I have a mind to stretch my legs."

Acquel looked at him. He still had not lifted his gaze from the shore. "A walk? Now?" He gave an awkward laugh.

"Come with me for a walk," Gregorvero repeated, his tone unchanged. He moved around Acquel and stepped up onto the steeply sloping gangway that connected the carrack to the dock. He thumped down the plank. Acquel knew something wasn't quite right but he was also curious and confused by the master's manner. He grabbed the opening in the gunwale, hopped up, and followed Gregorvero down to the dock.

He followed the rotund master and his rolling gait up the rickety dock and onto the stone quay and mole. They were heading to one of the braziers, the one with the men gathered around it.

"Master Gregorvero, where are we going?"

No answer followed. Acquel could now see those ahead: four men and a smaller figure that on closer view he saw to be a woman. As he drew near, he saw the men spread out, one coming towards him, the woman at his side. She drew back the hood of her cloak and he could see her long pale face illuminated in the firelight. He had never seen her before but somehow her expression made him believe she knew him. She was looking him straight in the eye—and nearly into his soul. He found himself sinking into her gaze, transfixed. A calming confidence settled on him like a warm blanket. He took a few hesitant steps towards her. *Did* he know her?

An instant later, burning pain lanced across his breastbone as if the amulet that dangled on his chest had become red hot. He bent forward, clutching at the jewel, his forward movement abruptly halted. Gregorvero stopped in his tracks, and shook his head as if he'd been punched. They were still about ten paces away. To Acquel, it appeared as if Gregorvero had been drugged or sleepwalking.

He heard the woman yell, "Take him!" and watched as the man next to her moved towards him, hands outstretched. Acquel jumped behind Gregorvero and drew his dagger. The amulet had now cooled as suddenly as it had heated. Another message from Elded delivered. He glimpsed a second man moving on his left and making a lunge to grab his arm. Acquel lashed out and slashed the assailant's wrist. The man fell back with a yell and a curse. The first man, tall and with features made sharper in the firelight, moved on him again. Acquel shoved Gregorvero with all his might, pushing him into the attacker. Gregorvero was coming out of his stupor and Acquel heard him swear an oath as the big seaman shoved the tall man backwards and then took a swing. The tall man in turn ducked the punch and made for Acquel again, drawing his own dagger as he moved.

Acquel went into a crouch, dagger forward as he heard the woman cry out again, "Don't kill him!"

The ship's master was now lashing out and careening into them all as if he had woken up in the middle of a street brawl.

Acquel cried out as loudly as he could. "Murder! Murder! Strykar!" Never losing sight of the man in front of him, he could still just make out the woman in the corner of his vision. He knew she was watching him, calling him. His eyes were desperate to follow her, pulled by her presence as if he were the needle to her beautiful, living and breathing lodestone.

His assailant shot forward, knocked Acquel's dagger to the side and tried for a kick to pull out his leg from under him. Acquel pivoted left, lashed out again at one of the other attackers who was trying to flank him, and then back-pedalled. He heard a woman scream somewhere behind him—Timandra he thought—and then the ship's bell was set to clanging.

The man was at him again, and this time, at this range, Acquel's memory ignited and he recognized the face of the man who had demanded his life on the road from Livorna: Flauros, the captain of the Temple guard. He parried a thrust and sidestepped again. Two of the attackers had now drawn swords and Gregorvero, having regained his senses, raised his hands and began backing away. Flauros yelled to his men.

"Get around behind him, damn you!"

Acquel roared and lunged at Flauros, straight for his throat. It was easily parried and he felt a fist slam into his cheek, sending him reeling. A yell sounded to his right and he saw a figure hurtle past, straight into the swordsmen. It was Strykar. Another soldier from the ship flew past Acquel and thrust through one of the attackers. Strykar took on two opponents at once, his sword swinging with such ferocity it sent the two reeling backwards. Acquel saw Flauros break off and dash over to the woman who herself was backing away from the fray. Flauros seized her arm and the two ran headlong for the piazza and the streets beyond. The other assailants, perhaps unaware that their captain had fled, redoubled their efforts and came on again, despite their worsening odds. Strykar parried a high cut which slammed down into the quillons of his sidesword but instantly gave a blow of his own with a snap-turn of the wrist, biting deep into his opponent's collarbone and nearly severing his head. The last attacker turned and made to run for it but the bolt of a crossbow brought him down, shot through the back.

Acquel sank to his knees, still clutching his dagger in his fist.

Strykar clasped Gregorvero by the back of the head. "Are you whole? Unhurt?"

The master nodded, rubbing his forehead.

Strykar looked down at Acquel. "By all the devils of hell, brother monk, what in the blessed Saint's name was that all about?"

Acquel hauled himself up off the stones. He was shaking. More of the crew had now appeared, surrounding them. He saw Timandra push her way through, mouth agape.

Strykar wheeled around and scanned the piazza before looking again at the dead men. He put a toe into one of them who lay sprawled on the blood-slicked cobbles. "Too well dressed for ruffians. They must have thought Master Gregorvero was Danamis." He cursed again, and turned back to Acquel. "They were having another go, damn them."

"No," said Acquel. "They were here for me."

FLAUROS DIDN'T STOP running until he was sure there was no pursuit. He and Lucinda had ducked down into the network of small alleyways on the far side of the piazza, no idea as to where they were headed. After a few anxious minutes, he slowed his pace, his hand still gripping her wrist, his sword in the other. He stopped with his back against a house and twisted her around to face him, gripping her upper arm tightly.

"You said he would follow you! That you could master him!" Flauros shook her with each outburst. "That nearly got all of us killed. The whole pirate's nest emptied into us, woman!" For a moment he saw her haughtiness crumble, self-doubt rising up. But she rallied, both arms flailing up to knock away his grasp.

"It *was* working!," she spat back. "But something broke the—" she was about to utter *charm* but the word stuck in her throat. "The monk has some protection from my gift."

"Tell that to my men lying dead back there. And now we've lost our chance. Lord knows where they will go next."

Her face grew hard and confident. "I know where he will go next. And so does my sister. He has questions. Questions for where there is only one place to get the answers."

Flauros growled and seized her arm again. "You're going to tell me everything, my lady. I shall not risk my neck again until I know the truth of it all."

She didn't pull away from him even though she could feel his grip crushing her bicep. She looked into his face. "You may not like where that truth leads you."

Flauros pulled her to his chest and kissed her hard. She did not resist him. The wound below her collarbone tingled slightly, a murmur only she could hear, and then was still.

Twenty-Five

THE LANTERNS BURNED all night upon the *Royal Grace*. The gangplank was drawn up, netting strung along the sides, bowmen set to pace the decks, and two seamen who'd drawn short straws crouched miserably in the crow's nest. A heavy, discomfited anticipation settled upon the ship. Danamis, sitting in his cabin, grey-faced and drawn, had demanded answers as to how and why. Answers that Acquel did not readily have. Danamis believed that the Temple guard might return in force, a concern bolstered by his new knowledge that the priesthood had conspired against him because of the myrra trade. How they could have possibly tracked Acquel so quickly he could not fathom, but he knew this business of the tomb and the amulet was at the heart of it. And why not just publicly arrest the monk and take him away by force? Why such a ruse as kidnapping by stealth? To his mind, it meant they feared what Acquel knew about the long-dead saint, and what he might tell others.

As for Acquel, as much as he wanted to share what he and Timandra had discovered about the amulet, he held his tongue, as did she. Strykar cursed himself for letting his guard down and wondered aloud who the blonde woman was and how she seemed to have almost bewitched the ship's master into wandering towards her. That was, if Acquel's account of the woman was to be believed. Poor Gregorvero was little help, for he had no recollection of even leaving the vessel, just lashing out as he awoke like a man from a deep, drunken stupor. At length, a tired and fractious Danamis announced that he would make sail in the morning light and that Perusia—and the king—could go to hell. The night wore on, the moon set, and those who could slumbered away the short remaining hours.

Shortly after dawn, Acquel awoke with a start from his thin horsehair mattress in the fo'c'sle, its peculiar nasty odour his first sensation of the new day. A few sailors snored around him, those from the last watch of the night he assumed. As with every morning, his damp clothing clung to his body. He rubbed his hand over the stubble of the tonsure and swallowed hard, his throat dry and sore. More dreams had plagued him through the night. Dreams that were now taking on a strange sort of narrative, almost making sense. Leading him.

As he emerged onto the main deck, eyes squinting in the brightness of the new day, he could see the final preparations being made for departure: men in the rigging making sails ready, the lateen spar being hoisted into place by half a dozen grunting sailors, the last few supplies being tossed and stowed below deck. A few of the crew gave him dark looks: they knew now he was at the centre of the fracas on the quay and they wanted to know why. After a few minutes, Acquel spotted Timandra emerging from the stern cabin and he went to her.

"We must speak," he said.

She looked to have slept badly, her eyes red, and she pulled up her shawl to cover her head. Acquel placed his hand on her arm.

"I had another dream."

She looked up at him. "And you wish to share this with me?"

"You need to know what I am... seeing."

She nodded, reluctant or resigned, he couldn't tell.

"I dreamt of the Ara back in Livorna," he said, his voice quiet as he lead her to the side of the stairs and out of the way of bellowing seamen. "The great cellars below the Temple and cloister. I have been down there many times but never too deep. But there is a door in my dream. A huge door of black oak, studded with iron and bound with bars and locks. Somehow, I know I must unlock this door, but I don't know how. I watch and the iron studs begin to glow red hot, each becoming a letter of script. I want to read what it says but the door recedes and I wake."

"Acquel," she said, shaking her head, "you could have summoned that up from your memory. How do you know it is a vision?"

"Because I had it three times last night. And then there was a fourth dream. I saw *him* again. So real..." The words halted in his throat as he struggled to express what his mind had unveiled; an unwelcome gift.

"Who?" said Timandra, gripping his hand.

"The saint of saints. Elded. He was on the beach where I had last dreamt of him. He had with him a wooden chest. He wanted me to open it."

Timandra felt a shudder of apprehension run through her. "Did he speak to you?"

"No. He gestured to the wooden chest... with that hand... such long fingers." Timandra watched Acquel's face contort at the recollection. "He smiled at me and beckoned."

"Then what happened?"

Acquel lowered his chin and shut his eyes. "I knelt down and reached out. And then I woke."

"It must be just a dream," she whispered.

"But what the amulet can do. What we found out yesterday. Can't you see? The great saint is working *through* me. I don't know what to do anymore!"

Timandra raised her two fingers rapidly to her forehead and then down to her chest in a blessing.

"I am part of this now," he said. "His spirit is guiding me towards something. Something I must do. Can't you see?"

"Come to Maresto," she pleaded. "Stay with the company. With *us*."

"Timandra, they will never leave me alone. They've hunted me all the way here. They will not give up. They will come to Maresto. I can't just wait for them to find me. I have to *do* something." He held her by her shoulders. "I need you with me—wherever I have to go."

She pulled his hands down, tears welling. "I can't follow you in this. I am a sinner... I'm—tainted." She swept past him and bounded up the stairs to the stern cabin.

He started to follow, her name on his lips, but a commotion had erupted on the deck and he turned to watch the crew pointing to something coming towards the ship along the quay, down from the piazza. He saw a grand palanquin borne by ten liveried men and an armed escort of halberdiers front and rear coming to a halt just opposite the *Royal Grace*. In an instant, fear washed over him. *Could they be here to take him?*

Gregorvero pushed past him and fair leapt up the stern staircase to alert Danamis and Strykar. Acquel felt as if his feet were nailed to the deck. The halberdiers, all giants it seemed, were dressed in the slashed multicolour fashion of Perusia, some wearing hose with each leg a different colour of fine wool. Every man wore a floppy black felt bonnet that sat at a rakish angle over one ear. As they stood, unmoving, two of the bearers, with practised skill and speed, deployed the wooden legs of the palanquin. Gently it was set down and the heavy curtain opened at one side. Two bearers moved closer to assist the occupant as they emerged.

At that moment, Danamis came down the stairs, his eyes wide at the small pageant on the quay. Acquel heard him muttering a well-known prayer as he reached the main deck, still fumbling with the buttons of his doublet. Strykar and Gregorvero were right behind. Their faces told Acquel that this was an unexpected visit and not one likely to be welcome.

A high-born woman was lifted out of the palanquin by her retainers. She wore a full court dress of saffron-coloured satin, slashed at the sleeves to show the fine pure white silk of her chemise. At her breast a set of golden necklaces adorned with pearls shimmered in the morning sunlight. Her white silk gauze veil dripped with pearls, all along its hem, each sparkling and vibrating as she took a few slow steps towards the ship. The veil was held in place by a circlet of gold, the crown of a queen.

Bassinio was now moving amongst the sailors crowding the starboard side of the deck, pushing them back and demanding their silence. Danamis quickly met Gregorvero's eye. The master gave him a stern look and toss of the head, telling Danamis to get down the gangplank. Slowly, he clambered up and then down the wooden board, his booted feet bouncing on the creaking wood of the dock, and he rapidly ascended the small set of stone steps up to the quay. He stopped and looked at the woman. She in turn gave a near imperceptible nod, motioning him to come forward. When Danamis reached her, he knelt down on one knee, his arms spread wide, palms upwards.

"My queen! We are honoured by your presence."

"You look terrible," she replied, like an amused mother trying to scold a precocious mud-caked child. "And do get up, Nico. I can't converse with you down there."

Danamis drank in her beauty, still as glowing as when he had first met and flirted with her as a boyish and brash commander when she was still just Cressida of House Guldi, the daughter of the Duke of Colonna. Not the queen of Valdur. And although she was six years older than he, a secret dalliance had ensued, one swiftly snuffed out by the duke's castellan, and luckily no one—not least the Duke—the wiser for it. She extended a ringed hand, which he gently grasped and kissed, and then he stood, somewhat inelegantly.

"That's better," she cooed, nodding. "I was anxious to come as early as possible as I had an inkling you would be departing rather soon. And I have learned of this attempt on your life. You were wounded. Does it trouble you? The royal chirurgeon should have been summoned for you but it appears my fool of a husband didn't think to offer it."

"The wound heals, my lady. It was a poorly aimed blow."

She clasped her hands. "Thank the saints for that, at least. I wanted you to know how very displeased I was by your treatment at the court. If he's trying to teach you some lesson about self-reliance it's... well, it's disgraceful given the service you and your family have given to the crown."

Danamis's gaze moved quickly to the retainers and guards. "I am most moved, my lady. But I am not sure it was politic to greet me in such a way."

"You mean so *publicly*? That was my main intent. I want the king to know I am displeased with how he treats his best commanders. And I don't want anyone to think I'm scheming behind his back. He'll damn well know I am displeased."

Danamis smiled, remembering her fearlessness and wondering how the fickle Sempronius dealt with her headstrong nature. "But I have no wish for your actions to bring down trouble down upon you, my lady."

She laughed, eyes crinkling, and Danamis could still see her as he had known her eight years before; full of life, wit and possessed of a generous soul. "I can deal with trouble, Nico. Have no fear on that account. Besides, he is fixed on these dealings with the Silk Empire. That unctuous Raganus and Captain Polo also... filling his head with notions about alliances and trade. What can we offer the Sinaens? Our wine? Some wool?" She shook her head in disgust. "They're just having a good look at *us.*"

Her scepticism and mistrust resonated in his own mind.

She hesitated a moment before continuing, her voice lower. "Do you know where you will go? I would understand if you do not wish to share that here... and now."

"I have few places left to go. But I know where I will end up eventually. Back in Palestro." He winked and she smiled again.

"I know that you will. And to further that particular end..." She gestured to one of her men who reached into the palanquin and withdrew a heavy linen sack before handing it to Danamis. "I want you to take these. Three hundred ducats for the cause."

Danamis felt a lump in his throat as he took the jangling sack and gave a bow of thanks. "My lady, I cannot express my gratitude enough. Not just for this. But because you believe in me."

She looked into his eyes and her voice took on a tone of silk-wrapped steel. "Teach him a lesson, Nico."

Danamis swallowed and nodded, not quite sure whether she meant Tetch or the king. "God willing, my queen!"

She smiled and signalled to her men. "Fare you well, admiral!" she called as she was escorted into the luxurious cocoon that would transport her back to the palace. He glimpsed two curly-tailed brown monkeys dressed in little blue doublets leaping about on the cushions inside, golden collars and chains around their necks. He took a few steps backwards and bowed low until she had disappeared inside, the curtains drawn. The bearers rapidly hefted the palanquin, the signal was given to the halberdiers, and the royal party wheeled out along the quay and back up into the city as it had come.

THE WINDS IN the white-capped expanse of the Bay of St. Blasius blew contrary all that day. Gregorvero, more grumpy than usual since his brush with the Temple guard, stomped about the poop ordering changes of sail at almost every hour. Their course zig-zagged south, not at the best of speed, but at least to the relief of Danamis and the *rondelieri*, they were rid of Perusia. Once out at the mouth of the bay, they would again enter the Sea of Valdur, sailing west across its length until they reached Maresto. If winds continued fickle, it might take them more than a week to reach their destination.

The visit by the queen, while not guaranteeing success, had at least bolstered Danamis's reputation aboard his ship. Especially among the new hands taken aboard, the send-off by Queen Cressida had raised his star to new heights, a token of changing fortune. Even Strykar had been impressed by her support—and the sum. It also made Strykar feel slightly less guilty for having taken what remained of Danamis's wealth in payment for debts incurred. But, knowing Fortune's wheel for what it was, as did any soldier or sailor, circumstances could change yet again and it was usually best not to worry one way or the other. That was how he had lived his life, taking his pay from the Count and enterprising what he could on the margins. Which is how he had met the Palestrian pirate, a man who was more prone to self-doubt (and now ill-luck) than any he had ever met.

That first night they dropped anchor in some shallows, barely cannon distance from the Torinian shore. It was an isolated stretch of coast where the wind ripped across sparse grassy dunes, devoid of any ports and where only poor fishermen eked out a living bludgeoning wolffish and giant seabass when not bludgeoning each other. But without a squadron to support them they were still on their own. They had to be wary: no pennon or standard flew from the mast and lookouts would stare all night into the darkness with bleary eyes, searching for tell-tale lantern lights on the water.

Danamis broke bread that evening with his ship's master, Strykar, and Bassinio, his spirits better for the visit by Cressida and her gift. Maresto was going to be another dice throw, he knew that full well. But he had survived an assassin's blade, a king's scorn, and a banker's claws all within the last week. He poured out the wine to each as they ate their meal of smoked fish in a watery stew, cheered up by some bread slops just two days old.

Strykar noisily swallowed a prodigious mouthful of gravy-soaked bread and then gulped some wine. "You talk of the need for more men and ships," he said, wine running down his chin, "but why can't you just avoid closing with an enemy and blast away until you sink them?"

The two other seamen exchanged smiles as Danamis waved his hand and again attempted to explain their situation to the mercenary.

"Ship's cannon is only accurate at close range," he said, "even a weapon such as a murderer or a curtow. We can't fire and reload fast enough to prevent them from getting their hooks into us and boarding. Understand? And then it is all about billhooks and swords and crossbows."

Strykar wiped his beard and then absently swiped his hand across his leather doublet. "Bollocks! Just fire them all at once into the enemy's hull, bugger off, and let them sink."

Gregorvero and Bassinio erupted into laughter and Danamis shook his head and grinned. Even Strykar began to chortle, seeing how he had amused them all.

"Have yet to see a piece of stone shot hole a ship enough to sink it," said Gregorvero. "Take out mast and spars... sweep a deck of her men? Of course! But rarely sink a ship on its own."

Bassinio, recovering, if still of ruined looks, nodded his agreement. "Stone shot breaks and scatters when it strikes a hull. Might as well be seagull shit."

Strykar threw up his hands. "Well! Use iron shot instead! Any blacksmith can cast that for you."

"Rare as hen's teeth," replied Danamis, beads of sweat running down his temples and cheeks. "And more likely to blow up our barrels than come out the muzzle."

"Bollocks," repeated Strykar, annoyed at being taken to task for his ignorance of maritime war. "I've seen cast iron shot made—and cast guns too. I've even seen one made from cast orichalcum being fired. A big beast of a gun with range to match."

The others looked at each other, grins of doubt blossoming.

"Orichalcum? Who knows how to smelt that?" asked Gregorvero.

"The forgemaster of Ivrea," replied Strykar, a smug look on his face. "I was there a year ago. Stronger than wrought iron they say because they are a single piece cast in the furnace. They load them from the muzzle end. And they shoot farther and with more power. Cast shot too." He crossed his arms over his chest.

"Bah!" moaned Gregorvero. "Why haven't we seen anything like that yet?"

Strykar shrugged. "The Ivreans don't make much use of warships themselves. But they've got those guns on their city walls facing out to sea."

Danamis had been silent in the exchange as the import of Strykar's words began to sink in. "Ivrea you say? I have never sailed there. Strange place, they say."

Strykar nodded. "Strange ain't even the beginning of it. Half of them down the mines, the other half doing their blessed best to keep to their own business, which is generally fleecing their fellows. Never seen a city with more ferocious merchants."

Danamis wiped his brow with his sleeve. He was tired. "And you say you saw these cast orichalcum guns fired?"

Strykar swirled the dregs around in his cup. "Well, yes... though it was just a ranging shot out to open sea. Mind you, I did speak with a captain of infantry there who had seen one hit its target. He told me, 'If those pieces ever get sent into the field they'll tear a hole into an army at nearly half a mile.'"

"Cast guns are treacherous. Likely as not to blow up in your face."

Strykar shook his head. "Not these. Orichalcum isn't brittle like iron."

There was silence in the cabin for a few moments, the ship's movement a gentle sway as it lay at anchor. Gregorvero stared at his captain. He knew him well enough to know that this talk of Ivrean guns had caught his interest—maybe worse. Danamis was looking into his cup, his thoughts elsewhere. Bassinio elbowed Gregorvero and tilted his head towards Danamis. He too was starting to worry.

Strykar caught the glance. "So nobody believes me," he said, his voice rough.

Danamis sat up straight on his bench. "I believe you, Strykar."

The mercenary leaned back, smirking, as happy as a dog praised by his master.

"Tell me, Strykar, how well do you know the forgemaster of Ivrea?"

"We hoisted a few jugs together when I was there. Not much more."

Danamis turned to Gregorvero. "I want to make for Nod's Rock as soon as we round the point."

The ship's master gawped and then looked to Bassinio to see his reaction. "Are you mad, Nico! After everything that's happened in the last fortnight! The trade with the merfolk is what turned the men against you—and the Temple. And now you want to start it all again?"

"I will seize any chance—*any*—to get back Palestro and the fleet," said Danamis, practically spitting his words. "The guns of Ivrea won't be bought cheap—assuming that they even can be bought. But I swear I will go there and get them."

Gregorvero looked first to Bassinio and then to the mercenary across from him, hoping he would find common cause, a voice of restraint. Bassinio cast his eyes downwards while Strykar wore an expression of amused detachment.

Gregorvero turned to Danamis, his shoulders hunched. "You are the captain—*my* captain," he said softly, the air of resignation in his voice barely concealed, "and the *Grace* is yours to command. We make course for Nod's Rock."

Danamis looked over to Strykar, wordless yet expectant. The mercenary took a breath and sat back. "Well, I and my men are only passengers on this voyage—and reluctant ones at that." He paused and scratched his beard. "However, it's *my* myrra that lies in your hold and, like you, I can only think of one party interested in it. So, my friend... shall we discuss the conditions of the loan for your war chest?"

Twenty-Six

THE SEA OF Valdur was always azure, and agreeably warm, even into the depths of winter when it turned merely a shade of darker blue, the waters cooling slightly as the air blew chill from the northeast. The sun of the late summer bathed the *Royal Grace* as it lay drifting without anchor in the lee of Nod's Rock. The smell of melting pitch rose from the timbers and beams, not unpleasant in itself and a far better alternative than the smell of the sweating seamen and soldiers that stood crowding the decks of the vessel, their anticipation waning as their skins reddened.

Captain Danamis made his way across the main deck, offering words of praise and encouragement, slapping shoulders, laughing, promising success and gold. A few of the men may have noticed his wobbling, slightly unsteady gait and remarked upon it for Danamis's sea legs were as good if not better than any man who had grown up on the water. For three hours they had waited there and though Danamis had ordered his father's conch horn sounded three times, this signal had failed to summon merfolk from the depths. Hope was fading and with it, that precious commodity: trust. While many of the crew had been with Danamis for years, near upon half were newly joined in Perusia. Talk of merfolk for these men was not a cause for rejoicing but for distrust and fear, so deeply were the tales ingrained.

Gregorvero stood on the poop looking forward, his gaze moving from the topmast with its furled sheets to the triangular fo'c'sle deck where he could see some two dozen soldiers and bowmen wilting in the heat under the eye of Captain Bassinio. He had convinced Danamis not to drop anchor nor to stow the powder charges belowdeck, for he knew they were exposed out in this well-travelled stretch of the sea betwixt Torinia and the Rock. His gaze moved downwards towards Danamis ambling amongst his men on the quarterdeck, smiling as he spoke, and for the first time he found himself wondering whether the young admiral would be able to overturn his infernal ill luck or if this was the beginning of the end.

"He's burning with fever." It was the Widow Pandarus.

Gregorvero turned to her. "I know. And I worry that I may have to make the decisions come the morning."

"I have tried to keep the wound clean," she said, "but there is precious little physik aboard for me to do much more. With God's help it will burn itself out."

Acquel was standing close by her. "How much longer do we wait here?"

Gregorvero continued to watch his captain. "Until he realizes they're not coming."

Danamis, dressed in his red velvet brigantine of plates, falchion at his hip, suddenly leapt down to the main deck and the larboard gunwale, one hand leaning on the barrel of a saker for support. He began pointing and then waving out to something he had seen out at sea. The lookout in the main mast was quiet and though others ran to Danamis's vantage and scanned the water, no one could see a thing.

"It is a chariot! Ten points off the bow! It's there, breaking the surface!"

Gregorvero moved quickly to the railing and shielded his brow from the glare of the high sun. An occasional whitecap erupted and flattened out beyond. He saw nothing. The men on the deck started to exchange glances and Gregorvero swore under his breath and struck the railing with his fist. He turned and grabbed a sailor by his shoulder. "You! Go and tell the captain I need to speak with him now!" The lad nodded and disappeared below.

The master turned back to Timandra. "Is there nothing more you can do for him? If I can convince him to take to his berth, can you tend to him?"

Timandra nodded. "I can sponge him with some wine and try to cool him down. Not much more."

When Danamis reached them Timandra realized how ill he had become. He was dripping with sweat, pale as death and eyes bloodshot. But his demeanour was disarmingly buoyant, almost ecstatic as he reported to Gregorvero that he had seen them briefly appear and then sink again.

"Nico, go below and take some rest," said Gregorvero, placing a hand on his shoulder. "Your fever is talking. The Widow Pandarus will redress your wound and make you comfortable."

Danamis gave a confused smile and quickly glanced at Timandra. "But, they may not come unless they see me here on deck."

Timandra spoke softly. "Captain, Brother Acquel and I can tend to you below. The master will keep a sharp watch."

Danamis shook his head and wiped his glistening brow. "I'm a bit low but I can still run this ship. Tend to me later."

Above them, there was a sharp cry from the crow's nest. "Sail ho!"

Gregorvero and Danamis cried out almost as one: "Where away?"

All heads craned towards the direction shouted down and they saw the square-rigged sails of a carrack emerge from around the western side of Nod's Rock, barely a mile away. In an instant, boredom turned to alarm and confusion. As Danamis moved to lean over the rail, staring at the newcomer, Gregorvero bellowed, "Raise all sail!" and seamen leapt to the ratlines and shrouds. Acquel found himself bowled down by two sailors who rushed past to free up the halyards tied to the mizzen.

"Talis! Get your bowmen up here! All of them." Gregorvero swore a streak at his own complacency but was interrupted by another shout from the top of the mainmast.

He looked out past their bow and saw a second ship— another large carrack—following in the wake of the first and, beyond that, a third. He squeezed the rail, his jaw going slack. "Saints preserve us," he muttered.

The *Firedrake* and her companions were swinging out wide from the island, preparing to take full advantage of the wind and bear down on them from the west. And it was a *Firedrake* confidently arrayed in striped mainsail of red and white, the three-dolphin flag of the Free City of Palestro flying over her top.

"Nico! It's Tetch!"

Danamis slowly turned to look at Gregorvero. "He has the devil Berithas himself at his shoulder," he replied, voice steady and without emotion.

Bassinio had already taken command in the fo'c'sle as more soldiers and gunners spread out to take their stations. On the main deck, the gunners had hastily donned their helms and were preparing to place shot and powder into the big guns. Above them, there was the loud snap of canvas as the huge mainsail was unfurled, flapping madly in a luff as the ship began nosing towards the north, painfully slow, until it filled.

Strykar arrived at the stairs to the poop, shouting the whole of the way up for Danamis. "Elded's bollocks! Tell me they're from Maresto or Perusia!"

Danamis swayed and steadied himself on the railing. "Tetch," he said, spitting the name. "It's sorcery. How can that bastard know what I intend to do at every turn? Damned sorcery."

Strykar, taken aback, glanced to Gregorvero. He gripped Danamis by the arm. "Where do you want me and my men?"

Danamis seemed distracted and his answer came haltingly as concentration seemed to fail him. "Strykar. Good. Take your men to the main deck and help mine deploy the netting above the guns. We'll need your swords if they try and board us."

Gregorvero stepped forward. "Captain, I'll swing us around to the east! We can then run south around the island with the wind at our backs and try and outdistance them."

Danamis's eyes suddenly grew large with absolute rage. "We sail straight *at* them, damn you! I'll have him this day! *Firedrake's* the lead vessel. Run us past his larboard and we'll fire a broadside into him and then come around."

Strykar heard the ship's master inhale loudly. In a flash, Gregorvero grabbed Danamis by the yoke of his brigantine and pulled him in close. "We can't sail into the wind! This is the fever talking!" he yelled. "We can't fight on these terms!"

Danamis bellowed like an enraged bull and shoved Gregorvero backwards. "We have at them! I will board him myself and take his head!"

In the distance a gun sounded. "Well," said Strykar, laconically, "one of you better decide before they're climbing over the rails."

Firedrake had rounded Nod's Rock and made its turn, bearing down on them wide so as to cut off the *Grace* and force it between Tetch's squadron and the island whose massive cliffs dropped down into the sea as steep as any castle wall.

Danamis staggered over to the centre of the poop and shouted down to the helmsman at the whipstaff on the quarterdeck beneath. "Steer for *Firedrake*! Take her on the larboard and don't let her flank us!"

Gregorvero started for Danamis but Strykar held out his arm. "He's the captain. He has command."

The master looked up at Strykar. "He will be the death of us all."

Strykar smiled and backed away. "Truth be told, I'm tired of running too." He turned and went down the stairs to re-join his men.

Acquel stood close by Timandra as they watched the disheartening exchange. "Come," he said quietly, "we'd better find some arms below. I didn't expect we would be doing this again so soon."

"We stay by Strykar in this," she replied, her voice sounding determined but with false confidence. "That will give us our best chance." She turned and looked up at him. "Tell me you'll pray to Elded for us."

Acquel nodded, trying to hide the fear that was crawling up inside his chest. "I will."

Torturously slow, the ship gathered momentum as her foresail and topsails filled more in the side-on breeze, her rudder assisting her manoeuvre downwind. But the enemy was bearing down from the windward, closing the distance between them at a rapid rate. A puff of white smoke billowed out from one of *Firedrake's* fo'c'sle falconets followed by the gun's report echoing off the water.

Danamis stood on the poop watching the carracks close while around him the tankard-like breech charges clunked into place on his own swivel guns. His soldiers were shouting at each other, the metallic cranking of the crossbow spanners carrying loudly across the poop deck. His head was now beginning to swim and a feeling of giddiness, almost abandon, welled within him. His feet seemed to be lifting off from the planks underneath and he felt the corners of his mouth turn up into a smile. He heard Gregorvero at his side, telling him something before he darted down the stairs again to the quarterdeck. Telling him they would get one fair pass on the larboard and a chance for a cannonade before falling off and coming about.

And within a few moments both ships were within range. Strykar, surrounded by Brognolo and his men, stood square near the mainmast and just behind the sakers. Acquel and Timandra found themselves on the inside of the mass of *rondelieri*, she brandishing a bill hook and he the same, ready to push off boarders that made for the netting. Acquel heard their fo'c'sle swivel guns sounding off and then flinched as the sound of whizzing shot through their own ratlines proved they were under fire too. As the bowsprit and fo'c'sle of *Firedrake* hove into view, he hunkered down, instinctively putting an arm around Timandra's back. An instant later he heard a loud explosion and saw a billowing tongue of flame shoot out from their deck guns. Within a heartbeat his face was spattered with debris, his ears ringing. A stone shot from *Firedrake's* sakers had ripped across their deck, shattering the gunwale and bowling over at least a dozen men near the fo'c'sle bulkhead. He staggered and reached for Timandra and, remarkably, they had escaped hurt. A pall of thick greyish smoke swirled and covered them. He felt the ship list under him, throwing him off balance. The *Grace* was turning hard over to starboard, and he heard the mainsail snap furiously as the wind filled it in a great blast, like the exhalation of an angry god.

The smoke drifted off the ship and Acquel could see the enemy moving into their own turn to try and cut off their run. Around him men were screaming as they writhed on the deck, heart-rending cries rising at high pitch amid the desperate babble of the unwounded.

Timandra had been knocked to the planks, but as far as Acquel could see, she was without a scratch. Aloud, he gave thanks to the saint who dogged him. "Timandra!" he called. "Help me!"

They began pulling the wounded, the two of them together, one man at a time from the centre of the deck to the fo'c'sle to get them out of the line of fire. As Acquel emerged a third time he looked aft to see Gregorvero yelling for Danamis. The master had sprung up the little steps leading to the poop deck. Strykar was close behind. Acquel yanked Timandra's arm and shouted close into her ear. "Something has happened to Danamis!"

They moved aft, stepping over the dead, discarded weapons and helms. Acquel ascended to the quarterdeck and looked up to Strykar on the poop. The mercenary's look of helpless shock told him the worst had occurred and he took the last set of stairs two at a time. Dead bowmen lay in a pile and blood was spattered across the deck. Gregorvero was bent over, hands on his knees, a mournful bellow pouring from him. The entire larboard rail was gone, ripped away by a cannon shot, and with it, Captain Danamis. A dull thud sounded, echoing on the water. Acquel looked up to see *Firedrake* in full sail, bearing down on them, her sister ships in her wake.

DANAMIS FELT HIMSELF going over the side, falling, and though his eyes had shut at the moment of the impact of the shot, his mind's eye was frozen on the image of Giacomo Tetch with his shining bald pate and flaming beard on the quarterdeck of the *Firedrake* as it passed, an instant before the falconets blasted his station. The shock of hitting the water jolted him. His eyes flew open, his arms spread wide, and he could feel himself sinking. A cloud of bubbles surrounded him as he sank, quickly rising up even as he plunged deeper. Somehow, he had managed a gulp of air before impact, and as he oriented himself in the blurry, blue water, he began kicking furiously to propel himself upwards. It was futile. His armour and the sword at his waist were dragging him to his death. He fought a retch, a large bubble of precious air escaping his mouth.

His hands fumbled at the harness buckles even as he began to feel the burning urge to exhale. His ears popped. He managed to free one shoulder buckle but the other he could not. His lungs ached and he swallowed, trying to gulp back escaping breath. And then he realized that he was drowning. He stopped fumbling at his harness and curled his body. His head now felt ready to explode.

Something knocked him from behind and the last of the air in his lungs blew out of his lips. Someone appeared in front of him; a dark face, blonde hair billowing. He felt a pair of arms embrace him and the face of a woman came close to his. Her eyes, a vibrant violet, were wide open as she pressed her mouth forcefully to his and blew a breath into him. Another set of arms, this time from behind, and he could feel himself rising upwards. He sucked in the air she had given him, his own eyes wide in near terror and disbelief. Then, once again, his lungs burned and he coughed out, the bubbles exploding in his face. Another woman leaned in toward him from his left and above, pressing her lips to his. He felt the air fill his mouth and throat and he inhaled again, nearly breaking the lip seal and sucking in seawater. The woman who held him in the embrace raised a long slender grey finger in admonition and her wide mouth broke into a smile.

His head fell back and above he could see the bright light of the sky through the crystal sea. Three mermaids lifted him effortlessly through the water, now less dark as he neared the surface. After what seemed an age, his heart hammering, Danamis broke the surface with such speed that his whole torso shot upwards, and he sounded a horrible strangling noise as he greedily gulped air. The same sound he had made as a child when his father had beaten him so hard that he had screamed his lungs empty. That first inhalation was always hard fought.

And with that painful breath he sank back, weaker than ever, and into the arms of the mermaids. One of them grasped his hair and held his head up.

"Danamis!" she spoke, his name strangely accented on her lips. His eyes focussed on her and he now recognized his rescuer. It was Citala. He managed a nod in return. Without any words spoken amongst them, only a few exchanged glances, they tilted him on his back and towed him, Citala and another mer taking each an arm while the third woman supported his back from underneath. He could feel himself being pushed and pulled along, far faster than he could have even swum naked. They were taking him towards Nod's Rock and as they drew closer they rose and fell with each huge swell. They were near to the cliffs and Citala looked at him again and spoke.

"Danamis, take breath again and hold it. Not long this time!"

Before he could protest he was under the water, his limbs flailing. Again he was pushed along and down, into the darkness but within a minute he had broken the surface again. This time, he was in a cavern with a ceiling barely head-height above the water. They pulled him along again in silence until he saw light from a jagged opening in the rocks ahead. The water became shallow and as he reached waist-deep he slipped to his knees. Undeterred, the three picked him up and supported him out and into an ankle-deep tidal pool. A tidal pool surrounded by verdant palm fronds and vines, the air filled with the pungent smell of earth and decaying vegetation. His head lolled. And then a deeper voice sounded in front of him and he turned.

Two lanky mer warriors emerged from the undergrowth and advanced on him, and Citala stepped forward only to be brushed aside by one of the mer who towered over Danamis by more than head and shoulders. Danamis was like some run-out rabbit, frozen where he stood. The merman, his sharp teeth flashing in a wide snarl of anger, seized him round his chest and then lifted him up right off his feet, dripping armour and all.

Twenty-Seven

DANAMIS KNEELED IN the clearing, his hands bound behind his back. A twisted vine canopy rose all around him, the sun streaking through the greenery. Surrounding him were a dozen warriors, sleek and grey, their heads adorned with what he had previously believed to have been long plaited hair but, having seen one mer pull it from his head, he now saw it was an elaborate plaited headdress fashioned of sea grass. Mermen had no hair upon their bodies at all, it seemed. Several had the long slender black swordfish spears he had seen before. As he began to fall forward from fever and exhaustion, one of them stepped in and prodded him in the chest.

He looked up to see mermen part and make way for a new arrival. It was Atalapah. He was talking low and fast in his tongue, too fast for him, but Danamis knew menace when he heard it. Atalapah snatched a spear from one of his warriors and moved towards him. He heard a woman's cry and saw Citala rush in front of her father, blocking his progress. Gesticulating, nearly raving, the chieftain bore down on his daughter, flecks of spittle flying from his wide mouth. She held her ground, at times throwing a hand behind her towards Danamis, and then reaching out to her father in supplication. Danamis caught a few words but not enough to understand their conversation. He wished he had been more attentive to his father's teaching but it was too late now.

And suddenly, Citala was calling over her shoulder in halting Valdurian.

"He is saying, Danamis, that I have sinned by bringing you here. You will not be suffered to live."

"I don't think I'll be leaving again anyway," he croaked. He could feel himself slipping away into a swoon.

Citala ran to his side and knelt, holding him up. She looked at her father and cried out to him again, her voice trilling and lilting. Atalapah grunted and motioned for her to move aside. She hauled herself up tall, pointed a shaking hand at him and spoke again. The other merfolk looked at one another, murmuring. Atalapah hefted the spear in his hand, lowered his head slightly and blinked a few times.

Citala propped Danamis up as he sagged yet again. She spoke softly. "I told him you saved his life on the ship when you jumped in front of him and shielded him from attack."

Danamis swallowed hard. "Ah, I had... forgotten that."

She spat out more words in the mer tongue, all laced with accusation.

Again, she whispered to Danamis. "I told him he owes you a blood debt."

Atalapah then spoke, pointing at Danamis. He turned the spear in his hand and drove it point first into the soft black soil. He gestured to his men-at-arms and turned, stalking off towards a large house fashioned of wood and palm fronds that lay on the far side of the clearing.

Danamis could sense Citala relaxing her shoulders. She eased him backwards. "He says he will decide your fate later.

No landsman can see where we live and return to Valdur to tell others."

Danamis finally felt blackness closing in on him. "Wouldn't... help to... promise him?"

And he fainted dead away in her arms.

HE AWOKE IN a strange hovel, its roof made of interlaced palm fronds. As he became more aware, he felt something moving over his naked chest. He lifted his head a little to see a mer woman running her hand gently through his chest hair as she stared wide-eyed at his torso. There was a cry and then Citala was looming over him, scolding the other. The mer woman, who like Citala was nearly naked except for a wrapping of some manner of fabric about her loins, bowed and scuttled away as Citala knelt over him.

"She has never seen one of your kind before. They are all amazed by how hairy you landsmen are."

He felt lucid again. His head fell back onto what appeared to be a straw mat and his eyes took in his surroundings. It was if he was inside some great bower, the round walls were made of living vines and light shone down from holes in the palms above.

He opened his mouth and struggled to speak, the words clinging to the inside of his parched throat. "Did... they... get away? My ship?"

Citala lifted his head and held a wooden cup to his lips. He drank the slightly bitter liquid it contained, and swallowed hard.

"We saw them run from the other ships. I do not know if they got away but it appeared they were outdistancing them."

Danamis shut his eyes. "Thank the saints."

"You have lain here two days. I had to reopen your wound

and clean it. It is now stitched up again. I think it will cause you pain."

"Better than being dead." His hand felt for the gash in his side and he could feel some sort of paste and leaves pressed into it. He pushed himself up on his elbows and Citala moved to assist him. Pain lanced his ribs as his muscles flexed. "Ah! You're right in that." He was clad only in a loincloth like the mermen wore, their version of braes. He winced and looked up at Citala's face and neck. "You have no gills? And you breathe air? And you are *here*... out of the sea?"

She looked intently at him. "We are not *fish*, Danamis. We breathe as you do. And we hold our breath under the water, as you do. Just better."

Danamis took in her round face and delicate features, alien yet feminine. Her skin looked as smooth as polished glass. Again, he was reminded how much it appeared like the sleek skin of a dolphin, almost glistening even when dry. "How do you know the Valdurian tongue?" he asked.

She leaned back on her knees. "Generations ago, most of my people spoke Valdurian. Now few have any reason to learn. One of our elders taught me. We have found books and scrolls at sea over the years. These too have I read."

"What will you do with me?"

She crossed her arms. "I am trying to convince Atalapah to spare your life. But even so, he may never let you leave here. We could not risk others finding us."

She spoke with authority and a certain coldness in her voice. But why had she bothered to save him from drowning? How had she even known he had fallen in unless she had been watching all along? He let himself slide back down and he focussed on the leafy ceiling above him.

"Then you might as well kill me."

"It may come to that," she replied, matter-of-factly. "But I would rather propose a new arrangement. When the time is right and when my father is in better humour."

"A new arrangement? I was *here* to do trade with *you*. You never came—but my enemy did."

She lithely regained her feet and seemed to be studying him, looking him up and down. "The myrra leaf is one reason I would make use of you," she said. "But not in the way you might think." She walked to the high-peaked opening of the hovel. "There are some truths about myrra you do not yet know. And it is a heavy responsibility your father bears in their creation. We will speak more of this later. Rest, Danamis." She stopped at the entrance and turned back to him. "Why did you try and save my father—or me—when we were on your ship that day?"

"I don't know why. It was my ship. My expedition. My men had disobeyed."

Citala considered this for a moment. "And why did they attack us?"

Danamis offered up his hand in guilt, maybe supplication. "Because they fear you. Because you are children of the old gods. Heathen."

She shook her head slowly, features hardening in disgust. But she did not reply. She slipped out through the entrance, leaving him alone.

Danamis frowned to himself and scanned the room. His filthy shirt and woollen hose were hanging tucked into the thick vines of the walls, sea-sodden boots below. But his sword belt was nowhere to be seen, nor his brigantine. He briefly toyed with stealing away but to where? And then the realization struck him as if he had been slapped in the face. He now truly had nothing except his miserable life left to him. He rolled over, curled up, and tried to sleep.

* * *

HE AWOKE TO the sound of birdsong, a noisy chatter in the canopy. It was still light outside, but weak. The air in the hovel smelled strongly of fish and he turned over to see a bowl by his side containing chunks of white fish and seaweed. Beside it were a few pieces of dark red fruit he did not recognize. He picked up a chunk of fish and saw that it was *cooked*. So the merfolk knew fire too. He dug his fingers in and ate it all, ravenous after his long fast. A large wooden drinking vessel, elaborately carved in swirling lines, stood nearby. He sniffed and then sipped. Water. Fresh and clear.

Holding his side, he managed to crawl onto his knees and then stand. The undergarment he now wore was a curious wrap of woven weeds, secured with a waist tie. He slowly retrieved his hose and after a few minutes of painful manoeuvring, he had them on. His own braes had disappeared. The shirt was blood-stained and stiff. He threw it down and hefted the boots. Still damp, but wearable. He rolled them down and slipped them on, pulling them up to mid-shin. A quick look outside and then he cautiously stepped from the hovel and surveyed the encampment. Merfolk were everywhere: females, children, and warriors. A gaggle of small ones came running up to him, laughing and gesturing before being chased away by two young mermaids, who in turn, stopped and stared at him, their heads tilting like curious cats.

But no one made to stop or challenge him. He walked unsteadily out into the open. There were dozens of hovels scattered around and he could see that he was near the base of tall cliffs, the same ones holding back the sea on the other side. Opposite this great wall of rock, the forest seemed to go on forever, though he could see the cliffs continue and curve away in the distance. Nod's Rock was hollow, it seemed, though to all of Valdur it was a barren stone mountain, unclimbable and there only to wreck ships that ventured too close. He smelled smoke. A large ring of stones surrounded a cooking fire nearby. Tendrils of thick white smoke rose up and dissipated over the cliffs, looking like the mist of a sea fog as it reached near the top. On all his voyages he had assumed that was what it was, never dreaming of its true source. Two young warriors walked past him, heading for a cave in the cliffs, both about his own height, each armed with spears and sacks of woven sea-grass. They eyed him suspiciously, exchanging words in a muttered, sullen way. Were they youths? Despite the distrustful stares from all, he was left alone and he continued walking, this time towards a group that were seated in a circle near the centre of the village.

One merman stood, reciting something in their rippling language while the others listened intently. And then, as he watched, he saw each and every one raise index and middle fingers of their right hand and press them to their foreheads, then dropping their hand to touch their hearts. On the ground he saw a symbol, something fashioned of bits of sticks and nut shells. It was a sunburst, its rays emanating outwards. The holy sign of the One Faith. He suddenly remembered Brother Acquel's dreams of Saint Elded and the merfolk. These were no heathen. They were believers.

Someone came up from behind and he turned. It was Citala, standing tall as he, eye-to-eye.

"Does this surprise you, Danamis son of Danamis?"

He nodded. "You all follow the One Faith?"

As he looked into her face he thought he saw deep pain and sadness. An instant later it had changed and she was the chieftain's daughter again.

"It is time for us to speak plainly. Speak the truth of both our peoples. Come with me."

They walked a short distance from the village towards the massive cliffs, winding their way down a well-worn track, birdsong following them. At length they came to a pool that spilled from a jagged opening in the cliff face, the water rising and receding as the waves crashed on the far side of the rock wall—the very cavern he had come through, half-drowned.

Citala entered the crystal clear pool, barely waist deep, and perched herself on a rock. Danamis glanced down at his sodden boots and decided to sit on an outcrop at the water's edge. She pointed to the jagged opening of the cavern.

"That is the only way in or out that you would be able to find, search as you might. It is the reason why my people are still here, alive."

Danamis folded his arms about his knees, his wound throbbing still. "How many of you dwell here in this place?"

"There are some thousand of us that remain. Far fewer than in the time of my forebears. But here, at least, we are safe from your people."

He took in her long limbs, her hands and feet; a lean beauty, though mer she was. Her strange hair, a mystery in itself, was thicker than a human's, almost like spun wool, the colour of snow. He smiled awkwardly, her prisoner, but at least alive.

"In Valdur, we have been told all manner of things of the merfolk. That you live under the sea, have gills like fish, worship devils..." He grew embarrassed.

"Your holy men planted those seeds. They have borne terrible fruit. Our storytellers remind us of a time when our peoples dwelled in peace and the mer lived on the shores of Valdur, from Saivona to Torinia. In the days of the saints we walked together as brothers and sisters."

"That sorrows me. I think my father was trying to learn more about the mer by trading with you. It was... a beginning."

"A beginning?" She pushed herself off the rock and dived down into the pool. She came up quickly and shook her head. "I bit my tongue over my father's decision to trade with you landsmen. *He* wanted it. And you know why. But it is a curse, Danamis son of Danamis." She emerged from the pool, the water beading on her skin. She looked down at him. "So who were those others chasing you down? You are a great admiral of Valdur, like your father was, says Atalapah. Why do you run?"

Danamis ran his hand over his beard. "I was a foolish man. I lost my fleet and the rule of my city. Lost because I was a poor judge of bad men and because I took the good men for granted."

"So you fight to regain your power to rule over Palestro?" Her hair dripped seawater onto his boots.

"That is so. But not terribly well up until now," he said, grinning.

"It seems to me that striving for the happiness of one's people is more worthy than striving for power alone."

"You do not understand the ways of Valdur."

"So, what is it you want?"

Danamis stood up, facing her. "I want to kill the man who stole my fleet and take back what is mine."

She looked into his eyes. "For which you will need more treasure, no doubt."

"I would not get very far without it."

Her tiny, flattened nose twitched, nostrils flaring. "Shall I show you what your myrra has accomplished?"

Danamis looked at her quizzically. "My lady?"

"Come with me."

They returned to the settlement and she took him deeper into its random and almost aimless arrangement, further than he had gone thus far. He saw womenfolk on their knees scraping the inside of some tree bark and peeling back the resulting white tissue. Others were rolling this and flattening it until they had small sheets of it.

"That is *tapua*," she told him. "What we make our cloth from."

They reached a large round-roofed hovel, far larger than the others that were scattered about the forest. She motioned for him to enter and she followed.

Danamis stopped immediately and saw a green glow of tree fungi in the roof space of the intertwined boughs above. It illuminated the windowless space of the roundhouse and revealed dozens of mermen lying near to one another as if asleep. But they were not. Their arms moved, they rubbed their heads, rolled over, and Danamis could see one who lay near him thrusting a fistful of myrra leaf into his mouth. Danamis turned and looked at Citala, not comprehending what he was seeing. She lowered her head, turned away and exited. Danamis reached out and touched her arm.

"What are they doing?"

"That is the truth of myrra. Most of our men do this every day. Lost to their senses even as landsmen succumb to their wine. They are as slaves. It is the she-mer—and our young— that fish and weave and work. Our warriors idle their hours in there. That is since your father began trading with us."

"But what does your father do to stop this?"

"Did you not see him in there? With the others?"

With this latest revelation Danamis felt unable to offer any words to her, either of explanation or comfort. He could not return her stare.

"Danamis, my people will not survive another generation living like this. There is another mer settlement near the island of Piso, but their numbers are less than ours. We are dying a slow death. A death your house has hastened."

Danamis finally turned back to her. His eyes were welling with tears. Tears for everything that had happened. "What would you have me do? Can you not see I have lost all? There will be no more myrra anyway. Not from me."

She raised her chin. "I mentioned a new arrangement between us. If I can convince my father. But I need to know you are a man who will stand by his word—and fight even unto death. As I would. There may be a way for you to gain your ships and for me to gain my people a future."

Twenty-Eight

"FAILED?" THE MAGISTER'S reply sounded plaintive, almost despairing. But he repeated it, this time with his composure regained. "Failed? What has she told you, woman?"

Lavinia raised her eyebrows. "Magister, we do not speak together as such. My gift doesn't work in that way."

Kodoris looked to see where Lavinia's servant was standing. Hopefully, out of earshot. He took two steps closer to the canoness, a picture of maidenly composure and beauty. He folded his arms, perhaps unconsciously, as he wanted to throttle her for her infuriating aloofness. "Then tell me what it is you do know. What has happened? You said a day ago they were closing in to take him."

A group of greyrobes shuffled across the courtyard a short distance from where they stood, leading whiterobes across from the monastery to the Temple Majoris for instruction. Kodoris waited until they had passed. The mood of the brethren had not improved in the past week and whispers throughout the Ara monastery carried far. Why had Brother Acquel done what he had? Where were the missing greyrobes? Kodoris turned back to Lavinia.

"Well?"

Lavinia toyed with her jet black hand mirror that dangled from a red ribbon. "I hear her *thoughts*, not her voice, Magister. The better when she consciously directs them to me. They tried to abduct him at the harbour. She failed."

"And what of Flauros and his party? What does she tell you of them?"

Lavinia pushed out her rose-red lips ever so slightly, eyes barely concealing amusement. "Flauros is with her... protecting her."

Kodoris shook his head in frustration. The High Priest had in the past two days experienced an unexpected spell of clarity and was asking what progress had been made in finding the greyrobe. In ending the threat of exposure. He had procrastinated. "So... they will try again and capture him?"

"No. I sense she is returning now. To Livorna."

The loud inhalation of breath by the Magister made her draw back, raising the mirror to her bosom protectively.

"I have not given her permission to return!"

Lavinia shook her head in vague regret. "She never listens to what I say. I'm not surprised she pays no heed to you. She didn't like what our father said to her and, well... he went away."

Kodoris swallowed. "You must tell her to try again! We need to bring that boy back here."

"But Magister, they have already departed. They are somewhere on the road in Torinia now."

Kodoris shut his eyes hard, teeth clenching. And then Lavinia began to giggle in her childlike way. He opened his eyes and grasped her arm. "You find this all amusing!"

Lavinia checked herself but a smile remained on her face. "No, Magister. But she is so very angry with herself. Because she failed."

Kodoris released her, his hand shaking.

"Do not fear, Magister. She believes that the greyrobe is returning here too. You see, she saw him briefly. She touched him briefly. He is seeking answers like you. And he thinks the answers are here at the Ara."

Kodoris looked at the young woman again. For the past few days, he had begun questioning his wisdom in making use of the sisters and their gifts. It was a decision made rashly in the shadow of the terrible events, he knew that, but there was something else to these creatures that seemed less than good. Perhaps even less than holy.

The loud slap of sandals on the flagstones brought Kodoris around and he gave a quick tug to cinch the purple velvet belt of his robes as a novice hurriedly approached and bowed his head.

"Magister, the Principals are awaiting you at the Night Stair."

Kodoris turned back to Lavinia, his voice a honey-coated caltrop. "Canoness, you will inform me of any further developments—without delay."

Lavinia giggled again, the jet mirror covering her mouth.

THE BRETHREN STOOD side-by-side at the foot of the Night Stairs which connected the dormitories to the choir archway of the Temple, the cowls of their robes raised over their heads. Kodoris approached and gave them a nod of respect.

"Brethren. Are we ready to proceed?"

They were ancient priests, far older than Kodoris, and their dark and wizened faces looked like tiny shrivelled dolls' heads, lost as they were in the voluminous woollen hoods. Kodoris worried that they would be unable to negotiate the steps down into the cellars below the Temple. But as the new member of the Grand Curia of the Nine, he was beholden to these two for their guidance—and the keys. He had been itching to glimpse the Black Texts since Brachus had told him of their existence. That itch had now turned to panic in light of the tidings from Perusia by way of Lucinda. He had to know more—to see more—to understand what was at stake.

One of the Nine, a Saivonan named Dromo, rasped out a reply. "It has been more than a few years since any of us have ventured down there. You are the first new Principal to even ask. But I have not forgotten the way."

Kodoris bowed and then retrieved two torches from the wall mount, where the wide stone staircase led downwards, under the very nave of the Temple. "I shall light the way," he said. The three descended and Dromo moved up to walk by his side. The other Principal followed silently behind.

This area of the cellars was known to all: vaulted ceilings held up by massive stone columns and dozens of wall niches for the remains of more important brethren, a large round ossuary for everyone else and for those bones so ancient that no monk could even put a name to them. At one end of this undercroft a single torch burned in an iron sconce at the foundation walls. Here a semi-circular chapel was carved out around the petrified remains of the pagan tree hacked down by Elded. An ancient axe hung on the stones, the one that tradition said the saint himself had wielded. The jagged stump, four feet in circumference, was now rock-like, blackish-brown with age. The little party gave it no heed but rather turned halfway down the length of cellars, and through an archway leading to a tunnel carved out of the earth and stone and left unlined for centuries. Dromo's first key opened a thick studded oak door and they passed through, the darkness held at bay by Kodoris's torches.

The tunnel continued, gradually sloping downwards, deeper under the Temple foundations and the Ara plateau. Several ancient doorways, some now bricked up, lay on either side. They came to another locked door, blocking their progress, and this too was opened. A few yards beyond, the tunnel abruptly ended. There were now two doors on either side. One was magnificently wrought, bronze and copper fittings and studs covering it. The other less so. Plain iron straps and petrified oak, a gap at top and bottom. It was this door that Dromo now opened. And as he opened it outwards, Kodoris saw that behind it lay yet another door. And this was far grander and stronger. Kodoris saw the lock mechanism that stood proud of the stout wooden planks: a heavy forged contraption, intricate and secure. Dromo dropped his hood and held up the last remaining key in the glow of the torches.

The key turned without effort and Kodoris heard the ratchets click the bolt open. Dromo gave him a wink. "There's at least a pint of hog fat greasing that lock."

Kodoris wondered how the silence of the locksmith had been assured given the significance of what lay beyond. Had the Curia used the same method as he had in Elded's tomb? Dromo lifted the latch and they entered, Kodoris first. The chamber was not large nor was the stone ceiling very high. It was almost claustrophobic. Out of the earth and stone walls had been hacked shelves upon which lay small bronze caskets, each easily shifted by a single man. Kodoris counted rapidly: fifteen. The other Principal now threw back his hood and stepped forward, placing a wrinkled hand on one of the boxes.

"Behold. The Black Texts."

Kodoris rammed one tallow torch into an iron stand and handed the other to Dromo. He moved next to the other and flicked the latch securing the lid. He opened it and peered inside. He saw more than a dozen vellum scrolls lying within.

"I assume you read *both* Old Valdurian scripts," remarked Dromo.

Kodoris reached in and pulled one out. It was not brittle as he had expected but still supple after centuries. He unrolled it and read, its borders decorated with sinuous foliage of green, yellow, and blue. It was an epistle of Elded among the merfolk, his teachings to them. He seized another and opened it. This one was an intricate map of what looked like Maresto and Saivona—he could tell from the shoreline. It indicated all areas of settlement, both human and mer, and where temples had been founded. He placed it back and took out another. This one was an account by Elded's contemporary, Saint Alonus, telling of his conversions of both mer and men in the east and how they had cast out the old gods.

He closed the lid and stood there, stunned by the enormity of these little scrolls.

"Is it what you expected to see?" asked Dromo.

Kodoris didn't reply. He moved to the next casket and opened it. A long scroll, dark brown, found its way into his hand. His eyes widened as he read. Nothing less than a history of the wars against the followers of Belial, the cutting and burning of worship trees, the valour of mer and men fighting together against the heathen. And then he found what he had been looking for. It was a wide scroll of the finest bleached vellum, delicately inscribed and illuminated. It bore the laws of Elded, given to him by the one true Lord of the Heavens. Ten laws. He read them, carefully. As he read the final three commandments he muttered a prayer and blessed himself. It was fire without flame. Enough to burn the One Faith to a cinder.

He turned to Dromo. "All of the Nine know of these? For centuries gone by? Have you studied these scrolls?"

The two Principals of the Grand Curia looked at each other. "It is enough to know they are declared heretical," replied Dromo. "Few if any in our lifetime have bothered to read them. Our task is to *safeguard* them."

"They are the words of the saints? Of Blessed Elded and his chosen companions?"

Dromo gave him a look of bemusement. "They are the words of the Saint. But delivered *after* Elded's mortal mind failed him. We cannot destroy them but we must not obey them either... to defend the Faith."

Kodoris knew that Acquel was in possession of some of these truths and that, like a small hole in a sack of grain, the breach in the Faith would quickly grow bigger. "You bear the knowledge that the Lawgiver was half-merman and yet none of the Nine have bothered to learn the secrets these contain?"

"No," said Dromo. "The question is... why are *you* so interested, Magister?"

HE BURNED FOR her. She knew that. And she had tempted him, returning his kisses. But she had not taken him to her bed. Not yet. A small but sharp push with her mind had been sufficient to deter him, for now. Lucinda watched Flauros as he built a fire for them. He was dependable, even ruthless, when required. Handsome as well. And though she could bend men's minds to her will, this only worked one man at a time. As she had already seen, a strong sword arm was often also required. He caught her stare and gave her a wink before leaning over the kindling with his tinderbox. They had made it back to the ruins where the ox of a soldier Demedrias had tried raping her. For an instant the memory enraged her. Berithas had dealt with him though, protecting her. Through her.

In the uplands of Valdur, summer was beginning to die away. The horses behind them whinnied as the flames took hold of the wood and sent out warmth to kill the chill in the clear night air. Flauros had draped her with a blanket and, comfortable enough on the ground, she now watched the fire crackle into life. Flauros seated himself opposite on a square slab of ancient temple ruins. He pulled his cloak about himself and set to watching her, a look of amused curiosity on his face.

"So, then, it is the Old Faith for you," he said as he threw a branch on the fire. "And yet you have chosen to confide that little heresy to the captain of the Temple guard."

She smiled a knowing smile. "I confided in a man whose heart I read well. A man who is sick of the lies and hypocrisy of the priesthood."

"The Temple pay their guardsmen well and have never required holy orders for those who sign for the service. For me, the Faith was never a consideration." He waggled a stick of firewood at her before tossing it into the rising flames. "How is it you can reach into a man's mind and control it? Or speak with someone who is far away as if they were in the same room? By what power or charm?"

She placed her hands upon her knees and sat up straight. "It is a gift. A gift of the Redeemer. The one who the craven priests call the Deceiver. Berithas."

Flauros poked at the fire with the toe of his boot. "The same Deceiver as was struck down by Elded after being revealed by Saint Dionei? Ironic that, considering the abbey you come from."

"I would say poetic retribution. And useful for my struggle."

Flauros chuckled quietly. "A cuckoo in the nest, eh?"

"If you will. But Berithas works through me to restore the old ways. To bring back the Tree of Life. Restore the old gods to their proper place. See the power of earth, tree and stone renewed. And show the sky god for what he is— powerless and uninterested in the affairs of men."

Flauros leaned back on his slab and patted it. "Well, here is one temple already thrown down. The others will not be so easy though. If you are discovered they will cut out your living heart and burn you."

She nodded. "They would. But Berithas will not let that happen. Nor will you. There is a path that the Redeemer has revealed to me. One which has a part for you to play."

"And what makes you think I will join with you and turn against the One Faith?"

"Because, Flauros, you already have. I can see it in your heart—and your mind."

He bristled slightly, back arching. "I do not like you doing that."

"Why? Because I can see that you desire me?"

"You don't have to look into my mind to see that. What is it you want me to do? Find that greyrobe and kill him for you? Take his amulet?"

Lucinda's eyes widened. "No, no, not that. Berithas has told me that the greyrobe is a seed we must nurture. But we must return to the Ara to do that, among other things."

Flauros frowned. "I will not be your pawn in this plan. If I am to follow you and stand with you then... I will need to know everything."

Lucinda stood up and let the blanket slip off of her shoulders. "For that you will need to swear to Berithas and to the Old Ones whom he serves—Belial, Beleth, and Andras." She moved around the fire and came to him, the satin dress she wore shimmering in the firelight. He reached out and pulled her in, burying his face into the mound of her womanhood and gripping her buttocks.

"And there will be rewards," she said, soothingly. She pulled his face away gently, tilting his chin upwards. "You must hear Berithas if he will speak through me."

She reached up and undid the first few ties of her dress and unlaced the ribbon of the neckline of her chemise. She bared her shoulder and Flauros stood up slowly, holding her at her waist. He saw the livid red scar that lay underneath her collarbone near where the curve of her bosom began.

"What? Have you been burned? Branded?" His eyes squinted in the light to make out the mark and he raised a hand to her shoulder. And then he saw the wound pulse and begin to glisten, the lips opened.

Flauros went rigid, his mouth moving wordlessly. Lucinda took him by his hands and squeezed.

"Do not be afraid. If you would have me then you must have Berithas. And hear his words."

And as the voice spoke, like the sound of a gently bubbling fountain, reassuring him, he began to understand everything.

Twenty-Nine

CITALA STOOD CLOSE by bare-chested Danamis as she addressed her father and the elders in the sacred circle. Danamis found it difficult to judge mermen by their faces since it seemed what features they had moved little with any emotion except perhaps anger. For his benefit, she addressed them slowly in Valdurian, assuring him that the elders would understand.

"We have talked many times before," she began, "of leaving this place to return to the old settlements on Valdur. By letting Danamis live we can make that happen."

"This man knows where we live. *How* we live." It was a merman hunched with age. "To release him would bring more landsmen down upon us. Last time this happened there was no debate. You know that, daughter of Atalapah."

Citala raised her finger. "Then you would consign your grandchildren to a meagre and uncertain existence. Time does not favour us and ignorance only flatters us."

The elder bristled. "See Atalapah, how your child is infatuated with her prize?"

Atalapah held out his hand to silence him.

Citala turned to her father. "This is no ordinary man. He

is the lord of Palestro and knows the princes of Valdur. He is Danamis son of Danamis."

"What interest does he have in our return?"

"We each can serve the need of the other," she replied, her eyes moving from elder to elder. "Danamis would return to destroy his enemy and retake Palestro. To do this he needs ships and men. We have the treasure he needs to buy them."

Atalapah twisted the haft of his spear in both hands. "And what do we receive in return, my daughter?"

Danamis took a step forward. "My lord, I will swear upon all the saints to undertake the protection of your people, to provide a safe haven for them, and to work with all my power to convince the dukes of Maresto and Saivona to afford your people peace and prosperity."

A few of the elders began making noises deep in their chest—*hurr, hurr, hurr.* It was the sound of mer laughter and Danamis felt himself foolish.

"I give you my word!" he pleaded.

An elder stepped forward, pushing aside two of his fellows. His head was a mass of black scars, his right eye missing. "And what of the myrra? Where is our myrra? What do you say to that, landsman!"

Citala had warned him this would be mentioned. He shot her a glance, looking for her reassurance. She gave him a nod in return.

"The myrra will more easily be traded with you in Valdur. Whatever you want."

The merman's thin lips parted, revealing sharp teeth. "So you say. But you are one man."

Atalapah spoke up again. "And if he fails to kill his enemy? What then?"

"I will die in the trying, my lord," said Danamis, puffing his chest out. "And you will have only lost a treasure you have little use for."

Atalapah nodded. "And if you give up and abandon your quest?"

Danamis bowed, his arms making a flourish. "Citala has sworn to find me at sea and to drown me. I now owe her *my* life, you see. It was she who pulled me from the depths."

The mermen exchanged looks and muttered amongst themselves. Atalapah raised his long grey arm. "We will now decide, Citala."

She bowed to her father and took Danamis by his hand to lead him away. They walked back to the end of the settlement, to the hovel where he had been kept.

"Will they listen?" he asked her.

Citala looked him in the eye. "I do not know."

"I fear I may never be able to convince the temple priests to relent of their poison. They have stirred up the mistrust for generations."

She took his hand. "I believe that you can, Danamis. So long as you yourself do not believe their tales." She allowed herself a small smile, her pearl-white teeth just showing. "I have had several dreams of late. Of a redeemer who seeks reconciliation between our peoples. He is a landsman, not mer." She leaned back against the tree post of the entryway; her haughtiness was melting as she confided in him. "It may only be a wishful dream, but… it makes me happy to think upon it. Just the same."

Danamis remembered his dream of the mer—the dream that had foreshadowed his fall into the sea a few days before. And she had not pulled him down, she had pulled him up. "Let us hope it is a harbinger of the future," he said, "for both our sakes."

He looked out into the lush forest beyond, filled with great creepers and vines and broad-leafed plants that dwarfed a man. Parrots called to each other, unseen, and green-backed monkeys leapt from palm to palm in search of fruit. "Some might consider this a perfect garden. A place to stay forever."

Citala followed his gaze. "And others would consider it a prison."

Danamis snapped back to attention as a group of mer made their way towards them. It was Atalapah and a band of warriors; as fearsome a sight as any he had ever witnessed. He stood up straight, ready to receive his death— or his freedom.

They halted a few paces in front of him and Citala. Atalapah held his short swordfish spear like a sword in his right hand, the pointed end resting in his left palm. His voice boomed as he made his pronouncement, as proud as any duke or king.

"Danamis, son of Danamis. We will accept your oath to Elded and the saints and seal our bargain. You may return to your people but we will hold you to your word."

Danamis bowed low, his heart thrumming so hard he could feel it pulsing in his ears.

WHATEVER SEA PHYSIK Citala had used on him, his wound had healed wondrously after only a few days. It still ached, but it was clean and scarring well. Most importantly, he could move his torso freely—and fight. It was time to leave. On the fifth day she led him and a party of mer warriors past the tidal pool and the grotto that led to the outside world. Further on they came to another cave, the repository of all they salvaged from wrecks lying on the bottom of the sea. The gold and gems were near knee-deep, spilling across the floor of the cave, silver goblets and chargers tossed amongst it all. Danamis, holding his torch aloft, watched the light dance and sparkle off the treasure and thought of his comrades. He tried to imagine Gregorvero's face if he could have witnessed such a pirate's dream. As it was, he could only stare in silent amazement as the mermen stuffed their sea grass sacks with fistfuls of gold coin and necklaces, emeralds, rubies, and sapphires. They filled fifteen sacks each as large as a *catana* melon and as the last sack was carried out, Citala's lilting voice echoed in the cave.

"Is this enough for you, Danamis?"

Danamis swallowed hard, nodding. "Aye, my lady, that ought to buy a few cannon and men!"

When they returned to the tidal pool, he saw that the mer had dragged a small longboat from out of the undergrowth. Both prow and sternpost had been ripped off at the gunwales but, as he walked around it, he thought that it appeared sound nonetheless. Citala told him that they had submerged it and dragged it through the tunnel many months ago. If they could drag it in they could drag it back out, bail it, and refloat it. Trouble was, he knew that *he* would have to be submerged again too, pulled through the grotto while his lungs felt ready to burst.

Citala, hands on hips, watched him as he clambered into the boat and ran his hand along the planks and seams, looking for holes and gaps.

"It was afloat when we found it so it will float again, Danamis," she said, sounding unconcerned. Not being mer, he felt differently about it.

"It will be low in the water with a load of treasure and me," he replied, standing as he ran his hand back through his long hair. "One good swell and I'm likely to be sunk."

She laughed, her confidence radiating like a burst of bright light. "You'll not be alone and you won't need a sail. You must trust me."

He looked at her and managed a grin. If he'd had more soldiers like her he'd never lose a battle. They both stood back as the mermen dragged the boat out to the pool and sank it, the sea roiling where they disappeared. After a time a few returned and with the help of others, they each took a sack of gold and dived in again to pass through the grotto. Lastly, he watched as his brigantine, sword, boots, and hose, all carefully wrapped in the same oilcloth he had used to deliver their myrra, were hefted by two warriors and thrown into the pool. The mer plunged in and disappeared. He stood watching, clad only in his braes to conceal his modesty from the she-mer. Citala turned to him, teeth flashing in a broad smile.

"Now then, Danamis son of Danamis. Are you ready?"

He nodded and waded into the pool, the warm water lapping at his chest. She followed him in and faced him.

"Grasp me tightly as I showed you," she ordered. "And take the deepest breath you can when we go down. I will give you air when you need it."

He hugged her about the waist like a lover embracing his beloved. And then they were under. She was preternaturally strong, swimming effortlessly with him clinging to her. It was pitch black despite his eyes being wide open. He could feel her powerful body pulling through the water, her legs kicking as fast as a shark could swing its tail. It seemed an age, she above him, her breasts pressed to his chest, her long arms cutting through the dark waters of the cave. His grasp slipped once and she gathered him close in an instant until he had locked his fingers behind her back, but precious air had escaped his mouth, bubbling out and up. He could see light again and he knew they must nearly be out. But he began to panic, his body bucking. A burst of air escaped his mouth. Her face was in front of his, those violet eyes wide. Her lips pressed his and he felt a blast of air enter him. He swallowed greedily and as he did so he felt them rising upwards. He could see everything again in a blur of greyish blue. She slipped further down, her hands on his waist propelling him upwards as she kicked. He exploded out of the water, mouth gaping as he drank in a lungful of air.

She laughed like a little girl as he spluttered and coughed. And then she pointed to the boat a short distance away. His arms shaking, Danamis hauled himself up and over the gunwale, falling inside on jingling sacks of treasure. Citala's head popped up, her delicately webbed hands grasping the side of the longboat.

"Now we make you a chariot!" she cried before disappearing below again. Danamis could see mermen at the broken prow where they had tied woven lines to what remained of the stem of the post. He felt the boat pitch up as something bumped it from underneath and he hurriedly grabbed at the gunwales. Four glistening dolphins broke the surface around him, cackling playfully. As he steadied himself amidships, he saw the mermen place them into harness which they readily accepted. The boat rocked again. It was as low on the waterline as he had feared. Citala burst from the surface, her hair swinging and splashing him.

"We are ready," she said, a hand on the gunwale. "Three warriors will come to guide the dolphins. We will not stop unless you wish it. If they are strong boys you will be in Maresto in a day and a night."

Danamis put his hand over hers. "If my ships could make such speed!" He looked about him: fresh water in a gourd and a sack of fruit, the sacks of gold neatly positioned from stem to stern. "Then give the word, Citala, and tell your men I am ready. I will not forget what you have done!"

She laughed again. "You will not be able to forget. I am coming with you." And she cried out in her tongue to the warriors. Before Danamis could protest, he was thrown backwards onto the treasure as the longboat shot forward. The bow shot spray backwards and the boat gathered speed as if a tempest was filling an invisible sail. He clambered upright and looked out ahead to see four white wakes and four straining ropes as the dolphins pulled their load. The mermen kept pace somehow, Citala too, and he saw her reach forward to grab a dorsal of the lead animal, their blue backs just breaking the surface. Behind him, an escort of what seemed an entire pod of dolphins sprang from the water as they followed. Nod's Rock began to grow smaller as the Sea of Valdur, gleaming in the bright sun and as smooth as mirror glass, opened before them. A day and a night to Maresto. He allowed himself an inward smile.

He was still dicing with Fate and he knew it. His enemies held his ships and his city. The priesthood and his king had abandoned him. And if Gregorvero and the *rondelieri* had made it back to Maresto safely he would have already been pronounced as lost at sea; like his father. But he had new allies now and he had a plan. In Valdur, gold can buy many things, a much greater tool than honeyed entreaties. Even so, in the back of his mind, a small voice warned him that grand promises—like grand compromises—can undo even the mightiest prince.

Thirty

CAPTAIN JULIANUS STRYKAR and his unlikely bodyguard—a greasy-looking lieutenant in a red sash, a redheaded woman in straw hat, brown kirtle and clogs, and a young man with a curious haircut dressed in a dark green wine-stained padded doublet and hose—crossed the great piazza and approached the main entry of Maresto's ancient and glorious ducal palace. It was a hulking and slightly menacing construction of red stone, its impressive series of arches faced in ochre sandstone at least affording it some measure of beauty. High above this long palace, a massive row of tooth-like dagged crenelations hinted at the fortress that lay at its core.

It was the second time in just over a week that Strykar, rather worn out from the adventure of the last fortnight, had come to the palace of his half-brother, Alonso. The first time he had arrived on his own, to tell of the untimely end of the rightful ruler of Palestro, the friend and ally of Maresto, and to relay news of the impending threat of Torinia in alliance with the Palestrian usurper, Giacomo Tetch. Now he was back again, this time at the direct summons of the Duke. Not likely to be a good omen, he thought, as the halberdiers at the portico stamped and saluted a stupidly grinning Lieutenant Poule before lifting the bar and pushing open the great door. He had never been on intimate terms with his half-brother, and never publicly acknowledged that he was of the blood, but the relationship was one of mutual respect. Yet he was worried as to why the presence of both Timandra Pandarus and Brother Acquel had been requested. He had confided in Alonso about the monk's journey and what curious artefact he held, the accusations of murder, and the botched attempt at kidnapping him. Alonso had told him that he would decide what to do later. Perhaps now was that time.

They were escorted through the high-ceilinged galleries, each boldly decorated with colourful murals of the city and the saints, all slightly darkened with age, before reaching the throne room. Strykar watched a nervous Acquel place his hands together while Timandra doffed her wide-brimmed hat. Poule tugged at his sash and took up station next to him. The throne room was empty except for the high-backed carved chair on the dais, and they were quickly marched to the room beyond—an antechamber. The lead guardsman gave a nod to Strykar as he unlocked the door to this private space. Strykar turned the bronze handle and entered, the others close behind.

It was a large chamber, big enough to hold fifty or more guests. As they entered, a palace guard at the other end knocked on an adjoining door and immediately opened it. Four people filed in and stood in front of the massive marble hearth. Duke Alonso, tall, with closely cropped greying hair and a neatly groomed beard, stood centre, dressed in a dark red velvet houppelande gown. A great golden medallion hung from a chain about his neck. Next to him stood his most trusted counsellor, Lord Renaldo, scion of the wealthiest merchant dynasty in the duchy. Two other figures, just taller than either the Duke or Renaldo, stood off slightly to one side. They both wore ankle length cloaks with hoods that obscured their faces. Strykar noticed Acquel pull up sharply for a moment, no doubt thinking they were clerics.

Strykar and his party halted and bowed to the Duke who, in turn, welcomed them with a sly smile and a diffident wave of his right hand.

"Captain Strykar and... companions!" The Duke's eyes settled briefly on Acquel and Timandra. "We welcome you."

"Your Grace," said Strykar, "we come at your service. You do us honour by requesting our presence."

"Good of you to say, Captain. But it was not me who asked for you." Alonso took a half step back and gestured to one of the cloaked figures. The man reached up and threw back his hood.

Timandra suppressed a gasp and Strykar bellowed, "Sweet God above!"

Danamis grinned at them like a village prankster and then Strykar seized him in a bear hug for a brief instant before remembering himself and holding back, his head shaking in disbelief.

"You were surely drowned! You were blown over the side—in your armour! How?"

Timandra and Acquel looked at each other, beaming, and she reached out for his arm. The Duke laughed, pleased by the triumph of his little surprise.

Danamis put his hands on his hips. "Aye, maybe half-drowned. I sank faster than a piece of shot. But... I had a rescuer." He reached over and gently pulled back the hood of his companion. Strykar took a step back without thinking and Timandra's sharp cry echoed off the frescoed walls. Poule swore softly, his eyes starting from his much-scarred face.

"This is the princess Citala, daughter of Atalapah, the chieftain of the merfolk of our waters."

Acquel looked at the mermaid and felt his heart nearly stop.

A creature, the same of his many dreams, now standing but two paces away. She was looking directly at him with a most curious expression that seemed almost one of recognition. He found her strangely beautiful with her high cheekbones, deep violet eyes and striking pale hair. Timandra was still gripping his forearm and he broke his gaze to look back at the Widow. She too was staring at the mermaid, her mouth gaping as she tried to believe what she was seeing.

"But," continued Danamis, "I would stay dead a while longer if you will assist in the deception. Far better for Tetch to believe me lost overboard when we begin our expedition."

Strykar turned to the Duke and then back to Danamis. "What expedition would that be?"

"It is imperative for Maresto that Torinia never control the Palestrian fleet," Duke Alonso said, his voice commanding. "Lord Renaldo has told me only this morning that a Palestrian warship boarded two of our merchantman yesterday and stripped them clean. They're goading us. The admiral has a plan to retake the fleet from Tetch and safeguard our trade. He also tells me you two had discussed it at sea, off Perusia."

Strykar frowned at Danamis. "Not Ivrea? That's a fool's errand." He quickly raised his hands in supplication. "Your Grace, forgive me."

The Duke looked down his long nose at his half-brother. "I forgive your outburst, Captain. But as Lord Danamis has explained to me his plan already, I find it has merit. And it's worth attempting." He gestured to Citala. "And he has entered into an alliance, of sorts, with the merfolk who have lent him a war chest to go to Ivrea with a respectable offer."

Citala nodded and Strykar looked again at Danamis, who he could tell from long acquaintance was hoping that he would approve of his new venture.

"Lord Danamis and I," said Citala, "have entered into an arrangement. In return for the treasure he needs to buy his navy, he will undertake to champion my people in Valdur."

"A not inconsiderable undertaking," replied Strykar, still amazed by her presence and by the fact that she could speak Valdurian.

"But you differ in your outlook?" said the Duke. "Don't you think these orichalcum guns would benefit the Black Rose in the field if we could successfully acquire them?"

"My lord, no, it is more surprise than any reservation," Strykar said. "Nor did I know about Danamis's new friends."

Lord Renaldo broke in, his weak and reedy voice sounding like a man dying of thirst. "We are entering dangerous times, captain, and the duchy is feeling a distinct chill in the air. We must move to secure new alliances before Torinia makes her next move."

"And more too," added the Duke, "I like not at all this talk of the Silk Empire and their newfound interest in the affairs of the kingdom. Is it only trade that they are interested in? Or perhaps spreading their empire westwards? Ursino sits in Torinia stirring the cauldron and I would wager my coronet that his alliance with Tetch is just the first part of his scheme. From what Lord Danamis tells, we can expect little in the way of decisive leadership from the king."

Strykar nodded. "I fear that is true, my lord."

"Then," said Alonso, "we cannot allow Palestro to remain in the hands of mutineers who are no more than puppets of Duke Ursino. Lord Danamis is prepared to do what he must to secure new ships and these new guns. For our part, we shall bolster the free companies including yours and I shall tell Count Malvolio exactly that later this day. The eastern towns are at risk."

"Yes, my lord," replied Strykar. "Do you wish me to again reconsider the Count's offer to take up promotion in the company?"

"Your continued lack of interest in seizing advancement

is always something of a puzzle to me, Captain, despite the fact that it has been often handed to you on a silver platter. But, no, I think your skills as a soldier would be better put to use in joining Danamis's expedition to Ivrea. He will need a few good swords at his side going into that lion's den."

Strykar felt himself blush. "I serve at your pleasure, my lord."

"For my part," said Danamis, "I would be grateful to have you watching my back. And you know Ivrea far better than I do."

Strykar blinked a few times. "Well then. Ivrea it is."

Duke Alonso clapped his hands once. "Excellent. The admiral tells me he will buy a merchant caravel here in Maresto and prepare for the voyage. His ship is the worse for wear and he tells me that it is not suited to his purpose. Something about needing speed."

Danamis nodded, looking pleased with himself. Strykar inclined his head in admiration for it seemed that his friend and trading partner had found something of his old fire again.

"I am sure that you all would like to discuss your plans further," the Duke said, gesturing them away as if shooing chickens, "and hear more of Lord Danamis and his charming companion. You will find refreshment ready for you in the gallery without the throne room."

Strykar bowed and withdrew, along with Acquel and Timandra. Danamis offered his arm to Citala, who at first gave him a quizzical look, then gently took it. He bowed to the Duke and she copied him.

Alonso smiled at them both, but more at her than Danamis. "My dear lady, I had always hoped to meet one of your kind. Now that wish has been fulfilled. Admiral, we shall talk further as your plans progress." As they withdrew the Duke called after them, "And remember, stay in the shadows. Maresto is not yet ready for merfolk walking the streets."

"If ever," mumbled Lord Renaldo, at his side.

MINUTES LATER, IN the grand gallery two chambers beyond, Lieutenant Poule took up his goblet, drank deeply and began studying the *puti* that frolicked above them on the painted cupola, its vibrant blue sky giving the illusion of open space and sunbeams. He shoved a handful of juicy black grapes into his mouth as he eyed an impish cherub with puckered lips that was spitting down at him. "Very fucking clever," he mumbled to himself, juice running down his chin.

Citala sniffed the contents of her goblet, her tiny flat nose flaring a moment before her nostrils sealed shut. She did not drink but held the silver vessel awkwardly in her hand. Strykar lifted his goblet to Danamis.

"Here's to your new beginning!"

"I can almost taste it," said Danamis, hefting his own cup. "Strykar, I had no wish for my return to be so dramatic. The Duke insisted on this little charade. But you took it well. Poor Gregorvero actually fainted dead away when he saw me. Hit the deck of the ship like a lead weight."

Strykar placed a hand on his shoulder. "The Duke has always enjoyed arranging little surprises when the opportunity presents itself. I've even been the butt of a few before. But this time, I am glad of the outcome."

Citala wandered off, fascinated by the scenes depicted around her; all a distant world compared to the one she had grown up in. Soldiers warred, masons built cities, townsfolk prayed to the saints, and noblemen wooed maidens in their green bowers overgrown with roses. Her lips parted in wonder for she had now entered the land she had long dreamt of.

Acquel approached her cautiously as if she might evaporate like a phantom if he touched her. She turned as he came. The monk wasn't sure what he wanted to say to her but he felt the urge to say something. It was she, however, who spoke up first.

"You are the holy man that Danamis has told me of?"

"I was a greyrobe of the monastery at Livorna," he replied sheepishly. "Suppose that I still am."

She nodded. "And I am told that Saint Elded works through you."

His discomfort increased. "Princess, I do not truly understand what the Lawgiver tells me. But I sense his presence and his... voice."

Citala took Acquel's hand; hers felt marble smooth and very cool in his own. "Sometimes the Lawgiver speaks to our people when we dream. I, too, have had such dreams of Telling." She smiled, her head tilting slightly. "And there is something about you that I sense. Something of a task not yet completed."

Acquel watched as her eyes moved downward to the amulet, even though it was concealed inside his shirt and doublet.

"You are as I imagined in every way," he said, quietly. "As I was shown... by Elded."

Citala smiled again and released his hand. "And I am pleased that we have met and opened our hearts, holy man."

Across the room, Poule called out again harshly. "Widow! Are you too grand a lady now to answer me?"

Timandra, startled, took her gaze from the mermaid and Acquel and turned to face the soldier. "What are you prattling about now, Poule!" she fired back as she recovered her composure.

"The arse on that one looks like yours!" he laughed, pointing upwards.

She gave him a look that would have curdled milk and then raised her goblet to her lips. But she was thinking about Acquel, thinking about what was running through his mind now that he had met merfolk in the flesh. Giving his dreams new significance, planting a dangerous seed of a plan that would take him away—probably to his death. In her heart, she knew that he was thinking of running. Running back to Livorna. And she was already dreading the moment when he would ask her help.

Danamis leaned in to whisper to Strykar. "Tonight, come alone and join me on the *Grace*. We have much to discuss."

Strykar nodded towards Citala. "You mean to discuss *her*?"

"Among other things. The Duke has told me if war with Torinia comes, he has no wish to anger the Temple priests unnecessarily and cause them to side with Duke Ursino. I fear that Brother Acquel may become a pawn—or a gesture of goodwill."

A low growl rumbled in Strykar's throat, his lips pursing in irritation. "That does not surprise me in the least." He turned and barked to the others, "Drink up, Poule! The revel is over and we're going back to camp!"

THAT NIGHT, AFTER sundown and when the moon had risen, Strykar made his way into Maresto again and wended his way through the crooked streets and down to the harbour. He was struck by the number of merchantmen sitting at anchor, their lanterns burning and the voices of their crew raised in jest or argument. Far too many, he thought. The *Royal Grace* was tied up where Gregorvero had left it nearly two weeks before. It looked battered and tired, even in the torchlight.

He pulled his cloak up higher on his shoulders and swung his side sword around so that the belt and scabbard rested on his left buttock. He hollered up to the deck and was met an instant later by the sight of Gregorvero looking down on him. The gangplank was lowered away and Strykar made his way up and over the gunwales, leaping lightly to the deck.

"Welcome aboard, Captain," said the master, an uncharacteristic smile on his mouth rather than the usual scowl he reserved for the *rondelieri*.

Strykar nodded. "Where is he?"

They climbed the stairs to the stern cabin and Gregorvero ushered him into the cramped space he now knew so well, its familiar fug hitting his nose like a fist.

"Captain Strykar," said Danamis from his seat at the chart table. "Sit down and join me for a drink."

Strykar pulled a bench underneath him and angled the hilt of his sword more comfortably as Danamis poured him some wine from the jug. Gregorvero sat down opposite and wrapped his fingers around the goblet that was already waiting there.

"So, how many know your secret?" asked Strykar.

Danamis raised his brow slightly. "Couldn't keep it a secret from the crew—but they're sworn to secrecy under penalty of losing every last dinari they own or are likely to see again. Far more effective than threatening to slit their throats."

Strykar swigged from his goblet and smacked his lips. "Well, barely a fortnight ago everyone hereabouts knew you were dead and gone. Some of the men actually mourned you."

Danamis shrugged. "All the better for it. Let's hope back in Palestro that the word is House Danamis is dead."

"I see the place is crowded with ships," said Strykar. "Far more than I've seen before at one time."

"Their captains are afraid to venture out without escort and Duke Alonso just does not have enough warships for that," Gregorvero said.

"Whether he believes it or not," added Danamis, "he is already at war with Torinia."

Strykar looked around the cabin. "So where is your new companion? Your mermaid rescuer."

Danamis looked straight at the mercenary. "She is the key to everything. And we have a bargain."

"My eyes nearly fell out when she threw back her cape.

How do they breathe air or even survive out of the sea? Shit, you would expect them to... dry out."

"They are not fish-men, despite what is said. They breathe as we do. How long they can stay out of the water I do not know. But she is there now."

Strykar nodded thoughtfully. "And the treasure? Same sunken coin that you get from them for the myrra, I assume."

"It is. And I'm taking no chances until we leave for Ivrea. It now lies on the bottom of the harbour and only she and her men know where it is."

Strykar chuckled. "No better hidey-hole than that! You reckon there's enough to convince the Ivreans?"

Danamis smiled. "It's a king's ransom. More than enough to tempt this Count Leonato, even if he is a High Steward. I have never seen such a haul in my life."

Strykar leaned in. "You've stayed with them? Seen their treasure trove?"

"We shall not speak of it. I am sworn to her and her people."

"Saints above! How can you deliver on that promise? You know how the priests and most folk feel about the mer. Even your own men distrust them. I don't even understand how Alonso welcomed her like he did into the palace. That was just as much a surprise as seeing you again."

"The Duke sees the potential of an alliance with the merfolk. As do I."

Strykar laughed. "He sees the potential of a chest spilling with gold and jewels, I reckon. A hundred years' worth of shipwrecks out there to plunder adds up to a fair old haul."

"But I am the one with the alliance."

"For now," mumbled Strykar.

Danamis ignored the jibe. "And Gregor here has found the perfect ship for us with an owner happy to sell."

"She's a three-masted caravel," said Gregorvero. "Saivonan-built, a strong and fast ship. As she's fore-and-aft rigged, we should be able to manoeuvre ourselves out of most trouble."

Danamis nodded. "No guns mounted. We'll be discreet leaving Maresto. Just another scared merchantman running the blockade."

"Just another merchantman running the fucking gauntlet under Tetch, you mean," said Strykar leaning back and folding his arms across his broad chest.

"We can do it," replied Danamis, his voice confident. "And when we come back, we will be a very different ship entirely."

"So then, how many of my men do you need?" Strykar's voice carried a hint of resignation.

"Bring me fifty. Your best sword and buckler men. Fully armed *rondelieri*. I'll pay each of them enough to be a captain of infantry."

Strykar closed his eyes and squeezed the bridge of his nose. "Sweet God above. How I'm still getting dragged into these things with you I'll never understand."

"You're an *aventuri*. What else is there to understand.? Now, what of Brother Acquel?"

"Aloysius's balls. He's like a ghost at a funeral. You know what he is carrying. The poor bastard doesn't know where he will end up."

Danamis looked into his goblet. "I know you told the Duke his story. And he asked me what I knew of the greyrobe. Alonso says that if the High Priest or the High Steward asks for his return—and he did say *if*—then he will send Acquel to them under escort. He says it's a matter for the Grand Curia. He doesn't want trouble with the Temple Majoris, not with war looming."

Strykar shook his head slowly. "Fucking hell. The Widow will take this badly. They are as thick as thieves those two. But you yourself have seen the signs... the amulet. I *know* what I have seen."

"Some people don't want to believe in miracles. Your brother is one of them. It makes them... worry."

"Half-brother," corrected Strykar flatly.

"Will you warn Acquel?"

Strykar hung his head and sighed loudly. "If I don't, Pandarus will never forgive me, that's for damn sure."

He then looked at Danamis, snorted, and shook his head. "You've been stabbed, blown overboard and drowned and now come back from the dead. Brother Acquel may have his amulet but I'd say you're the one who Elded is looking after."

Thirty-One

TIMANDRA FOUND HIM sitting on the trampled grass next to one of the iron-shod wheels of her sutler's wagon, head down and hands in his lap. Around him, the tents of the Black Rose's cook and armourer stood, smells and yells emanating from both. The *rondelieri* were billeted just outside the north town wall, much to the annoyance and disappointment of them all. The cavalry had taken precedent on the inside of Maresto and no further room remained. *Rondelieri* traded insults and dagger thrusts with a company of spearmen who also remained outcast on the far side of Maresto's walls.

Acquel had been despondent for a few days now. Seeing Captain Danamis had momentarily raised his spirits, but the weight of his burden had pressed down upon him again with all its suffocating doubt. Timandra sat down next to him and threw off her battered straw hat. He managed a smile and reached out to touch her hand. She was reluctant to tell him what she knew she must.

"Acquel, Strykar has confided something to me. Something that concerns you. Directly."

"I suppose that the Duke has finally decided what to do with me," he replied, not looking at her.

"In truth, he has not. But Strykar believes that if the Temple asks for your return—if they learn you are here—then the Duke will not save you." She put her other hand over his. "But *we* can hide you if it comes to that."

Acquel smiled at her. "Timandra, you know that cannot be. I must leave. I was going to tell you that anyway. My mind is made up."

"Where? Where can you go where you will be safe? You don't know a soul except for us here."

"I'm going back to Livorna. As I told you, that is where my fate lies for good or ill. The saint is pulling me there."

She squeezed his arm and her eyes grew harsh. "You fool. They will catch you and they will kill you. You won't even get the chance to explain your innocence. They don't want to know."

"I need your help to get on the road. Food and water for a start. Maybe some denari."

"You're not listening to me! You'll die there."

Acquel took both her hands in his. "No. I won't," he said quietly. "Elded is going to show me the way. Show me the truth." He released her and slowly climbed to his feet. "I would be grateful for your help. But even without it, I am leaving."

He wandered off into the thick of the encampment, a solitary figure who was neither soldier nor monk. Timandra watched him disappear as she chewed on her lower lip, her heart and head in battle with each other.

ACQUEL SPENT THE afternoon only half-aware of his surroundings and feeling more alone than he had in days. A group of unusually pious swordsmen spotted him passing by and asked him to lead them in prayers despite his soldier's garb. He complied, awkwardly spouting the words he knew by heart and they following his lead—

mumbling and sheepish. He rounded things off with a recital of Elded's Prime, and though this may have brought some comfort to the soldiers it brought little to him. He had already decided he would depart in the early hours, just before sunrise. It was a long walk to Livorna from Maresto—he knew that—but equally very few roads to have to worry about getting lost on, so long as he headed north. He threaded his way through the camp and back to Timandra's wagon just as the cook was finishing clearing up from the evening stew. Four mangy dogs were skulking about and fighting over the slops that had been thrown at the base of the town walls. He saw that the wagon steps were down. Timandra was inside. He poked his head around the corner and she saw him.

"I've been waiting for you," she said, her voice low but firm. "You need to come with me."

She led him across the camp and he quickly realised they were heading for the officers' enclosure. He stopped and turned to her. "You told him. So much for your friendship."

"Don't second guess me. This will be in your interest."

As they entered Strykar's tent he saw the captain and also Poule, standing and waiting for him. Timandra closed the flap and Acquel faced them both, hands at his side. Strykar said nothing but Poule walked to the wooden field chest that lay near Strykar's table and hefted a large bundle that lay on top. He tossed it down at Acquel's feet.

Strykar gestured towards it. "It contains a side sword and a pair of boots. It's all old but serviceable. And that wrapping is an oilskin cloak." He turned and scooped up a purse from his table. He handed it to Acquel who accepted it warily, his face screwed up in puzzlement.

"You're letting me go?"

"I would never force a man I've fought beside to put his head into a noose. There's little justice enough in this world without me making it worse. Go where you must, brother monk. And I wish you well." He extended his hand to Acquel.

"Too bad you're not staying a while longer," said Poule, smiling. "I could have shown you a *mandritto* cut that would have been useful. At least you already know your dagger fight."

Acquel swallowed hard and looked over at Timandra who was forcing a smile of support.

"You are a good man, Captain. I will pray that the saints look out for you. You will always have my thanks."

Strykar laughed. "You can put in a word with Elded for me." He waved his arm. "Go on, and try to be at least a *little* stealthy about sneaking away tonight."

Acquel smiled and picked up the bundle. "Farewell to you all!"

He gave a slight nod and then brushed past the tent flap, gone. Timandra turned to her cousin. "Thank you, Jules. I don't want him to go, but I know he must."

Strykar came to her and put an arm about her shoulders. "He's a miserable sod but I confess I will miss him. I do wish him well." He lifted her chin and saw the tears streaming.

"My God," he whispered, "you love him."

"CAN YOU NOT hear her singing?" Danamis had one foot on the railing, one precariously on the deck, and his right arm gripping a shroud line.

Strykar's wry grin widened. "I'm sure the music of your ship is wondrous. But I'm here at the orders of my prince. Your voyages tend to wear me out before my time."

The caravel had caught a good southwesterly, her huge amber-coloured triangular sails stretched full, and she was making excellent speed northwards past the west coast of Maresto. Danamis had named her the *Vendetta*, pleasing not only himself, but Gregorvero and the old hands too. They had run the gauntlet out of Maresto harbour under cover of night, spying the lanterns of two Palestrian warships close by. But there was no challenge. This was just as well as *Vendetta* carried no big guns. Only four falconets, two on the fore deck near the tall prow and two at the stern, the better to outrun any threat. Bassinio had been left behind in Maresto to command the old carrack and the remaining crew, who had been ordered to once again take to their tools to repair the battered vessel.

Vendetta had stopped only once so far, dropping anchor off the island of Piso. The crew had watched with approval as Citala had shed her cambric chemise and dived over the side. Most of the men assumed she needed a bellyful of raw fish as merfolk didn't eat pig or cow. But Danamis knew where she was going and why. She was gone for several hours but returned at the end of the day, clambering up over the side and disappearing into the stern cabin.

Now, as the sun dipped low on the horizon, the ship was running with the wind on the larboard quarter, the bow diving into the rougher waters of the great *Mare Infinitum*. Danamis leapt back to the deck and clapped Strykar on the shoulder.

"Come my friend, let's take our meal!"

Strykar was watching the mermaid as she walked fore of the mainmast, stopping to speak with the sailors, most of whom she towered over. "They seem to be used to her presence now where before they were wary."

Danamis nodded. "It was her idea to talk with the men. She says it is the only way to build trust between her people and ours."

"Still, it's all damned strange. They probably just want another look at her tits when she goes swimming. It's all I can do to keep Brognolo on the men's backs. But they can only keep their heads down so much you know, cleaning their harness and such."

Danamis scowled. "Your lot will treat her with respect on my ship. She has a part to play just as you. And she's clever. It was her idea to lead the men in morning prayer yesterday. That took them by surprise."

"Me too," Strykar snorted. "I imagine you'll create a stir in Ivrea when you meet with the Count."

Danamis lifted his chin and placed his hand on Strykar's bicep. "You're not questioning my wisdom in bringing her along, are you?"

The mercenary chuckled lightly and shrugged. "Me? It's your ship and expedition. I'm here to supply steel when needed. It's just... you need to be careful about assuming folk will accept the mermaid as easily as you... and me, of course."

Danamis released his hand. "I value your counsel, my friend, I truly do. But maybe I have more confidence in her charms and her wits than you do."

Strykar scowled. "Fie on you. I have great admiration for the lady—and the risks she's taking. I have far less admiration for tongue-wagging Ivrean merchants and their wives. That's what gives me bellyache."

Danamis nodded. "Don't worry. We will navigate those shoals if we meet them." He stepped to the side and shouted forward. "Citala! Join me in my cabin, if you will, my lady!"

The three, plus the ship's master, sat down in more generous confines than the ones aboard the *Royal Grace*. The *Vendetta*, though somewhat narrower of beam, was a longer vessel, the spaces a little less cramped. Danamis had stocked the galley well in Maresto: Gregorvero was almost humming to himself with joy as the diminutive and wizened cook they had signed on laid out the smoked ham and herring, black bread, cheeses and bowls of vinegar-soaked olives. The master hefted the brimming wine pot and splashed out a liberal dose into his cup.

Citala smiled. She was getting used to the company of these landsmen now, despite their strong and usually rank scent, and found their humour good-hearted and brash—like the mer themselves. But clothing was a different matter. She reached over and rubbed the chemise around her shoulder, pulling it away from her itching flesh.

"These clothes that I must wear... I find them uncomfortable. Rough. All of the time they are on me. I do not understand how you tolerate this... *feeling*."

Strykar suppressed a snigger. Danamis smiled at her. "We are accustomed to these things. You are not. But in our world it is not proper for a woman to go naked about the town."

"Well," remarked Gregorvero, "there are *some* women."

Citala blinked, not really understanding, and Strykar and Gregorvero shared a laugh. Danamis gritted his teeth and decided to change the subject.

"Strykar, since you came aboard you haven't mentioned Brother Acquel."

Strykar tore off a chunk of dark rye. "No. I haven't."

"Did you turn him over to Alonso's men?"

Strykar paused and looked at Danamis. "Do you think I would have done that? Send him back to the priests? I let him go. To hell with them all. Bad enough the Widow was moping about like some lost soul when I left her. She'll be a handful for poor old Poule in the next few weeks. She... she was close to the monk."

Citala smiled. "You speak of the holy man that I met at the Duke's palace. I liked him. But he is troubled. He carries what we call *na-kuli*."

"And what is that?" asked Danamis as he watched her thin dark lips sound out the word.

"It means a heavy burden. But more. That one is unable to share this fate, or to lessen it. He is alone."

Strykar exchanged a knowing glance with Danamis.

"That rings true enough," replied Danamis. Strykar grunted.

Citala looked down at her trencher, debating whether to share more of her feelings about the young holy man. But she thought better of it and kept quiet.

"My lady," said Danamis, "why did you send away your warriors after they loaded the treasure on board? Rarely does anyone in Valdur dispense with their guards by choice."

She placed the herring back on her trencher and rubbed her fingers. "Too much change, too fast, is not always good, Danamis. You saw the looks on your men's faces when my people climbed up over the side. Better for the Ivreans to see just one she-mer than several warriors when we get there." She smiled again. "We have sworn an oath, you and I. I *trust* you, Danamis. And your men." She levelled her gaze at Strykar and Gregorvero. "You will look out for me in this new city and... I will look out for you."

Strykar's eyebrows lifted. "Well spoken, my lady."

Gregorvero cleared his throat and looked about the table. "My lady... how is it you can *stay* out of the sea? I mean, for very long."

She laughed, that strange trilling noise, a sound of amusement that Danamis had come to like very much. "We are not so very different from you. I breathe the air you breathe. We don't live under the sea but we spend much time in it. We grow uncomfortable in our skin unless we return to it often."

Danamis thought she may have revealed too much already. For it begged the question: where did the mer live? He changed the subject before Citala could say more.

"When we make it to Ivrea port," he said, "we are a merchantman—not a warship—there to buy swords and guns for Maresto. Strykar, you should keep your men aboard to guard the treasure below. It will be hard enough explaining the presence of so many armed men on a humble merchant ship but I'll have to come up with some excuse that's believable."

Strykar nodded. "The lads won't be happy. But they'll obey."

"God willing," said Danamis, "we won't have to stay more than a few days."

"Assuming they will sell us the orichalcum guns," added Gregorvero, sprinkling a dose of pessimism. "Not to mention lending us the men who know how to fire them."

Danamis reached for his cup. "Every man has his price, master Gregorvero. We just have to find out what Count Leonato's is."

A WEEK PASSES slowly at sea. Although a few vessels were seen at a distance, none hailed them and the *Vendetta* was left to make its progress unhindered. Danamis had time to consider matters. His opening gambit with the Ivreans for one. And he caught himself watching Citala's daily promenades more and more often. He relished his playful words with her together as they stood on the raised quarterdeck, watching whales breach and gulls dive to feast. So too, he noticed her command of Valdurian growing stronger with each day and he marvelled at her quickness both in mind and body. Always, her strange eyes drew his own to hers. And slowly, but surely, his heart was starting to follow. As conscience pricked him lying in his berth, he would remind himself that infatuation with this exotic creature was understandable. But it would never be right. He forced himself to contemplate his courtesans, abandoned to their fates in Palestro. A reminder of the man he was.

On the morning of the ninth day, the high cliffs of Ivrea, mountains beyond, hove into view. All was grey: the sky, the sea, the city. A fine steady misting rain fell upon them, cold, soaking, and unwanted. The ship passed by the stone jetty of the city and made its turn into the harbour under the cannon of the round watchtowers and the gaze of the garrison. Danamis's standard snapped out defiantly in the steady breeze. From the stern, he stood with Strykar watching the parapets above. Citala stood near the mizzenmast, the hood of her long brown cloak pulled up, concealing her from view. A barbute-topped soldier leaned over the wall and gave them a wave of welcome. The *Vendetta* was skilfully eased up to a mooring, the dockmen lending a hand to secure the cables as the crew scampered to make the ship fast, Gregorvero's commands echoing off the fortifications that rose above them. Danamis counted the other vessels in the harbour. Six merchantmen and two war carracks flying Ivrea's standard. Not particularly busy for a free city of the kingdom.

He looked up towards the city, so different from the ones of the south. Ivrea clung like a mountain goat to the high slopes. Round turreted towers dotted the view, these seemingly preferred to the square towers of Perusia and Palestro. And where in the south red sandstone blocks were the preferred construction, here Danamis could see that rough stone and mortar was used, the result coarse, ugly and uninviting. But that fit with the reputation of the place.

Strykar elbowed him, drawing his attention back to the quay. A party from the garrison was approaching fast, polearms waving as they moved at a trot, their long-bearded commander at the fore.

"And so our Ivrean adventure begins," muttered Strykar. He added, "My men are below."

Danamis nodded, clapped him on the shoulder, and pounded down the stairs to the main deck. As the soldiers approached the edge of the quay, he took a station at the gunwale amidships, hands on the thick oak railing.

The garrison commander stepped forward and shouted up to them. "Palestro, are you?"

"That we are. I am Nicolo Danamis, Lord of Palestro and the king's admiral. I am here to request an audience with the High Steward."

The commander's scowl did not soften. He pulled at his unkempt beard for a second and then folded his arms across his blackened breastplate. "You still have to pay the mooring tithe."

Leaning forward over the side, Danamis flashed him a brash smile. "That we can do, sir! That we can do."

Thirty-Two

THE *RONDELIERI* COLUMN parted either side of the street as if the bouncing shot of a bombard had bowled through them. But it was a mastiff, nearly the size of a bear, that bounded past them all. It was wearing a purple tabard over its back and a cylindrical leather satchel around its neck that rested on its broad chest. It gave a booming bark that echoed off the houses and, without stopping, loped downhill.

Recovering from the surprise, Danamis looked over at Strykar for an explanation. Citala, wrapped in her cloak, clung to his arm as she pressed against him. She had only recently seen her first dog in Maresto, and that from a respectable distance. The beasts still filled her with apprehension and this huge brute the more so.

"Faster and more dependable as messengers than men," said Strykar as the column of ten soldiers regrouped and started up the cobbled street again. "The dogs are used by the High Steward and the Decurions as couriers on account of the steepness of the place. Some merchants use them too."

Danamis put his hand on his falchion hilt and resumed his climb on aching legs. "Dependable, you say?"

"Aye. And anyone who interferes with their run is likely to lose an arm. Each dog is trained to travel between only two stations. So a lot of dogs are needed. And a lot of shit to sweep."

They had ascended the main centre thoroughfare of the city to the halfway point. Here, there was a small market square from which a crossroad led to the east and west, the latter towards where Leonato's palazzo lay. The sky hung low on Ivrea like a damp and dirty woollen blanket. The cramped stone houses looked all the same and the air was filled with the stink of coal fires from the forges and the smelters. High above them the coal smoke mixed with the mist of the looming mountains where the great mines had been dug out over centuries. This was, after all, a city that belonged to the craft of ironwork.

More than a few stall holders and townsmen turned their heads as the group walked past. Danamis had felt a sullenness about the place since they had set out. It was like a plague town without the plague; a heaviness in the air that spoke of mistrust, unhappiness, or fear. He noticed that Ivreans dressed from his grandsire's era: knee-length tunics on the men secured with a waist belt and large hoods that covered their shoulders. Of the few women he had seen it was their fashion to cover their hair entirely by coiling it up into two great linen-swathed bunches either side of their heads. Some seemed to have shaved their hairline high, halfway up their crowns. And not one of them smiled.

They reached the hulking palazzo, a massive single fortress, round and squat where in the south such palaces were built four-square. A small company of soldiers stood guard at the large black studded oak door, watching apprehensively as Danamis and Strykar approached. And if they themselves looked dirty and stupid, thought Danamis, at least their armour and arms were of high quality. Side by side, he and

Strykar walked up to the post and the guards brought their polished glaives up to cross their chests.

"We seek audience with the High Steward," said Danamis. "I am the king's admiral, Nicolo Danamis. And he is expecting me."

One of the men, his eyes large, spoke up. "We was told you would be coming this afternoon." And he knocked three times upon the door and waited, looking back nervously towards Danamis as he did so. The door creaked open and a palace retainer, dressed in a breastplate and gorget as if expecting a fight, filled the doorway; a tall sallow-faced man who glowered down at the soldier who had already retreated a few paces.

The retainer looked over to Danamis and Strykar, then to the hooded form of Citala. He said nothing to the guards but addressed Danamis directly.

"My lord Danamis, you and your party may follow me."

The palace, ancient beyond memory, was ill-lit by natural light and torches burned on the walls. Half a dozen other armed retainers met them, all of Leonato's men wearing tabards of white and burgundy. The structure was like some great spiral and they were led up a wide stone stair to the second level. Here windows provided some dull light and they proceeded down the corridor. Danamis sniffed. The air was tinged with mould from the shabby worn tapestries and a whiff of old damp stone. He watched Strykar take in the surroundings with a soldier's eye, occasionally turning his head to watch his own men and the three retainers who were at the rear. Two mastiff messengers sat in the corridor, panting with tongues lolling. They watched as the party moved past, attentive but passive.

At length, they turned in toward the centre of the great round tower, through double doors, and were ushered into

Count Leonato's hall. Strykar gestured for the *rondelieri* to take up station outside and he noticed how an equal number of Leonato's men did the same, opposite his own.

Danamis took in his surroundings. Three rectangular windows looked out over the city. A heavy black-stained beamed ceiling rose up some twenty feet, and a huge stone hearth on the opposite side surrounded a cast iron brazier filled with burning coals. A round table the length of a longboat stood at the centre of the room, its gilded legs enveloped by carved serpents. It fair groaned under all manner of platters holding roasts and sweetmeats. A great silver wine ewer oversaw all.

"Welcome, welcome to the king's admiral of Palestro!"

Leonato came practically bounding into the hall from a small door near an immense but hideously discoloured tapestry, bringing two servants in tow.

Danamis and Strykar bowed. "We are pleased that you have been so kind to receive us with such little notice," said Danamis.

"Indeed, no notice at all," laughed Leonato. He was neither short nor tall, but well proportioned, of fair complexion with jet black hair and beard, the latter adorned by two plaits at either cheek. Danamis could not tell his age but he had heard the Count was well over fifty. The man before him did not look near so old. He wore a red velvet tunic over which was draped a black houppelande that made him appear big-shouldered and strong.

"Unavoidably so, my lord," replied Danamis, apologetically. "This is my companion, Captain Julianus Strykar of the Company of the Black Rose."

Strykar bowed his head slightly, never taking his eyes from the Count.

"And this, my other companion and ally from the south, Princess Citala, of the kingdom of the merfolk in the Sea of

Valdur." He knew he was going too far, but first impressions carried weight. Citala raised her long hands, the colour of pale lilac, and lowered the hood of her cloak.

"BY ALL THE blessed saints!" Leonato's dark eyes widened and he clapped his hands to his face. "A daughter of the merfolk here in Ivrea. Your people are never glimpsed in these northern waters, my lady. You are indeed most welcome here."

Citala managed an awkward smile and bowed her head, her long white tresses falling across her shoulders. This was the second time to be so greeted by a great Valdurian nobleman and she was unsure she liked the attention. The Count spread his arms wide and gestured to the table.

"Join me, please." The servants scooted forward and began lifting platters and pouring wine.

They ate sparingly, enough to show gratitude. The Count too partook little, it seemed to Danamis. Strykar took a good swig of wine, swallowed hard, and smacked his lips; the best of Milvorna. Danamis began to tell the Count of the journey from Maresto and of his desire to source swords and cannon for the fleet. But Leonato's eyes darted like a ferret's from Danamis to Citala and back again.

Danamis raised his voice slightly. "And I was hoping for a demonstration of your cannon on the battlements. The ones cast of orichalcum, to be exact."

Leonato's head shot back sharply towards Danamis. "Orichalcum guns, you say? So word has already spread to the southern duchies then. And Palestro would be the first to have them?"

"Captain Strykar here has told me of their superiority. And as an honest man I won't hide the fact that I might like to acquire a few. But we are able to pay. Handsomely."

Leonato smiled. "An honest pirate lord? After seeing this noble mermaid, my second surprise of the day. Of course we are willing to sell you swords and guns, Lord Danamis. Orichalcum possibly. The forgemaster has only just perfected his process he tells me. Much trial and error. And a few... accidents."

Danamis returned the smile as the game began. "As some already sit on your battlements one would assume they are ready."

"Oh, I believe that Master Alarbus is confident his casting formula is perfected. But as you can imagine, such a metal affords a new kind of power—and influence. I would not want to see these weapons in the hands of an enemy. Or a potential one."

Danamis nodded. "Indeed. Which is why I would propose an alliance between our two cities. As part of any arrangement we might come to."

Two knocks of a halberd announced a retainer and behind him, a dog padded in, the leather satchel at its neck swinging. Man and beast stopped a few paces from them and Leonato motioned to the retainer. He retrieved the note inside the satchel and handed it to the Count.

As he read its contents, bushy eyebrows beetling, Danamis and Strykar exchanged glances. So far, not an outright rejection. It would come down to the price then.

Leonato's hand closed slowly about the note he grasped. He held it aloft between two fingers as if it were a soiled snot rag. "I am sorry, but I must attend to this." He was addled, Danamis could see it.

"Please, enjoy more food and drink," he continued, folding the parchment again, roughly, his annoyance obvious. "Do you have irritations with your Council of Decurions in Palestro, my lord? Daily vexations from mine. Questioning me, demanding explanations."

Strykar tried not to grin. Danamis nodded in sympathy. "From time to time, my lord."

"Do they forget we are the king's representative—his very arm and hand—in these cities?"

Citala noticed that the mastiff was staring her down and it occurred to her that the creature had never seen one of her kind before. She directed a calming thought towards it, as she might to a dolphin. It licked its lips once and kept watching. Disappointed, she focussed instead on the exchange between the noblemen.

"My lord," said Danamis, "please attend to your business as needs require. We are content to wait upon your pleasure."

Leonato gave a slight bow and turned towards the door he had come through. He stopped after a few steps and turned back to Danamis. "And after I reply to the timewasting Council I will send word to the forgemaster to receive you later this day—for your demonstration." He smiled and then waved his hand towards the retainer who led the dog away.

When the Ivreans had left, Strykar turned to Danamis. "I don't like him," he growled. "Thinks he's clever."

Citala folded her arms. "That is of little importance. He holds what you want and you will have to make a bargain to get it."

"Bah!" grumbled the mercenary. "Where is everyone in this decrepit palazzo? Has he no *contessa*? No family?" He tilted his head and looked at Danamis. "An alliance? What will Duke Alonso have to say about that?"

"I'll worry about the consequences later. I need those guns."

They waited. Strykar amused himself by throwing almonds across the table at the gaping mouth of the giant sea bass that was arranged decoratively, if bizarrely, at the centre.

Citala turned to Danamis, who was staring into the middle distance. "What will you do if he says you cannot have them?"

Danamis started a little and turned to her. He grinned mischievously. "Then I will need another plan."

"Everything depends upon this. For both of us."

They turned as the door near the tapestry creaked open and Leonato appeared, apologising profusely for his delay. He strode across the room and bellowed for his retainers in the corridor outside.

"Get these out to their destinations!" he ordered, shoving his letters into the retainer's hands. "And do make sure you give them to the correct animals!" He wheeled and returned to the table, his hands on the facings of his gown which gave him the look of some oversized magpie.

"Now, Lord Danamis, we must continue our conversation." He stood next to the pirate and looked out over the feast. "I have been thinking on this matter. If you decide you want the orichalcum guns, I shall let you have them. But only four. As a gesture of my goodwill."

"I need eight," replied Danamis, his voice measured and assured.

Leonato, still staring at the sea bass, pouted. "Eight? Well, hardly enough to equip a fleet, I suppose. But still more than I am comfortable to part with." He turned and faced Danamis. "Shall we say six? A thousand ducats apiece?"

Danamis watched Strykar's eyes visibly widen.

"Five hundred each," replied Danamis.

"Eight."

Danamis placed his silver goblet back on the table. "Six hundred ducats, my lord."

Leonato said nothing for a moment. He smiled thinly and sniffed. "I would have thought if you had journeyed this far for these guns you would be willing to pay any price."

"Even pirates have finite purses, my lord."

Leonato turned slowly and walked part way across the chamber before spinning back towards his three guests. "I can agree to your offer. But only with one further condition."

"That being?"

Leonato looked towards Citala. "That the mer princess remain here as my guest." He held out his hands. "Only for the time it take you to fit out your ship and resupply. What could that be? A few days?"

Citala moved closer to Danamis and he shot her a glance before answering the Count. "That is a bold and, some might say, most improper condition."

Leonato laughed. "Nothing improper. She will have her own handmaiden that will accompany her everywhere. I will never have another chance to learn of her people— their history."

Danamis's voice was cold. "To what purpose, my lord?"

The Count dropped his arms. "To a very good purpose indeed. My history of Valdur. I have laboured on it for years. And it is sadly deficient in regard to the days, long past, when the merfolk lived among men. Citala could teach me much."

Danamis looked to the mermaid. He still found it difficult to judge the facial expressions of the mer. And now, her face displayed something resembling surprise and curiosity. "Citala is not some commodity to be bartered. She is in my charge. Let us keep to the matter before us. The money."

"Good my lord, the gold is quite secondary to me." His visage had now changed its cast, his eyes gaining an intensity where before there was playfulness. "My last condition is not negotiable."

Danamis felt Citala's strong hand wrap around his forearm. Her voice was quiet but insistent. "Danamis, I choose to remain. We both must play our part."

Strykar was shaking his head in silent objection. Danamis looked into Citala's eyes, liquid lavender and without trepidation. "Are you certain you wish to do this?"

She inclined her head and her lips parted slightly. "I do."

Danamis turned to Leonato. "And I too place a condition. That two of my *rondelieri* will remain as her bodyguard."

Strykar turned his head in surprise.

"Of course," said the Count. "I would expect no less."

Danamis leaned in close to Citala. "Is it possible for you to remain out of the sea for such a time? Can you do such a thing?"

"You should have asked me that before now. But, yes, I can."

"Then I will agree," he told her quietly. "We will be back for you in no more than three days."

"I know that you will."

He lifted her hand in his and turned back to the Count. "Then my lord, I deliver her into your good care. Until a few days hence." He beckoned for two of Strykar's soldiers to enter and then told them to accompany Citala. They both cast their eyes to their commander and Strykar nodded.

The Count walked forward and took her hand in his. "Come, my lady. We have centuries to catch up with!"

Citala pushed her shoulders back, swallowed the doubt that welled inside her, and let him lead her away.

Danamis's eyes followed her as she left the chamber. Deep down he was uneasy with the request and his conscience was already stirring within him. But he plucked at the sleeve of a distracted Strykar and turned to leave. As they reached the entrance, Strykar turned to look back into the room.

"Did you not see that big rat—or maybe it was a black cat? It went from under the table and scooted after them as they left for his apartments."

Danamis shook his head. "I saw nothing."

Strykar rubbed vigorously at his head as if trying to shake off the fug of too much wine. "For a moment—just a moment mind you—I thought it walked upon two legs." He looked again at Danamis and then snorted at his own foolishness. "Bah! Let's get back to the ship."

Thirty-Three

HE HAD TREKKED northwards for two days, always upon the road unless a group of horsemen were approaching. When he did spy others approaching, he would hurry into the high grass and hide until they had passed. He avoided every village and town, preferring to eat his meagre provisions and to sleep rough under the stars. But now his feet ached such that his mood had turned from cautious hope to self-pity borne of discomfort and loneliness.

It was nearly mid-day on the third day of his journey to Livorna. He assumed he was perhaps halfway, maybe more, and he could see ahead, in the rising landscape, scattered pockets of woodland, and the undulating grain fields of the northern reaches of Maresto. Further ahead, hazy and purplish, he could just make out the high hills around Livorna, beyond which the lands of Ivrea lay, a string of snow-capped mountain peaks forming a formidable border. Looking behind him as he trudged on the dusty rutted road (which he did every so often so as not to be taken by surprise) he saw a lone mounted figure leading another horse behind. Whoever it was, they were not even at a trot, just ambling. No doubt a trader bound to Livorna. As the hour went by, the figure drew nearer until he heard the rhythmic pound of hooves close behind him. He turned off the road and crouched in the tall grass, angling his head to get a look as the stranger passed him.

The rider was dressed in a dark cloak and hood and mounted not on a horse but on a mule, another in tow. As the person drew even with him, he slowly stood up, recognizing something oddly familiar about the small rider. Acquel raised a hand in a tentative greeting, one follower of the road to another. The figure reined in the mule and stopped. The hood fell back and there was Timandra, grinning. Acquel cried out and ran across the road. He reached up and threw one arm around her back, the other gripping her forearm.

"Timandra! Sweet God above I cannot believe you're here!"

She grasped his wrist and squeezed. "I'm here for you, greyrobe." She then jerked her thumb behind her. "And this one is yours, so climb on up so we can be on our way."

They rode on until the sun was low and blooded in the west. Timandra told him of her defection from the Black Rose, stealing away in the dead of night. Strykar had set sail with Danamis the day before. She had said farewell to her cousin, the parting markedly more poignant for what she was about to do. She also knew that Poule would no doubt be in an uproar when he discovered her gone, but she had left him a note saying the wagon and all her goods were his to do with as he pleased until she returned. As the light failed, they found themselves with a great wood on their left, rolling open fields on their right. Timandra suggested they make camp a short way into the trees and Acquel nodded, trusting her field skills. He had not even bothered to make a fire the previous night and had shivered himself to a fitful sleep.

Soon, he had his fire, a small blaze to nurture some hot embers to keep them warm but not large enough to draw attention. He swung his side sword across his lap as he sat underneath an old beech, still unaccustomed to wearing a blade. It did not suit him. Timandra threw some more wood onto the blaze and joined him. They faced the road, and watched the sun die, twilight throwing its shadows through the wood.

"Why did you come for me?" Acquel asked as she sat next to him, back against the smooth silver bark of the tree.

"Because I had to. You ended up with us for a reason... with me—for a reason. It wasn't right to let you return on your own."

Acquel gave her hand a squeeze. "You befriended me when I had no one. I am sorry if I rewarded that with... baseness, in Perusia. It's only that I care for you so deeply that it has shaken me to my core."

She gently turned his cheek towards her. "And I care deeply about you. But our love must remain a chaste one. You are a monk still. And I, a sinner. I can't return your love."

"Why?"

The hurt in his eyes made her look down. "Because... it might endanger your soul on the path the Saint has chosen for you."

Acquel glanced down at the amulet in his shirt. "I am glad you came for me, just the same."

They ate some bread and dried ham that Timandra sliced with her dagger, but as darkness fell their conversation grew less and less. It was almost as if what was unspoken had become a wall between them. The moon had risen and Acquel found himself nodding off, his head leaning against hers, the sound of hissing embers and the occasional cry of a night bird coming to his ears. And then, he was aware of another sound: breathing; slow long breaths. He lifted his head. It was not coming from Timandra. The high-pitched whinny of the mules brought him to his feet. They had ripped their reins from a sapling and were tearing through the trees towards the road.

Timandra swore and leapt up, her hand springing to her dagger. "What is it?" she hissed.

Looking beyond her, Acquel saw a human head staring at him no more than a few feet away; a head the size of a bull's. For a moment, it looked disembodied in the poor light of the dying fire. But now he saw that it was connected to a body, a body of a lion-like creature, as large as a great warhorse. Timandra swore and fell back into him. His own feet were frozen to the ground. The creature padded forward silently on its powerfully muscled legs until they could smell its rank and rancid breath. It was bearded, with thick brown lips and skin the colour of bronze. The hair on its head, black and matted, flowed into a lion's mane, the fur cascading wildly down its back and sides. It looked at them and tilted its head in an expression of puzzlement, so human in fact that Acquel instantly felt his guts turn to water and his balls shrivel. It was a *mantichora,* alive and breathing as if it had sprung from a woodcut illustration in the library of the monastery. It blinked slowly, eyes the size of cooking apples, and its mouth gaped in a horrible smile, aping human emotion. He saw rows of triangular teeth like those of a shark, whitish strips of chewed meat dangling between them. What Acquel thought was a giant serpent swaying behind the beast he now saw to be its swishing tail. He slowly moved his hand to the hilt of his sword. A sword he did not even know how to use. And then, it spoke. It was a voice so low it rumbled against Acquel's chest.

"I will have you before you draw it out halfway, man."

Acquel stood still, his eyes locked on the hideous face of the creature.

It sniffed loudly, nostrils crinkling. "Much choice there is here. You, woman, or both." Its eyes moved towards the road. "Or horseflesh… if I feel like running them down." Its words came from deep in its chest, bass and terrifyingly unearthly.

Acquel began muttering a prayer, a short one to Elded, over and over. The *mantichora's* eyes narrowed, the glistening greenish orbs shrinking to slivers. "There's something about you, man." It sniffed again and raised its head slightly. "I don't think I like you."

Acquel found his voice, albeit a timorous one. "Leave us be. We mean you no harm. Take a mule if you must."

"It's not having our mules *or* us," hissed Timandra as she sidestepped Acquel, her dagger drawn. "Get back to your hole or I will take out your eyes before I go down!"

The *mantichora's* rippling shoulders and forelegs drooped slightly, its head lowering. It broke into a broad grin and something like laughter issued from its throat. It pursed its massive lips and tilted its head, sniffing the air about Timandra.

"*This* one has fight. And another's blood. I can smell it upon her." A wide tongue spilled out and touched its lower lip. It took a half-step closer to Acquel, and then halted again, suspicious. "You carry something... different. I can smell that too." It let out what Acquel thought to be a sigh. "So much is changing. I can feel it around me. That which was sleeping is now waking again. It speaks upon the wind as it gathers strength. Do you not feel it under your feet?"

The *mantichora* edged forward two steps, its head shaking in amusement. "And what have I found? A strange fellow who reeks of the priesthood and a little she-killer with the heart of a marten. No, this is not for me to feast upon. Far too foul." It suddenly let out a cry of savage exultation and sprang past them through the trees, branches and twigs snapping and cracking under its great weight as it pounded into the forest. Acquel turned and reached for Timandra and they stood there, shaking, too fearful to move. Not long afterwards, a high-pitched neigh, a pitiful and helpless sound, echoed and was cut short. Acquel belatedly drew his side sword and backed himself against the tree. Timandra slumped down at its base, her head hanging.

"Do we try and find the other mule?" he whispered.

"No, we stay here until light. And pray it doesn't change its mind and return."

Acquel looked out into the wood, lit silver by the sinking moon and teeming with shadows. He kept thumbing the edge of his sword, finding some illusory comfort from the sharp steel in his untrained hand. After a minute, he spoke again to Timandra.

"What did it mean? About you. Another's blood. 'She-killer', it said."

"I told you I was a sinner." Her voice was flat, weary. "The creature spoke the truth."

Acquel sank down to his knees and huddled up close to her, the sword pushed into the soil. "What did you do, Timandra?"

She kept looking at the bed of moss at her feet. For a long moment she did not reply. And then she spoke, her words soft. "I am a murderess. That is my sin, Brother Acquel."

He looked at her, not quite believing or understanding. "What did you do?" he repeated, a note of fear creeping into his voice.

"Pandarus wasn't stabbed by a man. He was stabbed by me. I lied to the others—to Strykar—and said it had been someone my husband had cheated."

Acquel put his hand on her arm. "Your husband was... beating you? Had he tried to kill *you*?" He could feel her tears dripping onto his hand.

She shook her head and let out a sobbing laugh as the tears coursed down. "No! I just hated him. That's all. He was a brute with not an ounce of love in him. It enraged me, sweet God above, it enraged me. But he did not beat me. He *ignored* me. So I killed him." She shook her head. "I wasn't even drunk."

Acquel struggled to find words, any words, to give her comfort. But it was like groping for a coin on the ground in the dark. All these weeks with her, the many times she alluded to her sins and then changed the subject. Here now, at last, she had bared the truth. "Timandra, you have carried this on your soul for a long time. But so too can I see your pain and your regret. Elded forgives you. God will forgive you. "

She turned her wet face up to him. "Don't you see? It is why I needed you. Why I have looked after you. I wanted you to be my path to salvation. My holy man." She wiped the back of her hand across her eyes. "I thought that by helping you I might help myself. You are chosen by the Lawgiver for some purpose." She laughed weakly. "Even in that I was a calculating bitch. But I began to care too much for you."

Acquel felt his heart ache with sadness and yearning mixed such that he did not know his own emotions. He pulled her into his chest and hugged her tightly. And all her defiance melted at once and she held onto him, sobbing gently in the dark. He stroked her head and, both exhausted, they each nodded off, past caring about the return of the *mantichora*.

BIRDS AWOKE THEM both, the first rays of dawn shooting through the trees, turning the ground mist golden. Their clothes were sodden with morning dew. Acquel was cold, his stomach gnawing, and the events of the evening still only half-believed.

Timandra drew herself away from his chest. "I'd better see if we still have one mule," she muttered, pulling herself up and leaning on the tree for support.

Acquel climbed to his feet, stiff and pained. "Don't wander off too far."

"Do you still want me with you?"

He pushed her hair from her face. "I need you with me. And I will never tell anyone of your confession."

"And once in Livorna, what then?"

"I will go to the Temple. I have seen it in my dreams. I must find the door—the chamber—that the Saint has shown me. That's where the truth lies. The truth that has been hidden from all of us and the reason they killed the brethren. And then I must find the Magister."

She pulled her shawl up on her shoulders, a chill coursing through her back. "And what of the guardsmen? You'll be captured once you enter the Ara. What can you expect to do there? Kill the Magister?"

Acquel retrieved his sword, wiped it on his sleeve and returned it to its scabbard. "I'm not running anymore. Elded will guide me. I know how to get in by the gate at Low Town and where I can get a monk's robes. I will slip into the Temple at night and then down to the undercroft."

She looked at him, frightened. "Acquel, you don't have a blessed idea of what you're going to do. Or even of what you're looking for."

"No, I don't," he said, as he reached down for his satchel. "But I will once I get there."

KODORIS DID NOT pause to knock on the door to the chamber. He slammed the handle down and burst in. Lavinia was perched on the edge of the bed while Lucinda sat in a chair, a handmaiden brushing out her fine blonde hair. Lavinia sprang up but Lucinda didn't flinch as he strode across to where she sat.

"You," he motioned to the servant. "Leave us at once."

The horn hairbrush clattered to the tiles as the girl scrambled to gather her things, bowing and apologising. Lucinda looked up at the Magister, her eyes narrowing.

"You may be the Magister of the Ara but you still must knock before entering a woman's apartments, sir. This is plain boorishness."

Kodoris swallowed his rage. "We can discuss my manners another time, canoness. When were you planning on informing me of your return? Your empty-handed return."

"When I had made myself presentable and not caked with the dust of the road."

Kodoris crossed his arms as he stood over her. He was no longer a young man but he was yet a strong one, still broad of chest and taller than others in the priesthood. But Lucinda was not intimidated.

"I am beginning to doubt my faith in your abilities—both of you," he said, as he glanced over to Lavinia who had seated herself, hands folded in her lap. "It should have been a simple task, particularly since I lent you a contingent of the Temple guard. And where is Captain Flauros?"

"I am not responsible for Captain Flauros, Magister. Perhaps he has duties to attend to."

Kodoris's face began to match the colour of his robes. "I expect a full account of the journey. And why it was not successful. And I will have it now."

Lavinia giggled. "The greyrobe is on his way here, Magister. Just as I told you."

Kodoris looked at Lavinia and then back to her sister, his mouth falling open. "He's on his way? When?"

Lucinda smiled smugly. "He will be here, at the Ara, within a day. Two at the most. Lavinia has seen him."

"Them, sister," corrected Lavinia. "His woman companion is with him. It's her I see mainly."

Kodoris's brow arched as he turned back to Lucinda. "Will you know when he sets foot into the Temple and the cloisters?" His conscience was already prodding him, an ever more strident voice in his head, to weigh carefully what the sisters told him. And to guard his own counsel. For days, the revelations in the Black Texts had run through his head and the wall he had built around his own motives in defending the status quo was beginning to collapse as if it was made of sand.

"Perhaps," Lucinda replied. "The question is, what is he looking for? I think you know the answer to that."

Kodoris gritted his teeth, and then with great effort, relaxed his face into a thin smile. "And if you are committed to defending the One Faith, you will keep that secret to yourself, canoness. Leave the greyrobe to me. You just tell me when he arrives."

He knew she could easily read his mind if she chose to do so. But there was no familiar pulling sensation in his temple, no shooting pain in his forehead. She was not bothering. Which told him that she wasn't interested in what he was thinking. And that worried him greatly.

One resolute knock sounded on the door. Even as Kodoris turned, Lavinia was off the bed and dashing across the chamber. She opened the door and squealed.

"Captain Flauros!" She curtsied, arms flowing expansively as she backed into the room.

Flauros entered, dressed in his red cloak and black breastplate, and locked eyes with the Magister. He was expressionless but gave a bow of his head, his right arm folded against his stomach. His eyes shifted briefly to Lucinda, who was looking at him with amusement as if she enjoyed seeing his discomfort, knowing full well he had not reported to the Magister.

"Captain. Paying respects to your charge before reporting to me?"

"I was told you were here, Magister. That is why I am. I've been at the barracks since my return. Looking after the affairs of my men. My first concern."

The look of disdain from the captain, perhaps even loathing, hit Kodoris like a mailed fist. He had underestimated Lucinda. It appeared she had put her time with Flauros to good use.

He looked at Lucinda, her face perfectly composed, beaming. He turned back to the captain, his own face a mask of control. "You have found me, Captain. Now accompany me back to my chamber that you may tell me what happened in Perusia." He didn't wait for a reply but bowed curtly to Lucinda and Lavinia and left, Flauros sidestepping to allow him to pass.

Flauros bowed to Lavinia, who put her hand to mouth, eyes laughing, and then nodded to Lucinda, a knowing smile on his lips.

Lucinda returned it and sealed it with a gentle kiss of her fingers.

Thirty-Four

ALARBUS, FORGEMASTER OF Ivrea, dropped his arm. There was an abrupt deafening roar of an explosion mixed instantaneously with a *whump* that vibrated beneath the feet of everyone on the battlement. Danamis watched as a four-foot tongue of bright amber flame shot from the muzzle of the six-foot great saker, the gun jerking back on its wooden truck, ropes and pulleys snapping taut. A pungent cloud of white smoke drifted out over the walls, a few wisps blowing back over the gun carriage. Danamis could not prevent an enormous grin from splitting his face. Out over the water, at a distance of some 300 yards, a huge flume of spray erupted as the cast iron shot struck a swelling wave. He rubbed his hand along the still warm barrel of the orichalcum gun, his fingers tracing the elaborate embossed arms of Ivrea: a ram's head *guardant*.

"But can you hit anything at that range?" laughed Strykar.

Alarbus, a giant of a man, face pocked and scarred from years of having molten metal spat at him, looked at the mercenary, head lowered like a charging bull. "You can anchor your ship just where that shot struck if you want another demonstration," he said, before breaking into a mischievous smile.

"I'm convinced," said Danamis. "You say your iron shot will break solid oak planks at a hundred yards?"

Alarbus nodded, pulling up the scorched leather apron that covered his ample belly, his eyes falling lovingly on his creation. "We've pierced ship hulls and shattered masts ten inches thick. You fire *this* saker at point blank range—she's goddamn near enough a basilisk or a culverin—and you're going in one side and out the other!"

Danamis looked at the gun again. Far more slender and smooth than his own crude wrought iron sakers, it was the colour of a jaundiced Southlander, a yellowish copper. But firing these guns meant that powder and shot both had to be loaded down the muzzle with a rammer. And that meant leaning out over the side or pulling the gun back in first. Either way he would not be able to fire these quickly and every shot would have to find its mark.

Danamis turned and stuck his thumbs into his belt, the smell of gunpowder still filling his nostrils. "You say you have six guns of this calibre at the forge. And plenty of shot?"

Alarbus pulled at the myriad of plaits in his long red beard. "Aye. If you bring the treasure you say you have. The Count has told me the price you agreed."

"And I require a hundred side swords—plain, nothing fancy. And, another thing, I have need of a petard. Nothing too big. Can you manage that too?"

Alarbus shrugged. "The swords we take from the forge arsenal. But a petard? Bit unusual for a ship's captain to want one of those."

Strykar's eyebrow twitched. Danamis had no use for such a siege weapon. He was evidently scheming something new.

"I like to be prepared for anything, Master Alarbus. Could be useful one day against a corsair fort on Darfan," Danamis replied. Strykar rolled his eyes.

"Well," mumbled the forgemaster, "I suppose I could

fashion you one out of a small bronze bell I have lying around the forge. But that will cost you more, my lord."

Danamis smiled broadly. "Name your price, Master Alarbus."

IT TOOK ANOTHER day for the new sakers to make their way to the deck of the *Vendetta*. Brought down by teams of four mules from the forge, each gun was hoisted with a crane by a dozen cursing, sweating men and precariously lowered onto the ship. Danamis watched from the quarterdeck as Gregorvero directed the work, the carpenters hammering away at the wooden trucks, fixing metal eyes on the gunwales to feed the securing ropes. And throughout the day, the sound of the orichalcum cannon on the sea wall would reverberate as Danamis's gunners learnt their trade anew under the eyes of the Ivrean militia.

He thought about Citala often, left up at the palazzo with Leonato, and the more he ruminated the more worry ate away at him. This wasn't helped by Strykar berating him for his acquiescence in the Count's request. Leonato was a man they neither knew nor liked, Strykar had grumbled at him, though he could not say why he distrusted the Count. But it was peculiar at best that the mermaid stay up at that ramshackle palazzo. Danamis tried to assuage his doubts by telling himself that he would retrieve Citala after only one more day.

As the afternoon of the second day wore on, Danamis found himself looking up towards the dark city, black chimney smoke billowing from furnaces and sitting low over the houses and turrets of the battlements. From the main deck, Talis let out a curse and berated a sailor for dropping a piece of iron shot as the human chain of sailors and *rondelieri* loaded each iron ball into the wooden crates in the hold. Powder bags would come last. The side swords and a few longswords had already come aboard, wrapped in canvas. The work was nearly done. The *Vendetta* had now been transformed from a merchantman to a not-so-obvious warship. Gregorvero was still huffing about having to saw into the ship's railings larboard and starboard to allow the new guns to be run out, but as they sat low in their wheeled trucks the guns would never have fired level over the gunwales. Danamis tapped a nervous tattoo out on the bulkhead with his knuckles. He could not wait to be under way again, back to the south. He then caught sight of three gentlemen coming towards the ship, a gaggle of their retainers following behind. He descended to the main deck to meet the newcomers.

"Admiral Danamis!" one of the men shouted over. "May we come aboard?"

Danamis leaned over the side. "And who are you, my worthy brothers?"

The lead man gestured to his comrades with a sweep of the wide sleeve of his squirrel fur-trimmed robe. "We are from the Council of Decurions. And we would speak with you."

Danamis nodded and pointed the way to the gangplank as his sailors moved aside to let the party aboard. What business could these Decurions have with him? Unless it was to stir up trouble with the High Steward, if Leonato was to be believed. Or worse yet—countermand the permission to export the arms and guns he had just shipped. As the Decurions clambered up, Danamis saw Strykar's large bear-like head emerge from the hold. He whistled down and caught his attention.

"Captain Strykar! Join me in my cabin if you please!"

He ushered his visitors into the stern cabin and bade them sit at the table while he shouted out the hatchway for Talis to bring in some drink. The three Council members were wealthy, that was clear from their garb, all of some age, every one with greying hair. But they were also twitchy and suspicious, reluctant to state their business. After some minutes of empty cordiality, Danamis took another drink, set down his cup, and levelled his gaze at the three.

"If you desire something of me, gentlemen, I pray that you speak plainly. And as much as I enjoy a drink, I am preparing my ship to make voyage. What is it you want?"

They looked from one to another until one, Ugo Aratino—long-nosed, thin, and balding—cleared his throat and found his courage.

"You were at the palazzo two days ago. We are anxious to learn if you saw or heard anything out of the ordinary. You see... the High Steward has refused any of the Council entry there for months."

Danamis looked over to Strykar who stared back at him with a look that would wither a field of standing corn.

"I saw nothing," said Danamis. "But the Count spoke of your intransigence in matters of state. So it seems you don't get along very well."

One of the Decurions sat back and harrumphed. Signore Aratino nodded. "That is true. But it is not why we ask you what you have seen. In the last year, six women in the city have disappeared. Women of good families. The last, two months ago, a tailor's daughter."

A feeling of dread began to creep slowly into Danamis's stomach. "And you suspect the Count and his household in this?"

Aratino looked quickly to his comrades. "We do. Screams have been heard at the palazzo. His guards seldom venture out and never consort with the city militiamen. All is secrecy and stealth. That is why we ask you if you have seen or heard anything while you were there."

"We did not," said Danamis. "And a bit of shouting that someone may have overheard seems a weak reason to accuse him."

"Bartolo, show him."

One of the others, a short fat man, pulled out a small leather-bound book from a pocket of his robes. He handed it to Danamis.

"This was found beneath the palazzo walls last week. It had fallen from a window above where the Count's apartments lie. We do not know where it was printed."

Danamis picked it up and flicked through the pages. It was in a strange tongue he could not read yet it was the images that it contained that focused his attention. Leaping horned demons, savage ancient beasts, and women and men being nailed to strange-looking trees. He swallowed and turned the pages further. He stopped when he saw a picture of a living woman having her heart plucked from her breast. Danamis pushed it back to Aratino.

"He says he is writing a history of Valdur. This must be an old book he is using."

"You don't understand," protested the fat man. "This book is not old. It was recently made. And it is a manual of the Old Faith. It is of the worship of Andras, and Belial. The banished ones."

Strykar took a deep breath and pursed his lips. "I've heard enough. I knew Leonato had the stink of evil on him. And you damned well left her with the man."

Aratino looked at Danamis. "Who is this you speak of with the Count now?

Danamis looked down. "An ally... and a friend."

"You must go back there and bring her out. She could be in grave danger."

Strykar was on his feet, his face flushed. "Danamis, will you wait any longer?"

Danamis pushed his stool back and looked up at the bristling mercenary. "I've not been blind, my friend. Why do you think I asked the forgemaster for a petard? Just in case."

Strykar shook his head and gave a grim smile. "You bastard. I knew you were planning something in that devious head of yours."

Danamis placed his hands on the table. "Gentlemen. Will the Council support me if I storm the palazzo?"

The Decurions looked hesitant, then nodded their agreement. Aratino cleared his throat. "You are the king's admiral of Palestro and a High Steward of Valdur. We will sanction you."

Danamis nodded. "And I will hold you to that, gentlemen. As we are going to blow his gate in tonight, you had better be right. We have no real proof and this is one very big wager."

CITALA STOOD AT the arched window in her chamber, shivering in her kirtle and mantle. The sun had set an hour ago, and the chamber had grown increasingly cold. Two candles guttered on a small table, the only other piece of furniture was the tall bedstead. Her skin was so dry it felt as if beetles were crawling all over her body. Looking at her arms she saw that tiny fissures had erupted on them, oozing clear liquid. She could feel herself growing weaker by degrees. She had lied to Danamis. She had never spent more than one day out of the sea in her life. Danamis would have been shocked to learn that execution among the mer consisted of the guilty being tied to a tree and left to dry out like a landed fish.

For nearly two days she had humoured the Count and in that time she had grown ever more suspicious of him. He prattled endlessly of his studies, delving into the ancient past of Valdur. He asked of life among her people but only in passing. As if he actually already knew what he wanted. He spent far more time lecturing her on the war against the Old Faith and of how Elded's disciples and followers, aided by the merfolk, had driven the old gods down, killing their followers throughout the island kingdom. When Citala had enquired of his family, he had only said that the *contessa* had died a year ago and then changed the subject. The handmaiden provided for her was a withered crone who said little, merely bringing her food to her chamber (half of which she could not stomach). After she had refused wine she was brought brackish water instead. And now, as she had grown ill, she had finally requested to take her leave. Leonato had come up with a raft of excuses why she had to stay until the next day. Most telling of all, Strykar's swordsmen had disappeared from her door. When she had asked after them, she was told they were down in the buttery, having a meal. That was hours gone.

It was time to go. And she hoped that by now, Danamis would have his guns and supplies. Her door was unlocked but the crone was always lurking. When she opened it, she had decided upon a ruse to enable her to get to the main hall of the palazzo.

"I have remembered something that the Count asked of me," she said to the woman. "Something that he was very keen to know. Something urgent."

The woman had risen from the chair outside, her face set in stone. "Then I will call for a retainer to tell him," she said. "And *he* can decide if he wishes to see you now."

Citala blinked rapidly. She could feel the panic rising up inside her. For some reason, she was no longer a guest but a prisoner. That which made her mer suddenly took hold. Without a sound, she lunged forward and her long fingers wrapped around the throat of the woman, stifling her attempt to cry out. Although she was weakened, she pushed the crone across the corridor, nearly lifting her off the floor. They ran into the far wall, the woman's eyes wide in horror as her head struck the harsh rag stone. With a loud exhalation she sank down into a heap at Citala's feet.

Citala was breathing heavily, arms shaking. She knew she had to find her way out but these great houses of stone, structures she had only just encountered in the last days, were alien to her. She at least knew how to find the staircase to the next level. Down she went, the wide stairs spiralling around and around. She passed two more floors, and, disorientated, she kept moving, afraid that she would run into some of the guardsmen. She heard men's voices and laughter and ran the other way, trying to remember the way to the gate of the palazzo. A mastiff sitting on the floor regarded her as she passed it and she prayed it would not attack. She saw a large studded door on the left side of the corridor that was partly ajar. Men were now approaching and without thinking, she pushed the door open further and entered.

The chamber was cavernous, a vaulted undercroft of sorts. She now realized she had gone too far down and that she was below ground. The space was lit by wall torches and as she looked across to the opposite side of the vast chamber, she saw—rather impossibly—a tree. It grew from a break in the flagstone floor, tiles pushed up all around its trunk. It was like no other tree she had ever seen. Its leaves were of many different shapes, waxy and green-black. The trunk was smooth and grey, almost flesh-like, and it soared up, the branches brushing the brick ceiling. Citala walked down a flight of steps into the chamber, agog at the strange sight. How could such a thing grow and flourish under the earth? And then she heard a moan, a weak cry of pain. It was only then that she saw a person at the base of the great tree.

It was a woman. Naked, dirty and deathly white. Citala ran to her and knelt. She gasped when she saw that the woman's legs and hips were inside the tree, the tree which was consuming her. Citala reached out and tried to lift her but she cried out in agony, held fast in the breach. As Citala set her down again the tree seemed to shiver, its leaves trembling. A hundred small whispering voices filled the air, and as Citala looked up she saw the fruit that the tree bore. Small heads, the size of apples, dangled from the branches, faces like unborn babies with eyes closed and button noses. Their lips moved continually and the chamber began to fill with their strange insistent hissing. Citala recoiled, not believing what she was seeing. Beyond the base of the tree and near the far wall she now spied a pile of yellow bones, ribcages and a skull.

"Is it not magnificent?"

Citala pushed herself up off the floor and saw Leonato standing at the doorway, one of his retainers at his side. She shook her head and began backing away from the shivering monstrosity.

"You have no right!" she said, "Let me go from here."

The Count smiled. "You have spoiled your surprise, Citala. I was going to introduce you to this place soon enough but here you are." He took a few steps forward, motioning for the guardsman to remain where they stood. "You know, the tree has grown remarkably since I discovered the tiny shoot coming through the stones. I had prayed and prayed to Andras, and it grew. As you can see."

Citala unlaced her mantle and took a few slow steps towards him. "What have you done here? How many have you killed?"

"Killed? *Sacrificed*. And your exotic flesh will be offered as well. A fitting tribute to the Tree of Life for the perfidy of the merfolk in the war against the Old Faith."

Citala whipped the mantle from her shoulders as she sprang at him. She whirled it and tossed it over him but the Count sidestepped and brushed it away. She raked him once with her left hand but he delivered a backhanded blow that sent her sprawling to the flagstones. Her head was spinning as she pushed herself up into a crouch. She could taste blood in her mouth. "Lord Danamis is coming," she rasped, her rage undiminished.

Leonato shook his head and bent over her. He seized her hair and yanked her head upwards. "Your pirate lord will need more than a few *rondelieri* to take this fortress. But that won't happen, as you will write him a note to say you are staying here with me."

Citala spat at him and he shook her like he was chastising a child. "Behave now, my mermaid! Accept your fate and you shall have a sleeping draught such as we gave your bodyguard. No more suffering than necessary."

DANAMIS AND STRYKAR stood well back in the shadows across the cobblestoned piazza that led to the palazzo doors. Behind them, twenty-five *rondelieri* stood, their round shields unslung and swords unsheathed. None spoke, but the sound of jangling harness and the rasp of chain mail on helms carried across the street telling its own story to those who listened at their shutters. Danamis watched intently as Aratino and two other Decurions addressed the militiamen guarding the keep. They were ordering them to withdraw in the name of the Council. Danamis could see arms waving and hear raised voices as the discussion grew hot and then calmed. He nodded to himself and smiled as he watched the five guards follow the Decurions back across the piazza, leaving the door unguarded.

Strykar whistled sharply and two of his men came forward, orange torchlight reflecting off their steel sallets. They carried a large square board with iron rings. Sitting at its centre, like some sugarloaf on a feasting trestle, was a bronze bell, drilled and bolted on. Strykar and Danamis sprinted forward across the distance up to the doors. Danamis winced as his side wound, still tender, gave a twinge. Swinging a sword this evening wouldn't help that, he thought. The two of them worked quickly, helping the soldiers affix the board to the grandly engraved bronze knob at the centre of the door and hanging it there. Danamis gave the signal to Strykar who touched his glowing taper to the fuse at the top of the bell. And they ran.

The explosion reverberated across the piazza and was quickly followed by the sound of chunks of oak and iron pinging and clinking as they rained down on the cobbles. A great gushing cloud of smoke billowed out in the torchlight from the doorway and without waiting, Strykar gave a battle cry and rushed forward, his *rondelieri* at his heels. The door was still on one hinge and standing, but four *rondelieri* put their shoulders into it and it collapsed inwards, a smoking wreck. Strykar was inside first and took on an advancing pole-arm man nearly as wide as the door they had just blown. Strykar brought his shield up, deflected the thrust of the glaive while instantly stepping in past the shaft and hacking down into the collarbone of its wielder.

Just ahead, he could see a dozen more armed men forming up to engage them, covering the width of the hall. Danamis moved up alongside Strykar, hefting his falchion in both hands.

"Are you ready Captain Strykar? Looks like we have started a war."

"Then let's end it in our favour," said the mercenary, and the *rondelieri* charged.

CITALA COLLAPSED AS Leonato released her hair. She looked across the floor and saw the poor girl writhing, her arms helplessly flailing. It appeared as if the tree was sucking her in little by little. Citala tried to crawl past the Count and towards the stairs. Her struggle had nearly sapped her of her last strength. She looked up at the High Steward who was observing the death throes of the woman with a curious detachment.

"Why?" demanded Citala, her voice a croak of frustration and anger.

Leonato turned to her. "Why? Because the earth is waking again, my dear. Those that have been silent for centuries are arising to take what was theirs. To right the wrong. To wipe clean the works of Elded the usurper." He let out a loud sigh and drew a dagger from his belt and pointed it at the dark tree.

"This is testimony to my faith, and to the old ways." Skirting Citala, he walked to where the woman lay. He knelt, lifted her up by her hair, and drew his blade across her throat. A red cascade splashed the roots around her and Citala watched, her mouth agape, as they pulsated and throbbed at the pooling lifeblood, relishing the liquid.

Citala closed her eyes. "Help me," she whispered. "Help, me. I beg you. Come to my aid." She opened her mind despite her terror, reaching out as she would reach out to her dolphins and whales in the deep. "Please, please, help me." She could see the mastiffs in her mind's eye. She focused all her entreaties, her desperate pleas, on the beasts that sat outside in the corridor.

"Are you saying your prayers to your sky god? To Elded's spirit?" Leonato wiped his knife and re-sheathed it. "Their time has come to an end, my beautiful creature." He gestured to the guard who stood in the doorway, his face filled with adoration of the Tree of Life. "Help me lift her up. She must be tied to the tree. A very special offering."

Citala's lips moved rapidly, repeating her call, eyes tightly shut. And then she opened them again. At the doorway, a large square brown head and short muzzle pushed between the frame and the door. It padded into the chamber and down the stairs. A second mastiff followed. Their eyes, black and glassy, bore into Citala's with heightened sentience. The great dogs both stopped, rigid as statues.

"Help me," said Citala.

Leonato roughly grasped her by her armpit, her kirtle tearing, and she cried out in pain. The guard bent down and yanked her forearm up, jerking her into a sitting position. And without a sound, the dogs sprang. One took the guard out, clamping its huge jaws into the meat of his thigh and bowling him over. The other leapt high and tackled Leonato with its paws on his chest, bringing him down to the floor. Citala heard the dog growl deeply as it sank its jaws into Leonato's throat and shook its head savagely, ripping the Count's neck and showering the flagstones with his blood. The other dog had the guard's head in its mouth as it bit at his face, the man screaming. It released him and dived in again, ripping his throat out. As quickly as they had attacked, the mastiffs retreated without looking back, loping out of the chamber.

Count Leonato's hands clawed at his wound as he tried to stop the pulsing flow, his life ebbing. His eyes were large, fixed in shock, and looking straight at Citala. He tried to form words but nothing came. Citala hauled herself up again to her knees, swaying.

"You had no right!" she cried. "No right."

She watched as his hands ceased their shaking and went limp, his mouth wide. And the sound of the explosion, like a rolling thunderclap, made her collapse to her elbows; some new terror. The Tree of Life began to wail, a high-pitched scree of protest.

Not long after, she became aware that someone was lifting her up. She felt numb all over. Opening her almond-shaped eyes, she looked into Danamis's sea-grey ones as he cradled her in his arms.

"Please forgive me, Citala," he said as he hefted her and held her tightly.

She spoke so quietly that he had to place his ear close to her mouth to hear her.

"The sea," she whispered. "The sea."

The three Decurions were standing together, aghast at the evil that stretched upwards before them, a thing that by rights should not exist in the world. They saw the pitiful human remains strewn at the base of its glistening trunk and one of the men began to sob.

"Blessed Elded save us!" said Aratino. "This is the blasphemy and murder we feared." Strykar joined them before the dreadful tree, wiping his flushed and sweaty face and still clenching his dripping side sword. Aratino muttered, half to himself, "What shall we do?"

Strykar looked up at a tiny homunculus head suspended by a stem. It had opened its eyes and was glaring at him, it little lips moving in some cursed tongue.

"Burn it," he growled. "Burn the damned thing to the ground."

Thirty-Five

As THEY PASSED through the east gate of Livorna, unhindered, Acquel felt a sense of elation despite the fear that a gauntleted hand might descend upon his shoulder at any moment. He was home again after weeks of misadventures on sea and land. Although he knew it could never truly be home, his memories held him up as he entered the market square, leading Timandra upon the remaining mule.

They had salvaged what supplies they could find, thrown by the more unfortunate of the two mules as it was dragged down and torn to shreds by the *mantichora*. Whether by accident or by that strange terrifying creature's generosity, the other mule they had found wandering, its cruppers a-tremble. To onlookers, they would have appeared as nothing more than two new arrivals to the free city, a travelling merchant and his wife. He watched as Timandra took in the scene around her: a jumble of limewashed houses with undulating terracotta roofs, a hundred market stalls teeming with hawkers and buyers, a group of white-robed novices huddled in a knot as they made their way across the street, heading uphill towards the Ara, a flock of sparrows swooping down to liberate a dropped crust of bread. He smiled up at her.

"And where are you taking me now?" she asked him. "For proper fare and drink I should hope after what we've been through."

Acquel nodded. "I know of a few hostelries down in the Low Town. We shall stay there this night." He gave her a reassuring smile. She had spoken little since her revelation, no doubt from deep shame and the worry of how he would judge her in light of it. Indeed, he could still not reconcile the bluff but big-hearted woman he knew with some cold-hearted murderess. Whether he realised it or not, Acquel had subconsciously diluted her crime, convincing himself that she *must* have had good motive for killing the man. For Acquel, she still held his heart in her hand.

They saw not a single Temple guardsman as they wended their way through the narrow streets down to the poorer end of the small city. As for Livorna's militia, they never ventured far from the gates and walls, and something in the way the town felt—the normal throb of daily life—told Acquel that they were not even looking for him. They stopped at the first creaking shingle they saw for an inn and entered the stone arch into the stable yard. They took a room as man and wife and the bitterness of this was not lost on Acquel as he wistfully shut the door to the cramped chamber in the roof space and turned to face her. "You take the bed and get some rest," he told her.

There was hardly room for two. She nodded and sat on the mattress, the rope bedstead groaning. "When do you want to…"

"Break into the Temple? Tonight. I dreamt again last night of the door… some chamber beyond it. The secrets of Elded lie in there. I've seen it more clearly than since last I dreamt of it."

She reached out and took his hand. "And what do want with these secrets? What *can* you do with them even if you find them and read them?"

He looked away for a moment and then back to her. "I mean to share them with everyone. With the world. The truth of the Saint has been buried far too long. The priesthood is rotten." A vision of poor Brother Kell, of innocent Silvio, passed before his eyes.

"And what will the people do when they learn that the Blessed Elded had mer blood?"

She watched as his face grew suddenly hard. "They will accept it. All the old lies will be shed. Cast off like dead skin."

She felt cold, her eyes moving to the chain that hung around his neck. Unexpectedly, for the first time since she could remember, she felt not in control of her own life. "I have pledged myself to help you, Acquel. Come what may. If it brings me closer to Elded's blessing and God's forgiveness, then I will be happy."

Acquel went down on a bended knee, his sword thumping on the rush-strewn floorboards. "Dear Timandra, you mean everything to me. But I cannot ask you to risk your life. Help me get into the undercroft unseen and then wait for me to return. That is all I ask of you. The Temple guard does not know of you and we must keep it that way if I fail."

She felt tears come, another surprise, stinging her eyes. "Tell me what I must do."

THE MANSERVANT HAD just closed the leaded glass casement to the High Priest's apartments now that the sun had set and the night chill had descended. A knock sounded on the door of the antechamber and Brachus looked up from his table, annoyed at the interruption. He dropped a paperweight upon the vellum scroll he was reading and sat back in his chair.

"See who that is, boy. If it is the Magister you may send him through. Anyone else may wait until the morning."

Brachus had forgotten the servant's name again and so had taken to calling him "boy" instead. Indeed, he was finding himself more tongue-tied than usual these past weeks, no doubt, he thought, due to the bad business in the tomb and wretched Kodoris's bumbling of the affair. He sighed as he looked at the curling vellum scroll. He was forgetting the liturgy now as well and needed to read it every night. More than a minute had passed and "boy" had not returned. He pushed back his heavy chair, the feet scraping loudly on the tiles. But then the servant did return, opening the door to the private apartments widely and stepping to one side. Brachus was about to ask the dolt why he stood so mute when a woman in blue taffeta entered the room.

Brachus pushed himself up into a standing position, the great sunburst medallion jangling at his chest. His rheumy eyes squinted at the visitor. "Why, it is the canoness is it not? I recognize you." His slippers scuffed as he began to move around the table. "What brings you to seek me out—and at this hour?"

Lucinda della Rovera gave him a knowing smile. "Good evening to you, Holiness. I bring you good tidings."

Brachus cleared his throat. "That may be so but this is not the hour, or even the proper manner of doing so. You should speak with the Magister."

"Good news such as mine should not wait. And I must insist that you hear it because it does involve you to some extent." She gestured and the servant, his face vacant, walked over to Brachus. He gripped the High Priest roughly and forced him into his chair.

Brachus resisted, sputtering his protests. "Boy! Unhand me!" He looked over at Lucinda who was observing with an expression of confident knowing. "What is the meaning of this outrage?"

She moved closer to the table and ran a hand along the fine marble top. "It is about the new order of things. I am here to tell you that today is the beginning of the end. The end of Elded's new faith and the beginning of the restitution of the old." She spread her hands wide and lifted them. "To the everlasting glory of the eternal three. To Belial. To Beleth. To Andras."

"Sacrilege! Abomination!" Brachus stuttered and tried to rise but the servant clamped his hands upon the old man's shoulders and forced him down.

Lucinda raised a pale hand to her left shoulder and her fine silken chemise. "I am chosen. The spirit of the Revealer fills me, guides me. Berithas has told me what I must do."

Brachus had stopped his struggling, his eyes wide with fear and dread at the names filling the chamber, uttered in the canoness's beautiful crystal voice. His lips repeated the name of the great Deceiver, the one whom Elded had cast down. "Berithas?"

She nodded slowly, the smile broadening. "Yes. And the Tree of Life, the great wellspring of the faith, will be reborn. From the Ara, the newly nourished roots will spread deep throughout the land. The followers will rise up, no longer in the shadows. And now, your Holiness, you must play your part in the great plan." She reached behind her back and drew out a curved dagger. Brachus watched in horror as she focused her gaze on the servant. She was instructing him, wordlessly. He tried to push himself up again but an arm pushed him back. Lucinda held out the dagger and the servant reached for it and took it in his grasp.

"She-devil!" hissed Brachus. "Witch! You will burn. I swear to almighty God you will burn."

Lucinda's eyes rested briefly upon a squat, silver-lidded clay drinking pot that rested on the table. She picked it up and slowly poured out upon the floor the dregs of wine that it held. "So as this, will your life pour out, Holiness. To give rise to what once was." She lifted her chin and looked at the servant. There was a moment of hesitation in the youth, but Lucinda's blue eyes bored deeply. With his left arm, he held the High Priest firmly in the chair and with his right hand he drew the silver blade deeply and rapidly across the old man's throat. Brachus kicked out, gave a stifled gurgling cry, and a spray of crimson shot out over the table, spattering the parchment and books that lay there. Brachus's own grip on the servant sagged, and his eyes looked out past Lucinda, still wide, but now unfocussed. She quickly moved to the carved arm of the blackwood chair and held out the pot to the pulsing fountain of blood that ran down the High Priest's purple robes. A metallic smell began to permeate the room as the blood dripped and pooled on the floor. The little pot filled quickly and she knocked the lid shut, the sleeve of her dress somehow unsullied. She then calmly picked up a vellum page—a prayer for a good harvest—and carefully wiped the vessel clean before tossing the sticky and stained vellum back to the table. Her head tilted to one side as she beheld her work.

She then looked back to the servant. "Well done. Now you know what you must do next."

The youth walked drunkenly to the casement window and opened the latch. He hesitated, bringing a hand to his head.

Lucinda picked up the dagger he had let clatter to the floor and wiped it clean before slipping it back into the sheath she wore on her jewelled girdle. She saw that the servant had turned to face her, silently fighting her will. She tutted. "Come now, that won't do at all." And suddenly, the youth went rigid. Slowly, he turned back to the window, climbing up onto the ledge. He kneeled. The hinges squeaked as he pushed the window open as far as it could go.

"Go ahead..." she coaxed, as if speaking to a child reluctant to walk out into a summer shower. The youth leaned forward and then was gone, three storeys down to the courtyard below. Lucinda raised the clay vessel, admiring its glazed beauty and the swirled engraving on the silver lid. She smiled, its contents warming her hand.

Outside the antechamber, Lucinda brushed past the still frozen Temple guardsman, lost in strange dreams where he stood. Awareness would return to him later, and with it, a surprise to be discovered in the High Priest's room. Lucinda walked briskly to her apartments on the other side of the Ara palazzo, along half-lit porticos, her dress swishing as it dragged across the well-worn flagstones. She clutched the clay pot to her bosom, safeguarding the precious liquid. And she was not alone. The voice filled her head but the whispers carried to her ear as well, emanating from the mouth below her collarbone.

She is failing us.

Lucinda's voice was hushed as she replied. "She is weak. Always was."

She has sent for the Magister. To reveal all.

A wave of anger washed over her as her delicate velvet shoes slapped on the stones. "She wouldn't! She does not know everything. I have not revealed it."

She knows more than you have supposed. Now she has failed you... and the Faith.

"I will punish her."

If you desire her power you must take it from her.

Lucinda stopped and stared down at the flagstones.

Only then you will be equal to the task before us. You must do it.

"Then I shall."

When she reached the apartments, Lavinia was standing in the centre of the bedchamber, expecting her arrival. She wore only her chemise, her long blonde hair tied back behind her neck. Her expression was nervous, surreptitious even.

Lucinda did not need Berithas's warning that her sister had done that which she should not.

She placed the ceramic vessel on a table. "Dear sister, why have you betrayed us?"

Lavinia hugged herself and looked away. "You told me stories of the olden times. Tales of long ago. But they were *true*. Not legends."

Lucinda's pale visage shone orange in the candlelight of the room. Her features, sharp and fox-like, were as though chiselled from stone. Cold and unmoving. "Tell me what you have done, sister."

Lavinia looked into her sister's eyes. She normally would not even need to give voice to her thoughts. They would share them instantaneously. Not now. "You are planning something bad. Very bad. I thought that it was a game... imaginings. But it is real."

Lucinda paced slowly to close the space between them. "You have sent word to the Magister, haven't you?"

Lavinia shook her head. "You mustn't hurt him. I like him. He reminds me of father." Her voice trembled.

Lucinda smiled and reached out to touch her cheek. "What we do we do for the Faith, *our* Faith. Not theirs. We must make sacrifices. All of us."

Lavinia struck her sister's hand away. "You killed our father! And our mother!" She leapt for the entranceway, seizing the iron ring and yanking the great oaken door open. Captain Flauros blocked her way and she gasped, falling backwards into the chamber. Lucinda closed the door and led Lavinia back to the canopied bed.

"Our parents died of weak hearts," she soothed. "Maybe broken hearts. I have told you that before."

Lavinia shook her head furiously and placed her hands over her ears. "The greyrobe is coming. I must warn him too!"

Lucinda pushed Lavinia onto the thick, soft mattress and

held her there. "I am not going to hurt the greyrobe, sister. I am going to meet him soon."

Lavinia whimpered and tried to roll herself into a ball. "It's all wrong! We've done wrong."

"Lie yourself down."

Lavinia exploded forward, shoving Lucinda backwards, a look of fear and rage mixed on her face, tears streaming. "Go away!" she screamed. "You are not my sister! You're a monster!"

Take her gift!

Lavinia's eyes darted to her sister's shoulder, from where the commanding voice had come. And then she looked at her sister again, head shaking in a silent plea. Lucinda reached behind her back and drew out the long thin blade. Her left hand, as fast as a striking serpent, reached forward and grasped the top of Lavinia's chemise, holding her fast. Her voice was steady and certain. "I offer you to the gods, my sister. Sleep you well." And she plunged the dagger into Lavinia's throat, up to the hilt. The girl arched her body in spasm and fell back onto the bed, clutching at her neck. As Lavinia went limp, Lucinda felt her head fill with a thousand images, flashing through her mind's eye. She staggered and threw her arms around the bed post, her fingers gripping the barley-twist carvings. She could see anew. Those she sought. Those who sought her.

She was lightheaded as she fell into Flauros's arms. But she quickly pushed herself away. "The Magister is here," she said. "Do nothing unless I tell you."

Flauros smoothed her shoulders. "Just give me the word and he is dead."

The knock sounded a moment later and Flauros moved off to the side of the chamber. Lucinda bade the visitor to enter and Kodoris rushed in, slightly out of breath. Flauros shut the door behind him. Immediately the Magister saw the arc of crimson across Lucinda's dress and then his eyes fell to the figure sprawled upon the bed.

"What have you done, you miserable creature!" He strode forward ready to seize the canoness where she stood. But then he felt something heavy lie on his left shoulder and saw twenty inches of naked steel resting there. He slowly turned to see the unsmiling captain of the Temple guard, whose gloved hand now held the short sword at this throat.

"Ah. She has bewitched you too. I thought as much. So much for your oath." He backed away towards the table, realizing now, too late, that he had been well and truly cozened. "More fool me though. There were always enough signs if I had not been so blinded by desperation."

Lucinda's voice was calm, but a trace of triumph rose up to the surface. "Magister, how can you say that? I am about to complete my task. The task you set out for me. I will deliver the greyrobe to you this evening."

Kodoris looked over at the body of Lavinia. "Why did you kill her? She was trusting of you. She had the mind of a child."

Lucinda's piercing eyes narrowed. "You know why. She betrayed me. And the cause."

"The Tree of Life," Kodoris whispered. "Lavinia tried to tell me. You are truly so mad as to serve the pagan gods and kill for them. They are dead. Gone these centuries. Your crimes—your heresy—will be punished."

A wide grin broke out on the face of the canoness. "I suppose you did not stop by the High Priest's bedchamber before coming here. You would have found an even more interesting surprise than you have seen here."

Kodoris went cold. Lucinda walked to the table and carefully lifted the ceramic vessel. She opened the lid and dipped a finger. She held it out and daubed the blood on the long bony bridge of the Magister's nose.

"Murderess!" he spat.

She waggled her finger at him. "Hypocrisy is a great sin, Magister. Do not forget that I have read your own thoughts these past days. You might have done the deed yourself."

Kodoris felt weak, as if his strength and manhood had all but dried up, withered away. "What is it you mean to do?"

"Why, I told you. We are going to see Brother Acquel. I believe he is at this moment down in the bowels of the Temple, finding what he has long sought. What *you* have already seen. The Ten Commandments of Elded and all the other truths of your One Faith that your priesthood has laboured so long to hide." She beckoned to Flauros who stepped forward and roughly seized Kodoris high up on his arm with his left hand. The point of his sword pricked the cords of the Magister's neck. "It is time for me to fulfil my promise to you," she said. "And to fulfil another. One I made to Berithas."

Kodoris snorted. "The Deceiver. *Trickster.*"

Lucinda puffed out her chest. She struck Kodoris across his cheek. "Berithas the Redeemer."

Thirty-Six

LIKE DRIFTING SHADOWS, Acquel and Timandra, dressed in the black robes of the priesthood, moved to the bottom of the stairs and held close to the ancient sandstone blocks of the undercroft. A few torches sputtered in their iron sconces but most of the vaults were in darkness. From high up on the stairs, the sound of many voices raised in song floated down to their ears.

May their souls fly upon the wings of doves;
Upwards, ever higher, unto the comfort of His bosom;
Glory to the Faith, glory to the Saints
In Heaven's seat the Lord reposes, wisdom and power,
everlasting.

Acquel gathered up Timandra in his arms. He could feel her shaking. "Do you hear them above us? They are singing the evening lament. All the brotherhood gathered."

She nodded. "Except for you."

He managed a smile. He gently clasped her face and kissed her on both cheeks tenderly. "We will leave here together and spread the word to all who will listen. The truth of

Elded. Your shame and mine will be washed clean."

She covered his hand with hers. "Companions together for as long as fate allows."

He reached up and grasped a torch before leading her deeper into the vaults. "There, that tunnel on the right. That is it." He turned back to face her. "Wait here for me. I will bring out whatever I find. If I can."

Timandra's fingers tightened nervously around the hilt of the dagger she wore on her belt. "I will wait for as long as it takes. If someone approaches then I will follow you down to warn you."

They reached the tunnel entrance and Acquel turned to her. "Stay here, in the shadows."

She gave his hand one last squeeze. "May the Blessed Saint guide and protect you!"

"And you, my dear Timandra. And you."

He pulled his robes close and set off into the narrow passage and she watched him grow smaller, a tiny circle of light about him. A damp chill blew along the tunnel and she crouched down, pulling the hood of her robe around her face.

Acquel felt the temperature plunge as he descended. The amulet against his bare skin grew warmer and began to tingle. He held the torch out as he stepped along the uneven floor, hacked out centuries ago. There were no turns or other open passages, only a few bricked off. The tunnel walls ran as straight and true as a mason's plumb could ever make. At length, he saw an ancient, heavily studded door before him. He turned the large cast iron knob at its centre and gently pushed. It was unlocked. As he stepped through he found himself at the very end of the tunnel, a wall of jagged rock in front of him. And on each side, great oak doors, one vastly ornate with curling bronze fittings, the other plain and undecorated, its hinges and lock blooming with orange rust. A strong sense directed him towards the plainer of the doors, an intuition that, as he stood facing it, was rewarded by the throb of the amulet. It pulsed as if alive; a warm thing clinging to his chest. As his hand reached for the great iron ring, he leapt back at the grinding metallic sound of clicking tumblers in the lock. Elded was beckoning. He pulled the door open only to find an even stouter one behind it. But a mere touch of his palm upon its planks and it too creaked open, swinging inwards with barely a push.

Acquel stepped into the chamber he had seen in his dreams. The rows of little metal caskets in niches hewn out of the bedrock were just as he had seen in his mind. He held aloft the torch to illuminate the chamber. It was no more than twenty paces square. He spotted a torch rammed into a sconce and touched his own to it. The fat-impregnated rags ignited, telling him that someone had been here not long previously. He set his own in another sconce and faced the row of caskets, without rust despite their age. His eyes flitted from one little box to another. Where to begin?

Another impulse seized him. He threw back his hood and reached into his unbuttoned doublet, down into his shirt. He pulled off the amulet and let it dangle before him on its chain. The gold and lapis sparkled, seemingly brighter than he had ever seen it. As he watched it, it moved; moved like a lodestone attracted to iron, suspended nearly sideways and pointing to the caskets on the left. Acquel took a few steps towards them and the amulet wavered again, jutting out, and pointing to just one casket.

He found himself shaking as he dropped the amulet back over his head. The casket rasped along the stone shelf as he pulled it towards him. He undid the hasp and opened it. The folded vellum inside practically cried out to him. He reached in and withdrew it. The ancient Valdurian script that stared back at him suddenly seemed to mutate as he held it. Where a second ago he could barely decipher it, now it was as clear as any text he might have penned himself. It was the Ten Commandments of Saint Elded, the same as was on his amulet. He was reading—comprehending—the old language of Valdur. He laughed aloud as the wonder of the discovery filled him. He opened other caskets, unrolling the scrolls within, devouring the words they contained, the words of Elded and his disciples. The story of the first days of the Faith unfolded before him. He saw the pagan trees fall, the armies of men and mer battling satyrs and dragons, driving the worshippers of the old gods into the wilds, the stones of the first temples being set into the ground where once innocent blood was sacrificed to dread Belial on corrupted trees bent to dark worship. He grew lightheaded and fell back against a wall, his breaths coming fast. The knowledge of 800 years poured into him, filling his head like a brimming wine jar, and prayers he had never uttered before poured from his lips.

TIMANDRA JUMPED WHEN she heard the voices and saw the torchlight spilling down the wide stone steps. She crouched even lower as she watched three figures turn the corner and enter the undercroft. One was a woman, her full skirts seeming to float across the stone floor as she walked under the arches of the vaulted ceiling. Then two men, one wearing the robes of a priest or monk. The other, taller, wore a long cloak and she could see his blackened breastplate and the glint of a drawn sword. They were walking with purpose, luckily not towards her and the tunnel but rather across the length of the undercroft. The woman lit other tallow torches with hers as they walked and soon the red bricks of the undercroft were illuminated with their orange glow. She bit her lip. If she went down the tunnel to warn Acquel, they would both be trapped. The visitors might not even be looking for them. She saw that the three had gone to the far side of the undercroft to where a shallow nave of stone had been set. The woman was speaking; the monk protesting, raising his voice. She watched as the soldier backhanded him and hauled him up by the hood of his robes.

Timandra slowly raised herself up and moved to a massive pillar some distance closer to the figures. She poked her head around it and strained to hear what they saying.

"SACRILEGE! MONSTROUS SACRILEGE!" yelled Kodoris, held fast in the grip of Captain Flauros. As he cried out for help, Flauros pommeled him on his collarbone, dropping the Magister to his knees.

Lucinda paid him no heed. She looked at the blackened stump that was before them. "The first Tree of Life, the Ur-spring of the True Faith that nourished the people even as it was nourished by them. Hacked and burned by the usurpers, Magister!"

Kodoris looked up at her. "Defeated by the power of God and his chosen servant, Elded the Blessed!"

She bent over Kodoris, one hand on her knee, the other raising up the vessel of Brachus's blood. "This night the war resumes, Magister. And the roots of *this* tree grow deep. Deep down and across the breadth of the kingdom. Where they slumber still. Until now."

She smiled knowingly and stood up, raising the vessel over her head in both hands. "Berithas," she intoned, "I give you the blood of the great usurper." She opened the silver lid and held out her arm, pouring the blood over the stump. It ran and collected into little pools in the gouged ancient wood. It sank in, all of it, as if the dead tree had lapped it up greedily. Lucinda tossed the lidded ceramic pot and it shattered on the stone wall.

* * *

TIMANDRA BECAME AWARE of a vibration at her feet. The entire floor of the vaults seemed to hum. She heard cracking noises and saw the large flagstones buckle as they heaved, undulating. As quickly as it had started, all became silent. But she knew something terrible had happened just the same. Something profoundly evil.

She saw the monk roughly roused to his feet and the woman pick up her torch again. They moved towards her and she ducked back, creeping around the pillar as they passed. And to her horror, they made straight for the tunnel leading to Acquel.

ACQUEL CLUTCHED AT his chest. The amulet had suddenly become red hot and he cried out with the pain and shock of it. That was when he heard the footfalls. He turned towards the doorway and backed himself to a far wall. A whirl of burgundy came tumbling into the chamber. A man rolled across the rough limestone floor and somehow managed to pull himself up to his hands and knees, his face contorted in pain. As he raised his head, Acquel saw who it was. Kodoris threw back his open robe and Acquel's right hand flew to the hilt of his side sword.

A woman's voice sounded, clear and melodious. "Brother Acquel, I greet you well."

She glided into the stone chamber, Flauros immediately behind. Acquel drew his sword, awkwardly catching it on his robes. Flauros chuckled but Lucinda raised her hand to silence him. Acquel at once recognised the two as the ones who had tried to kill him at the harbour side in Perusia. Flauros he remembered, captain of the Temple guard, but the noblewoman was a mystery. And why in God's name had they just thrown the Magister into the chamber head first? Had they found and hurt Timandra out in the undercroft?

He looked at the woman. She seemed unnaturally beautiful, her alabaster face almost glowing in the torchlight. But something else, far more than the tingling amulet, set his heart pumping faster. Her countenance shone with a malevolence that made him shiver, her penetrating eyes reminding him of a lizard on a fence post about to snatch a fly.

"I trust you have found what you were looking for, Brother Acquel?" She moved across the chamber, staring him down as she did so. He felt a dull ache in his head. The amulet flared again, briefly, and he felt the pain in his brain evaporate. She reached Kodoris who still crouched on the floor, dazed, and tousled his grey curls.

Acquel raised his sword but could not keep the blade from shaking slightly. "What do you want of me? Why have you pursued me? It was not I who killed the brethren in the tomb." He pointed his sword at Kodoris. "There is your man!"

Flauros had moved slowly along the wall, trying to flank him. Acquel turned slightly and opened his guard towards him. Flauros's taut face remain unchanged but he stopped where he stood.

"We know you did not murder them," Lucinda replied, her voice as unctuous as flowing oil. "And you should thank me for allowing you to find this place. For revealing what was hidden from view."

"She is a witch," said Kodoris weakly as he pulled himself towards the far wall. "She follows the Old Ones, the gods that were thrown down. Do not listen to her, Brother Acquel!"

Acquel waggled his sword. His voice shook. "Listen to her! Why should I listen to *you*? You killed Kell! Silvio! All of them!"

Kodoris pulled himself up, his hands gripping the lip of the stone niche above him. "I was wrong. I know that. I sacrificed the brethren to protect the Faith. But it was wrong. I was blind to the truth. To them!"

Flauros hefted his sword and moved towards the middle of the chamber. "Shut it, old man! I know it was you who murdered my soldiers. I cannot wait to sink my blade into your guts!"

Kodoris put his head into his hands and groaned. Lucinda reached out and laid a hand on Flauros. "And you shall, my brave one. When we are done. I have fed the Tree of Life and now I must plant a new seed, as Berithas directs."

She moved to the stone alcove and opened a casket. "Brother Acquel, take what you need to feed your fire of faith."

"Berithas?" The word left Acquel's lips as his head shook in confusion.

"The Trickster!" shouted Kodoris. He lunged for Lucinda. Flauros swept her back with his free arm, sending her spinning, and brought his sword up high, poised to cleave the Magister with a downward blow. Before he realised what he had done, Acquel found himself flying forward, his blade parrying Flauros's downward swing. Flauros snarled and let Acquel's momentum continue, the greyrobe's sword following through and down. He then turned his wrist upwards, gathering Acquel's blade with his own. With a grunt of exertion and a flex, he sent Acquel's blade flying and clattering off a wall. A second later he back-handed Acquel across the cheek with his hilt and the greyrobe staggered, his hand moving to his head as his knees began to buckle.

Flauros cursed and turned full-on towards Acquel, raising his sword to cleave him through. Acquel raised his head and lifted his right arm—a reflexive but futile gesture. Suddenly, Flauros fell forward, a black-robed figure flailing upon his back like some huge flapping crow. It was Timandra, Acquel saw, dagger in her fist, as she struck at Flauros's neck. He howled as the blade went in at the base of his collarbone. His forward movement and her momentum sent Timandra tumbling over his head and onto the floor. Acquel, head down, bulled into the guardsman, but a balled fist sent him sprawling. He turned to see Flauros drive his sword into Timandra as she lay on her back.

Acquel's cry of desperation and rage, like some wounded beast, filled the chamber. But it did not stop Flauros from raising his sword again and advancing unsteadily on Acquel a second time.

"That's enough of you!" he hissed breathlessly as both arms raised to deliver the blow.

"Bastard!" Acquel screamed with all the energy he could summon. And then he saw Flauros's head suddenly split open, a spout of gore spattering him like raindrops. Flauros dropped to his knees and then forward, Acquel's side sword lodged halfway through his skull. Behind stood Kodoris, blinking rapidly and swaying on his feet. Near the door stood Lucinda, her mouth agape and a bleeding graze on her forehead. She recovered herself, blue eyes bulging in rage, and she raised a long trembling finger at Kodoris. Kodoris stiffened and turned towards her.

"No!" yelled Acquel, pushing himself to his feet, his head still swimming. The canoness whirled to face him, her eyes seeking out his. A stabbing pain in his head staggered him but as soon as the bright nail entered his skull, he felt the amulet burst into fire once again. The pain winked out and he saw Lucinda's concentration waver and collapse. She stepped back, a curious look of surprise that quickly changed to recognition—as if she had seen someone, or something, new. Acquel saw her move her gaze down to the shattered remains of Captain Flauros, a look of disappointment, even disapproval, showing on her face. An instant later she turned about and dashed from the chamber.

Acquel tottered, barely upright. Half crawling, he made it to where Timandra lay. He gathered her up into his arms, the smell of blood strong in his nostrils. Her head fell back and he supported the back of her neck as he cradled her. A feeling of sickness overwhelmed him as he looked on her. He held her close and rocked her, muttering helplessly, imploring Elded to save her. Timandra's eyelids fluttered, though her body remained limp. Acquel looked down at the wound in her stomach. It had been a deep thrust and was steadily oozing blood, a rhythmic pulsing. He knew it was mortal. He stroked her head and called her name. Again her eyes fluttered, opened, and she saw him. She tried to move her lips and he felt her hand tighten on his arm.

"Forgive me," she breathed. "You were... my confessor." Her ashen face contorted in pain. "But I came to love you. Could not help it."

Acquel's tears dropped on her neck and lips. "Your sins are forgiven, dear Timandra. Forgiven by God. Hush." And he cried as he felt the life flow out of her, the first woman he had lost his heart to. He held her tightly for some time, heedless of the Magister who leaned against the stones near him, breathing heavily, exhausted.

"Brother Acquel."

He looked up at the old man.

"I am sorry," said Kodoris. "Sorry for all I have caused."

Acquel gently lowered Timandra to the floor. His arms were shaking. He sucked in a deep breath and stood, his face numb where he had been punched. Seizing Kodoris by his robes, Acquel shoved him hard against the rough-hewn rock of the chamber wall.

"I did what I thought necessary to protect the Faith! Brother Kell understood!" Kodoris sputtered.

Acquel lifted and slammed him against the rock wall again. "You murdered to protect a lie! To hide the truth of the holy word! By Blessed Elded you will work with me to repair what has been done! I swear it!"

Kodoris could not look him in the eye, his chin falling as Acquel spoke.

"You must atone for the blood on your hands. And you will do that by working with me. Working to spread the truth of Elded's teaching. None of my brethren—nor Timandra—will have died in vain. These texts, the sacred words of the saints, will be taught to all. Every man, woman and child. Do you understand me?" Acquel bunched the fabric of Kodoris's robes around the old man's throat.

Kodoris raised his eyes to the greyrobe, glistening with tears, and nodded his assent.

Acquel gestured with his head over to where Flauros lay in a heap. "And there is the murderer you have sought. Your scapegoat. That is the one lie I will permit to save us both that we may carry out our mission. You will proclaim my innocence."

Kodoris nodded slowly. "Elded's will be done," he croaked.

Out in the vast undercroft, in the glow of sputtering torchlight, a hundred cracks had spread across the rippling flagstones like the tendrils of a kraken. If a soul had been there to witness, looking closely at those rent paving stones, they would have glimpsed the tiny blackish-green shoots of vegetation that had already burst upwards from the foul-smelling earth below.

Thirty-Seven

TWO MILES OFF the west coast of the Duchy of Maresto, and just beyond the Gulf of Saivona, the anchor of the *Vendetta* dragged along the sandy shallows until it snagged on a jumble of thongweed-encrusted rocks. The caravel stopped its drift and its bow gradually swung into the direction of the prevailing current.

From his command on the quarterdeck, Danamis watched, a smile on his lips, as Citala swam around the ship, her undulating motions propelling her faster than he had ever seen anyone swim before. A large dolphin broke the surface near her and she glided straight to it. He could hear her laughter even from a distance. She grasped its dorsal fin and it took her away at even greater speed, out across the smooth blue water, occasionally disappearing beneath gentle swells and then bursting forth again. He had marvelled at how quickly she had recovered from her wounds, her cracked and peeling skin wondrously healing after only a few days of her re-acquaintance with the sea.

"She is an interesting creature, I'll give you that." Strykar had joined him at the rail, stretching his tall broad frame. "I'm still trying to puzzle out why the dogs attacked the

Count but not her too. Hoy! You down there! I told you bastards no dicing on the main deck!" Strykar's ear had caught the sounds of merriment and argument and he had poked his head over the forward rail, narrowly avoiding smashing his forehead on the mizzen spar. "Brognolo! Damn you, give these fools a boxing and get them below where they belong!"

He was truly well pleased with the conduct of his men but he wasn't about to stint on discipline when it warranted. And he was thankful the two he had left at the palazzo to guard Citala had been found alive, chained in a storeroom but none the worse for wear. He shuddered to think that they might have shared a terrible fate, far worse than falling in battle. He and his *rondelieri*, chafing at the days of confinement despite the brief mayhem at the palazzo, were happy to be returning to Maresto but Strykar knew his service with Danamis would not end there. Now that the orichalcum guns were theirs, it would soon be time to engage Giacomo Tetch and the mutineers. Though he was by his own admission no sailor, Strykar was taking a dim view of a single caravel—even one well-armed—taking on the Palestrian war fleet.

"That has bothered me too," said Danamis as Citala waved up at him. "She says that she has no memory of how the dogs came to attack. Damned peculiar since they were Leonato's own beasts. Thank Elded that they left her untouched. I imagine the curs had been driven mad by the sight of that horrible tree."

"Mad?" Strykar laughed. "The townsmen have declared those mastiffs heroes for killing the bastard. They even gave them new tabards! Little thanks we got."

"I am pleased enough with the guns—and Citala's deliverance," said Danamis as he watched the mermaid swim towards them. "I suppose the treasure will go to the

Decurions now, and they will remember its provenance. No bad thing if we need to visit again."

"And what will the Ivreans do now that they've learned their High Steward was a murdering devil worshipper?" Strykar shook his head in disgust. "Still can't believe that fucking monstrous tree. A Decurion told me it howled like a man when they poured the pitch on and torched it."

"And they hanged all of his household. Makes one wonder who they missed out. No one keeps a secret that terrible without help in many places," Danamis called out over his shoulder as he moved to the steps leading down to the main deck. "The king will have to be told by the Ivrean Council. And then Sempronius will have to appoint another High Steward to clean out the horrors there." He held out a silken gown for Citala as she clambered up the side at the waist of the ship, as nimble as a cat leaping up a tree.

"I am in no doubt, my lady, that you could out-race this vessel if you had a mind to." He was grinning like a fool.

Citala smiled as she let him drape the gown over her shoulders, covering her nakedness. From his vantage on the quarterdeck, Strykar cocked an eyebrow and pursed his lips. "Besotted. And no good will come of it."

ALL THE NEXT day, the *Vendetta* worked to windward, beating its way southeast along the coast, a back-breaking time for the crew who had little respite as the ship groaned and tossed, the rigging whistling. Danamis worried that if the wind grew stronger, they might have to come about and head out further to sea to avoid being blown onshore. But as the sun dipped low on the horizon, the island of Piso rising up before them in the distance, the stiff wind lessened and a sweeter breeze from eastwards began to ease them onto the desired course. Others vessels hove into view that afternoon, old cogs with their single great square mainsails, a stately merchant carrack probably bound for the city of Saivona at the head of the Gulf, even a long graceful galley of the king's fleet was glimpsed from far off but much closer to the tree-lined shore.

Since leaving Ivrea, once a day Danamis had ordered practice on the new guns. He had managed to get one of Ivrea's master gunners to take his bounty (after also paying off the commander of the guard). Tadeo Verano had proved a good instructor and diplomat, somehow managing not to offend Danamis's own gunners and mates as he warned them of the deadly peculiarities of the orichalcum pieces. A few water casks lashed together and fitted with a spare spar for a mast served as their target and the crew of the *Vendetta* laboured hard to judge the roll of the ship, up and down, when firing. The difference, at range, could mean a shot passing through rigging and sails or bouncing on the water. They had to learn in little more than a week how to shatter hull and masts from distances they had never engaged at before. Or they would die.

On the morning of the sixth day, the ship dropped her mizzen and mainsails along the southern edge of Piso, her speed becoming lazy as the foresail alone took in the light wind. The sea ahead of them was a familiar azure now that they had left the tumultuous white-flecked swells of the dark *Mare Infinitum*. Danamis could not tell Gregorvero exactly where they should drop sail, that was for Citala to decide. She had not revealed to him where the Pisoan colony of the mer lay, whether on the main island or one of the many smaller islets that surrounded Piso like so many children around their mother. That was a secret he agreed needed to be kept. She emerged from the stern cabin, her yellow silk gown wrapped about her tall frame, and joined Danamis on the main deck as he surveyed the scrub-covered rocky island. Its wind-tortured *amelasia* trees ranged on the cliffs, waving their evergreen branches frantically as if to ward off all comers.

She stood beside him, looking outwards. "We are nearly there. And... I am ready to go."

Danamis looked at her and nodded. "Come, speak with me up on the quarterdeck."

For the moment at least, they were alone, and he walked the mermaid to the stern rail. "Everything depends upon you bringing the mermen out with you. If they do not come, I will likely lose it all. Everything."

Citala raised her chin a little, her violet eyes growing slightly larger. "They made their promise to me that they will join me—and you. I told them what was at stake."

"That was near upon a fortnight ago."

Citala smiled, her purplish lips parting, teeth sparkling, not nearly so ragged and sharp as those of mermen. "For the mer, a fortnight is no time at all, Danamis. They have given me their word."

"And you can again explain what I need them to do? Your warriors need to be as ghosts. Working by stealth. If the fleet thinks merfolk are attacking how can I deliver your people back to Valdur? No shedding of blood."

"Danamis son of Danamis! They were in full agreement when I told them before. They will do as you have asked. It is an admirable plan. And they too want to go home."

Danamis smiled, embarrassed, and took her hand. "Are you well enough now? I would never have left you had I known what would have happened. Not someone I owe my very life to."

She moved her head from side to side, inviting him to inspect her skin. And he saw how smooth it was again, blue-grey at her bosom, fading to pale lilac under her throat and chin. He laughed and she burst into a wide smile, her strange yarn-like hair caught in the wind that whipped around them.

A silence fell between them as they regarded each other. And then Danamis asked her what had worried him. "Why did you lie to me, Citala? When I asked if you could remain out of the sea."

She looked away a second before facing him again. "I knew that if I told you the truth you would have taken me back to the ship, and you would not get your guns. It was a risk that had to be taken. I thought that I could survive until you returned."

Danamis frowned. "I might have come up with another plan; indeed I had one to *steal* the guns if needs must. Is that the *only* reason you risked your life?"

She blinked. "I did not want you to think... that I was not like your kind. That I was more fish than woman. For that is what your people call us."

Danamis grasped her hand, his countenance flushing. "Dear Citala, from the first I beheld you I never thought you anything less than the most beautiful creature I had ever seen. And no less a woman than any that walk the land of Valdur."

She placed her fine, long hand over his, her slightly webbed fingers fanning out. "And I never doubted that you would come back for me."

Gregorvero bounded up the stairs, bellowing back to some sailor as he came, and Danamis released her.

"Begging your pardon, Captain. The helmsman is asking what course you want now. God knows I can't tell him what it is." Gregorvero belatedly gave a curt bow to Citala.

Danamis looked at her. "Tell us where we need to sail."

She nodded and moved to the edge of the quarterdeck facing the bow. She raised an arm and gestured. "Over there, off that spit of land on the island. From there I can reach where I must go."

* * *

A_N HOUR LATER, Danamis and Strykar stood amidships between two of the sleek sakers, gleaming golden and bronze in the sun. Citala emerged from her cabin, clutching her silk gown about her as she joined them. Sailors and soldiers alike parted to make way for her, silent and respectful.

Danamis stood close to her. "I didn't forget what you asked for. Will this do?" And he handed her a long thin dagger in a sheath, an amethyst set in its silver pommel. She took it from him and turned it over in her hand.

"Thank you. I pray that I won't need to use it."

Strykar smiled. "Use it on who?"

"Why, sharks of course," she replied, somewhat surprised by his ignorance. She thrust it into her woven *tapua* braes and made sure the hangar of its sheath was lodged securely at her hip.

Strykar's eyes widened at the thought.

Danamis placed his hands on both her shoulders. "Look for my ships off Palestro in six days' time. My enemy will be coming to meet us there. Bring me your news before they reach us if you can."

She nodded and turned to look at the crew ranged across the deck. "God's speed to you all!" she cried out. "May the saints watch over you!" And Danamis was amazed as nearly every man acknowledged her with a nod, a bow, or a gesture of blessing, forehead to breast.

She turned to Danamis and peeled the silken gown off of her shoulders. "Keep this safe for me, Danamis son of Danamis. I am beginning to like it."

"God keep you," he said, a large part of him not wanting her to leave, though leave she must. Citala gave them both one last flash of a smile and slipped over the side and slid into the sea with hardly a sound, disappearing beneath the surface without a trace.

* * *

Duke Alonso swept into the receiving chamber, his advisors following at his heels like so many fretting hens.

"Lord Danamis returned from the north! And I am told you have brought back that which you sought." He clapped his hands first on Danamis and then his half-brother Strykar, his many golden rings clacking together as he did so. "Now, I will expect the both of you this night at my table but do tell me if you dodged the blockade without incident. Your erstwhile uncle's ships are still pestering us here."

"Good my lord! We slipped in quickly before one of their carracks could manoeuvre to cut us off. I think it was *Hammerblow*. A fine ship but not a particularly fast sailer. If they had known it was me, I dare say they would have laid on the speed."

Alonso laughed and waved his arm behind him to fend off a councillor who was trying to thrust some letter or other into his hands. "And Captain Strykar, how does the Black Rose contingent fare?"

Strykar gave a polite bow of his head. "They gave good service in Ivrea, your Grace, but are glad of heart to be in Maresto once again." He glanced over to Danamis. "And they have not forgotten that they will be called upon again shortly. They won't have long to dry off." He made light of it but his own heart was troubled. As he and his *rondelieri* had returned to camp that morning, Poule had given him the news of the widow's abandonment of the company to pursue the young monk. He was now regretting having ever released the greyrobe. Or even ever finding him. Poule was dragging his tail about the camp like a forlorn lover and the boy Poule had left in charge of the sutler's wagon had thieved what he fancied and run clear away. With war against Torinia now likely within weeks, how could he even hope to go in search of her?

"They are the best of soldiers without doubt," added Danamis. "We mean to make sail for Palestro to seek out Tetch and give battle as quickly as we can ready *Royal Grace*."

The Duke shook his head in disgust, pointing to the letter that the little man behind him was still fluttering in a shaking hand. "Another demand from Torinia. They want payment for the services of the Palestrian fleet in protecting our merchants from attack by Southland corsairs. Services indeed! The insolence of it makes me sick! They are now stopping and boarding our ships to confiscate cargo as payment."

"The Torinians won't have the services of Palestro for much longer," said Danamis. "I promise you that. But I have a request to make of you, my lord. Business with the Temple priesthood. Is it within your power to direct the High Prelate of Maresto to deliver a message for me? A message to the Prelate of Palestro."

"He damned well will do so if I tell him to. Give my councillor the message and I will see that it is done immediately."

GIACOMO TETCH LOOKED down from the quarterdeck of *Firedrake*, his lower lip protruding in displeasure. Assembled on the main deck were most of his crew with one sailor in particular looking clearly unhappy with his situation. His arms were pinioned behind, a capstan bar shoved behind his back and he had been paraded to a position just aft of the mainmast. Tetch blinked away a bead of sweat that trickled into his eye and then tugged at the tuft of his newly dyed flame-orange goatee. On the Palestro quay, another hundred sailors and soldiers jostled for a view. His voice boomed out across the ship and reverberated along the dockside where it was moored.

"I have given you dogs the world! The Sea of Valdur is yours for the taking! And I have been repaid with bellyaching and babbling. Vile discontent and vague whispers."

A low roar of outrage swept across the deck and quayside as the pirates growled their support, all outdoing each other in their vocal backing for the new admiral of the fleet. And although many more missed Captain Danamis, few were brave enough to mumble under their breath or tell a comrade. The few including the unfortunate soul who was now facing Tetch's wrath.

"Well, my lads. This miserable shit of a sandworm you see standing before me is undeserving of the leniency I am about to deliver to him."

Tetch gave a slow dramatic nod of his head and a soldier moved towards the prisoner, a set of tongs in one hand and an iron rod in the other. The poor man tried to back away but a lift of the capstan bar stopped him. His eyes bulged in terror as the iron rod, cherry red at one end, came down on his bare chest. As he screamed, the soldier reached forward and clamped his tongue with the tongs. The next instant he had brought the round iron down on the man's extended tongue, piercing it with a hiss that was drowned out by another (but more muffled) scream of agony.

Tetch put both his hands on the rail before him and leaned out. "Next time it's heads that will decorate my bowsprit!"

Ramus appeared from the dock, jumping up onto the gangway and onto *Firedrake*. He mounted the stern stairs and approached Tetch with a salute to his rusty sallet.

"This has come from the priests, sir. By way of Maresto." He handed Tetch a folded bit of parchment. Tetch wiped his shining pate and then swiped his palm across his doublet before seizing the note. He opened it to find that a smaller strip of paper had been glued onto it, the actual message. A miserly scrawl, the letters closed up tight, he had trouble reading it. But this was a tiny message delivered by pigeon and his one good eye devoured it. First he gave a frown, and then a slow shake of his head. Finally a chuckle erupted which rapidly grew into a hacking fit of laughter.

"Clever, clever boy!"

Ramus, took half a step backwards, not knowing whether his commander was angry or amused.

Tetch looked down at the message again.

Uncle, will you not come out and play? I will be waiting for you with open arms a league from Palestro on the Feast of Aloysius.

Tetch reached over and grabbed Ramus by his collar of his doublet. "When is Aloysius? The feast day?"

Ramus stuttered. "It is in two days' time, my lord."

Tetch crumpled the letter in his fist. "Send word for my captains! We are going to sea!"

Ramus looked as if he'd swallowed a fly. The word "why" was on his lips but yet unspoken. Tetch clapped a grimy paw on his shoulder and shot him a rotten, gap-toothed grin. "To slay a ghost, my friend!"

Thirty-Eight

THE SEA WAS a patchwork of grey and blue as the boiling sky sent low clouds drifting past. In the far distance, a great waterspout stretched upwards, the squall around it a dirty white swirling mass against an approaching clear blue sky. Danamis watched as some of his men pointed and jabbered. For them it was an omen. But he knew the morning's storms were now passing. The afternoon would be clear and, God willing, the stiff breeze would continue. If he was becalmed in the next few hours, he would be ripped to pieces by Tetch.

The *Vendetta* had dropped some sail, but was yet pushing ahead east against an oncoming wind, a slow steady run. In her lee followed *Royal Grace*, packed with as many swordsmen, pole arms, and crossbowmen as Danamis could pack onto her deck. Danamis saw his own personal standard whipping furiously from her mainmast top, a strange sight since he was not on her deck. For the *Grace* was to be a ruse, a goat tied to a stake to lure the wolves in. Bassinio was now her captain, and having lost *Salamander* at Palestro, as well as being burned and maimed, he was itching to take his satisfaction against Tetch no matter what the odds. He would fight his ship with every ounce of cunning he possessed. Danamis heard a long low holler ring out from the crow's nest and his eyes moved to see where the crewman was pointing. He saw the sails on the larboard bow: five vessels, perhaps more behind and all moving towards them. Long odds indeed. A ripple of excited voices echoed from bow to stern as the enemy hove into view.

Danamis tasted blood. He had bitten through his lip without realizing it. He shifted his red leather brigantine, its rivets now blooming with green from the dunking it had suffered, and cinched his sword-belt a notch tighter. His crew trusted him. They trusted him when he said the mer would fight for them. But the mer had not as yet surfaced. Were they even there at all? Gregorvero joined him on the quarterdeck, his face an island of peaceful calm despite the impending battle.

"Your course, Captain?"

Danamis turned to him and smiled. "Raise all sail. Steer us a few points east by northeast. I want to run wide past them if we can and then come about with the wind on our quarter."

Gregorvero raised an eyebrow. "Aye, well, I hope that the *Grace* can keep up. She's sailing about as close to this wind as she can now."

Danamis nodded. "Bassinio will do his best."

The master barked his orders down to the helm and sailors scurried to hoist the great lateen sails. Danamis looked behind to see the *Grace* respond with her own men scrambling up top. The dance had now begun. Bassinio knew that the *Grace* would have to try to avoid direct engagement if it could. He also knew that the mer would play their part when the time came—if Citala had convinced them.

Danamis looked forward out over the wide foredeck of the *Vendetta*. It was full of Strykar's *rondelieri*, many carrying spears with which to repel boarders if it came to that. But amidships was taken up by his six great guns and their crews. Though there were many crossbowmen cranking their bows as he watched, they would be joining him up on the quarterdeck, leaving the main deck to the gunners. And being the lowest part of his ship, that would be the likeliest place for Tetch to try boarding him. Everything depended upon the *Vendetta* avoiding that outcome.

"Remember," said Danamis, "we concentrate our fire on *Firedrake* alone if possible. I want you to take me within a cable length of them and we'll give fire as we run by. We'll then come about smartly after we pass their stern so we may strike them with our starboard guns as the larboard crews reload theirs. We will have a following wind at our backs then."

Gregorvero shook his head and sighed loudly. "And getting onto that port tack means we will slow to a crawl before the wind fills our sails. Risky. I would be a little more confident if we'd practiced that some, Nico." He fiddled with the buckle of his steel corselet, trying to hook the clasp, but his pudgy fingers were hindering him and he muttered a curse.

Danamis smiled. "Let me," he said, and cinched him in, slapping him on the back. "I believe in Citala. She will come through."

Gregorvero looked at him. "Nico, I understand why you're doing it this way. You're right; making war on your own people is no way to make friends. And you can't force a man into loyalty by splitting his skull. I just pray that God rewards your restraint. And that the merfolk do as you bid."

Danamis placed a gauntleted hand on the master's shoulder. "I seem to remember when we were fleeing Palestro with barely half a ship under us, you told me some hard truths. One of them was that you can't guarantee loyalty by merely paying for it. If we can kill Tetch, the battle is ours. The fleet will come back to me."

"You're starting to look old these days," said Gregorvero. "But you wear it well upon you. I even see a little wisdom showing. Your father would indeed have been proud, so never think otherwise." And he suddenly clapped his arms around Danamis in a bear hug. "Now let us find the one-eyed bald bastard son of a whore and send him to hell." Gregorvero laughed awkwardly. "I think our helmsman will need all the help he can get on this run. I'm going down now to make sure he keeps both hands on the whipstaff."

Danamis followed him down and strode the main deck. Words were cheap but he offered them anyway. A clap on the shoulder, a laugh, a smile. He looked into the faces of his men: sweaty, unshaven, scarred, broken-nosed, confident, worried. And even as he cajoled, joked, and praised, his own thoughts were filled with gnawing anxiety. Before he reached the steps to the foredeck, he glanced out over the larboard side. The five ships were growing closer, having altered their course to intercept him. And still, he had not a clue whether the mer were out there, ready to engage. As he ascended the steps onto the fore deck, the *rondelieri* broke into a ragged cheer. He acknowledged their salute with a deep bow.

"God save the Black Rose!" he cried out, raising both his arms high. The armoured men roared their approval, stamped their spear butts on the deck and clapped their round shields with their steel gauntlets. Danamis seized Strykar's shoulder and gave him a shake.

"My dear friend, I give you joy! And I would rather have no one else to fight by my side this day."

"I'll be damned if I know how you manage it, my boy," replied Strykar, his eyes bright, "but let us pray to the saints your luck holds this day too."

There was a shout from a gun crew behind them and Danamis turned to see the men crowding the gunwale and jostling excitedly. He sprang to the railing and seized a stay line, hauling himself up on the railing. He saw what had been spotted, less than a hundred yards away and moving towards them. It was a small pilot whale, glistening and as black as night. Upon its back was a figure, sitting high. Danamis could just discern the flowing white mane of hair of the rider as the whale rose and fell, slicing through the swell. It was Citala.

His heart leapt as he watched her close on them. As the crew recognized the mermaid, a great cheer rose up from stem to stern. She drew near, and he saw that she was in a saddle of sorts, sea grass harness and reins upon the grampus. A great explosion of spray erupted from the creature's blowhole and Citala waved to him, shaking her swordfish-bill weapon in her fist. He waved madly back, like some overexcited boy at a fair. She and her mount drew alongside, pacing the ship as it cut through the water. He looked down at her, her mouth wide in a near rapturous smile, and their eyes locked together. Danamis gave her a deep nod as he clung to the stay, his body leaning out over the side. Citala dipped her own head, and then gave a jerk to her reins. The whale turned away and dove, taking them both down under in a splash of foaming white spray. Danamis exhaled loudly and breathed in a lungful of salt-laden air. Now, *now* he had a chance.

At last, Gregorvero put the caravel through its first turn a few points north by northeast, further filling the vessel's three great sails. As it altered course, the *Vendetta* quickened with a side wind coming in over its beam. Danamis was amidships, near the main mast, looking to single-out *Firedrake* from the line of ships that were closing. He saw it, the second vessel in the procession, the *Hammerblow* in the van. His increased speed would give him the position he wanted. He would run past *Hammerblow*, and save his guns for *Firedrake* once in closer range. If he was lucky, *Hammerblow* might veer off to take on the *Grace* following in his wake while he engaged Tetch's flagship. *Firedrake* sprang into clarity, her garishly decorated sterncastle gleaming in the now unhindered sunlight as the *Vendetta* gained on her. Danamis watched as crossbowmen leaned over the quarterdeck on Tetch's ship and two falconets were swivelled to face them.

Danamis allowed himself a small smile. *We'll not be close enough for that to prick us.*

He looked over to Tadeo Verano who was bracing himself in the roll of the ship, feet spread apart, a burning linstock in his hand whose saltpetre fuse was protected by a flap of soft leather against the spray of the sea.

"Master Verano! At the ready, if you please. And fifty ducats to you if you take down a mast!"

The gunner nodded and moved to his crews on the larboard. He ordered the three guns run forward, their muzzles just peeking out beyond the side of the ship. The *Vendetta* had nearly reached *Firedrake*. Gregorvero tapped the helmsman hard and the sailor grunted as he put his shoulder to the long whipstaff. The ship responded and angled left, bringing it parallel to *Firedrake* as it ran past. A heartbeat later and Verano levelled his linstock to the touch hole of the first gun while another gunner touched his linstock to the third. Two tremendous cracking thuds in quick succession and two tongues of yellow flame shot out. Verano jumped to the second gun and ignited it, sending the little truck recoiling back on the deck. The crews hauled on their lines bringing them back in to reload while Verano and the other firer moved to the starboard side.

Through the white smoke, Danamis saw splinters and bits of deck and railing flying off of Tetch's ship. A falconet fired at them impotently from their stern as *Vendetta* overtook them and he heard crossbow bolts tearing through his canvas overhead. He could see men running like ants around the decks of *Firedrake* and her mainsail lines were cut on one side, the great canvas flapping outwards, uncontrolled. As the *Vendetta* surged past it now began a tight turn to starboard. The canvas shuddered on the masts as the *Vendetta* went into irons, the wind hitting it fully on the bow. This ship slowed, only its earlier momentum sending it forward and into the turn. At last, the sails billowed anew, sending the ship surging ahead. Danamis caught sight of the third of Tetch's ships—*Swiftsure*—passing off their starboard bow. They fired a few falconets at him, too far away to do any harm. As the *Swiftsure* sped past at distance, Strykar caught a glimpse of two dark figures clambering on the rudder mounts at the transom. They were mermen, and they were lashing the huge rudder with ropes, working rapidly to foul it completely. He swore softly. The luck of Danamis was shining through after all.

Firedrake, her mainsail flapping uselessly, fumbled her turn to follow the *Vendetta* and was overtaken by *Swiftsure*. Danamis crouched near the starboard guns, biting his lip, as they completed their own turn and ran by for a second pass of Tetch's ship. They were closer this time and a hail of iron-barbed shafts came raining in, striking the deck, deflecting off mens' helms with a dull clang, or finding flesh. A few screams echoed around him. He watched as Verano waited for the moment, then signalled to the other gunner. The orichalcum guns sang out again, abrupt, crisp cracks of thunder and not the dull thuds of his old cast iron pieces on the *Grace*. He heard a slow rending sound of ripping canvas and the squeak of wood giving way, and then he caught sight of the *Firedrake's* foremast starting to tilt and then topple. One of the other shots had cleared a bloody swath across the main deck, a pile of bodies lying stacked on one another as the iron ball had bowled through them. Just below her stern cabin, a huge hole had been blown through just above the waterline of the vessel.

Even as their own stern passed the bow of *Firedrake*, a huge explosion rent the air. Danamis sprang up and looked backwards at Tetch's ship, his eyes frantically looking for a view of his nemesis. One of *Firedrake's* guns had blown up in the breech, sending pieces of iron across the deck, killing many. But Giacomo Tetch was nowhere to be seen.

There were other things to worry about. The carracks *Fortuna* and *Bonaventura* were bearing down on them under full sail, eager to join the battle. So too, he spied one of his old caravels, the *Seafox*, coming up on a different tack. Danamis sprang to the quarterdeck as the gunners worked furiously to reload under Verano's ear-burning tirade. He saw a few of his men being pulled below, quarrels still protruding from leg or chest. Once on the higher deck he quickly took in his situation. The *Grace* had managed to outsail *Hammerblow* and was following now in his wake. She might have to be his last defence if they were run to ground and boarded as she had far more soldiers and bowmen than he did. As he watched, he saw that *Hammerblow,* in pursuing the *Grace,* had completed her turn and had kept turning, her rudder jammed. He nodded and smiled. Now the merfolk had to disable the others in the fleet if they could manage. He laughed as *Hammerblow* began to drop sail, her people hanging over the transom, a few sailors flailing their arms about madly. *Firedrake* was drifting too, fire having broken out on her main deck.

Danamis leaned over the railing and called down to the master. "Gregor! Bring us about again! I want Tetch taken!"

His gun crews were working furiously to swab out the long barrels, awkwardly leaning over the gunwales to ram the scrubbers through before handing a canvas bag of blackpowder to the loader to be poked down the muzzle and then seated home. The heavy iron shot was passed man to man and then awkwardly pushed in the muzzle and rammed down. Verano shoved his stiletto in and out of the touchhole of the guns as if he was dispatching a hated foe, ripping the canvas bag inside to spill the powder charge for his match.

Two rolling booms sounded across the expanse of sapphire sea and Danamis raised his head to see *Royal Grace* coming under fire from the two carracks. Yet even as they reached firing distance, he saw *Bonaventura* lean away and veer off. No master would have ordered such by choice when closing on an enemy. Something had fouled their steering too. Another ship out of the fight—for the moment. *Fortuna* was still bearing down on the *Grace*, she in turn still faithfully sailing after his own ship on an easterly course again. The caravel *Seafox* had altered course directly for the *Vendetta*, leaving the pursuit of the *Grace*. Danamis jumped down to the main deck again and rushed forward. He would soon be in hailing distance on the next pass as his ship turned to starboard ready to come up on the starboard side of *Firedrake*. He could see men crowding the sterncastle and the main deck, smoke still billowing. She was also taking on water and was already sitting lower as every large swell sloshed more of the sea into the ragged hole torn in her hull. Danamis pushed in among the heaving *rondelieri* on the foredeck, making his way to the bow. Less than a hundred yards from her, Gregorvero ordered the sails slackened and the *Vendetta* began to slow as she closed. Danamis now had the option to fire again and then board if he chose. But *Seafox* would be upon him in minutes.

Strykar and his men hunched down, awaiting a flurry of arrows or a cloud of stone shot from *Firedrake*. They reached her bow moving dead-slow. Danamis cupped his hands and bellowed across the distance.

"Yield to me now!"

A voice cried out in reply from somewhere up on the stern. "Mercy!"

And then others took up the cry, plaintive calls sounding across the ship. Danamis leaned over the gunwale.

"Tetch! Show yourself to me!"

The cries of "mercy" kept echoing, almost becoming a fervent chant, a group prayer. A cheer went up on the *Vendetta* as the *Firedrake's* pennant came fluttering down, cut off by one sailor who had had enough.

"Give me Tetch, damn you!"

Danamis saw a sallet helm peek up higher than those around him.

"Spare us, Lord Danamis! Our master is slain! Captain Tetch is not aboard."

"Where?" bellowed Danamis. "Where is he?"

Another voice spoke up from somewhere on the sterncastle. "He captains the *Seafox*!"

Danamis's eyes met those of Strykar at the same moment. "Sweet God," he muttered, falling back and pushing his way down to the main deck.

"Gregor! Give us speed! Away!"

Behind them, the *Seafox* had already overhauled the *Grace*, ignoring her and pushing on to catch Danamis, her bow throwing up a mighty wake of churning sea. She was a fast ship and just as capable of squeezing out speed in a headwind as was *Vendetta*. In her wake, she dragged a merman, a crossbow bolt through the top of his skull, a sea grass rope tangled about his ankle.

Her lines hauled taut, the triangular sails of *Vendetta* billowed again as she pushed on east by northeast. But she had lost precious time. Gregorvero muttered a prayer to Aloysius as he urged his ship onwards. Once they had increased speed they could tack into the wind and then cut back westwards to stand a chance at a passing broadside on *Seafox*. But it was torturously slow and Danamis stood silent as he watched Tetch close the distance between them.

Further back, orange flashes and thuds told him that *Grace* was now taking fire from the *Fortuna* and God willing, was giving it back. If they grappled, he would be on his own against Tetch.

He wiped his hand over his thin sweat-soaked beard. "Gregor, we need to come about. Now."

The master looked at him doubtfully. "Nico, we'll lose even more speed if we do so now."

"If he takes us with grapples at the stern we won't be able to bring the guns to bear. We've got to turn around and strike him hard before he can."

Gregorvero frowned, his face glistening red as an overripe medlar. He then nodded and his cheek twitched in a half-smile. "Aye, then. Ready about! And God save us." He shouted his orders to the helmsman and as the whipstaff groaned, the *Vendetta* obeyed, her spars swinging outwards, sails shivering as she heeled to starboard. Danamis watched as *Seafox* bore down on them, nearly amidships and head-on off their starboard. If he could circle her, he could fire a broadside but *Vendetta* was stumbling on her turn, her momentum bled nearly dry.

"Master Verano! We will have one chance, sir! Ready your guns! You may give fire at your command." He then scanned the sterncastle for his commander of the soldiery. "Talis! Ready your archers and gunners!"

Tadeo Verano pushed his great flopping red beret over his right ear and hefted his linstock. He crouched over the first gun and grabbed hold of the wooden quoin and yanked it towards him, raising the piece slightly as he sighted down the barrel and gave it a pat.

"Stand back, lads!"

The saker belched with a jump, its fiery tongue licking out. Danamis saw the foresail of *Seafox* twitch as the shot pierced it, speeding on to carry away rigging. Verano was onto the next gun, muttering loudly to himself as the soldiers around him stepped back, entranced as if they were watching a street magician. Verano grunted as he gave the quoin a shove. He kissed his fingers and then touched his cannon. The linstock followed. Danamis saw the bow rail of *Seafox* shatter, men flying over the side. But the ship came on. The third shot raked across the deck diagonally, missing the mainmast but surely killing a score of the closely-packed soldiers and gunners. Danamis knew that by the time they reloaded, Tetch would be on top of them. It would now come down to steel in hand. *So be it,* he thought. He drew his falchion from its scabbard and ascended to the foredeck.

NEAR UPON A mile distant, the *Royal Grace* manoeuvred to the rear quarter of the *Fortuna*, her painted transom in full view. They were in shouting distance of each other and deep inside the range of a well-aimed crossbow. But all was quiet as the two vessels drifted. Bassinio had his orders to refrain from shedding the blood of Palestrians and astonishingly, the crew and captain of *Fortuna* seemed to feel the same. From his vantage, Bassinio could see the tangle of green sea grass wrapped about *Fortuna's* rudder pinions, the great slab of wood pressed hard-over to one side. Between the ships, three mermen bobbed, waving their greetings to the slack-jawed crews.

"What do we do now?" asked his tall grizzled sailing master, shaking his head in wonder.

Bassinio rubbed his face, weighing his options. "I reckon it will take them time to clear that fouling. Half of it is below the waterline." He looked over to the poop of the *Fortuna* and recognized her captain, a man he had fought with and hoisted tankards with years gone by. He slowly lifted his plumed hat from his head and bowed to him. The other man, after a moment's pause, did the same. "Get us under way again," said Bassinio to the master. "Captain Danamis may need us."

Danamis was already beginning to think the same thought as the *Seafox* drew near, her gunwales and fo'c'sle still crowded with spear points and bills. Strykar was grim-faced as they met.

"I thought you could hole her before they could board," he chided as Danamis sidled up to him.

"We missed," said Danamis, his voice flat.

"Ah."

Danamis stared intently at the approaching caravel, his eyes searching out for his enemy. If he could slay that one man, he could end the fight. He knew it.

"Can your buckler men shield me if *we* board first?"

Strykar turned to him and pushed up the rim of his sallet. "Take the fight over to them?"

"Not all of them. Get me close enough to Tetch. We board at whichever end he is at."

Strykar nodded. "Better than getting sliced bit by bit where we stand."

Gregorvero's voice boomed out below them. "Brace!"

The *Vendetta* shuddered as the bowsprit of the *Seafox* hit them amidships and dug aft along the side, stripping the railings and snapping the shroud lines of the main mast. The ship rocked, men stumbled and there was a moment of deathly silence before grapnel hooks and lines came flying across and thudding onto the decks. A whispering swarm of arrows descended upon them. The bow gunner in front of Strykar aimed his swivel mount across and up towards the low sterncastle of *Seafox* and touched his fuse. The fist-sized shot tore away railing and elicited several screams as it struck. *Rondelieri* bucklers flew up as another hailstorm of crossbow bolts rained down. Danamis craned his neck, oblivious to the hiss of missiles around him, searching to find the one-eyed devil. And he found him, waving his sword, a battle cry on his lips, urging on his men as they stormed to their starboard, the ships pulled even tighter together in a death embrace.

Danamis gripped Strykar's shoulder, the latter just peering over the rim of his shield. "There! Amidships!"

Strykar nodded and rallied those around him. They jostled and pushed their way off the fore deck and down to the main deck. Where the orichalcum guns were lashed down was now a mass of straining and yelling men, spears jutting outwards to defend against those thrusting towards them. Two giants from *Seafox* stepped over the heads of their comrades and rolled onto the deck of *Vendetta*. One struck down two of Danamis's crew with his sword before a crossbowman sent a bolt into his face. The other scrambled to his feet, dazed, and this spelt death for him as he was hacked to the planks.

Strykar and about twenty of his men pushed past, running towards the stern, Danamis in their midst. They climbed to the stern deck and Strykar waved his sword, marshalling them all to where there was a short drop down to the bow and fore deck of *Seafox*. Brognolo, his face a bristling angular mask of short white whiskers came last, puffing.

"Stay back with the others, Sergeant!" Strykar called over to him.

"Captain, they'll be no others left to come back to unless we take these bastards! I'm jumping with you."

"Suit yourself, you old fool!" laughed Strykar and he bounded off the deck, landing on a stupefied pirate and slamming him with his buckler, while the other men followed him across. Tetch's men had crowded together on the main deck as they pushed to gain footing on Danamis's ship. But they had left the fore deck lightly held and those who did not give way were chopped down by the *rondelieri*. They locked shield rims and raised their swords high in a hanging guard, moving as one, foot by foot.

Danamis kept a hawk's eye on Tetch who still had not noticed that his own vessel had now been boarded. The remainder of the *rondelieri* were now reinforcing the inwardly bulging wall of soldiers on *Vendetta*, barely holding back the press of Tetch's crew. Others were trying to board across the gap nearer *Vendetta's* foredeck. But a poorly timed jump and a large swell saw two of them tumble down to sink like stones. On-board *Seafox*, a cry went up as the *rondelieri* came down the short steps from the foredeck. A group of thirty polearm men peeled off to face them as they advanced, Giacomo Tetch behind them. The mass of men now swirled into melee, steel-barbed shafts thrusting at waist level and at head. A muffled cry of pain or deep grunt and a man would sink down to be trodden on as the lines shifted, a maelstrom of flashing blades high and low.

"Uncle! Come to me!" yelled Danamis, revealing himself. Between a gap in the armoured men, Danamis caught a glimpse of a bald head. Their eyes met and Tetch grinned. His baleful red marble eye made him look monstrous. But Danamis's heart burned with revenge and it was for him a beacon to guide him to the kill. A *rondelieri* next to Strykar fell, a bolt through the eye. Another buckler man stepped in to close up the gap.

"Fight me, you whoreson!" Danamis spat as he tried to push his way forward, breaking through to Tetch. Already, his side wound was aching as if a blade had pierced him anew.

Strykar barely managed to block a fast spear thrust to his face, just catching it with the rim of his shield. "Danamis! Goddamn you, hold!" But Tetch, wearing his studded brigantine of blue velvet and a rusty gorget, was also working his way through the press to meet Danamis, cackling with joy.

"Over here, boy! This way! Found one of your fish-men fiddling with my ship!" Tetch sidestepped around the mainmast, trying to flank Danamis. "Did you think you could fool me, clever boy? I knew you'd be on the fastest ship you could find. So I got me one too."

Danamis managed to push between two of the *rondelieri* and found himself four feet from Tetch. A throng of men around Tetch caught sight of him. And Danamis recognised faces among them, comrades and crew who had fought at his side. A strange lull fell amongst them, first upon those who had seen Danamis emerge, and then spreading to others as awareness built. The furious hammering of poleaxe and sword, spear and shield now subsided into half-hearted blows and parries as the main deck fight slowed.

"Look out there!" said Danamis, hefting his falchion in both hands. "Your fleet is mine again. This is the only vessel you command and that won't be for long." And the men around him receded, wordlessly creating a stage for the two captains. Strykar watched, realizing he was helpless to stop the single combat. A crossbowman now, in the uncertainty of the moment, could take Danamis down like an executioner.

Tetch licked his lips as his head darted about, taking in the new situation. Danamis looked past Tetch to see the billowing sails of the *Grace* closing in. Others had seen her arrival, Tetch included. He hawked and spat on the deck.

"Well," he said, "Better we end it this way. Save the lads from shedding brother's blood, right? I will forgive them all after I've taken your head." He glanced over his shoulder and gestured for the curtle-axe that one soldier held. The man tossed it to him and Tetch caught it by the haft.

It was then that Danamis recognised the blade in his other hand. A curving and delicate Southlander sword whose pommel was a golden ball. Escalus's sword. A weapon Tetch would not be holding if Escalus yet took breath.

"Lord Danamis!" A *rondelieri* offered his own side sword, hilt forward. Danamis took it in his left hand and bent his knees slightly, each sword held waist high.

The deck had gone near silent all around them, despite the great number of men. Danamis's voice carried across both vessels and all eyes were upon him, barely a breath taken. "Look around you!" he cried. "You are known for the traitor you are. A black-hearted dog who betrayed those closest to him. The Palestrian dead today are laid at your feet, not mine."

Tetch smiled again and huffed, tilting his head.

"It will matter little when I kill you, my boy."

He lunged forward with a downward swipe of his hand-axe to force a block from Danamis, even as he swung the light Southland blade down at Danamis's left arm. Danamis parried the attack and converted his ward, chopping at Tetch's neck even as he raised the weapon in his left hand to intercept the pirate's next blow. Their arms whirled, trading blow for blow, each parrying the other. They circled each other, moving the fight towards the larboard, and, as one, the crews turned to follow them.

The pain in Danamis's ribs was sharp and he was slowing already, far sooner than he had expected. An instant later and Tetch's lighter sword had twisted round his side sword. Tetch bent his wrist and the sidesword clattered to the deck. Danamis leapt back and gripped his falchion with both hands in a high guard.

Tetch gave a retching laugh, his breath short. "Your memento from Perusia giving you trouble?"

Danamis cursed him, his arms shaking. "Your aim was poor then and will be again today!"

Tetch laughed raucously. "*My* aim? Guess again, my boy. You think I'd waste gold for someone else to slay you?"

Danamis blinked as the words sank in. He had assumed too much. Like having only one enemy. Not even dreaming that others wished him ill as well. The anger swelled in him until it burst forth in a cry of fury. He rushed forward and heedlessly aimed a vicious cut—with all his might—down at Tetch's head. Tetch's sword struck Danamis but the light blade bounced from his brigantine while Tetch's axe caught the falchion on its haft. The falchion slid down into Tetch's gloved hand and he hissed with pain as the axe flew from his grip. Danamis yelled as he dropped his own weapon and seized Tetch by the neck with both hands. He tightened his grip, staring into the unblinking red eye. Tetch whirled, still holding his sword but unable now to wield it. In desperation, he slammed Danamis into the mainmast but Danamis was like an eagle, his claws firmly gripping his prey. Tetch tripped on the deck and they both went down, cursing and snarling. Tetch's bloody fist struck Danamis in the cheek, and then a second time. Flashing lights filled his vision and his grip on Tetch loosened.

Strykar was as tense as a spanned bow, ready to spring forward. If Danamis fell, the battle would continue despite what Tetch would order. If he intervened now, it might erupt immediately. He continued to watch, his mouth agape. Either way, he swore he would kill Giacomo Tetch before he went down himself.

Tetch's right arm flew up, bringing the pommel of his sword into Danamis's head. Tetch rolled and threw him off but Danamis, eyes burning with madness, grabbed the hilt and the blade with both his hands and twisted it round. Tetch fell back on the deck again and Danamis was on him, an elbow into his chest. He flexed his left wrist and the sword sprang from Tetch's hand. In one move, the pommel pointing skyward and Danamis's right hand holding the blade about seven inches from the tip, he leaned forward with all his weight and brought Escalus's sword down into Tetch's good eye. The pirate screamed in agony, his hands still clawing and pushing at Danamis's arms, straining to push away the narrow blade tip. Danamis thought of Escalus and all the others that his own blindness had caused to die. All dead because he had played the fool. And with a final cry he sent six inches of Southlander steel into Giacomo Tetch's brain.

Thirty-Nine

"Why isn't he buried yet?" Acquel stood in the cloister gardens of the Ara, again clothed in his robes of grey. The air had grown warm and humid, as if the tail end of summer was fighting against the normal passage of the seasons.

"Why, it would be unseemly for the High Priest to be buried any sooner," Kodoris gently chided, his hands concealed in his sleeves as the two stood together in the sunlight of the dying afternoon.

"You need to be invested *now*," replied Acquel. "You must take the purple and I my final vows in the black."

Kodoris lowered his voice deferentially. "But four of the Nine Principals have left the city. You know this."

"Then the rump can elect new ones. Our work must not falter. You are yet Magister. Put the ceremony in place." It was not a suggestion and there was more than impatience in his tone. Kodoris bowed his head. Not far from where they stood, Timandra lay in her lavender-strewn grave. Acquel wanted her there in the gardens, near to him, not in the burial ground outside the town walls among the grey stones. Hers was not the only innocent death that day of revelation beneath the Temple Majoris; one of wonder and of evil mixed. The boy in him had died as well. And in his heart, he had accepted what had been put before him, his future path.

The High Priest-elect shifted nervously, his eyes falling to the amulet that rested outside Acquel's robes. "The undercroft of the Temple is yet unclean, I fear, even though we have burned the black roots into char. We may not have stopped its growth. Deeper down."

"It signifies not. I have removed all of the sacred texts from the chamber. Even now they are being transcribed. The plates for the Temple presses will be readied soon. We must waste no time. The Faith depends upon it."

Kodoris tried to accommodate his new ally. "Agreed, Brother Acquelonius. But twenty blackrobes have already abandoned the monastery. They will find common cause with others who do not accept the revealed truth. How many more will we lose if we... push things too quickly? You have set us upon a difficult road—strewn with obstacles."

"Twenty have left but many more have embraced the newfound texts with joy." Acquel's face was haggard and though he spoke of joy there was little of it in his voice. "I have promised to deliver the truth of the Word. Some will not like it. But the Truth is the Truth and shall remain so."

Kodoris seemed to find a little of his old authority once again. "In the tomb... did Elded's amulet find you or did you find it? I am asking if you stole it from the Saint's body."

Acquel looked again at Kodoris, emotionless, his eyes locked onto those of the Magister. There was a moment of silence as Kodoris returned the iron stare. Then Acquel answered, his voice steady, almost matter-of-fact. "I stole it. Yes. And it has paid me hundredfold for my rashness. But I accept my fate."

"Your destiny. The Saint would have found another if you were not meant to bear its message. You told me how the amulet can choose who it will remain with. It could have chosen someone after you. But it has not." Kodoris placed his hand on Acquel's arm and the greyrobe tensed at the touch. "Know that I follow not only out of penance, but out of choice. My own choice. I have read the Black Texts. I embrace them. And you are anointed of the Saints. But, I fear that prayers and incense will not be enough to combat what has been unleashed on Valdur."

"Where has she gone?"

Kodoris shook his head. "She has fled Livorna. But we know not where. She is a powerful enchantress and I will carry to my grave the sin of having empowered her. But she must be pursued or the old evil will take root elsewhere."

Acquel's back straightened. "I know that. And I will need your blessing and seal for what I plan to do."

Kodoris looked up, his brow creasing.

"The Temple guard will never be suitable for the task that lies ahead," said Acquel. "I will found an order—a holy order of the Temple—a fighting order. One as once there was at the Priory of Saivona. And all who will bear arms in its name shall be ordained brothers, greyrobes and blackrobes. You know of what I speak. *You* were in such a holy order before it was disbanded after the last war among the dukes."

Kodoris's thin lips parted slightly and he nodded. "I was. And I have told few of that part of my life."

"You told enough. It was not hard to find out. But I suspected it, seeing you could wield a sword."

"The Duke feared us. Forced our disbandment." Kodoris sounded distant as the memory flooded back to him.

"But *we* will be stronger. A thousand strong if the Lord so inspires." Acquel brightened visibly with internal fire as he spoke, his hands spread wide. "Monks from throughout Valdur shall come and take the new vow. The Order of Saint Elded and of the Temple Majoris at Livorna. And you will appoint me its captain-general."

Kodoris, his eyes still distant, slowly moved his hand to his forehead and then to the medallion on his breast, making the sign of blessing. "A Temple army," he whispered.

Brother Acquelonius Galenus nodded, a smile spreading upon his lips for the first time since Timandra had fallen; fallen having saved him from death. "I will defend the True Faith to my last breath, *Holiness*. And so will you."

LADY DELLA ROVERA watched dispassionately as the brigand seized the bridle of her mount while his comrade, equally ugly enough to be his brother, guffawed at his side. A noblewoman riding on her own at dusk was either mad or looking to change her profession. Either way, he thought, luck was smiling at him. He moved a greasy hand towards her daintily shod foot resting in the stirrup. His grubby blackened fingers stroked her ankle, but only once. The last thing he felt was his comrade's knife as it rapidly cut across his throat.

Lucinda gave the other a kindly smile of gratitude and dipped her chin to him.

"You know what to do now, good sir," she said quietly.

The remaining brigand, his face a picture of contentment, gave her a gap-toothed grin, plunged the knife into his own belly, and staggered silently to the side of the road where he fell, conveniently, into a ditch.

Around her was silence but for the raucous cawing of some crows. Tied stacks of newly mown hay stood on either side of the road, mute sentinels to the event. She clucked to her horse. Its ears twitched and she resumed her ride deeper into the Duchy of Torinia.

"They are talking about me," she said, her voice low. "I can see them when they do. I can *feel* what they say. They talk of the Tree of Life and how they will burn it."

They will not succeed. You have planted two seeds, my daughter. The newly blooded Tree and the young monk. Both will bear fruit in time.

Lucinda ran her tongue along her teeth as the lips in her shoulder tingled. "You have said that the roots are deep. Now I have nourished them."

Deeper and wider than any in Valdur can imagine. You have done well.

She smiled to herself, considering it, before moving to another thought. "And is the Duke of Torinia a handsome man? And what of his *duchessa*? I do not think she will welcome me."

He is a prince most handsome. She is a frail woman whose heart is weak. And you are a most captivating creature, my daughter. The Duke will be glad of your comfort and counsel.

Lucinda giggled in excitement at the prospect. "And will the gods look upon me kindly? Will they help me?"

You are beloved of the gods. Beloved because you are the vanguard of hope. Belial, Beleth and Andras shine the brighter because of you. That which has slept an age is now awakening!

Not too far distant, she could make out the red-tiled roofs of a small town, nestled into a hillside, the smoke of hearth fires rising up and dissipating on the light breeze. The prospect of a bed and a meal pleased her. Refreshment and a bath perhaps. The palazzo of the Duke, not two days further journey, beckoned to her, a perfect sparkling beacon in her mind's eye.

THE GUNS ON the slime-coated sea wall rang out as Danamis entered the harbour of Palestro. But this time they were not firing at him, and Tadeo Varano answered the salute with powder and wad from one of the orichalcum sakers. Lord Nicolo Danamis stood on the battered and ripped bow of *Vendetta* as it passed the two chain towers, his personal standard flying at the mainmast, the crimson and gold griffon banner of the kingdom of Valdur at the mizzen. And halfway up the foremast, Giacomo Tetch swung limply like a grotesque marionette as the ship bobbed. Behind them, the *Royal Grace* rolled majestically in the wake of her lee, the flag of the Free City of Palestro billowing out at her mizzen. As the canvas dropped and they neared the dockside, Danamis waved an arm and two trumpeters gave a spirited fanfare that brought cheers from the crowed already gathering, more people running down from the square.

As the ships were made fast, he had stood there, alone, a watchful eye upon those thronging the docks and quay. All cheering, hailing his return. But what of those who had betrayed him along with Tetch? Were they beaming away up at him with false cheer or had they fled? Even before he had disembarked he had summoned Talis to his side and given him one order: arrest every single Decurion of the Council. And when he judged that the fisherfolk, soldiers, seamen, tradesmen, and chandler men had swelled sufficiently, he moved forward and leapt to the bow rail, grasping a stay. He had again signalled the trumpeters for a blast and then raised an arm to command silence. A subsiding wave, the crowd quietened, except for the occasional raucous yell of support. And he had spoken to them.

"People of Palestro!" he had cried. "Here hangs the man who deceived you! The disloyal dog that tricked many of you good folk into betrayal of your chosen ruler! Know you all— and tell all you see this day—that I pardon every man who lifted arms against me." He had gestured widely towards the other ships that slowly entered the harbour. "All these have I forgiven! Every captain has sworn his allegiance anew!"

And the cheers had risen high, rolling from the quayside up to the terraces of the city. And he had walked home.

Now, the sun dipped low on the horizon. In his deserted palazzo, the dying light of day shone through the nobly arched windows, sunbeams casting long shadows. Danamis prodded a pile of broken shards with the toe of his boot, the remains of a clay jug thrown against a pillar. The black and white marble tiles told a tale: blood stains and wine, muddy tracks and vomit puddles. The scent of urine rose from every corner, like some fetid dungeon. Poor Escalus. He hoped in his heart that the ghost of his castellan did not haunt the sad remains of this house. He hefted a small wooden wine cask, brought up from the *Vendetta*, and poured out a generous measure in a half-crushed brass goblet and handed it to Strykar, an apologetic smile on his bruised face. He did the same for himself and then noisily pulled up the remains of a carved oak folding chair, its leather back slashed away.

He held up his goblet to the mercenary. "To you, my friend. For standing by my side these past weeks. So that I could bring you back… to this." And he let out a tired but sincere chuckle before taking a long swig of the sweet liquid.

Strykar tipped his goblet and drank too, drops spilling into the salt and pepper curls of his square-cut beard. "Why are you thanking me? You paid me after all, and that is, of course, my profession. The only one I shall ever know."

"You could have taken my gold and stayed in Maresto."

"Nay, my friend. We've had an arrangement these past few years. Men of commerce. I'll not shit on that. But what of your fleet? Will they bite your hand again?"

Danamis looked hard at Strykar and the mercenary saw now how the adventures of the last month had worn his friend at the edges, his eyes ringed dark. "Dear Strykar, I can only pray that my trust will be repaid in trust."

Strykar nodded and gave him a brotherly look of affection. "Your father—and you in turn—took men who were pirates and made them pirate-hunters. And traders. You can't turn a wolf into a dog. You must watch your back, Nico."

"And never make more enemies than you can fight at one time," added Danamis with a self-derisory snort. "Well, the myrra trade is at an end. For now at least. Citala is dead set against resuming it. The leaf has enslaved her menfolk and this I have seen with my own eyes."

Strykar lowered his goblet. "But I've still got a fortune's worth on your ship!"

Danamis shrugged. "The price of an alliance. And not the only condition at that."

The mercenary scratched the stubble under his neck. "Hmm. Mayhaps I should try giving it a chew myself. I wonder if it has medicinal properties."

Danamis smiled wanly. "It may indeed."

Strykar took a drink and belched quietly. "The *other* conditions. It will be a small mountain to climb to settle the merfolk here. The priests will fight you, for one." He inclined his goblet towards Danamis. "That said, Duke Alonso has given you his support for the enterprise."

"He smells the promise of merfolk gold."

"Ah, Nico. Every man needs a reason to do something. In my experience it is rarely the result of the milk of human kindness."

Danamis rose up from the creaking chair and drained his goblet. "Will you take ship soon for Maresto?"

Strykar leaned back and laughed. "Ship? I think I've had my fill of voyages by sea! We return by road this time, my friend. Another day or so. After the lads have had time to fill their bellies and empty their cods. Lord knows what news awaits us when we get back there."

"Stay here tonight if you wish. Saints willing, you and

your men will find beds that don't smell of piss. I go now to meet a friend."

A wry look broke upon the mercenary's craggy face. "I suppose that is well deserved. Please give my greetings to the blue lady." And he stood and held out his hand.

Danamis gripped it warmly. "Fare you well, Captain Strykar!"

Epilogue

HE RODE A borrowed horse down to the east gate. The weather had grown humid again and the heat made him heedless of fashion or his station. He was dressed only in a cambric shirt, hole-shot green hose, and salt-rimed boots, a threadbare brown woollen cloak thrown over his shoulders, hood up. His falchion bounced at his waist as his mount walked down the narrow cobbled street. Most of those he passed did not recognize him, the few that did paused and watched him pass, bemused at his shabbiness and his solo ride with night drawing in.

He mused that if any wound-licking mutineers lurked in the alleys, they would have an easy time of him. His fatigue lay upon him like a succubus, pulling him down and down with heaviness. The gate was yet open and two guards of the militia eyed him as he passed under the portcullis and through the heavy oak doors. He carried on down the road and turned off on a trail that ran down to the sea. The town walls rose up on his right, past palm and scrub until the woods opened and he found himself at a tiny cove and sandy beach, a place he had known since boyhood, and for the moment deserted. At one end of the cove stood the chain tower but to his left the great expanse of the Sea of Valdur rolled out before him. He looped his mount's reins to an *amelasia* tree, standing forlorn, bent and twisted like an old man.

As he stood on the bleached white sand, wrist resting on his sword hilt, he saw her rise from the water and walk towards him, glistening in the twilight. She was near-naked as when he had first seen her that fateful day on the deck of the *Grace,* a wild creature, tall and lithe. And his heart sang at the sight of her, his melancholy and weariness lifting away. She drew near and her white smile flashed brightly, the almond-shaped eyes wide and full. Danamis smiled too, breathing deeply, and held out his arms for her. She took both his forearms in her long-fingered hands, squeezing gently, and seawater soaked his sleeves.

"Danamis! It is a great victory as you had hoped. My heart gladdens at the sight of you again!"

Danamis grasped her forearms in return. "A victory not possible without you and your people. I owe my life to you—twice over. How fare your warriors?"

Citala lowered her chin. "One dead. A sacrifice that all would have made for the prize. A return here."

"It is one too many. I am sorry for that."

Citala half-turned to face the water, moving one hand to grasp his. "They have returned to Piso. They understand that the time is not right to show themselves plainly. That lies ahead, in time. I must return also, to the island. My father must be told of your success—and the hope that it brings."

"I have pledged my honour to restore you. And I will do all in my power to bring this to pass. You must believe me."

She raised a hand to his cheek, brushing the still livid boss of his bruise. "And I believed in you from when first we met. A landsman I could trust."

He winced slightly as she touched the cut on his brow.

"Your wounds have not been seen to," she said quietly.

"The sea is healing. Come." And she undid his cloak and pulled up his shirt over his head. Danamis unbuckled his sword belt and placed it on the beach. She laughed as he struggled, off-balance, with his boots. And he was laughing too as he unlaced his codpiece and peeled off the hose. He stood there in only his braes, the warm slight breeze invigorating him. Citala nodded and extended her hand to him. They waded into the water of the sheltered cove, the surf gently lapping the shoreline. She pulled him out further until the sea was just over their waists. He pulled her back and their eyes met again. She blinked, the pools of shining violet wider than before. And then he folded his arms about her and leaned in. She did not shun his gentle embrace and their lips met as her hands splayed upon his shoulders. She tasted of the sea, bracing and fresh, bitter and briny. They sank down together under the surface, still in each other's arms.

DANAMIS AWOKE ABRUPTLY to the sound of thumping oars and harsh voices. He rolled over on his crumpled cloak, still naked, and, shaking his head, stood up. A small fishing shallop had been dragged up onto the beach a few dozen yards from him. The men were laughing at him. He wiped his arm across his sand-crusted face. Citala was gone. They had lain together on the beach until he had drifted off, at peace and contented. He could still smell her hair, a scent of peppercorn and sea. He frowned and retrieved his clothes, hastily pulling everything on, sticky and sand-coated. His horse, still patiently tethered, watched him and then flapped its lips out of boredom.

As he hefted his sword belt and scabbard, a cannon up on the harbour wall thundered. A moment later, a second gun boomed out.

"Shit."

Danamis cinched in the prong of the buckle in his worn leather belt—next to last hole—and twisted it around, the hilt of the sword far back on his left hip. He left the cloak, hurriedly untied the horse's reins, threw himself up into the saddle and spurred up the path back towards the gate. Ambling merchants scattered as he shouted a warning and trotted under the portcullis of the gatehouse, the horse's hooves scrabbling on the cobbles. He should never have let his guard slip as he had, his foolish lax ways returning like a bad acquaintance. He had not even left any orders for the defence of the harbour and only Gregorvero and Bassinio— God willing—were down there to lead the men. He was no great horseman, and the creature whinnied and snorted as it navigated the precarious downward streets, losing its footing more than once. Danamis held on tight, his mind filling with every conceivable threat.

Again, guns sounded, further off this time. It was a ship. He rounded a corner and the piazza and quayside were before him. People were running down to the docks from every direction. He kicked the horse and shot forward, his eyes taking in the scene. He slowed, his breaths coming fast, and then reined in. He blinked, then squinted, only half-believing what he was seeing.

A large carrack had entered Palestro, sailing proudly between the two towers of the chain. Another of its deck guns boomed out in greeting. It was a vessel he knew very well. A great twin-tailed standard, twenty feet long, trailed out from the mainmast, shivering in the breeze. Upon it was a blue seawolf, its scaly tail coiling three times. His father's personal badge.

Lord Valerian Danamis, the lost admiral of Valdur, had found his way home again.

Acknowledgements

FIRST AND FOREMOST I must give thanks to my wife for putting up with the solitary (and often grumpy) reality that is a writer's life. Thanks also to the team at Rebellion Publishing and Solaris Books, in particular my talented and near-omniscient editor Jonathan Oliver for helping bring the text to life. I also doff my cap to my accomplished cover artist, Adam S Doyle, for giving the early script a read and offering encouragement. Finally, I am grateful for the continuing support and sage wisdom of my agent at Sheil Land Associates, Ian Drury.

About the Author

CLIFFORD BEAL, AN international journalist for 20 years, is a Fellow of the Royal Aeronautical Society, and was the editor-in-chief of *Jane's Defence Weekly* in London before turning his attention to writing history, historical fiction and epic fantasy. Over the years he has been flung about in military aircraft, fought in full medieval armour, trained in 17th century rapier combat, fired flintlock pistols, messed about in boats, and ridden both horses and motorcycles. When not writing and imbibing endless mugs of tea he is reading and imbibing endless mugs of tea. He lives in Surrey, England, with a fiery redhead of a wife and a Boston Terrier named Buzz.

You can follow his blog at cliffordbeal.com and on Twitter @clifford_beal

1653: Two plots to kill Cromwell.
One to restore the King.
The other to set the Devil on the throne.

GIDEON'S ANGEL

1653. The long, bloody English Civil War is at an end. King Charles is dead and Oliver Cromwell rules the land. Richard Treadwell, Royalist, exile, and now soldier for the King of France, burns for revenge on those who deprived him of his family and fortune. He returns to England in secret to assassinate Cromwell.

But his is not the only plot in motion. A secret army run by a deluded Puritan is bent on the same quest, guided by the Devil's hand. When demonic entities are summoned, Treadwell finds his fortunes reversed: he must save Cromwell, or consign England to Hell...

But first he has to contend with a wife he left in Devon who believes she's a widow, a furious Parisian mistress who has trailed him to England, and a young Musketeer named d'Artagnan, sent to drag him back to France. It's a dangerous new Republic, for an old Cavalier coming home.

ISBN: 978-1-78108-083-7 ☆ £7.99